KU-248-993

WHERE THE MISSING GATHER

THE BURROWHEAD MYSTERIES

HELEN SEDGWICK

POINT BLANK

A Point Blank Book

First published in Great Britain, the Republic of Ireland and Australia
by Point Blank, an imprint of Oneworld Publications, 2021
This mass market paperback edition published 2022

Copyright © Helen Sedgwick, 2021

The moral right of Helen Sedgwick to be identified as the Author of this work has been
asserted by her in accordance with the Copyright, Designs, and Patents Act 1988

All rights reserved
Copyright under Berne Convention
A CIP record for this title is available from the British Library

ISBN 9-780-86154-193-5
ISBN 9-781-78607-978-7 (ebook)

Typeset by Geethik Technologies
Printed and bound in Great Britain by Clays Ltd, Elcograf S.p.A.

This book is a work of fiction. Names, characters, businesses,
organisations, places and events are either the product of the author's
imagination or are used fictitiously. Any resemblance to actual
persons, living or dead, events or locales is entirely coincidental.

Oneworld Publications
10 Bloomsbury Street
London WC1B 3SR
England

Stay up to date with the latest books,
special offers, and exclusive content from
Oneworld with our newsletter

Sign up on our website
oneworld-publications.com/point-blank

MIX
Paper from
responsible sources
FSC® C018072

30119 029 143 31 2

05/22
CHE

'Book two in the Burrowhead Mysteries series is another triumph. A masterful blend of crime and psychological suspense, with a hint of the supernatural for added chill... An immersive, haunting read.'

Mary Paulson-Ellis, author of *Emily Noble's Disgrace*

'Unputdownable. *When the Dead Come Calling* tracks the toxin which seeped into a village. If you read closer you will see who the "key workers" are. Helen Sedgwick saw into the future and that future is now! It's an incredible book! READ IT.'

Lemn Sissay, author of *My Name Is Why*

'Creepy, atmospheric and spine-tingling, *When the Dead Come Calling* is the kind of mystery so deviously plotted it left me reeling. Brilliant.'

Chris Whitaker, author of *We Begin at the End*

'*When the Dead Come Calling* confirms what many of us already knew: Helen Sedgwick is one of Scotland's finest contemporary storytellers.'

Claire Askew, author of *All the Hidden Truths*

'Beautifully written, beguiling and mysterious, the sort of book that would reward a second (and third) read.'

Fiona Erskine, author of *The Chemical Detective*

'A multi-layered tale from a range of viewpoints that reaches back into history and poses as many questions as it answers... A thumpingly good read shot through with some beautiful prose.'

Herald on Sunday

'The dense narrative moves back and forth, incorporating horrors from the past and fears and resentments from the present. The final twist works well and adds an extra layer to the story that is both surprising and moving.'

Literary Review

'By combining up-to-the-minute themes, well-tuned dialogue and warm and witty details of everyday life with a deep, impressionistic sense of dread, Sedgwick produces a mystery as addictive as it is anxiety-inducing… Deserves to be a stonking series with wide appeal that should run and run.'

Molly Flatt, author of *The Charmed Life of Alex Moore*

'Sedgwick's writing is minutely observational, clever and warm. One minute you are transported by her descriptions of the landscape, the next she is raising the hairs on the back of your neck with her dreamlike descriptions of whatever lurks in the cave at the foot of the cliffs. It is her portrayal of the closed world of a remote community, however, that will chill you to the bone.'

Scotsman

'This is a stunning, complex, out-of-the mainstream novel that's completely immersive.'

Mystery People

'Helen Sedgwick weaves a clever combination of psychological suspense and low-key police procedural.'

Crime Review

'*When the Dead Come Calling* is assured, engaging and beautifully layered. Intriguing characters meet contemporary issues, and historical whispers, in a haunting landscape. A must-read!'

Scottish Book Trust, picked as a 2020 Great Scottish Novel

'It's the poetic quality of her writing that makes this a moodily engrossing, and rather uneasy, opening to the series.'

Peterborough Telegraph

'An ethereal, supernatural take on the crime genre.'

Huntly Express

For Mavis
1922–2020

LOST

A WAY BACK

Deborah-Jane can still hear the scratching, the terrible scratching like cracked fingernails on wood. It follows her as she runs, like the rasping breath under the wind – the air is filled with it – and the mud that slips and sinks beneath her soles, pulling her down. That noise.

The scratching.

Shapes are moving around her, crouched but tall, solid then rippling in the wind that finds its way down the back of her neck, and then she is leaping the fence and racing into the dense woodlands: ash and silver birch, gnarled oaks, sharp brambles crawling about their roots and the sudden glint of animal eyes that are gone sooner than she can believe what she's seen. A squirrel. A pine marten, some kind of weasel, that's all, that must be all, but she runs faster and there are scratches at her ankles, twigs twisting their way through her hair – and she sees jagged tufts of hair, lighter than her own, baby blonde matted with blood from where scissors had hacked – no, no, she mustn't look, she mustn't remember, the bushes are head height now, thicker and darker, sharp-nailed—

She screams.

A deep scratch, clawed into her cheek.

She spins around: twisted and brittle mimosa, groaning in the wind. A snapped branch, jagged at the fracture. She swipes at it and then she's off again, thrashing and fighting everything in her way, kicking the bushes that snatch at her clothes until she hears the

3

sound behind her. It's close and deliberate: crunched undergrowth, a step, a pause. Another step. It can't be a person. She's frozen. That scratching. Scratching.

Then something tugging at her stomach, at her insides.

Move.

Move!

Running again, faster than before, forcing her way through clawing bushes and jagged gorse, eyes glinting out from the undergrowth, and she's leaping the logs and stones in her path, yelling out in the dark to keep going, to get through the woods. What she saw. She mustn't think about what she saw. Keep running, keep lashing out. Her hand strikes something fleshy but she keeps moving and racing and yelling and her paces get wider and her back gets longer and soon she's taller than the trees themselves, tall enough to crush the gorse underfoot and let the creatures cling around her wrists like cobwebs and then she is out: the open, the wind, the night sky with its stars glinting freely above the cloud; she's running through the cold fresh chill of the clearest, brightest night she has ever seen and she'll never be able to get back what she has lost, but nothing can stop her now.

TODAY

The coffee smells good. Georgie likes a good cup of coffee of a morning – and Fergus does too, she knows. He tends not to bring her breakfast in bed these days, though she can hardly blame him for that. Still, midsummer. That could be some kind of turning point, maybe, after a spring of such darkness it changed her; changed the way she works, the way she looks. She's been watching Fergus too, looking for signs of a change in him, though it's when she glimpses the old Fergus, sees him putting seeds out for the birds or dead-heading his roses with such tenderness that she feels a pang for what they've lost. That's the new Georgie thinking, though. The old Georgie would just have wrapped her arms around his waist and given him a squeeze.

'That coffee smells good,' he says. 'Thanks.'

He's showered, dressed, ready for work. His new haircut is short and neat; it gives him fewer curls and a lighter shade of auburn.

'Toast?'

He shakes his head.

Georgie puts two pieces in anyway – she'll eat them even if he doesn't. She's got an ongoing dispute about tyre slashing in the village and a pub that routinely serves underage kids, not to mention a talk for the school to write, a police station to paint.

Fergus stands, looks around, brushes non-existent crumbs off his clothes.

'Don't want to be late, love.'

Georgie looks at him. He's taken to ironing his top, even though the T-shirt fabric hardly needs it, and he wears his smart trousers since they told him it was his choice. The kids might wear jeans or joggers to work on the tills but not him, not Fergus.

'I'm having my breakfast,' she says.

'Of course, I didn't mean to rush you, I… I'm sorry—'

'No, I didn't mean to… It's okay. It's okay.'

He sits back down and waits while she coats her toast with peanut butter and jam, and then he seems to sit a bit higher in his chair as he says what he must have been saving up for a while:

'I've got a new member of the archaeological society. Someone you might be interested in.'

Her eyes flick up to his. She can see he's trying to help, trying to reach out to her.

'It's Natalie Prowle. You know, from the museum?'

'Lee's mum?'

He smiles – he knows that already. Mind you, the whole village knows Lee Prowle and Andy Barr were arrested for attacking Pamali and vandalising the Spar; knows they've both been let off with community service too.

'What did she say?'

'Nothing much yet, she joined up using the form on the website. But she's the chair of the community council and they've invited me to their meeting tonight, to give a wee talk about the excavation now we've got permission to go ahead. So I'm thinking that'll be good.'

'Hmm.'

'And that professor from the university is very interested in my iron figurine.'

The image of it settles somewhere behind her eyes, the vicious beaks for hands, the broken wrists, the peaked hood and claw feet.

'It's hardly yours, Fergus.'

She shouldn't have said that – he loves that little idol or whatever it is. The villagers seem to care about it too. Perhaps there are advantages to having a husband who found something that the people round here want; not to mention a husband who's so white folk forget who he's married to long enough to let their prejudice show.

'I just meant the one I found in the motte,' he says quietly. 'It's nice that a professional is interested, that's all.'

'Of course it is,' she says. 'And I'm interested too. You know that, right?'

Their kitchen windows look out into their garden, which has become overgrown this year, untended – she hadn't realised how much work he was doing out there, before, while she was at work elsewhere. Now there's leaf mulch under the cherry tree, long-dead daffodils collapsed under their own weight, twigs blown down in the spring winds still lying where they fell and brown leaves of montbretia cascading over flower beds; she wonders what might be underneath it all, struggling to grow.

'I'm not meaning to rush you, not at all, but...'

Her toast, only half eaten, is soggy anyway.

'Okay,' she says. 'I'm ready. Let's go.'

They've always shared a car, her and Fergus, though she knows he's frustrated at having to rely on her for a lift all the way to Crackenbridge. He cycles sometimes, though it takes him a good couple of hours – she guesses he does it for the independence – but he's on the early shift this morning and she offered the lift. It's something to do before she has to take that deep breath and turn herself back into DI Georgie Strachan. She puts the radio on as a way to fill the silence, and even though the sky is a spectacular golden peach this morning, layered with streaks of soft white cloud, neither of them comments on it. Fergus notices it though, same as she does. She's fairly sure about that.

'Are you okay, love?' he says.

She glances over, gives a brief nod and takes the coast road up to Warphill, past the derelict flats, because she likes to keep an eye on them these days – no sign of life in there – then turns on to the main road to get up to Crackenbridge as fast as possible.

'It's just…ever since…'

She pulls to a stop at the first red light.

'Ever since the case…'

'Ever since Alexis was killed and my best friend was attacked by those racist kids you mean?'

Fergus almost winces as she says it.

'It's what they did, Fergus. It's what they did to Pamali. Andy Barr and Lee Prowle, and don't you ever forget it.'

'I wouldn't, Georgie, I couldn't, everything that happened was so awful, but…'

'But?'

'It's just you seem angry at me.'

Georgie breathes before answering, keeping her voice quiet, cautious.

'I'm not angry at you, love.'

'Angry at everyone, then.'

She blinks.

'And why aren't *you*?'

'No one here means us any harm, Georgie. Not… I mean, not really.'

The lights change and she drives on slowly, careful not to rev the engine. Roads are quiet this time of the morning, but that's no reason to drive thoughtlessly.

'I just want us to get back to how things were,' he says.

The smell of the abattoir fills the car then is replaced by manure.

'I know, because of what happened to your brother—'

'This is nothing to do with Errol.'

'It's just…' He sounds almost nervous. 'Anger never solved anything.'

'Says the white man—'

'What?'

She'd close her eyes if she could, but instead she lets a moment of quiet soften what she says next.

'Well you are, aren't you?'

'No. No!'

She indicates, calmly overtakes the tractor chugging along at twenty.

'I mean' – Fergus is still talking – 'well obviously I am, but I'm not, you know what I mean… I'm not English either, am I, I'm not local…anyway, you don't see the colour of my skin, surely?'

There are more cars around now, the roads filling up with every mile.

'And since when have I ever cared about the colour of yours?' he says, defensive.

Georgie watches the road, the traffic, drives on in silence. Indicates in good time at the roundabout. She wishes she didn't feel so bloody tired.

'Here we go,' she says at last, taking the exit to the retail park outside Crackenbridge and driving into the first parking spot she sees. It's a massive car park here, God knows how many people they were expecting to do their shopping all at once.

'Okay. Maybe I misunderstood,' he says, taking a deep breath then letting it out. 'Thanks for the lift. Bye, love.'

He goes to kiss her, as usual, and she lets him, as usual, but they both know something's lacking.

He sits back in the seat. There's a twist in Georgie's stomach. She wishes she remembered how to give him a hug, a big genuine hug.

'I don't understand where we're at, Georgie.'

They lock eyes, and that's something.

'We're giving each other some time,' she says.

'But I'm on your side, love—'

'I just need some time, that's all. This year has been so…'

He sighs, not angry but resigned, and gets out of the car, closes the door gently, raises his hand in a wave then strides off past the trolley stacks to the supermarket entrance.

Georgie – who hadn't turned the engine off – reverses out of the Kaltonn car park and begins the drive back to Burrowhead police station. Maybe it's true. Maybe he is on her side. She always believed he was before, so what's changed? But as she approaches the village, she sees people, young people, leaving the caravan park and heading over to Ricky Barr's brown-and-yellow fields and her thoughts leave Fergus behind. They're here to work on Ricky's farm for the season. Those kids. Local kids. She slows down to get a good look at their faces. Sees plenty she recognises, and a few she doesn't. Lee and his older brother Aaron are among them – she notices them, and they notice her too. They stare right in through her window, that same look of spite on their faces as Lee had when she arrested him earlier this year, the same look he probably had when he was attacking Pamali and vandalising the Spar; they stare at her as though nothing in this world could stop them and Georgie clasps the steering wheel and waits exactly where she is until they are out of sight, and that's when she gets the call.

TIME WELL SPENT

Shona is standing by the potato harvester waiting for Kev. Not that she's keen to get the work started; she'd be happy never to see another potato again, soil-covered misshapen little gnome heads that they are. It's been so hot this summer she'd worked in a T-shirt on her first day – rookie mistake, and she had the cuts to prove it, woke up to find weeds tangled in her hair, blotches on her skin. Today she's got her hoody sleeves pulled down and her gloves up to her wrists and she can still feel the itching. She wonders if there's some kind of venom in the ugly little leaves. But the potato work was one of the main things Ricky was hiring for, that and the drivers (she wishes now she'd learned to drive a tractor). It's a mixed farm, Ricky Barr's, but he doesn't seem keen on letting any of the summer kids near the livestock. Presumably there isn't too much they could do wrong with the potatoes.

'They need lifted and checked and packed,' Ricky had said as he directed them to stand in one of three huddles on their first day. 'You lot are on the silage with me. Andy: you're on the baler. We've got a dry few weeks coming up. Good news all round, eh?'

Then Lee had been put on driving duty for the potato harvester – though why anyone would trust him around heavy machinery Shona had no idea – and Kev had been sent over to stand with Lee and his brother Aaron, who'd walked out of his job at the butchers just to be here apparently, and then Ricky Barr's eyes had fallen on her.

'There's weeding to be done in the garden,' he'd said.

Shona had silently walked over to stand with the boys on pota-to-lifting duty and Ricky had grinned.

'Never let it be said I'm not for equal rights. You're on sorting with Aaron. Kev?'

'Yep?'

'You can drive the trailer?'

'Course. Did last summer over at Dummigan's, north a Warphill.'

'Aye, I know it. Right. Questions?' Then he'd glanced at Shona again. 'Aaron'll keep you right.'

So today Shona is riding the back of the harvester with Aaron beside her, gloves pulled up over her wrists, sweat clinging to her upper lip that she can't spare a hand to wipe, as she grabs at the weeds and stalks in among the ever-moving conveyor belt of pota-toes dug up by the harvester before they're dropped into the trailer Kev is driving beside them. Him and Lee are yelling to each other, windows rolled down and voices loud and gruff over the engines, play-acting at being weathered old farmers like Ricky Barr, 'stead of kids just out a school with crap A levels and nowhere to live but a bedroom at their mam's. That was a large part of the appeal of this job, and Ricky knew it too – he could get away with paying them way under by offering them living space in the caravans for the season. That's where they're all staying now, Shona included.

Lee keeps going on about how great it is, Ricky taking on so many local kids. 'Need more of that round here,' he says. 'Why shouldn't we get priority, eh?'

'He shouldn't have taken on those posh twats though,' Kev yells back. 'D'you see that one in his pink festival trousers?'

'Cunt.'

'Aye.'

'Shut it you two,' Aaron shouts from beside her. He doesn't say much but when he does it's usually an order, and it's usually obeyed, for a couple of minutes at least.

Riding the potato harvester with someone so sullen as Aaron Prowle is giving Shona plenty of time to think. Especially now her hands have got into the rhythm of it and her eyes have adjusted to the searing light of the sun on the metal edges of the runner that spits the potatoes at her. It becomes mechanical after a while, an automatic glance for weeds or roots, a grab at what shouldn't be there, the quick flick of a wrist to throw out whatever is unwanted, and then on. Now and then Aaron gives her a sideways glance, when he thinks she's too engrossed to notice, like he's checking up on her but not wanting her to know it.

She never knew Aaron much at school – he wouldn't have been seen dead mixing with younger kids, didn't even acknowledge his own brother – but Lee used to boast about him, go on about how he worked for Ricky Barr, how he got that motorbike he drives around on. Rachel used to feel sorry for Lee, when he started going on like that, but not Shona – not then and not now. She wasn't even surprised when she heard he'd attacked Pamali in the Spar, or that Andy had tagged along with him like a puppy dog; the two of them had been looking for trouble all year. The surprise was they'd both been let off with community service. Bobby Helmsteading had led them astray, that was their defence, and there was some mess-up by the police, a lack of responsible adults present. Now that she can believe – there's a shortage of responsible adults in this place. Maybe that's why she can't make up her mind about where to turn. She'd have told Rachel, if she could. But Rachel is dead and she's on her own, at least until she gets something she can write a proper article about and the paper finally puts her on the payroll.

A voice from beside her: 'The girl, though. I'd do her.'

When Kev is like this it makes Shona feel more unwelcome than all the rough talk of all the shitty boys this side of Crackenbridge. She wishes she hadn't signed up for this, thinks about walking away – they're not on contracts so Ricky Barr can't make her stay, none of them can. The decision to keep hanging round with them is hers, and where is she getting with all this? No exposé in sight, just her own guilt and a feeling of something dangerous beyond her grasp. She still can't shake the unease of how Kev had treated Pauly, how they all had – not that she'd realised at the time how often she'd think about it afterwards, wishing things had played out differently. Then there's the sharp chill she gets when Kev calls his sister Penny-Ann a dyke or joins in a fight down the pub, no hesitation, kicks, punches, barges his way into the middle of it all, and the spite that comes out his mouth sometimes; could it really all be an act? But then he turns, looks at her with that grin and she remembers, like she always does, the gang of them: her and Rachel, Kev and Pauly, Andy and Lee, the six of them when they were just kids, before everything got so fucked up.

They had a party once round at Rachel's, before her mam got sick; it was her thirteenth birthday and her mam had let them have cans of Diamond White and Tennent's, which they all thought was pretty cool. Out in the garden she'd made a bonfire and they had sticks with marshmallows on to roast, and they'd been having a really good time out there for a while, before the boys had started flicking the roasted marshmallows at the windows where they splodged and stuck. Trust Lee to ruin a good night, even then.

Eventually Rachel's mam had said it was late and the party was over, which was probably less about the marshmallows and more about finding Shona and Rachel smoking behind the shed – Shona could tell Rachel would be in for a bollocking after they left – but they all filed out and said thanks and happy birthday and that. She supposed now they were all a bit ashamed of ruining it. But as they were leaving Lee made some excuse to go back inside and when he met them out on the street it was obvious he had something stashed in his jacket. 'What've you done?' Shona said, and they were all thinking he'd nicked a bottle of vodka or something, but then he pulled it out with a flourish and it was weird because it was just this glass vase thing that Rachel had asked them all to be careful of, because it was her mam's favourite. God only knew what he wanted with it. He was like, let's chuck it, and no one knew what to say, but then he hurled it up into a tree and it lodged there, between the branches.

After a while wandering the streets Kev said he was headed home, and even today Shona's not sure what it was that made her do it, but she waited till he was far enough on that he wouldn't notice and then she followed him. He looped round back to Rachel's house and went straight to the tree where Lee had chucked the vase and started to climb. He was a good climber, Kev, strong enough to pull himself up to that first branch, confident enough that he didn't have a fear of falling to get in his way. He got the vase, got back down, and only then did he see Shona watching him. She could see him thinking about how to explain; she even wondered if he was about to throw the vase away again, but then he looked straight at her and said, 'I'm giving it back.'

He did, too. Didn't land Lee in it or say anything very much when Rachel's mam opened the door, just passed it to her and said sorry and walked off with his hands in his pockets and Shona kept following him till he turned and said, 'What?'

She could feel herself making a choice in that moment: to carry on the act or push through it to something else; acknowledge what she now knew about him. It was the sudden softness in the way he didn't quite smile, perhaps, something almost goofy, verging on embarrassed, but at the same time he wasn't denying what had happened, wasn't making excuses or pushing her away or being a dick about it.

'I see you, Kevin Taylor,' she'd said quietly, moving closer to him, till her body was touching his and she saw a flush spread up his neck. He could've put his hands round her waist if he wanted to, kissed her – that was what she'd wanted – but he didn't.

'You talk tough all you like to them others,' she'd said. 'But you can't fool me.'

There's a cruel edge to his laugh now though; whatever it was Lee just said, it must have been spiteful or sexist. It's the kind of laugh that tells Shona she'd have hated the comment that sparked it, so she bites her tongue, focuses on the potatoes, grabs some twisted roots, a bit of…what the fuck is that? It's white, smooth. Different to anything else that's been lifted from the ground. Potatoes are speeding past on the conveyor belt along with weeds and dirt but she can't stop staring at what she's got in her hand. It's warm, it's… it's a bit of bone, that's what it is, about six centimetres long, thicker than a feather's spine.

'The fuck?' she says.

Aaron just glances at her, his hands keep moving.

'Chuck it,' he says.

'But it's—'

'From a dead bird or something, chuck it.'

The potatoes keep coming, weeds and stalks and all, but she's got the bone in her palm, held there by some force she doesn't understand, tight against her skin.

'It's not from a bird.'

'Christ, a fox then. Chuck it away!'

But Shona's doing no such thing.

She stuffs it into her jeans pocket, where it settles in, pressing through the fabric right into her thigh, and there's a heat to it that makes her think maybe it's worth her while being here after all.

MAKING THINGS RIGHT

The blood is everywhere. There's no shelter here in the clearing; the sun feels low and angry, stretching shadows from the trees against their will, sinking down to brand the clearing itself with searing light. The past few weeks have left the soil dry and parched – it's gulping in every drop of the blood that's collecting on the outer rim of the stone until it has momentum enough to fall. Georgie wishes there were something to hold, to steady herself. She's got that rising nausea again, the prickling of sweat on her forehead. The last time she was out here was to find old Walt Mackie, after he'd disappeared from home, scared Trish half to death – though she'd tried to hide it, of course. DC Trish Mackie doesn't like anyone to see her softer side, especially not when it comes to her Uncle Walt. But Georgie had known there was something wrong about the place then, too. The way Walt had been lying out on the stone like a willing sacrifice – that stone right here, where the blood's collected. Said he was waiting for his ancestors to come and save him.

She pulls out the bottle of water she's taken to carrying everywhere with her, tips her head back and gulps. The ice has melted but it's still cool, thank God. Folk round here aren't used to this heat, but Georgie's got some tricks to beat it. The clearing is maybe twenty metres across; beyond that are the parallel trunks of silver birch and swathes of wild garlic, woodland that shimmers with life this time of year and echoes with tall, frozen shadows in the winter. In the spring there were snowdrops here, late snowdrops – and mud and rain and the deep groan of a sky ready to burst. Now it's thirst and matted feathers and grass up to her shins, vivid red blood filling the circles within circles etched into the stone slab that make up the ancient carving of the cup and ring, and a bee buzzing around her hair. She shakes her head, swipes at it, takes a step forward.

The stone itself lies flat on the ground, rectangular and heavy, like a low altar, bang in the middle of the clearing where there are no other features at all. The blood is fresh. The slaughter happened recently, in the morning light. They were arrogant, the people who did this. No fear of being seen.

'My God,' says Simon, arriving behind her and keeping a step back.

'Si,' Georgie says, glad he's arrived. He's a good PC, and one of the few people she still trusts around here. The sight of more blood can't be easy on him though, so soon; not that he talks much about what he's been through. He's been working harder than ever. She put him on liaison with the city's investigation into the drug-supply networks in the area, though she's not convinced their approach is going to help. Every time they arrest one group in Crackenbridge another has taken their place within hours. Heroin- and methadone-misuse deaths are spiking all along the coast but there's no money for harm reduction, for treatment services. Besides, there's something desperate happening to a place when you're faced with a scene like this.

The horse is lying across one half of the stone slab, its throat severed but its head still attached. Not for want of trying, by the looks of it. The knife got stuck; it's still there, hanging out of the poor creature's throat, the handle soaked with blood. It looks like an ordinary carving knife – no wonder they couldn't cut through. Above, the horse's face is intact. Its eyes are open, dark and unnervingly human. Beneath the jagged wound, its black fur is matted. Georgie can imagine the blood spurting from its throat as someone hacked at the poor creature. It must have been drugged, surely. In a circle around the stone – about a metre in diameter – are the sinewy carcasses of six dead gulls and their white feathers, plucked. Neither Georgie nor Simon have stepped into the circle.

'This is disgusting,' Simon says.

Georgie swallows, tries to block out the smell but it's hanging heavy in the air. Flies are starting to crawl on the carcass.

'But is it…'

'What, Si?'

'Is it an actual crime scene? I mean—'

'We need to know who owned this horse.'

It's not human, of course, but it is a killing – that's what Georgie knows – and someone had to be sick to do it.

'So we could be looking into poaching? I mean, that'd be the charge?'

Georgie chews the inside of her mouth. The feathers remind her of something, though she can't place what it is.

'But what if the owners did this?'

Georgie frowns.

'Or…could it be wild?'

'I've not seen any wild horses round here.'

Simon exhales and pushes his hair back from his forehead – he's sweating too. This bloody heat, it's not normal.

'So what should we do?'

'Find the owner, Si. Top priority. And…and call the RSPCA,' says Georgie. Her accent is strong this morning, the faded North Carolina lilt of it. 'I'll tell Cal to get the forensics team down here. We need to check that knife for prints and get the blood tested, just to make sure.'

'Make sure of what?'

'That it all came from that poor creature and not…' She feels Simon tense up behind her, the way the air changes, the mood, so she lets her voice trail off. Sends that text to Cal. 'A horse this size, and it wouldn't have lain down willingly, I shouldn't think. So did they drug it?'

'They?'

'Must have been more than one guy at any rate. They had to get it here. Sedate it. Her, I mean. She's a mare. And they had to get close enough to cut her throat.'

Georgie's phone vibrates, and she checks the message.

'That's Cal on his way?'

Georgie nods. 'This was where I found Walt, last time he went a wander.'

'Isn't he on his trial week just now, at the care home?'

'That's what Trish said.'

Simon glances at her.

'Want me to check in on him?'

'Yeah. Ask him about…ask him if he's seen anything like this before.'

It's not just the heat, not just the smell, it's the stillness of it – the air is hanging over them, thick and bloated. She looks down at her feet, at the yellowing grass and parched soil, imagines looking deeper; are there more stones under there? Fergus has started talking about an ancient henge buried somewhere beneath the ground.

'There's, er…'

'What is it, Si?'

He lowers his voice, though Suze is over by the birches setting up a cordon round the clearing and there's no one else within earshot. It was Suze that called it in. She was out here for her morning run.

'There's something else I've been wanting to…'

Georgie feels something creeping subtly round her neck, like a nail filed to a point being scratched on her skin so faintly it's hardly there at all.

'…I think Alexis might have been on to something.' He pauses, breathes out. This is hard for him; she can see that. 'More than what happened to Dawn, I mean. The way he was being targeted, the way he was questioning Elise—'

'Si—'

'The way he was being so secretive, even from me.'

'The case is closed, Si.'

'But it's not over though, is it. Not for you and not for me.'

'I know it would have felt…different if we'd have been able to arrest Bobby Helmsteading, get a confession – get some closure for you. I'm sorry we didn't get that. I truly am.'

'It's not that.'

She looks at him, doubtful, but he's pressing on and she can see that she needs to let him. There's a look on his face she's getting used to now, though she'd never seen it before the spring, before the murders. It's something more than determination, something verging on conviction.

'Remember Pauly and Rachel?'

'Of course. The suicides last year.'

'You still sure about that?'

Georgie doesn't reply.

'Because I'm not.' He almost whispers that last bit. 'When they were found, there was animal blood as well, wasn't there?'

'In their stomachs, Si. They'd ingested it.'

'But it's a link. Isn't it?'

It is a link, and a lot of things are starting to feel linked to Georgie, in this place, but she knows better than to go saying that out loud.

'That case is closed too, Si.'

He swallows, looks over his shoulder, then back again in the direction of the cup and ring, the horse's legs, bent and collapsed under its body. Her body. The unnatural angle of the way her head is hanging there, the glistening red inside her throat. It's not the horse he's staring at though. She can see his eyes moving back and forth, as though watching a person pacing in front of him.

'I want to make things right,' he says, eventually.

'Then help me with this,' she says. 'This is what we have to deal with right now. Find the owner of this horse.' She lowers her voice. 'And a fresh case could be our best chance of finding out what's really going on.'

MEANWHILE, IN THE CITY

DS Frazer and DC McConnell are standing outside North Hill View nursing home, waiting with increasing impatience. They've rung the bell twice already, because the place has a security entrance system, but no one seems to be in the spacious and remarkably floral reception. They can see in easily enough – the secured front doors are generously proportioned and made of thick triple glazing – inside the walls are white and the pictures are of flower arrangements and there is a large bouquet on the reception desk, where the lack of receptionist is particularly noticeable.

It is far and away the nicest-looking care home Frazer has ever seen. Not at all like the one his wife's mum is in, which has worn old carpets and a smell of cooked vegetables, though to be fair there is always someone on reception there and he's never had to wait to be let in. The thought makes him shift on his feet and he feels his hands twist with the familiar need to hear his wife's voice, but instead he rings the buzzer again, this time leaning his thumb on the button for longer than would be polite.

Behind them, there are works being done along one side of the road, insistent drilling, men in bright orange fluorescent jackets, temporary traffic lights in place and a queue of restless cars blaring their horns. Someone's got their window down, the grating beat of rap barging its way out into the street. A siren wails in the distance. There's a child throwing a tantrum round the corner. The waft of cigarettes as a huddle of students walk by, their conversation all laughter and swear words and snatches of something that happened last night that they probably wouldn't be talking about if Frazer and McConnell hadn't been plain clothes. Someone has seen them, though. Someone's emerged from the double doors that lead into the depths of the building, and Frazer knocks on the glass with his knuckles just to make doubly sure. The woman nods as she steps behind reception and prepares to talk to them through the intercom.

'Fuck's sake,' mumbles McConnell. 'This place is more secure than the station.'

Frazer doesn't reply. Just clears his throat.

'DS Daniel Frazer and DC Jess McConnell,' he says, leaning close to the microphone bit of the intercom. 'You called us.'

She doesn't reply, but does finally buzz them in. The noise of the roadworks vanishes in an instant, replaced by the suffocating smell of potpourri as the door swings shut behind them and locks automatically. They walk to the desk, hold up their IDs. Beside him, McConnell smiles as though she finds the atmosphere soothing, welcoming even. He doesn't. The smell has intensified the headache he's had for the past two months – since getting back from that godawful case on the coast. It'd help if he didn't keep thinking about it. It's not like anyone cares about Burrowhead here, so why his mind keeps pulling him back there he has no idea. He even thought about calling Trish Mackie once. She's a spiky one. There's something about her he'd like to understand a bit better. Not out there though; he's not going back out there.

The receptionist is wearing smart maroon trousers and heels. Her hair is silver-blonde, gold threads over grey. She clocks their badges, leans forward slightly over the desk and thanks them for coming.

'I was the one who called,' she says. 'I wasn't sure if I should but, well, I'm glad you didn't just laugh it off this time. I know it might be a false alarm, what with her dementia and everything...'

Frazer raises his eyebrows. He doesn't believe he has ever laughed anything off.

'It was the way she kept describing that place...'

God but his head is suddenly pounding.

'I know it well myself, but to Betty it's so vivid, you know what I mean? And I'm not someone who'd normally...' Her voice trails off for a second and she looks like she's trying to decide something. 'Have you ever been out there? To Burrowhead?'

Just the name of the village is enough to make Frazer's shoulders tighten, his spine start to itch. He doesn't reply though. Please God, he thinks, don't let this be about Burrowhead.

She's still waiting, the receptionist, until he shakes his head in what he tells himself isn't a lie, just a way of saying he doesn't want to talk about it, doesn't want to think about it.

'Well,' she says. 'Not many have, I suppose. But that's what made me—'

'Will we be able to interview her today?' Frazer says. It comes out more abruptly than he means it to, but suddenly he can hardly breathe. He needs to get this interview done and get out of here.

He pushes his fingers against the bridge of his nose, then glances back up at the receptionist. She looks almost hurt.

'I...' He clears his throat. 'Apologies, Ma'am, but her first-hand account would be—'

'Of course.'

When she purses her lips they almost disappear entirely.

She pushes the chair back from her desk without elaborating and leads them through the locked internal doors and into a corridor that most certainly does not smell of potpourri. It's just a front then, being so different on the outside. He can hear a desperate sort of wailing coming from one of the rooms. Growing old seems to be a crappy experience however much money you have to throw at the process.

'That's just bath time,' the receptionist says, as though that should make some kind of sense. 'But don't worry, Betty Marshall is as calm as they come, most of the time.' She's talking to McConnell now, not him, Frazer notices. 'Like I say, normally we might not have taken her story too seriously, but she was so adamant and I thought, seeing as how I know the village and—'

'It's always best to call us,' McConnell says with a reassuring smile. Maybe it's because she's older than the rest of the team, maybe it's something to do with the gentle, familiar sort of face she has, but McConnell seems to put people at ease in a way Frazer has never managed. One glance at him and everyone seems to get defensive. It wears him down, some days. Other days it spurs him on.

'Here we are,' says the receptionist. 'Shall I leave you to it?'

'Please.'

'Call if you need anything. Tea and sandwiches are at twelve.'

Once the door is shut and McConnell has introduced them again – DS Daniel Frazer and DC Jess McConnell – Frazer can get a proper look at the old lady sitting, straight-backed and smartly dressed, in front of him. She doesn't look as though she belongs in here. Her hair is freshly washed and dried, grey but bobbed neatly under her chin. Her eyes are bright, searching. Her shirt is done up to the top button, blue-and-white striped, vaguely nautical, and her navy trousers beneath end in the only sign that she is in a care home rather than at a business meeting – red fluffy slippers. She clears her throat.

'It's about time you showed up,' she says, looking them up and down, clearly finding them wanting. 'No one else round here believes me, but I knew I could trust Debs. I need to report a murder.'

TRUSTING TIME, PART ONE

Trish Mackie had arrived at the police station first thing. She likes to be the one to open up, likes a few minutes to think through her day before Georgie and Simon arrive. She's got big plans, Trish, and choosing to work in Burrowhead doesn't make them any the less important. This is her home and it's in a mess and if she doesn't fix it then who will? Pamali washing the graffiti off her shop window every morning isn't going to do it. Mind you, the station's in an even worse state than the rest of the village: paint peeling off, rusty smears running down from the guttering, and the inside looks like it got stuck in small-town England in the 1970s, with a smell to match.

Trish has suggested plenty of local guys who could paint the place up – mates' rates they'd give her too – but Georgie keeps making excuses not to call them. After Andy made his mistake, standing by while Lee Prowle attacked the Spar, Georgie is being very cautious about who she lets near the station. Trish could say she's seeming a bit paranoid. So they're stuck here, in a grimy old building with ancient buzzing fluorescent lights in the ceiling and windows that won't open in this unbelievable heat, and her DI's doing nothing about it, despite the fact Trish can see her looking at the building every day with something verging on revulsion.

It's heading for lunchtime now though and she's still the only one here, and that is weird. Something's going on and she's not been called. Makes her itchy. She walks through the building, flicking all the lights on and off, checking every room: reception, kitchen, two offices, interview room opposite, cell at the back. The old broom cupboard. It's the cleanest room in the station since Andy did his work on it. He's turning things around, that kid. There's a good heart in him, like many of the folk around here – she can see that. If the world would just give them a chance, 'stead of crushing them down more every year. Shop closures, bank closures, library's gone, even the GPs in Warphill is being shut and what are folk to do who can't travel up to Crackenbridge, who need help? It's a bloody disgrace. No cinema, nowhere for the kids to go, nothing for folk to do. That big Kaltonn has put the last of the local newsagents out of business. Warphill is an angry shell of a place now; how Pamali manages to hang on at the Spar in Burrowhead Trish doesn't know. Bit of investment, that's what's needed, community services, incentives for local business, a grant to do up the fountain, get some tourists back. And one other thing: she needs to get Ricky fucking Barr out of Burrowhead and locked up once and for all.

Trish storms back down the corridor having proved that all the lights are at least working, and all the rooms are indeed empty, before turning back to her computer and hammering restlessly at the keys as she checks her email. There is no new email. The sun is bright, its light only dappled by the dirt on the windows. Georgie wants her on The Queen's Head in Warphill. They've been serving adolescents apparently – well, presumably. They always used to. Trish drank in there herself as a teenager. They all did. She'll give the staff a slap on the wrist but they're not going to stop and she reckons the pub's a safer place for the kids to be than the alternatives. She found a hypodermic needle up on the cliffs the other day and it's not the first time.

She was out walking with Suze and when they saw it Trish became so aware of the sun's heat on the back of her head she felt like it was burning. They're meeting up tonight as well. It's good, working with Suze. She's easier to get on with than Georgie, and she wants to make a difference. Plus she's a PC, so Trish gets to give the orders instead of following them. Just a drink later though, and that's the other reason Trish made sure she was in first thing: means she's got a perfectly valid reason for leaving early, should anyone ask.

Not that she's got anything to hide. Trish has nothing to hide whatsoever.

Her phone vibrates. Finally, a bloody text message. That'll be Georgie, telling her where they all are, what the hell is going on. But no, it's Suze. Again.

Just checking we're still on for tonight?

Good grief, woman, Trish types. *I said yes already.*

Maybe that was a bit harsh.

She follows up with a second text message: a smiley face.

Trish is smiley. Course she is. It's just she's surrounded by people who are neither as fast nor as smart as her, and no one seems to appreciate just how capable she is, and frankly it gets bloody frustrating.

TRUSTING TIME, PART TWO

As Georgie walks down the dim hallway to her office she can hear Trish pummelling away on her keyboard. Trish seemed to take it as some kind of punishment when Georgie suggested she could look into a transfer to Crackenbridge, but with every month that goes by Georgie is more afraid of closure and making sure Trish had a firm footing in a bigger station seemed like the best way to secure her a future. She didn't say that though. She doesn't want them to worry, not Trish and not Si.

'Morning, Trish,' she says, standing at the door.

'Ma'am.'

Trish has become more formal with her recently. It's been a month since she last called her Georgie instead of Ma'am; a month since Andy and Lee got their community service and Georgie was as angry as Trish was relieved. Now, it's like the pair of them are holding each other at arm's length and Georgie's not sure which of them is keeping it that way. Pamali thinks she's being too hard on her; that Trish is dealing with things the best way she knows how. Georgie's starting to think Pami is too kind to the world.

'Has something happened?'

She's a local through and through, DC Trish Mackie, just like her Uncle Walt. Is that all it is? Is it just that she loves these villages, this place Georgie suspects of something she can't even name?

'Give me a few minutes, Trish. When Simon gets here we'll fill you in.'

Georgie backs away and walks the four paces to her own office. How can there be a chill in here with that heat outside? They used to have coffee together of a morning, a couple of chocolate digestives, but now they've all taken to bringing in their own flasks – coffee's better that way at least. Still, Georgie's never felt so isolated, so much like an outsider as she has this year. Fergus could change that, she wishes he would, but he's too preoccupied with his amateur archaeological society and bringing in minimum wage to notice. Meanwhile she's got some kind of wet rot infestation in the interview room and a smell coming from the cell at the back that no amount of mopping seems to shift.

She asked Simon the other day if he could smell it too and he looked at her like she was going mad. He did his best to check it out, though, walked into the room and gave a few sniffs. He's been doing the same thing every morning this week, like he's checking it for her. Maybe it's the smell of Andy Barr's racism and Lee Prowle's spite and the villagers' fear of everything beyond themselves that has made its way into the station for Georgie alone to recognise. Trish tells her weekly how well Andy's doing, and Georgie can't shake the irritation that flares up in her every time. So much easier to forgive racism if you know it'll never be directed against you.

'That's him now,' Trish says, making her jump.

'What, Andy?' Georgie snaps.

'No, of course not.' Trish looks genuinely confused, almost hurt. 'Simon's back. I thought you were going to fill me in. I thought… Sorry, Ma'am.'

'No, no. My fault, Trish.'

God but Georgie wants to shake this feeling, wants to be able to laugh, share a moment of friendship.

'Let's get us all on the same page, shall we?'

If only she could.

TRUSTING TIME, PART THREE

Standing in the cell at the back of the station, Simon can smell something – though it's not the damp rotting fungus that Georgie has described to him. He's drawn here every morning, every time he walks into the station; it's why he's standing in the cell right now, even though Georgie has already called him into her office. Two minutes, he'd called back, hoping neither Georgie nor Trish would step out into the hall to see what he's doing. The smell in here, it reminds him of the salt water pooling on the cave's floor, of Dawn's hair when she'd hugged him and given him a way to move forward. Standing here for a few seconds, with that smell, he remembers what she told him: Alexis saved her life.

Simon loves him for that; loves him for who he was and for what he did. Christ, he thinks it's easier to love Alexis unconditionally now he's dead. He's so far from being over him that he feels more committed to him than ever. Trish asked him a few weeks back if he was seeing anyone new and he'd glared at her like she was something evil before he caught himself and shook his head and mumbled about not being ready.

'Si, you okay?'

Georgie has followed him out here, of course. She seems to be checking up on him all the time these days.

'I've asked around about the horse, just to get a preliminary sense – checked with the villagers I know who ride – but no one recognises it from the description so I'll start making calls now.'

'Good,' Georgie nods. 'Thanks.'

'And I went by the care home too,' he says. 'To see if I could pop in for a chat, but they said he wasn't up for visitors this morning. I figured it could wait till the afternoon.'

'What?' Trish says, making Simon jump. 'What care home? What's going on?'

She's standing behind them in the hall.

'Trish.' Georgie turns, her movements as slow as that cautious southern twang of hers. 'Now we're all together.'

'What's *happened*?'

Beside him, Georgie takes a deep breath, lets it out slowly before speaking.

'We've got an animal killing to investigate.'

'Animal?'

Georgie pauses and Trish looks so desperate for information Simon can't help but fill the gap.

'Someone's slaughtered a horse,' he says, 'and left the body out in Mungrid Woods. A black mare.'

Trish's mouth falls open, just a fraction, but Simon sees it.

'Jesus, that's… Where in the woods?'

'By the stone with the cup and ring,' Georgie says.

'You mean exactly where we found Uncle Walt after he disappeared?'

Georgie nods. 'That's why I asked Simon to go visit him in the care home, see if he can shed some light on what they might've been up to. It looks like a…'

'Like some kind of ritual.' Simon finishes her sentence, which he wouldn't normally do, but it had seemed for a minute there like Georgie couldn't bring herself to say it.

'I'll talk to him,' snaps Trish.

Simon can sense Georgie's posture changing beside him.

'I need you on the pub—'

'But he's my uncle.'

'Precisely.'

Trish opens her mouth to argue, then presumably thinks better of it, thank God.

'I'll be gentle with him,' Si says.

'Well, aye.' Trish's voice is softer now. 'He's uppity in that care home – doesn't think he needs to be there. But what if he goes another wander and no one can find him? He could have died out there in Mungrid—'

'Trish?' says Si. 'It's okay. I'll be gentle with him, I promise.'

'It's fine.' She turns, heads for the office, leaving Simon and Georgie standing outside the cell, leaving Simon to carry on worrying about her. Though, truth is, Simon's got something else on his mind.

Two months ago, coming home from Alexis's funeral, seeing the 'Sorry we missed you' card the postman had put through the door still sitting on the hall table. It had been on the floor when he'd got home from the pub that awful Monday night, Alexis's last. He'd thrown it onto the table and there it had stayed, every day for nearly two weeks. Box ticked: signature required.

Then after the funeral, needing to get out the house, to do something, he'd picked up the card and walked to the bus stop through the bitter wind, collected the package from the depot in Crackenbridge and recognised the writing on the envelope immediately: Alexis's own. He'd sent him a package.

'This afternoon then, Si.'

'What?'

It's Georgie; he's in the police station, at work, on duty, still standing in the hall.

'Interview Walt Mackie?'

'Of course, I'm on it.'

Simon swallows, strides to the office to make the call. The care home staff don't try to put him off again – he's welcome any time after two. Head in hands, just for a second. There'd been other things written by Alexis as well, in that package, things that gave him that familiar kick to the chest, left him nauseous and struggling for breath.

You have been the best part of my life.

That was the good bit. The bit that reminded him how much they'd loved each other, their walks along the cliffs, days outside sketching, plans for a future together.

Forgive me.

There had been no need to ask; Alexis was forgiven, of course he was, and he was missed. It was Simon who needed to be forgiven now.

But there is something very wrong in these villages.

'Si?'

It's Georgie again. She has this way of telling when you're somewhere else, and he wishes she hadn't. He's heard folk round here call her sensitive, though that could be a euphemism.

'You know…' She pulls up a chair. 'If there's anything you need to talk about…'

He shakes his head – he can't get it all to fit, that's the problem. Alexis hadn't pieced it together, or if he had, he hadn't explained. All Simon has to go on are the tapes in the package, each one labelled with a name: Dawn Helmsteading, Elise Robertson, Natalie Prowle.

Don't trust anyone from Burrowhead.

'Honestly, I need to be working. Things are…'

Don't trust anyone from Warphill.

'Things are getting better. I promise. You don't have to worry about me.'

Don't trust the police.

And there it was. The reason Alexis hadn't trusted him, at least not until he was afraid for his life. The reason Simon can't talk to Trish, or Suze, no matter how often they offer. The reason he can't trust Georgie.

CHANGELING

As Betty Marshall talks, as DS Frazer and DC Jess McConnell listen, her face seems to veer between that of an exhausted old woman and an elegant, self-assured seventy-year-old, though she must be in her eighties at least. She sits very straight in her chair – so straight and still, in fact, it's unclear whether she's able to leave it – and the only parts of her body that move as she tells her story are her face and her right hand, continually moving between the rings that decorate every finger up to the knuckles of her left. There's a slight droop to her left eye and mouth, and Frazer wonders if she once had a stroke.

'I was known as quite the party animal, let me tell you,' she said. 'So you can put that doubtful expression away. Yes, I mean you.'

She nods accusingly at Frazer.

'This is just my face, Mrs Marshall.'

As he speaks, he catches McConnell suppressing a smile.

'It's Ms.'

'My apologies.'

'This late after the event, though,' McConnell says, more gently than Frazer thinks Ms Marshall would like. 'It's not only going to be hard to prove anything, but there's the question of why you didn't report it before, immediately after you saw it happening.'

'I was afraid.'

'The next morning then.'

'Are you not listening? I told you, no one would have believed me. I tried, I told the staff at the hotel, but no one wanted to know.

Besides, they had some story that Abigail had given her notice, left the night before.'

'And you believed them?'

A ripple of doubt creases her forehead, and she is an old woman again, and Frazer feels a pang of sympathy more intense than he can explain.

'Can you talk us through it again, Ms Marshall? Stick to specific memories, if you can. I know it was a long time ago but don't fill in the blanks – just tell us what you saw.'

'I don't *fill in blanks*,' she says, but her hand has fluttered up to the navy silk scarf at her neck. 'We were all there, all of us girls. It was our midsummer bash and it'd been a long season and it was so hot and out there on the coast... We were young. It was the Sixties. I wouldn't expect you to understand.'

Frazer has no idea why people are always assuming he's never had fun in his life, but he thinks it's unfair. For a second he wonders if there's some malice behind her story. But directed against whom?

'So that's why no one would have believed me. That's why *I* hardly believed me. I wanted it to be a hallucination; I could wake up from it then, get on with my life. Only there comes a time when you can't live with a decision like that. Debs understands. You should talk to her too.'

'Who?'

'The receptionist,' McConnell says under her breath.

Frazer shakes his head, just slightly. 'Start earlier, before that night, if you can. Start with what you know for sure.'

'Without filling in any blanks?'

For a fleeting second, her sarcasm reminds him of DC Trish Mackie back in Burrowhead, but he shakes it off. Maybe everyone who spends time out in the villages ends up with a streak of it.

'Yes please.'

'Well, it was more than just a summer job for me. It was the first time I'd left home, the first time I was earning enough to make me

37

feel independent. It's a good feeling, at eighteen. The work wasn't so bad either, cleaning the rooms, early starts, but the girls were good company and I liked looking in all the rooms, imagining how the guests lived. It was an expensive hotel, Wyndham Manor. Is it still there?'

McConnell shrugs and looks at Frazer.

'I've not heard of it, Ma'am. But we'll be looking into it after this.'

'I'd like to know if it's still standing. It was away from any towns, any villages – ten miles from Burrowhead, and that was the nearest.'

Frazer clenches his teeth.

'The seclusion was part of the appeal, of course. The gardens stretched for acres. They were landscaped near the manor then they spread out into wild flowers and mixed woodland you could wind through for hours. There was a shallow stream at the edge of the property with enough pebbles that you could cross to the other side and see back across all the gardens to the manor itself and it was beautiful, it truly was. I started there just before the season, at the end of April, so by midsummer I'd had a couple of months with the girls and we'd got to know each other pretty well. Abby too, though I didn't know her as well as some of the others. She wasn't always around because of how she lived so much nearer than any of us, she was a local, you see, and she only worked part-time, but I liked her. She seemed…just like us.

'That night, the night of the midsummer party in the staff quarters, we were all there, all the girls, the lads from the kitchen, the gardeners – all us summer staff. The permanent staff, they tended to keep to themselves, I don't remember them being around. They might have disapproved. I had a new miniskirt and it was really modern, bright yellow, I'd got it in a shop called Lady Janine in town after seeing it in a magazine, the first thing I bought with my wages. I wouldn't have imagined a detail like that now, would I?'

Her eyes search Frazer's face.

'Only, I don't remember much about the party itself. It was busy, and it was hot – the windows were wide open and it was late, but I was sweating, we all were.'

She clears her throat.

'It wasn't the first time LSD had been passed round.' She leans forward, just slightly, lowers her voice as though she'd not want the other old folks to hear. 'It was—'

'The Sixties?' Frazer smiles, but she scowls back, straightens her shoulders. He hadn't meant it to sound patronising.

'My point is, there was no reason for me to *react* badly. I don't believe that was what happened.'

Frazer sits back in his seat, tries to give her a bit more space, but there's something so proper about her now, so irreproachable, it's hard to reconcile her appearance with her story. She pauses when he breaks eye contact. He looks back at her.

'I'm afraid I don't remember whose idea it was to go down to the stream to swim. It just got passed through the group, the way things did, and that's what I remember next, being out in the dark – but it wasn't fully dark, it was that summer night's dark where the sky seems more purple than black, you know? The girls were stripping off, jumping into the water, boys too, everyone – soon there were only a few of us left on the bank, and then it was just me, standing there on my own.

'I don't know why I didn't join them, but I didn't. Instead, I started walking away into the woods and my friends' voices disappeared into the splashes of water but then…it was strange, but then some voices re-emerged, more hushed, in front of me. I didn't understand. It was getting harder to see because the air was darker, somehow, and the trees seemed denser, but I couldn't have looped round on myself. Don't look at me like that.'

Frazer opens his mouth to deny looking at her like anything, but she doesn't even let him speak.

'I could hear voices, I'm telling you, some kind of singing in front of me, so I kept following the stream. There were birds, woodpeckers I think, large and bright-red-breasted with black and golden heads, dozens of them. Deer too, darting in and out of the trees along my path, and owls – I remember the call and answer of owls.'

Frazer shifts his weight. He doesn't believe all of her story, but he's not going to interrupt. Her hands are clasped onto her silk scarf, as though it's tight around her neck. Her breathing is shallow.

'Are you okay, Ms—'

She grabs his wrist and he can't finish his question.

'There were a dozen of them at least, in a circle, and they were chanting – I heard them. I hid. I don't know what the language was, but not English. I couldn't understand the words. It was a low, swelling sort of noise. I hid in the bushes, trying not to breathe, like I told you. The owls were there, still calling to each other, and there was a clawing, a scratching, like maybe there were badgers or weasels in the undergrowth. And moths, fluttering about my head.' She swipes at the air around her head now, the heavy, scented air. 'I hate moths, but I couldn't move to brush them away. They were everywhere.'

She gives Frazer such a searching look that his own breath catches in his throat. Her hand is still clasped round his wrist, a thin sheen of sweat between their skins.

'That was when I saw her. The circle of people were moving back, their arms raised, swaying and dancing around in this inhuman way, and their voices became shrieks and they were holding a knife up over her throat and between the shapes of them I could see her eyes, wide open, rolling back in her head like…like she was in ecstasy.'

Her clasp tightens.

'It was her. It was Abigail.'

There's something outside, a noise, a rhythmical scratching, clunking.

'What did you do?'

40

The smell of urine wafts across the room and it's enough to make Frazer blink himself back to reality. He pulls his wrist from her hand, looks behind him at the door – he should call the nurse. She's wet herself. She needs to be cleaned, changed. Is that a nurse in the corridor, wheeling a trolley?

'I don't know...' Betty Marshall is still saying, as the damp patch spreads across her smart blue trousers. 'Isn't that awful? I don't know what happened next. I woke up in the morning and I thought maybe it hadn't been real, so I went to see her. Abigail, I mean. Her room was just along the corridor. I went in my nightdress, it felt that urgent – I had to know she was safe – and it was before anyone was awake, but there was no one in her room. It was totally empty. There was no sign of her. I mean, it had been completely cleared out. Her clothes, her bag, her make-up – all of it, gone. So I got dressed and I went to Mrs Pettigrew. She was the full-time housekeeper at the manor and she told me Abigail had given notice and walked out the night before and I...'

Ms Marshall shakes her head, her hand fluttering to her mouth as her eyes fall on her trousers. She looks up at him, unwilling to acknowledge what has happened, and crosses her ankles together. They are so thin and frail, Frazer can almost see her bones through the skin. He wants to help, wants to tell her it will be alright. What would that mean, though? The old people in these places, they're here until they die. No amount of potpourri or tea and sandwiches can change that.

'Do you remember her full name?' he asks. 'We can check if there are records of her working there, if she ever made it home.'

'Of course I remember. I was never going to forget her name, even if I did try to. The subconscious has a way of storing what we need along with what can destroy us, don't you think?'

Frazer has the sudden urge to tell the staff that she doesn't belong here, to sign her out right now. He doesn't though, of course.

'Her name,' says Ms Marshall, straight-backed again, 'her name was Abigail Moss.'

There's a knock on the door. None of them reply, but a young man comes into the room anyway, with a tray from the trolley.

'Salmon and cucumber today, Betty,' he says. 'Your favourite.'

He places the tray down on the chest of drawers, turns to face Frazer and McConnell. 'I saved it till last, to give you as much time as possible, but I think I'd better…'

Frazer stands, McConnell too. 'Of course,' she says.

'Goodbye, Ms Marshall.'

Frazer holds out his hand, but she's stopped looking at him and doesn't take it. His arm falls awkwardly back to his side. His feet don't move. The young man who brought the tray has popped outside and is calling the nurse, saying there's a little accident to deal with. Why does he suddenly feel like this is his last chance?

'Thank you for… And if you remember anything else… The names of the other staff or…'

But Betty Marshall has already taken hold of her salmon and cucumber sandwich, and she looks at him like he has no right whatsoever to be in her room.

ALL THE HAUNTED PLACES

Georgie sets off on her rounds after Simon leaves the station and without telling Trish where she's going. Just a quick word to let her know she's on duty should anyone call and that she'll be back in an hour, and then she's out the door and in her car alone, just how she likes it. The first time, Trish had plenty of questions. Si too. But she's not been answering their questions for so long now they both seem to have stopped asking.

She starts by heading into Burrowhead, where all along the street windows are sparkling with such sharp green and golden light it's hard for her to see who might be watching. No hint of curtains moving though, no one in the centre of the village – the whole place has been oddly empty of tourists this summer. She wonders if it's because news of the murders has spread or just the impression that people outside these villages have, of the whole area worsening year on year with unemployment and drugs and shop closures, with TAKE BACK CONTROL scrawled desperately across the empty units; no wonder they'd choose cheap flights to somewhere with proper beaches and cocktails. She doesn't check the fountain, saves that for last. Instead, she turns down Church Street and allows herself to be thankful for the dappled light under the heavy foliage before mentally noting the litter, the cigarette butts and cans thrown by the side of the road, and pulling into the space beside the old church ruin.

Every day it's the same now. Deserted. Stale with the heat. She doesn't even know what she's looking for, but still she looks.

Increasing splatters of bird shit on the old walls, the old pews. No chip packets or cans here any more – not since she arrested Andy and Lee, and Fergus came by to clear every last speck of litter from the grounds – but no flowers either, no sign of folk visiting the graves. The cherry tree by the gate has fourteen flaps of white fabric tied around its lower branches, though. The first ones appeared when news of the murders got out and folk started getting more superstitious. Now Georgie counts the increasing number of them every time she's here, and lets the sense of lost lives settle in around her shoulders.

She walks through the ruin and steps over the crumbled stones to look at the dead tree that fell down in the storms earlier this year. It's still lying where it fell – the flat circular plate of its roots sticking out of the ground like a broken bone – but there is something new here, today. There are buds on one of the branches; there's still some life in it. She likes that enough to leave the ruin and get on with her work.

It's the old shed next, out behind Simon's place. A few minutes' drive and she's parked up beside what used to be the community field of Burrowhead, that used to have a kids' play area and a usable shed where they served juice and biscuits and kept a rounders bat, some tennis balls, skipping ropes. Today: nettles and gorse snagging plastic bags carried here on the wind, a padlock against the shed's door, its roof darkened by rot and a boarded-up scar where the window should have been. At least the gorse acts as a good deterrent – there's never anyone here, and even Georgie doesn't push her way through the gorse to the shed itself – but she keeps coming back for a glance, for the fleeting expectation of a set of eyes peering out from the edge of the boarded window.

The empty council flats outside of the village, though, those she does patrol. It's the focus of her trip, after Bobby Helmsteading was murdered here with such undisturbed ease. Two blocks facing one another so from the front room of each flat you can see into the window of the flat opposite: the matching old furniture, the lives abandoned and left to sink under decades of dust. She stands at the door to the room where they found the body, finds it hard for a second to distinguish between the way it looks now and the way it did then, blood seeping into the carpet. She can still see the stain of it. Then checking the bedroom, the kitchen, the next flat, the floor above, for signs of people sleeping or hiding – and unlike the church ruin or the old community shed, there's plenty people still use these buildings, she's just not managed to catch them at it yet. She can follow their footsteps in the dust, see the scattered evidence of them. She's asked for them to be demolished. She's asked for CCTV. She's asked.

By the time she's looped back round to Burrowhead and pulled up beside the fountain, they are waiting for her: Mrs Dover and Mrs Smyth, at their windows; Whelan pottering about in his front garden, pretending to be deadheading his roses. But she gets out of her car as she does every day and walks up to the fountain, places her hands on the rim. She tries to remember, even closes her eyes for a second: has she ever seen that black mare before? Being ridden by someone? In one of the fields on the outskirts of the village? She doesn't think so. In fact, she's sure of it. She opens her eyes and peers into the circular stone basin.

She looks, first, for any teeth.

She looks for signs of blood, though she has never seen any.

She looks for bones.

She looks at the latest collection of pebbles and feathers and animal hair, hears a door open and glances up to see Pamali waving from across the road, showing her a friendly face. Georgie could cry at how hard she's trying. She raises an arm, waves back, tries to force a smile. Pamali's been scrubbing the shop front again, trying to get the graffiti off, but the words WHITE MINORITY are still visible, scratched across the Perspex that replaced the glass last time it was shattered. Then she sees a flash of light – Walt's window catching the sun – and walks, head up, past Whelan and his roses, past Mrs Smyth and Mrs Dover's kitchen windows where the net curtains fall back as she approaches, past the butcher's with its lamb chops and kidneys and liver on display, to Walt's house where every window is dressed with hanging feathers, strung along the tops of the frames. Seagull feathers, crow feathers, blackbird, pigeon and gannet and occasionally something larger; they used to be hanging over the doorway, to ward off evil so Trish had told her, but now they're in every window, swaying in a breeze she can't explain other than that houses breathe, in their way, and it's giving the impression that his home is occupied even though she knows it's empty.

Then she sees it, on the living-room windowsill, where Walt would be looking if he were sat in his favourite comfy chair: an elongated oval face, twice the size of a human head. It's been carved out of wood, shaped and lined, then darkened with varnish. The scooped-out circles of its eyes, its mouth, its nostrils, are sprouting green tendrils of vines that twist and grasp, reaching out of the roughly carved contours of a frozen expression. The stems cascading from the eyes and nose make it look like it's bleeding. Like the curls of blood seeping from that poor animal in Mungrid Woods. He must have made it before Trish checked him into the home, so before the horse was killed, but after he disappeared out to the woods himself. A superstitious old man's prediction of what was to come. She stares at it, unmoving, as the sun beats down on her neck and every person on the street watches her.

A WAY BACK

The water cascades in three big arcs from the open mouths of the angels at the top of the fountain, twinkling in the late autumn sun. They're standing together, the circle of them, holding hands all around the edge of the fountain, balancing on the basin's rim as they start to sing.

Ring-a-ring o' roses

Deborah-Jane's not in the ring – she's never in the circle of them – but she's watching as they edge their way around, slowly at first, school shoes balancing on stone. They're all from her class, Alfred and Whelan and Camellia, already starting to wobble and giggle. It's thinner than the length of a foot, that rim, slippery where it gets splashed. The grown-ups sit on the edge sometimes, reach back for a palmful of water, but there are no grown-ups here, which is why they're able to play. The game: faster and faster as they sing, pulling each other along until someone falls in, clothes soaked, a telling-off when they get home, a tooth smashed if they're lucky. The bigger the fall the better. But she's never in the circle with them; she's just watching.

The king has sent his daughter
To fetch a pail of water

She's not the only one watching either. That's Amanda over there.

Amanda Mackie from two years above is leaning against the porch of her uncle's house. No one else has noticed she's there. The size of her now – she's stopped coming into the school, what with her belly growing so big. Some of the other kids didn't even know what that meant at first, and then it was all anyone wanted to talk about. The way Amanda's leaning back into the shade like that, though, like she doesn't want to be seen? Well maybe she's not allowed to be out here at all. Maybe they really do have her locked up like everyone's saying.

The wedding bells are ringing

As if.

'No one's going to marry that girl now,' is what her mam said when the news got out and everyone was trying to guess the father.

'She's refusing to say,' the grown-ups kept telling each other. 'Still refusing to name him.'

'Well, that's that then,' her mam had said, closing the topic down once and for all. Though with Deborah-Jane's baby brother still wanting to be fed at all hours of the night, her mam is not feeling particularly generous to the world.

It's great having a little brother though, even if her mam is in a bad mood all the time and her da is more silent than ever – she's always wanted a little brother and she's had to wait *years* for it to finally happen. She's going to take care of him, that she knows. She's going to teach him all the games they play and how to fight and how to swear so he can be tougher than the lot of them. And then, when he's ready, she's going to take her little brother and run away from Burrowhead and never come back.

The boys and girls are singing

Singing and laughing and they're getting faster now, they're almost running around the edge and pulling each other along and screaming and then there's a loud clap of hands and everything stops. Camellia wobbles, tries to steady herself, grabs Whelan's shoulder and he pushes her off and she topples to the ground.

'Down. All of you. Now.'

The stern voice rings out across the village square and everyone knows when you hear Nora Prowle's voice you obey.

The other kids jump down and scatter and Camellia picks herself up and rubs at her grazed knee before limping away. Over by the porch of her uncle's house, Amanda has disappeared back inside, like a ghost. Like she was never there at all.

Nora Prowle turns, her shoes click-clacking against the paving stones as she walks away, leaving silence in her wake. Time to go back to the farm, then. Time to see her little brother again, whisper to him about how no one is ever going to lock *them* up, no matter what they do, and tell him the story of how one day they are going to escape from Burrowhead and never, ever come back again.

TAKING CARE

The Burrowhead care home is a ways out of Burrowhead, and it seems to the residents that this is a way of helping the non-residents forget they're even there. Indeed, the non-residents rarely think of the care home at all unless, like Trish, they have a relative staying there whom they love enough to visit. That's who Walt Mackie assumes it's going to be when he hears the knock on the door that the staff agreed to use – two taps, a break, and a third knock. He was perfectly specific in his instruction, and they follow it to the letter.

Anyways, it's Trish he's expecting when the door pushes open, so it's hardly surprising that for a second the person standing in the doorway looks more like a giant than a man. Broad and tall and big-booted, shoulders the width of the door frame, with that wild crumple of blonde hair and blue eyes that Walt is sure were never so piercing in the past. Then he remembers. Probably the grief that did it.

He sits up a bit. 'Simon,' he says. 'How nice. Get yourself in here.'

'It's good to see you, Walt. How have you been keeping?'

Walt sweeps his arms around his room. 'I am imprisoned here for the week.' He looks down, brushes the biscuit crumbs from his thigh, then says under his breath, 'Trish made me promise to give it a go.'

'Seems like a nice place,' Simon offers.

Walt just looks around for his tea, which is over on the window ledge.

'Will I get it for you?'

'No, no—'

But the cup is already in his hand. 'It's empty, Walt. Will I ask them to—'

'Leave it!' Walt shouts. He doesn't mean to do that, but sometimes his temper gets the better of him these days, and he can't even remember putting the tea over there, why would he have done that? Simon's sat down on the guest chair at the end of the bed, and Walt has no idea why he's here. He'd thought it was Trish. He wants Trish.

'Reception tell me you've been spending some time down in the common room, Walt. That's good news, I think. Getting to know the residents, eh?'

'What, that lot? No, no…' Walt taps his finger against the side of his forehead. 'That lot downstairs are barmy.'

'So, erm…' Simon clears his throat. 'The thing is, Walt, we're investigating an animal killing. It's a bit unusual, and DI Strachan and I—'

'You mean Georgie?'

'Yes, Georgie and I were wondering if we could pick your brains about it. After all, no one knows the area like you do—'

'Lived here all my life.'

'Exactly Walt, all your life, and we were just wondering—'

'It was salted!'

'What?'

'The tea! I knew there was a reason I'd thrown it out of the window.' Makes total sense. He's getting home soon, not staying in this place. Salted tea indeed. He's going to get on at them about that. Trish won't like that.

Simon's still chatting away though.

'It was a horse, you see. They'd cut its throat.'

Walt looks up at that, catches his eye – piercing blue – puts his guard up. None of the police's business, the rituals, no reason for

51

them to be talking about that, and they'll get nothing from him. Something's nagging at the back of his mind, something about Georgie but he can't reach it, like that itch he gets between his shoulders.

'So do you know of any similar cases, animals being slaughtered illegally or… Walt, is there anything you remember happening before that might be relevant? Anything about the cup and ring, perhaps?'

Walt knows he's got to be careful here. Stay alert. That's the trouble, what with the window the way it is and the drugs they're forcing on him at this place – God knows he doesn't want to take them – but he's not as clear as he used to be, not so certain of what he's said and what he's seen. Like that time out in the woods when Georgie came and the Others didn't want her there. It wasn't until later that he realised they'd been coming for him after all, but she was in the way. What does that mean? He's fond of Georgie, and she's sensitive, she's got the sixth sense, same as him – he's always been able to see it in people – but if the Others don't want her here then there must be a reason.

'Walt…?'

Simon is looking all concerned. Probably expected him to be senile, locked up in this place.

'Look.' Walt glances over to the door, keeps his voice a low whisper. 'I can't hear anything, and I don't know anything.'

But Simon misses the point entirely and repeats his question about the sacrifice.

'Well…' Walt says, a deep sigh making his chest rise and fall. At least he's got his old armchair – it was good of Trish to bring that in here. He wishes his Trish were here. 'There was a thing with the farmers…' Simon leans closer. 'Killing the foxes…'

'That's not what I mean, Walt,' he says, straightening up again.

'I need the bathroom,' Walt says. 'Can you help me to the bathroom?'

Simon looks over his shoulder, like he thinks maybe the staff are going to appear, but they're never here when you need them, that lot. Walt's not staying here, that's for sure. He lets Simon take his whole weight, almost carry him to the toilet room, then says, 'Right, you can go.'

Once the bathroom door's shut he sits on the toilet and waits. He's getting pretty good at just sitting and waiting and after a while he hears Simon call out goodbye. Another minute, just to be sure, and Walt leaves the bathroom and makes his way to the window. He has a view out the back of the care home: grass, trees, fields beyond, the lass from reception standing outside the fire door having her fag. They'll kill you, they will. The staff in here, they should be the ones incarcerated for their own good, not him, not Walt Mackie.

He tries the window but it won't open more than a few inches. Not enough space to climb out. They must've done that on purpose; they try to send you mad, in this place, so as you can never leave. Mind you, that'll be plenty space enough for the Others to get in. He's been telling folk for long enough: they're coming. After everything he's done for them, of course they're coming. Though it's not even about him now – Walt wouldn't want anyone thinking it's all about him – no, there's plenty reason for them to come again. The village needs to be saved. He loves this village and it needs saving.

WHAT GETS LEFT BEHIND

'Well, I was right about them drugging her,' Georgie says, putting the phone down, aware Trish is standing quietly behind her. That poor creature; they made sure she was helpless. She was still conscious though, Georgie is sure of that. Her eyes were so wide open.

'Ma'am? What can I do?'

'Okay, Trish,' Georgie says with a sigh. As she turns on her seat she has this strange feeling that Trish is closer now, right behind her, close enough to reach her neck. She's not, though, she's at the door. 'You can leave the pub investigation for now. We need all hands—'

'That's great news, thank—'

Trish stops mid-thank you as Georgie holds up her hand; she doesn't want thanks for any of it.

'Simon's had no luck finding the owner of the horse locally, so help with that, will you? Get on to all the vets between here and Crackenbridge, farm and domestic. See if any of them have horses registered that match our mare... And I want to know which of them use ketamine, or keep it on site, and if *any* of them have had a theft recently.'

'Yes Ma'am, ketamine.' Trish risks a smile. 'That was Cal on the phone then?'

'He's finished at the scene and run a drugs test on the blood already—'

'That was quick.'

HELEN SEDGWICK

'It's becoming his field of expertise.'

A silence settles between them, the unspoken acknowledgement of the drugs flowing along the coast. Trish's smile has faded.

'It's no just out here the drugs are a problem,' she starts. 'They're in every town and city—'

'Not now, Trish.'

She looks hurt, but Georgie is tired of hearing her defend these villagers. Trish and Fergus both. What is it about this place that makes them so determined to excuse the inexcusable in one another? Someone drugged an innocent creature then hacked away at her throat with a knife, leaving her to bleed out for God's sake.

'It was a standard carving knife they used.'

'The one still in the horse's neck?'

Georgie nods.

'It's horrible,' Trish says. 'I wasn't even there and I keep seeing the image of it. That poor creature's throat all slashed away at like it was—'

'Her,' Georgie says. 'Not it, her.'

Trish swallows.

'And whoever was holding the knife was smart enough to wear gloves, it seems. There are no prints on the handle or blade and no identifying features – could have come from anywhere.'

Georgie looks at Trish, who is nodding, not taking offence to Georgie's sharp tone. It makes Georgie feel a little ashamed of herself.

'So the ketamine is all we have to go on,' she continues, softer.

'I'll get started then,' Trish says. 'If I may?'

Georgie nods. 'Yes. Thank *you*, Trish. Let me know when you've got something.'

She watches her leave the room.

But there was something else, actually. Karen had found it in the woods, about five hundred metres back from the clearing: a bit of rope, frayed, well used, chucked into the undergrowth as if they'd thrown it there on their way back to the village. Cal was excited about the rope, more so than he was about the ketamine. He seemed to think there might even be a chance of some skin cells that could yield DNA – and *that* could point them to at least one of the men who'd done this. They might have been smart enough to avoid getting prints on the knife, but would they have even thought about skin cells getting on the rope?

'I'm sending it off now,' he'd said, and Georgie had wondered if he was getting more and more upbeat to counteract her own mood, though when she'd asked about the timing he'd gone back to his old self. 'There is no chance, Georgie, of fast-tracking a horse-killing,' he'd said. 'No chance at all, and that's *with* me calling in some favours. We'll just have to wait.'

So Georgie will wait.

Her eyes stray around the office, to the stains below the window where the water's been getting in, to the ancient radio and cassette player they still have plugged in over on the spare desk. Fergus donated it to the station years back, after having a clear-out of all the old stuff he'd brought down from Glasgow – he wouldn't throw any of it away, spent ages on trips to charity shops and rehoming what he could, mending stuff nobody wanted, trying to upcycle – but it's been a while since any of them felt like playing music in here. So it just sits there, useless.

Ketamine though, there's been a bit around, not in Burrowhead but up in Crackenbridge. There was a teenager ended up in hospital last year, mentioned Aaron Prowle by name too, though they'd never been able to find so much as a trace of drugs on him. A couple of other lads seemed to be involved too, though they were fairly clueless; Crackenbridge had made a few charges of possession, none yet of supply. But that only meant they hadn't found who was dealing it yet.

The mare's eyes, she can't stop picturing them. The deep brown of them. The fear in them.

Down the hall she can hear Trish's voice on the phone, cheerfully calling round the vets as instructed, clearly finding no news of the horse or a break-in, but here in her office Georgie is imagining what it would be like to have someone drug you into losing control of your own body. To dissociate and have to watch someone gliding a knife under your skin, unable to move away, unable to fight back. Unable to stop them.

Suddenly Trish is back, standing in her office again though Georgie hadn't even heard her arrive.

'I was just thinking, Ma'am, if I can trace it—'

She sounds excited; as excited as Cal was about that frayed bit of rope.

'I mean, if we can find who's supplying the ketamine, then... Well, I know you don't like me to jump to any conclusions, Ma'am, and I've learned my lesson about that, truly I have, but I just wanted to say, if we can find who's supplying the drugs then...'

Trish is actually grinning now, and her hair's spikier than ever.

'...Well, Ma'am, this could be about so much more than a dead horse.'

CLOCKING-OFF TIME

The clock on the till is close to four and Fergus has his THIS AISLE IS CLOSED sign up. He's got through another day. He tries to stay cheerful, Fergus, but some days. Well.

Just so long as Georgie doesn't see how much it's getting him down, that's the main thing. Fergus is pretty good at not complaining. He's never wanted to be someone who complains; he prefers to look on the bright side. It's a job, at least, after all this time. It's a job. And he likes it when parents bring their babies along.

Just now there was a lass swinging her legs from the trolley seat and squealing with delight at every beep from the till. She can't have been more than two, two and a half maybe. There was such an unguarded joy to her Fergus couldn't help but play along – pausing before scanning each item, joining in with her anticipation, clapping when she did, even cheering when they got to the end. Her dad had said thanks, too, and the wee girl had called out 'ta'. It made such a change, to feel like someone appreciated him, he'd actually found it hard to wave goodbye. Most of the adults that come in don't bother talking to him at all, though he always asks them how they're doing. He's lucky if he gets a nod, and even a glower is better than when they ignore him completely. If folk hate it in here so much he doesn't know why they shop here, but they all do. It's non-stop, has been since it opened. But now, at least, he's done for another day.

As of tomorrow, he'll be on night shifts.

On the bus back to Warphill – to the community council meeting in Warphill Community Hall – he pulls his shirt over the bright red T-shirt they make him wear on the tills. He was worried when he first went for the job that they'd say he was too old for it, but there's folk older than him working there. Might have only been teenagers needed a till job a few years back, but it's everyone now. He does miss wearing a suit and tie, though, especially when it's folk from the village who notice him. Must be something about his face that makes it hard for people to take him seriously. The suit and tie used to help with that. The shirt helps now, too.

The bus to Warphill takes a while at the best of times but, as Fergus reminds himself, it is a beautiful drive: along past Mungrid Woods, close enough to see the beeches, the tangle of blueberry bushes, a haze of insects swarming in the heat. Then from the other window there's the motte, the site of the excavation, and that is something to look forward to – the professor is coming from the university tomorrow to get the dig going on, hence the need for his night shifts. And there's Warphill coming into view already. That didn't take so long, and he's excited because he's got lots to tell the community council.

He nods at the bus driver and walks the few paces to the community hall door, which he pushes. It doesn't budge. He tries again. Is it locked?

They said five, he's sure they said five, so he's only a few minutes early; he knocks. Laughs at himself quietly to dispel his nerves. Finally: a noise from within.

Natalie Prowle opens the door with a generous smile and a clasping of his hand. She must have come in early, to set up and welcome him in. Since he realised it was her working at the museum in Crackenbridge they seem to bump into each other all over the place. But a few steps later he can see he's not the first at all, he's the last. Twelve, he counts, no, fourteen people. They're all here, the locals who organise the spring fair and plant pansies in the barrel planters on Main Street every summer, who get up petitions to get the bins collected more often and request the mobile library and meals on wheels for the old folk. Bessie Wilkie and Colin Spence, Mrs Dover and Mrs Smyth from Burrowhead, Camellia Taylor from the Warphill estate and her daughter too, Esme, though there's no sign of Kevin – this wouldn't be his scene. Whelan and June, of course, holding hands as always. It used to make him smile, that, though today he feels a pang of envy that he shakes off with a friendly wave of his hand. He wishes Georgie were here; wishes she wanted to be here.

There's a scraping of chairs as he walks towards them. The chairs are in a semicircle around a central point – the point where Natalie's guiding him with that hand on his shoulder. He's standing in the middle, on his own. He clears his throat.

'Hi! Everyone, hi. Erm…'

Natalie Prowle holds out her hand and nods at someone scribbling in a notepad – the committee secretary? Fergus recognises him, too. He runs the garage on the way into Warphill. Terry, that's his name.

'Please all welcome Fergus Strachan,' she says, announcing him like a guest of honour. 'He has come to ask our permission for an archaeological dig at the motte.'

'Well, no, I… I'd like to tell you about…'

He doesn't need their permission; he really doesn't need their permission. The *actual* council have given their permission, and their MP has expressed an interest too. Or her PA has, via her office. Fergus does things properly; it's important to him. And he needs to know, should Georgie ever look into it, that she'd be proud of the way he arranged it all.

'Well, I… I'd like to tell you about our plans, that is, myself and the archaeological department from UHCN led by Professor, erm, to instigate a thorough excavation of the motte…'

The secretary is scribbling wildly, and two of the women at the back are whispering to each other.

'It's a very exciting opportunity to learn more about our local heritage and the lives of the people who lived in our villages before us. Even the size of our...'

Scraping of chairs. Scraping of pen on paper.

'...our population in the past is unknown, and the true purpose of the motte...'

It's such a strange feeling, the way it comes over him, the sense they all know something he doesn't. That he's on the outside. Just like Georgie says. Not another migraine, that's the last thing he needs.

'...the true purpose of the motte is still unknown, though an excavation in the, erm, several decades ago uncovered a ceremonial cauldron that could have had ceremonial...I mean, religious significance or...and a recent find—'

'Do you mean the Iron Age man?'

'I, yes, I...'

'We've all been wondering about that,' Natalie Prowle says with an encouraging smile. 'Can you tell us where it is now?'

'It's, well, it's a small figurine, only three inches high and it was—'

'Where, not what.'

Her smile again, and there is something reassuring about it, despite her tone – Fergus is sure there's no need for him to be getting so anxious.

'It's at the university,' he says. 'They're trying to date it, running comparisons to similar finds from England and, and Scotland. We have similar finds in Scotland...'

His voice trails off. Someone is standing up. It's Elise, Elise Robertson – he's not seen her since her dad passed away, poor girl.

'Scuse me,' she says quickly, her eyes darting to his and away again. 'Don't stop on my account, it's just I've got plans to meet some friends this evening.'

She's not addressing him, Fergus realises, she's talking to Natalie Prowle, who gives her a brisk nod, and with that she leaves the circle and walks from the community hall and Fergus turns back to Natalie Prowle, who is smiling at him again, and the circle of them, all around him, watching him and waiting, and as he wipes the sweat that's starting to gather on his forehead he realises he has no idea what else to say.

EVENING'S MEETING

As Trish leaves the police station she feels like her body physically changes with each step away she takes – her shoulders relax, her hand rises to spike her hair up, her calves release tension like a coiled spring and she runs a couple of blocks just to stretch it all out. She's early; she could run the whole way there. She's got her running kit in her bag, a set of trainers, why not? She'll be there within the hour.

Trish loves a good run. Kept her sane when she was growing up – even as a kid she could and did run miles, always on her own. She didn't bother with races, wasn't looking for medals, she was looking to clear her head, get her lungs filled properly after the suffocating fog of that school. Maybe that's what the station reminds her of, the school. Both official buildings, there for the good of the community; both crumbling and decayed, temporary solutions installed by people who never used them and have long since gone back to where they came from. But after hours of watching what she says, of following instructions, she can finally let herself go, pushing faster as she leaves Burrowhead and joins the coastal path to run undisturbed all the way to Warphill and the pub where she's meeting Suze for a catch-up and a bevvy.

By the time she arrives she's drenched in sweat, her hair slicked back with the water she's poured over her head. She nods at Dan behind the bar and heads for the loos, where she strips down to her vest and pants, shoves her leggings and trainers into her bag and pulls her work clothes back on. Some arse has been filling the basin with wet paper towels again – plug's all blocked. She scoops it out with her bare hands, dumps the clogged mess in the bin while she's catching her breath. That was a good run, that. She looks a little crazy in the mirror, and she likes it. The door opens and it's Suze, a wine glass in each hand, grinning like she knows something Trish doesn't.

'You've been working too hard,' Suze says.

'With nothing much to show for it, aye.'

'You need a sparkle.'

'You *know* I can't.'

'Just kidding!' Suze is grinning, passing her a sparkling wine. 'You remember the old days though. Sneaking in here, topping up our drinks…'

'*Before* I was a police officer. Before *you* were a police officer!'

Trish has taken the wine though, had a gulp – it's good to let her hair down, or spike it up some more. She likes this new cut she's got; she fancies dyeing it red or orange next, something with a bit of fire.

'Come on,' she says. 'I'm not drinking in the loos like a bloody teenager. Why'd you follow me in here?'

'I saw you racing through the pub when you arrived. Wanted to know what was going on.'

'Nothing's going on; I ran here.'

'What, from Burrowhead?'

Trish shrugs, grins, heads out to the bar. Suze has got them a booth by the window.

'Cheers.'

Suze has made an effort actually, navy jeans and a sparkly silver top, a black velvet choker looped around her neck. It looks retro, but good. She's staring at the wall, and Trish follows her gaze to find a large painting of a single brown horse.

'You know a bit about horses, right?'

Suze takes a swig of her drink and shrugs, glances round the pub. 'I can ride. Not as good as Elise, mind.'

Trish's glass is already empty. That didn't last long. She'll take her time with the next one – wouldn't do for a DC to be seen tipsy in the local she's been investigating.

'And you didn't recognise that black mare at all?'

'Never seen that horse before in my life.'

She'd have told them straight away if she had, of course. She's a good PC, Suze.

'So how d'you think anyone could have got a horse out to the woods and cut its throat like that? It can't have been easy, can it?'

'Tranquilliser, I'd guess. Lead it out first, maybe ride it. Then give it a shot.'

Trish isn't exactly sure why she's not mentioning the ketamine, the results from the blood analysis. Suze is police too, after all, she was there at the crime scene – and Trish wasn't.

'So you think anyone could get hold of some horse tranquilliser?'

'Course not. As you know full well – what is this, an interrogation?'

Trish laughs. 'Hardly. I'm thinking out loud, that's all.'

'Well,' Suze says under her breath, '*someone* has taken up where Bobby Helmsteading left off. My money's on Aaron Prowle.'

Trish frowns.

'Have you seen the state of him?'

She has. She's been watching him. That's why she doubts he'd be running any kind of business, illegal or otherwise.

'Don't believe me?'

'I didn't say that.'

'Well, whatever... Fact is, if you needed to get hold of some restricted medications around here, veterinary or otherwise, Aaron Prowle is where you'd start.'

Trish shakes her head, though it's not a denial. 'His mam running the community council, and all. She's always—'

'I know. Telling folk off for not collecting their dog shit.'

'Keeping an eye on everyone, I was going to say.'

Suze laughs. 'Aye, that too. Makes it even worse for her, I'd guess – her two boys both off the rails. You got to wonder what's happening to the place.'

'There's always been drugs, come on. You're the one remembering old times.'

'I know, but not like this. This is…'

Trish chews on her lip. 'It was disgusting, what they did to that horse. Don't you think? You've got to be wrong in the head to do something like that.'

'Maybe,' Suze says. 'But there's talk of something else too.'

'What do you mean?'

Suze shakes her head. 'Just seems to me things are getting bad, is all. And no one's doing anything about it.'

'Look, if you know something then—'

'Go to the police?' Suze laughs, and Trish finds herself joining in.

'I'll get us another,' Trish says. 'Same again?'

There's a mirror running the length of the bar, slanted and misty; in it you can see the pub but not see it at the same time. As Trish waits for their wines, she watches the people behind her – Suze, phone in hand, a couple of young lads having a pint – their faces hazy and their expressions lost in the black spots of the glass. She sways on her feet. Is that the wine? It's muggy and stale in here, years of smoke still clinging to the carpets. This is where she used to come, as a kid, a teenager, reeling from the loss of her mam and drinking herself to oblivion – not a time she wants reminded of. She wishes she were back outside, running by the coast, in the fresh salt air.

Dan's poured already; he's waiting for the cash. She hands over a tenner. A glance up in the mirror again and for a split second she sees more people there, shadows behind the tables, at the windows, reaching out to the bar. Just the clouded glass, the dirt. She turns and it's Suze, the lads, the same pub she's always known.

'I've invited Elise along tonight,' Suze says as she sits down again.
Trish doesn't like Elise Robertson.

'Did you have to?'

Her da was pals with Uncle Walt and the two of them were always
trying to push them together, but there's something about being
expected to play with someone you don't want to play with – you
can't force friendship like that. By the time Trish was an angry
teenager without a mam, Elise Robertson was the most popular girl
at school, and she knew it too.

'Come on, it was only a couple a months ago her da passed. She's
having a hard time.'

It does the trick – Trish goes quiet. But there's someone by the
window. Elise, here already. Looking at her. Suze nods and a few
seconds later she's sitting opposite Trish and she doesn't look like
someone lost in grief, she looks like someone who knows exactly
what she's doing and finally Trish realises: they've planned this.

'Tell me what this is really about, Suze,' she says, suddenly sober
again.

NIGHT MOTHS

Shona waits, restlessly, until it's long dark – and it takes a while for the night to fall out here, at midsummer – before opening the door to her caravan as quietly as she can. The guys are sharing but she's got hers to herself. Good thing too. Aaron's been watching her, she's sure of it, his twitchy eyes flicking over her body, to her pocket, to where she's been keeping the bone. Or is it something else he's looking at? He was on edge all afternoon, that's for sure. It was so hot he'd stripped off his T-shirt and she could see the bones of his spine sticking out, the way he kept crunching his shoulders like that. Gave her the creeps.

She keeps low to the ground so as not to be visible through the windows of the caravans she passes. The whole site is on a hill, feels like it's ready to slip all the way down and crash into the motorhomes parked by the electric charge points but for Ricky Barr's static caravans tethering it against its will from their uncomfortable perch right at the top. They've been there for decades. Ricky bought them when they were being sold off cheap, when the caravan park was hopeless – he bought the whole lot, meaning the caravan park could live on and Ricky Barr's seasonal workers had a coveted place to stay. It was shrewd. He owns all the land round here now, and what he doesn't farm he rents out – Shona's done her research.

Over by the gate: the red spark of a lit cigarette. Fuck.

She slips between two of the caravans, tries to silence her breath. Is that Aaron, having a fag? That's just what she needs.

Peering out, though, she sees it's too bulky to be him; Aaron and Lee are as wiry as Ricky himself but the shape there, smoking, humming, has some substance to it. She smiles, leaves her hiding place and walks more confidently over to where Kev's waiting. They've got him sharing with one of the students – they all know each other apparently, spend their time moaning about student loans and fees and fuck knows what else – but Kev's pretty good at being left alone when he wants to be.

'What you doing out here?' she whispers.

'That guy's snoring like a wildebeest.'

'Give us a drag.'

'Give us a kiss.'

'You first.'

'You're the boss.'

She inhales deeply, exhales through a silent laugh.

'You got that right.'

She pulls him into the kiss, holds his face with both hands like she needs to remind herself it's still him, still Kev, and not that brute driving the trailer.

'You okay?' he says.

She stuffs her hands in her pockets, doesn't want to stand here smoking a cigarette of her own. But there in her pocket: the bone.

'What is it, Shona?'

'Nothing.'

He reaches for her arm, and her hand is holding the bone; she's letting him see it. She hadn't meant to do that.

'I found it,' she says.

He reaches out and takes it. She watches him as he holds it in his open palm exactly the way she had – something about it seems to invite people to do that – and strokes the top of it with the index finger of his other hand.

'It's like, an animal bone or something?'

69

She shrugs, then realises he can't see in the dark, pulls a mobile out of her pocket and aims the torch end at his hand. The light makes the bone almost glow.

'It's smooth,' he says. 'Does that mean it's old?'

'I'm not sure.'

She instinctively takes it back off him and he doesn't try to stop her.

'Is it a finger?'

In the silence she can hear the scratch of an animal, a squirrel maybe, something small but clawed. She holds it against her own hand; it stretches from her wrist almost to her nail: a single, long, perfectly smooth bone.

'Can't be,' she says, but in her mind an image is forming, a long hand, fingers pointed and clawing out towards her.

'Let me have it again?'

She slips it back into her pocket with a shudder.

'Come on, Shona.'

There's something fluttering around her face: wings, fucking moths, loads of them. She swipes away at them, rubs at her skin where she felt them quivering.

'I've got to get out of here.'

'Where to?'

She edges back from him; she can still feel those wings flapping against her face, her neck. Jesus, this summer.

'I'll come.'

'Don't say anything, Kev.'

'What?'

'Please, just— These fucking creatures!'

'There's nothing there, Shona. Not even one of those bees that are bloody everywhere. What's going on?'

But she's turned away from him and she's on the track down the side of the caravan park to the gate and she's got the bone safe in her pocket. Kev won't say anything to Aaron. And maybe it *is* just an animal bone. It's probably not important at all. Besides, she can trust Kev.

Can't she?

And then, there: a light. A torch, a good one, with a strong beam. Handheld, from the way it's moving, slowly, joltingly, along the lane she was about to take herself, the one that leads from the village and out towards Ricky's farm. There's someone else out here. Walking, in the dark, with a torch.

All she can do is hold her breath and wait as the beam from their torch sways up towards the caravan park, to the track where she's standing, the exact spot where she is standing, right into her eyes and then away again, as though she is nothing at all.

LATE SECRETS

Two of them at least, Ricky counts, up in the caravan park – the would-be journalist down by the charge points and one of the lads up the top, couldn't tell which from the distance he was at. The girl though, she's distinctive. Shona. She saw him too, but she'd not recognised him, he'd bet. She'd no torch in her hand and she'd not have been able to see his face anyway, no one would – Ricky's well used to moving about this damn place unseen when he wants to.

He had to wait fucking hours in Warphill this evening, and make it back to Burrowhead on foot. Andy would've seen the van missing if he'd taken it, and the kid's been watching too close recently, spying for the police maybe, for that Trish Mackie or someone else. Or just for himself. He's asking questions and he's not so daft as he used to be. Ricky could almost feel proud of him for that.

Still, he keeps his footfall silent as he walks up to the house, checking the lights downstairs are off, listening from the hall to make sure Andy's upstairs. Kid could be sleeping, could be sulking up there, but so long as he's upstairs he'll not be able to see Ricky's face as he gets home. It's a struggle, keeping his breath quiet, but he manages. In the kitchen, he sits at the table, lets his hand rest on the familiar lined oak of it. His fingertips follow the shapes carved into wood. He'll no be sleeping tonight, and that's fine with him. He doesn't sleep well, these nights, anyhow, and each morning he wakes in such a sweat it disgusts him.

The stove under the oven is cold – in this damn heat neither he nor Andy want it on – though he could have used it now. Instead, he pulls the papers from his bag, picks up the firelighter and clicks for the flame. Once the first page is alight, he lays it in the stove and watches it burn down to flecks of black invisible among the ashes, glad for once he's not cleaned it and not told Andy to clean it; or if he did, Andy ignored the instruction and left it full of dirt. That swell of pride again. It's coming more often these days, and he's not sure what to do with it. The next page shrivels at the touch of a flame, and the one after that. There's plenty to get through. No rush to get it done. He's going to burn them one by one, to make sure, and they'll all be gone by morning. He doesn't need the written trail of what his life has become. Instead, he watches the way the paper twists and curls, and finds a beauty in it that makes him smile. Then, sitting there in the dark, he thinks about that girl Shona creeping about the caravan park, and that look she gets in her eye sometimes when she's watching him.

SOMETIME TOWARDS DAWN

Georgie can't sleep. She hasn't been able to sleep all night. Conversations are running through her mind, with Fergus, with Trish, her own words coming back to haunt her. Georgie can't sleep at all and so eventually she gives up trying, looks at Fergus beside her, his eyes closed, the contented rise and fall of him.

The benefit of the doubt. That's what she'd always tried to give folk. Believe in the good in people, that's what the old Georgie would say. And she's right, isn't she? Here, in her home, she needs to start having a bit of faith in Fergus again. His kindness. Without that, what is she? All this suspicion, it's exhausting, and it's not how she wants to live, not why she moved here – peace and kindness, that's what she was looking for. A job where she could help folk.

Besides, maybe she's wrong about things. It could happen – it's happened before. Georgie knows she's as capable of being wrong as anyone. Simon said poor old Walt seemed like a shell of himself in the care home, confused and scared. Maybe that's all it is, the feathers, the wooden face in his window, just the behaviour of a scared old man who needs her friendship. When did she get so suspicious of the villagers that she stopped offering her friendship?

One of the things she remembers most about her little brother was the way he offered his friendship out like that, all the time. No suspicion in him. He went through a phase of it when he was, what, eight maybe, nine. Meeting a stranger, another kid, an adult, a stray cat, Errol would give them that open grin of his and yell *We should*

74

be friends! Grabbing their hand – or in the case of the cat, the poor creature's tail – without waiting for a response. Georgie has spent years trying to be like that, trying to be the person she lost, though it's the man lying beside her who's a natural.

'Love?' Fergus says, his eyes still closed, rolling onto his side to be closer to her.

She imagines running her fingers through his hair. It looks bristly these days. She misses it being long, the way it used to curl and flop around his face.

'What's wrong, love?' he says, opening his eyes and looking up into hers.

'It was a bad day at work.'

She hadn't mentioned it over dinner, and now she's not sure why.

'What happened?'

'We found...' It's been a while since she confided in him about anything, but tonight she needs to talk to someone. 'We found a dead horse.'

'A horse?'

'Someone had tried to cut its head off. It had bled out.'

'Oh my God,' Fergus says, looking up at her. 'Why on earth would anyone do that?'

Something in his eyes, the warmth of his face, his genuine horror at what she just said, makes her reach out a hand to stroke his hair the way she'd been imagining.

'I've no idea,' she says, as he leans into her touch. Then she reconsiders. 'It's in their nature, maybe?'

'What do you mean?'

His voice is husky and there's something soothing about the way the bristles of his hair nestle into her palm, prickle between her fingers then, on reversing her movement, smooth out lush as velvet.

'It seemed like they were copying something, or... I'm not sure yet. You said the archaeology suggests there were sacrifices held in the area, once.'

'You think it might have been some kind of sacrifice?'

Georgie lets herself look into his eyes. 'That's what it seemed like.'

Suddenly she sees the image on that cauldron in the museum, the one Fergus thinks is so amazing, excavated decades ago and displayed in pride of place: a stag-man towering over a circling mob, a single figure dipped head first into a giant pot, being boiled alive. Her fingers stop moving through his hair.

'We don't know for sure if there was ever anything like that round here,' he says. 'There were some other finds, further south… But that was thousands of years ago.'

'I'm not sure people change very much, Fergus.'

'People can change,' he says.

She pulls her hand away from his head but he stops her, holds it back against his hair and smiles sheepishly.

'Don't stop, love,' he says. 'Please.'

It feels like the most intimate moment they've shared in months. Maybe it's time to start replacing her suspicion with something gentler, here at home.

'The thing is,' he says, leaning his body against hers, 'that's *why* we have to learn about the past, isn't it? We discover what we did before so we can acknowledge it and do better in the future. So we can change.'

'Is that why you've arranged the excavation?'

'I don't know. I've never phrased it quite like that to myself, but maybe.'

The warmth of him.

'Natalie Prowle is interested too. She's asked to come along tomorrow, to watch the dig on behalf of the community council.'

He pauses, and she waits.

'So maybe there's hope for the villagers yet,' he says, voice cautious, slow. 'If they're willing to learn.'

'Maybe,' she says.

She can feel his body relax at that, and he presses his lips against her shoulder, reaches an arm around to pull her closer, but she gently moves away.

Fergus swallows, clears his throat.

'We've not been able to trace the owner of the horse,' she says. 'We've no idea who she belonged to.'

'Would you like me to ask around?'

'No, no. I've got this.'

'So…'

'So?'

'So there's nothing I can do, then?'

'I…' Georgie feels a familiar lurch of impatience and then hates herself for it. 'Thanks for the offer, though. Go back to sleep, love.'

He rolls over, facing away from her, though whether his eyes are closed or not she can't tell. There must be something wrong with her, she thinks. They are so lucky to be here, together, aren't they, with this comfortable home and their beautiful garden outside. She's going to spend more time in the garden, that's what she's going to do. Clear some space for all that fresh growth that's been trying to push its way up. She just needs some time. Beside her, Fergus's breath gradually slows and settles into the even rhythm of sleep again. There is something so untroubled about the way he can fall into a deep sleep. It's nearly dawn, though, and Georgie hasn't slept a wink.

She gets up, silently, and makes her way to the window. When she looks out there's just the purple spill of predawn and the first birds waking up. Then she hears a crunch, round the side of the house. Approaching the front door. Footsteps.

Her stomach twists.

She pulls her dressing gown on, ties the belt in a knot, makes her way to the stairs, careful not to alert anyone to the fact she's awake. Whoever it is creeping around outside, she'll have the upper hand. She takes the stairs slowly, in the dark. Stands flat behind the door, listening. They're right there.

There's someone right there.

Georgie opens the door fast and is met by a frightened gasp. Standing on the doorstep: a girl in a baggy orange hoody, jeans, trainers. Hair pulled back in a messy ponytail. She knows her. The intern from the paper. The one who wants to be a journalist.

'Shona?'

'God but you gave me a start.'

'This is my *house*, Shona. It's the middle of the night.'

Shona looks over her shoulder, back at Georgie, shaking her head.

'I'm sorry. I know.'

She looks twitchy, nervous.

'I didn't know if I should come, but I just… I couldn't stop worrying—'

'About what?'

Shona's got her hand in her pocket, like she's holding something there. The sea is making a soft scratching noise on the rocks, dragging the seaweed back and forth. It rots in this heat, that seaweed covering the beach.

'I'm sorry to wake you,' Shona says, her voice a whisper.

'I was awake.'

Shona nods. 'I didn't know what to do. It might be nothing. I just…'

'It's not nothing, to bring you out here at this time.'

From her pocket, Shona pulls out a small, straight, smooth white bone.

'I think there's something buried under Ricky Barr's farm,' she says.

Her fingers are still curled around the bone – it seems as though it takes a conscious effort for her to release them, to hold it out to Georgie.

'This was in the ground. The harvester pulled it up and I found it in with the potatoes. I'm working there for the summer.'

Georgie raises her eyebrows.

'It's not like that. I'm not…looking for a story. There's something going on and I think Ricky is involved. He was selling something to Rachel and Pauly last year and I don't know what, but everyone knows he's involved with dealing, though he gets younger lads to do all the work. So I signed up for the summer, to find out what's been going on. And I found this.'

At last the bone falls from Shona's palm and into Georgie's. There's a heat to it that could almost burn her skin.

'I thought maybe it was…'

Georgie rolls the bone across her palm and nods, just once. She sways on her feet – the shadows moving again, a prickling at her neck.

'What is it? I mean, do you think…?'

Georgie doesn't reply, she just opens the door wider because she knows, deep in her gut where she'd been trying to smother all that suspicion: Shona has discovered a human bone in one of the fields of Ricky Barr's farm.

FOUND

UNDER THE SOIL

Georgie is standing to the side of the large, burled tree at the edge of Ricky Barr's potato field when the shout goes up. It's from Karen. Her voice is rough, like she needs to clear her throat. This is it, then.

The sun is blistering hot today. Georgie's never felt anything like it here. Reminds her of the way the tar used to melt and seep along the roads back home – strange, the way she's started to think of that as home again, as though her mind needs to place home somewhere, and if it's not here in Burrowhead then it's going to have to be where she grew up. With Errol. He's still a kid in her mind, still exactly like he was before he died – her home, then, her family, stuck where she can never reach it.

It's a few paces to the trench where Karen's working with three others from Cal's team. They're near where the harvester was when it spat up the bone, and somehow Georgie knows – though she'd never say it out loud – knows there's a body there; she knew before the shout, before she even arrived this morning. Maybe she's known it for months, since Ricky Barr caught her eye that time in the station and whatever it was inside him made her recoil. There's a job to do today though, and there's enough superstition in this village without her adding a word to it. No one's going to hear about her feelings, not today.

She was the first to arrive on the scene, bringing Shona with her, calling forensics and Trish and Si to come and meet her – though there's still no sign of Trish – getting the cordon set up wide, from behind the trees at the field's edge and taking in more than half the width of the field that the harvester had been travelling along when the bone surfaced. Soon as Cal arrived he set up trenches running along the ground, and the dogs are out too – it's a big area to be searching for human remains. She was right about the bone though. It's not a long, stretched finger, like Shona had thought. It's part of an arm, the ulna, and a small one at that.

Maybe that's why she doesn't want to look. The thought that it might be a child.

Or could it be that she knows Ricky Barr beats his own son – she's seen how afraid Andy is of him – and a man capable of hurting his own child like that could well have hurt someone else's child even worse.

He's standing there now, Ricky Barr, watching her.

Trouble is, the bone that Shona found looked old. If it'd had some flesh on it, if it was still decaying, here on his land, she'd have taken him straight in for questioning, but they've no idea yet how long it's been here. Decades. Could be centuries even. And this land's been used for farming for generations, dug up with machinery, ploughed, changed hands, turned over. Could have been buried long before Ricky Barr lived here. Besides, he'd have to be stupid to bury a body on his own working farmland – and she doesn't believe for a second that Ricky Barr is stupid. That's not the word for him.

Georgie takes in a deep breath of the sweltering air and looks down into the dry soil where Karen and Cal are now crouched together, both covered head to toe in their protective gear. They must be sweating in their suits. God but this heat. She glances back to where she made Shona wait beyond the edge of the field; she's been pacing back and forth there for a while now. Anxious. Keen to get some answers? It's possible that she genuinely cares; it's also possible she wants a story for that local paper she writes for – and the right one could get her a job somewhere far away from here. Georgie doesn't much trust journalists. Shona's just a kid though,

84

really, and she seemed pretty freaked out at four o'clock this morning.

'What's there?' Shona calls over. 'What is it?'

No one answers.

The way the heat has saturated the air, it's like all sounds have been dampened down. The birds sound distant, there's not a bark of a dog or the growl of an engine. Once Shona's shout is gone, all Georgie can hear is her own breath resonating in her head, the muffled pounding of her pulse. A text message vibrates its arrival in her pocket. She clenches her teeth. She can hear that, too, the grinding of it. Down in the soil, through the dried grass and roots and weeds that have been carefully excavated by the forensics team, she can see the curve of a skull lodged in the ground.

It's hard to tell the size of it yet. It's not fully visible. There's no doubt it's human, though. Georgie feels a shudder run along the back of her neck despite the heat. How long has it, he or she, been buried there, unnoticed and unmissed? She tries to think back over missing persons in the area – nothing unsolved, not since she's been here. At least, no one that's been reported missing to the police, except teenagers disappearing off for a night or two, wives leaving husbands, husbands leaving wives. Walt Mackie going walkabout.

Georgie remembers what he said to her, old Walt. Out at the cup and ring in Mungrid Woods, when she found him in the middle of the night, shivering and soaked after disappearing for two days, leaving everyone terrified he'd killed himself – but there he was, gazing at the sky and waiting for 'the Others'.

We villagers, we take care of our own. That's how it's always been.

Ricky is glaring at her like she has no right to be digging up his land, but it's getting clear she has every right. She meets his gaze, tries to see what's lurking there beneath the hostility. Knowledge? Fear?

Andy's expressions are easier to read, but he's in the house, whether by choice or his dad's orders she's not sure. Now and then she catches a glimpse of him watching them from the kitchen window and remembers his words from earlier this year, fired out at her from his cell, *They're stealing all the jobs and houses and…* Her eyes turn back to the mud, to the skull. Karen is carefully brushing soil away from it, revealing more of its shape. It looks oddly frail there in the dirt. Thin and vulnerable, like it could have been made out of paper.

She pulls out her phone and reads:

I missed waking up beside you this morning.

Fergus. She returns her phone to her pocket, leaving the message unanswered.

'What's that?' she says, pointing to a mud-covered shape below the skull.

Karen glances up at her, shakes her head.

'Could it be a blanket? Something the body was wrapped in?'

That's what Georgie sees: an old blanket. No longer distinguishable as fabric and colour, caked solid with dirt and age, but still.

'We're going to need some time,' Cal says, standing up to stretch his back, surveying the scene. 'You're right, a course. Could be blanket, clothes, who knows. I'd say we've got at least a partial skull and skeleton. We need to get it uncovered then back to the lab. I'll get a tent up too, keep the sun off, and let my people work in the shade. We don't know how long it has all been buried here, so we could be dealing with some fragile materials.'

'Anything that could tell us who it is…'

Christ, her phone again.

PS Remember the good in people. I love you.

Followed by a smiley face.

This time she throws the phone into her bag and zips it up tight.

Below her, Cal is hunkering down beside Karen to help with the work. He's right – there are more bones down there. She doesn't know why the arm bone would have been brought to the surface first, without the rest of it. Unless that was how the body was buried: on their back, with their arms up, reaching. Like maybe they were buried alive and died trying to claw their way out of the ground.

ABOVE THE LAND

Si knocks on the caravan door. There's some kind of movement beyond the closed curtains, and a sound, though what exactly he's not sure. Maybe they were asleep. He doesn't know what time they'd have been expected to start work, on a normal day. Could be they don't even know about the crime scene yet. He could use that to his advantage.

Georgie's told him to interview them all – every kid working on the farm for the summer, especially the ones staying on-site. Not that they're suspects, but they could be witnesses, could have seen something strange. Could have something to say about Ricky Barr. 'Everyone's a suspect and we're making no assumptions,' she'd said, but of course they all know Ricky must be involved. Ricky Barr is involved with everything that goes on out of sight around here, he's just mighty good at keeping his hands clean and so they've been waiting – the whole village has been waiting – for some proof against him.

Si wasn't surprised to hear Shona had been snooping around either. She's up to something, and he likes that about her. She's got her eyes open, and there's not many folk in these villages you can really say that about. He wants to talk to her too, but wants to do it on his own. He's got questions.

There's a grumbly coughing from behind the door, and then it swings open to reveal a scruffy blonde-haired lad in baggy turquoise trousers pulled tight around each ankle and what appears to be a maroon knitted vest. Behind him, Simon can see Kevin Taylor – jeans and a black T-shirt – grinning at him in that infuriating way he has.

'I'm going to need a word with you both,' Simon says.

'Who are you?' asks the blonde one, with an accent and a confidence that marks him clearly as not from around here, nor from any school that costs less than ten grand a term. He's suddenly straightened up, hands on hips, and Simon can see him graduating from uni in a couple of years, ditching the festival get-up and donning a Ralph Lauren suit and tie for work at a financial consultancy firm.

'PC Simon Hunter. Burrowhead Police.'

The lad frowns at Simon's badge, takes a step back from the door. 'You'd better come in then.'

Said like it's his own house, his own front door, his choice.

Behind him, Kevin Taylor snorts and flops down on the chair, twirling his unlit roll-up between his fingers.

'You not going to light that, Kev?' Simon says.

'The ventilation's not up to scratch,' he says with a smile. 'Wouldn't want the furnishings to absorb any bad smells, would we?'

'Do you two know each other?' Turquoise trousers has sat down too, on a low bench that might double up as one of the beds, his knees almost touching Simon's across the small room that counts as a lounge. You couldn't say they were spacious, these caravans. He starts vaping with an innocent look on his face, something sickly sweet.

'What did you say your name was?'

'Orlando Joyce.'

'Well, Orlando, I'm afraid we've had a report of a crime here on the farm and we need to ask if you've seen anything suspicious since you've been—'

'What kind of crime?' says Kev, leaning forward. So now he's interested. Simon wonders if he's still going out with Shona – and if so, how much she might have told him already. His eyes keep catching Simon's then darting away, and beneath his practised nonchalance Simon can see the flicker of intelligence that he remembers from the last time they spoke. Kevin Taylor, what a strange one.

'What brought you to work here, Orlando?'

'It's a summer job, good as any.'

Simon raises his eyebrows, and Orlando deflates slightly.

'I didn't get the internship I was banking on, so I needed to find something last minute... It's not bad for a bit of pocket money, you know how it is.'

'It's what I'm living on, mate,' says Kev, drily, refusing to raise his voice.

'And have you seen anyone...acting strangely?'

Orlando shrugs. 'It's all pretty much what I imagined it would be, working in a place like this.'

'Oh aye?' says Kev.

'I mean, it's boring but physical, so you get a good workout at least. Mr Barr seems to be in a bad mood most of the time. He likes barking orders.'

'Actually, I think there's something wrong with him,' Kev says.

'Meaning?'

'He's out of breath, coughing all the time, angrier than usual.'

'I thought that was just, like—'

'How we are out here?'

Orlando rolls his eyes as though the sensitivity of the locals, along with their bad moods, is all a bit too childish to bother with. Kev looks like he wants to hit him. Only for a second, but Si is watching – he hasn't stopped watching Kevin Taylor, as it happens.

'Well, I've not seen anything I'd call suspicious,' says Orlando. 'Except Kevin sneaking around outside with his girlfriend after midnight.'

Kev rolls his eyes but doesn't deny it.

So he and Shona are still an item then.

'Okay, well.' Simon stands up with a sigh. 'We've declared the farm a crime scene, so there'll be no work for now.'

'What?' Kev scowls.

'Like working, do you?'

'I like getting paid.'

'Well, don't worry, it'll not be for long,' Simon says. 'And we're asking everyone to stay put, please.'

'It's something serious then?' Orlando says. 'Do we need to take any precautions?'

Kev snorts and Orlando fires him a glare.

One thing you could say for Ricky Barr, he must have a sense of humour if he put these two in a caravan together for the season.

'There's nothing for you to worry about,' Simon says. 'Think of it as a day off.'

'Hardly, if we can't bloody well leave,' he says.

Simon smiles and makes his way back outside, pausing to stretch his back soon as he's climbed down the tiny little steps – he couldn't stand staying in a place like that. Felt like if he stretched his arms out too far he'd smash right through the walls.

'Right mate?'

Kev's followed him out.

'Thought you might want, you know, a private chat...'

'About?'

Kev drops the act.

'I've seen the bone.'

Simon waves his hands over towards the edge of the caravan park. Kev plants his cigarette in his mouth and finally lights it, inhaling deeply, and the two walk in silence over to the fence. Simon stops at a patch where the ground is covered in a good dozen or so fag ends.

'This your usual smoking spot?'

Si waits for him to put his guard back up, take a drag and shrug his shoulders, but Kev doesn't. Seems to be making some kind of decision to act like a bloody adult at last. Though really, if the sarcastic delinquent he usually sees in Kevin Taylor is an act – as Shona once told him it was – it must be exhausting, keeping it up all the time.

'It's Aaron and Lee you want to be talking to.'

Simon clears his throat. Can't decide whether the smell of that cigarette is making him nauseous or desperate to light one of his own.

'Why's that?'

'You're the police, you find out.'

For a second there's a glimmer of threat in his eyes.

'You grew up here too, didn't you, PC Hunter?'

He lets his cigarette fall to the ground and stubs it underfoot.

'We all grew up here,' Simon says, but Kevin has already swung his leg over the fence and is striding towards the woods with his hands stuffed in his pockets.

FROM THE SKY

The haze falls fast and thick when the heat's this strong in Burrowhead, and Trish feels it more than most, though why that should be the case she doesn't know. Something to do with how she likes the cold, the sea air, a winter's frost. Her mam was the opposite – Trish still remembers the heat in that flat they lived in when she was a kid. She always felt it pressing in about her, unnaturally. This land about here, it's not made for scorching, it's not designed to be parched, it only feels right when it's soggy; the mud should cling to your skin, not fall like fine sand between your fingers.

It's not overhead though, that heat haze, it's down around her mouth, her nose, in the air she's trying to breathe, gathering like a swarm of microscopic insects filling the space between the ground and the sky. Her head's pounding too – she'd blame that on the heat if she could – and she's late and she's not answered any of the messages from Si because she doesn't trust herself to speak just yet. There's a churning in her stomach that she gets when she's anxious, when there's something that needs to be done and she doesn't know how to do it.

Bloody Suze. Bloody Elise. Why did they have to go and put all that on her in the pub? Ambushing her like that. What did they *think* she was going to say? She's got to talk to Uncle Walt first, that's all she knows, though what she's going to say, what she has to ask him… No, she's got to get her head straight and her eyes clear, that's what, and she's got to get the fuck away from this heat.

Christ, she could throw up.

The paving stones around the fountain look damp with the heat, though they're dry as bone to touch, and the fountain could almost be beautiful, the way the ornate twirls above the three faces on the central carving disappear out of view. Back when it worked – which was before Trish was born, and she couldn't tell you how long before, none of the villagers seem quite sure – the water spouted from the mouths of the three faces, making three glistening arcs that splashed into the basin below; regardless of what angle you approached it from, you could always see water.

Trish needs a fucking drink.

When she arrives at the edge of Ricky Barr's farm she can see Georgie, standing above Cal and all the suited forensics team. They must be in a trench dug around the body, with Georgie up on the grass beside those three ugly old trees. How they fail to produce blossom, fruit or foliage in this heat is beyond her. Everywhere else is overgrown to a height that threatens to dwarf the village. In that last text Georgie sent her, she'd told her not to bother rushing in – just come along as and when, she'd said. It was her reply to Trish's apology, a genuine one too, sent soon as she woke up. She didn't sound cross. It was much worse than that. She sounded dismissive. As though on some level she was perfectly happy with Trish not being involved in the case at all. Trish could do with someone to speak to this morning, but it can't be Georgie, not any more.

She takes a deep breath and a long swig from her bottle. Even the water looks misty and parched; that must be some kind of optical illusion. Maybe it's the plastic from the bottle itself. She drinks anyway, downs it, feels a bit better, shakes off the haze, swallows down the nausea and marches towards the field.

So, what she knows so far: they've found a body. Well, some bones, a partial human skeleton. In Ricky Barr's field. And it sounds like they could be old. But *how* old? That's the real question.

She doesn't slow her pace as she approaches Georgie, marches straight on up to her before coming to an abrupt halt.

'Apologies again, Ma'am,' she says. 'No excuses. Won't happen again.'

Georgie nods, barely perceptibly, and doesn't turn to face her. That might not mean anything though. Her eyes are fixed on the ground, the layers of soil from where the curve of a skull is visible, lodged in the dirt. It looks like a number of other bones have been uncovered as well. It looks curled, the body – as though whoever it was had scrunched in on themselves. Hard to tell, until it's been fully excavated, examined in the lab. Could have been knocked about, what with this being a working farm. But there's something else too. Looks like a bit of cloth or fabric, about a foot away from where the skull is. Muddy of course, browned and rotted, hard to tell what it is. She gets that scratching at her neck that tells her it's important though.

'There,' she says, pointing. This time Georgie does look at her. 'What's that? An old…a bit of their clothes or…?'

'I'll get it back to the lab for some proper testing,' Cal calls up impatiently.

Cal likes questions to be kept internal, till he has the answers ready to give.

'I think what we're looking at is a child,' Georgie says quietly, under her breath. Not because she doesn't want Cal to hear – or so Trish guesses anyway – but because she's thinking it through. She's not talking to any of them; she's talking to herself, and the words she's saying are horrifying to her.

Ricky Barr is watching them. He's standing away, separate, over near the house. Trish can feel his gaze like a claw on her skin. Doesn't want to look back at him, at least doesn't want him to see her looking back at him, but the way he's hunched up, arms around his body like that, almost swaying on his feet… Glancing at him out of the corner of her eye she could almost think he looks scared. He's lost weight this year. He was always skinny, mind, lean and scowling. Suddenly Trish realises he's not staring over at her, at Trish, he's staring at Georgie, and there's something passing between the two of them.

Just then Suze comes striding up to them, planting herself in between Trish and Georgie and giving her a friendly nudge.

'You made it out in the end, then?'

Trish doesn't reply. In fact, no one says anything more at all. Georgie has withdrawn into herself and Trish, well, Trish hasn't decided what she's going to do about Suze and Elise, not in the slightest, and so the best thing for her to say right now is nothing at all. She edges away though, just a fraction, to give her the space to imagine Uncle Walt standing here beside her; just enough to stop the scratching at her neck getting any worse.

WAYS TO NEVER BE HURT

'I said no, Patricia.'

Trish's mam is lying on the sofa that she dragged across the threadbare carpet last year and placed right there opposite the window – Trish thinks it's unfair because there's only the one sofa and when her mam's on it like that there's no room for Trish. Her mam says it's so she can watch the sea, though when Trish tries that she can't even see the sea from the window, lying down like that, all she can see is the sky through the smudges on the window and there's nothing so interesting about that.

She pulls on her mam's hand for a bit, tugs and leans back and pulls with all her weight, but it's no good. Her mam's not moving today. She could have guessed that from when she used her long name that Trish doesn't even like and no one else ever uses.

'Please?'

'Those bees are dangerous, Trish.'

'Uncle Walt says they'd never hurt me.'

'That's nonsense,' she says.

'And we wear the special suits—'

'I'm looking out for you, Trish.'

'You're looking out the window.'

'It's still a no.'

Though her mam's eyes have closed now so they're not even looking at the sky any more, they're looking at nothing at all and Trish gives up, lets go of her hand, and tips all the jigsaw pieces from the 500 Pieces puzzle she got for her tenth birthday all over the floor. It's so hot in here, so so hot that sometimes Trish feels like she can't breathe but her mam says there's cold in her bones and so they need the heating, even in the summer, even if it means they can't afford the telephone. Sitting cross-legged on the carpet, she starts sorting edge pieces from middle pieces and glances up every few minutes to check her mam's eyes and sometimes they're open and empty and staring out into the distance and sometimes they're closed.

The jigsaw is a photo of a field with lots of bright red flowers in but the picture on some of the pieces is peeling up at the corners and one time when Trish was angry she pulled at one of them until it peeled right off. Her mam was upset about that and started crying and asking her why she would do that to her present, she kept saying that it was a present, and why would Trish do that, until she seemed to forget Trish was even there and was just crying into her hands so Trish sneaked through to their bedroom where they kept the craft books and found the glue, smearing it over the broken jigsaw piece and pressing the picture back on. 'It's a present,' she said to her mam when she showed her, and her mam had held her and cried into her hair and Trish hadn't known what else to do until her Uncle Walt came round and suddenly she was lifted and spun in the air and laughing, and they were outside, running along the beach, splashing into the cold waves.

Her mam's eyes haven't opened in a while now and Trish stops pretending to do the jigsaw and watches closely as her mam's body rises and falls with her breathing. She's waiting till she's asleep, just to be sure, though oftentimes Trish has managed the same trick while she was just resting her eyes or staring at the sea and she was back home before her mam even noticed she was gone. It's different with Uncle Walt and the bees though, her mam *really* doesn't like the bees, she doesn't like them almost as much as Trish loves them. But Trish has got Uncle Walt on her side and that means she'll win.

Standing, edging to the door – no movement from her mam – reaching on tiptoes to open the front door latch as quietly, quietly as she can and then, out at the top of the stairs, clutching her trainers in her hand and counting her way down in her bare feet, eight stairs and a turn, eight more and the landing where the Taylors live, eight stairs and the turn with the pot of marigolds, eight stairs to the ground floor and she's out, pulling on her shoes, running, running away from the flats and towards the village and it is cooler, it is wonderfully cool and bright with the salt in the air from the sea and the breeze from the beach helping her on her way. The village is gleaming in the light, the roses in the gardens are orange and pink and yellow and red, and there's green ivy climbing the buildings and the fountain with the angels and she's here, she's at Uncle Walt's house and he's opening the door and lifting her high in his arms and saying:

'Your mam agreed at last, did she, my Trisha?'

Trish nods and grins and her nod turns into a shake of her head 'cause she can't lie to Uncle Walt, she can't, no one could.

'Did you sneak out again, Trish?'

'Mam's sleeping. She'll never know…'

Uncle Walt is grinning his grin and he's so fun, he's not going to tell on her; he's on her side.

'One hour,' he says. 'Then home safe and sound.'

She's jumping and clapping and hugging him and he laughs his big jolly laugh.

'It just so happens I have a new suit in your size, Trisha. I chose you a bright yellow one – do you approve?'

The beekeeping suit is the best thing Trish has ever seen and she pulls it on over her trousers and T-shirt as they stand in the field, side by side, getting ready. Inside the suit she is safe, safe as she is with Uncle Walt, which is as safe as she can ever be, the hood up over her head, every bit of her protected and look: the hives are glinting in the sun, and the promise of all those fluffy bees is just seconds away.

A RELUCTANT DRIVE BEFORE LUNCH

'You're not serious,' DS Frazer says.

He's not normally one to talk back, but it just forces its way out. Of all the places he absolutely doesn't want to go, Burrowhead is at the very top of the list. When he was called into her office he thought maybe Betty Marshall's case was going to be passed on to someone junior who had nothing better to do.

'Ma'am. I mean…' He clears his throat. 'There's no reason—'

'There's a very good reason. Three, in fact.'

Frazer wants to close his eyes but he's not going to give her the satisfaction, so he straightens up, looks straight at her as she counts her reasons off on her fingers.

'One, the Wyndham Manor hotel, as was, is only ten miles down the coast from the village. It's derelict now, but if anyone's going to remember your missing girl it'll be the residents of Burrowhead. There's a chance some of the older ones might even have worked there. Or know some people who did.'

That, unfortunately, is true.

'Two, DI Strachan has been in touch this morning to tell me they've found human remains, decades old, buried in the field of one of the farms near the village. Now, your witness claims she saw a murder taking place in the 1960s, am I right?'

Frazer nods. 'Ma'am.'

'DI Strachan has found what appears to be fragments of cloth or clothing that she's having analysed. If they can date them, and the dates match your case, then I want *you* on site. Reporting directly back to me. Understood?'

'Ma'am.'

'Good. Dismissed.'

Frazer turns to leave, but stops by the door. It's glass, top to base, and the blinds aren't even closed – everyone can see him. Not that anyone's looking. He takes a deep breath and turns back into the room.

'But what's…'

The look she gives him is piercing. Those sharp green eyes, skin so pale she looks like she's made of glass herself – though they all know damn well she's not.

'Is there something else?'

She'd already turned her attention back to her computer, is annoyed at being interrupted, though she was the one who called him in.

'I was just wondering what your third reason for sending me out there again was. Ma'am.'

'Oh. Well, I just thought a cold case like this, nothing too strenuous, knowing what you've been through recently—'

Frazer feels his shoulders tighten, and in response she's on her feet and stepping closer to him. In her large window, overlooking the office blocks and the river snaking through the city, the glare is low and sharp, and they're both reflected in the glass.

'—and the rise in Islamophobia we're seeing in the city since the attacks can't be easy for you—'

'What, because I'm black?'

'No, no. I just thought a quieter—'

'They're racist out in the villages too, Ma'am, believe me.'

'Look, I just thought a cold case might suit you.'

Her voice has changed now. Softer. It's the sympathy again – God he hates the sympathy.

'There shouldn't be anything too violent going on out there, not this time. Take a few days by the sea and give yourself a chance to breathe. Alright?'

Frazer's jaw is tight and he wants to argue but he can't find the words. It's been over six months since his compassionate leave and he came back to work in January for a reason – and the time he spent in Burrowhead in the spring was in no way helpful; Christ, he felt like he was going mad out there.

'Good,' she says, her pale hand resting briefly on his arm before she turns her back again. He can't think of a reason to stay in the room, though by the time he's left the building and is in his car all the arguments he could have used to avoid having to go back out to Burrowhead are crowding into his mind – not least the simmering anger of the place he's still not got out from under his skin. At least you can avoid looking straight at it, in the city, if you're inclined to turn the other cheek.

He's parked in the basement garage, where it's cool and shaded, but soon as he's driven up the ramp and out the blue sky seems to be taunting him. Maybe it'll be cooler out there, at least. Maybe that wild beach will have managed to keep the heatwave away. Trish will be there. No doubt with plenty to fight about again. Some people just seem to want a fight. More and more people these days, it seems to him. He pulls off his suit jacket while he's stopped at the traffic lights. His air con is up but it's no match for the sun pouring in the windows. At least this time he has a case of his own to focus on. Betty Marshall has reported seeing a murder, and he for one is going to take her seriously.

But how the hell is it getting hotter?

He checks the dial, which is turned all the way to cold, his eyes flicking back up to the road before holding his hand over the air vents. Lukewarm air is coming through. Cooler than the outside, yes, but not enough. He pulls off his tie too. It's not like anyone will be smart where he's headed. He was fairly sure they spent the duration of his last visit laughing about how he'd got mud on his suit. They see dirt as a stamp of pride, that lot. Trish especially, and that farmer Ricky Barr. Though she'd be fuming if she heard him mention them in the same sentence. Far as Trish was concerned Ricky Barr was the enemy of the village, but it looked to Frazer more like they were all versions of the same person: prickly and bitter, quick to judge and equally quick to blame, pretending to be tough when really they're clinging to the village like they're scared of the outside world. Trish seemed to wear it like an identity, with her buckled-up boots and tattoos that she never quite managed to hide under her sleeve. Tiny girl that she is. Young too, to be carrying round so much anger – though Frazer is often called young himself, so he knows plenty can happen before the age of thirty to show you what the world can do. Still, Trish took an instant dislike to him, and he doesn't want to think too hard about why she did or why he cares so much.

The road feels strangely familiar. This single track that leads to the coast and to Warphill, he's only travelled it the once – back in the spring – and then of course on the return journey, leaving that ragged brutal beach and the faces looming out of the dark, pleading with him, as far away as possible. He's got enough nightmares of his own to deal with.

He's going slower now though. He's not going to make the same mistake as he did last time – there are deer in these woods, all too comfortable with wandering into the road. He taps the brake, keeps his eyes focused on the heat haze above the tarmac, sticky with the sun. Careful with each curve of the road, looking as far ahead as he can, trying to anticipate. The heat is doing something strange to the air out here. In the city, sure, it's muggy and sweaty and dense, but out here the air's loaded with it, like the heat is visible, glimmering, suspended between the surface of the road and the canopy of the tree arch overhead – and it is familiar but also strangely different, he doesn't remember so many trees, such an intense covering of green that the light takes on an underwater ripple. Of course, it was early spring before, bare-branched and frosty. He doesn't remember leaves because there weren't any, just the sharp threat of pine needles and the twist of branches like old men's fingers. Today, the foliage turns this stretch of road into a shimmering green tunnel, the sky visible only in fleeting gaps that twinkle like stars; for the first time he can see how beautiful it is. How could a few months have made such a difference? It's not like that in the city. He puts on his shades and even then he has to squint in the light, the texture of it, glistening, truly.

A bead of sweat rolls down his forehead and he brushes it away with the back of his hand. This air conditioning is useless. He hits a button and the automatic windows open. There it is: the smell of the coast. Salt and fish and seaweed, baked in the heat, and something sweeter too, now, something that wasn't here before. He licks his lips and realises they are dry and parched. The bottle of water he brought with him from the city is lying on the passenger seat, empty, though he can't for the life of him remember drinking it all.

CASTING BLAME

Aaron and Lee's caravan is right at the end, and Simon's being meticulous – he's suffered through uninformative interviews with the locals and students in every one of the caravans in between. Ricky has actually separated all possible friendship groups; there's a local and a student per caravan, and not a pair of them can stand each other. It's almost funny. The students are intrigued by the idea of a crime but think themselves above it, while the locals are all acting like they couldn't give a shit and, occasionally, glancing over to where Aaron and Lee's caravan is waiting. The two brothers together. So Ricky didn't split them up. Maybe he was thinking of the students' safety.

He knocks, once, hard, and Lee opens the door. The last time Simon had been this close to him, they were sat opposite each other in the cell at Burrowhead police station and he'd been left reeling with the spite of him. He looks a bit different today, mind. More hunched in on himself, his pretty face scrawny and rougher somehow, the hint of some bruising around the jawline – is that his brother's doing? Aaron is standing behind him, his hair clipped close to the scalp, the smell of unwashed men about the pair of them.

Simon pushes his way in, sits down on the makeshift bench all the caravans have, and asks them – like he has asked everyone else – if they've seen anyone or heard anything suspicious since starting work here.

'I take this job seriously,' Aaron says. 'Quit the butchers to be here, the work's that good.'

'I'm keeping my head down, aye,' Lee pipes up. 'Keeping my head down like yous lot wanted me to and now what, questioning me over nothing and all I'm doing is trying to work and it's hard enough to get work and I've done my community—'

'Shut it,' Aaron snaps.

They're kids, that's the thing. Unpleasant, sure, Aaron's a right bully and Lee's a spiteful little shite, but they're too young to have had anything to do with the remains Shona found on the farm, surely. If the body was buried thirty years back – and Cal seems to suspect it could be much longer than that – they wouldn't even have been born. Still, he's here, and the only suspicious things any of the others have hinted at involve Aaron and Lee Prowle being, well, unpleasant and suspicious.

'You'll no mind if I take a look around then?' Simon says, standing, casually walking over to the cupboards and opening the doors – a couple of mugs, stained black, no sign of food except for a tin of corned beef, a damp-looking half-used pack of sugar and some lentils.

'You making a dhal?' Simon says.

'Don't eat foreign food—'

'That crap was here when we arrived,' Aaron says, shrugging. 'And the whole place was dirty, weren't it.'

'Aye, dirty.

'So we cleaned it up. Mam'd be proud.'

'Mam *is* proud.'

Lee smirks, but Aaron's staring at him like he means it.

My boys. Simon can hear Natalie's voice saying it; he has heard it. *My two boys.* And then Alexis's writing swims up again, *Don't trust anyone from Warphill*, and those notes they sent him, the notes Lee sent him. *FOREIGN SCUM.* Simon feels a stab of rage and loss, pushes it back down, tells himself to focus on the job.

There's a constant tapping noise – the heel of Lee's shoe against the base of the bed, his knee jigging relentlessly.

Simon pulls his gaze away, pushes the mugs to the side and reaches deeper into the cupboard. It can't be this easy. But of course Kev wasn't talking about the bone, he was talking about the drugs. If they're working for Ricky, *dealing* for Ricky, it makes sense he'd have them staying here, in the caravan nearest the farm, and let them share – no city kids to push their noses in.

'What's this then?' he says, pulling out a dark brown glass vial, unlabelled, with a small quantity of liquid in the bottom.

Aaron sighs exaggeratedly, Lee's knee keeps going, Aaron kicks him in the shin, Lee's knee stops and he starts chewing at his gums.

'It was all here,' Aaron says, slowly, as though Simon were an idiot, 'when. We. Moved. In. You'd better interview the owner about that, eh.'

'You mean I can take it away? Ta.'

Simon is careful to only hold it around the base, keep his prints off as much as possible. Lee seems to be trying to clear his throat again and again.

'What's wrong with you?' Simon says, looking to Lee for an answer but getting one from Aaron instead.

'There's nowt wrong with him. What's happened anyway, what suspicious thing should we have seen round here recently?'

Simon shakes his head – no need to tell this pair a thing.

'Is that your motorbike out the side, Aaron?'

'It's mine now!' Lee shouts, standing, sitting again.

'Fuck's sake man, I've said you can have it – he's been after that bike for years I tell you.'

'And you don't need it any more?'

'I've got a car.'

'Ricky must pay well.'

Aaron just sits back at that, his jaw clenched – but from the look of his lips, Simon would say he's been chewing at his own mouth almost as much as Lee is doing now. Just learned to do it when no one's watching.

'Well, if you see or hear anything…'

'We'll call you,' Aaron grins. 'Thank you for your concern, PC Hunter.'

Simon leaves the door open behind him, and neither Aaron nor Lee moves to close it. They're not afraid of the police, that's for sure. Could be nothing in the vial, could be something. He's not thinking about the skeleton in the ground, he's thinking about the poor unidentified horse out in Mungrid Woods, and he can just picture the pair of them sawing away at the innocent creature's throat.

TWO OF THE GOOD VILLAGERS

'I brought you a nice bit a home-baked muffin,' Natalie says gently, still standing facing the door which is open only a crack – just wide enough for Elise to be peering out at her. 'They're cranberry and cardamom. Good for the soul.'

Elise's eyes look sore. Natalie noticed that the other day too – like they've been wet so much the skin has cracked and now it stings in the corners, making her eyes weep all the more. A vicious cycle.

'How are you today, Elise?' she says. 'Can I no come in, just for a quick cuppa?'

Elise nods and opens the door wider – she's still not dressed, Natalie realises, she's got her out of bed. Well, this time a morning, that's probably a good thing.

The house is a state too. She's not been doing the hoovering, not been doing the washing-up; not even been putting the bins out, by the smell of it. Natalie can help with that.

'You put the kettle on now,' she says. 'Nice cup of English breakfast, eh? I'll tidy up a bit for you.' But Elise is just standing there looking at her, as though she thinks she's lost it completely. 'We all miss him,' Natalie says, though at that Elise looks like she could slap her. 'Not as much as you, of course,' she adds hastily. 'He was your da, Elise. You miss your dear da.'

'I feel sick.'

Her voice is strong at least – Natalie's glad to hear that.

'The kettle now, pet.'

Elise opens her mouth, closes it again. The pyjamas she's wearing are a pair of knee-length grey leggings and a bright pink baggy T-shirt that screams the word QUIET. She shakes her head, but turns towards the kitchen. Once she's in the other room, Natalie sets to work. Cushions off the sofa, the seat cushions, the back cushions, all off and wiped and put back in place; the drawer under the TV pulled open – nothing but DVD boxes in there – so she adds in the boxes that were littering the floor. Clothes strewn on the chair by the window – she folds them into a neat pile. The bins in the kitchen – she'll have to get that later, the upstairs too, but there's a desk against the wall, the roll-top, with a key in the lock; she turns it, hastily looks under the piles of stuff, just junk, cards and bills and a flowery writing pad that's yellowing at the edges, pens, Sellotape, stamps, no, no, no.

'I told you already,' Elise says. 'He didn't leave it for me.' She's standing in the doorway, two mugs of tea in her hand.

'That's good,' Natalie says with a smile. 'You sound a bit more like yourself now.'

Elise looks at the mugs, slops them down on the table, slumps into the sofa and gives a bitter laugh. Natalie glances round for a tissue then wipes up the spilled tea. Sits down beside her.

'How are you, Elise? Really, now?'

'He didn't trust me.'

'He loved you, Elise. He was your da and he loved you so much.'

She takes her hand and Elise's eyes fill again, though she doesn't let the tears fall.

'Well,' she says. 'He's gone now, so…'

'It'll take time.'

'So people keep saying.'

'But you're strong, Elise. Always have been.'

Elise grabs a tissue and blows her nose, thoroughly.

'That's right,' Natalie says. 'You let it all out, pet.'

Elise glances up at her, tissue still at her nose, and lets out a reluctant laugh.

'That's better now,' Natalie says, smiling too.

Elise scrunches up the tissue and plonks it on the table.

'Well. And how are *you*, Natalie?'

'Me? I'm busy, you know...there's always so much to do with the community council and I'm worried about you, Elise, and I'm—'

'How are your boys?'

Natalie shakes her head; maybe she's pushing Elise too far, expecting too much of her – Art's death has hit her hard and she's a sweet girl, Elise.

'You must be so worried,' Elise says.

Natalie suddenly feels like her throat's constricted, like she needs to swallow again and again; she reaches for her tea, takes a big gulp but it burns her tongue.

'Can't be easy,' Elise is saying, 'being a single mam all these years, for those two—'

'They're good boys.'

Elise smiles gently. 'Of course they are, Natalie, of course. We all know that deep down. And thank you, for tidying up a bit.'

'My pleasure,' she says. 'It's the least I can do, really, and... I don't mean to be... I'm worried, Elise.'

'Have you been keeping an eye?'

'Where I can.'

'Well, that's all we can do now, Natalie. Everyone has your back, you know that? We all know what you've been through.'

'What folk are saying though, about Aaron and...it's not...they wouldn't do that, not for Ricky Barr, they wouldn't—'

'It's not their fault, Natalie. And it's not your fault either.'

Natalie is looking at her tea, but she doesn't want to drink it, can't imagine sitting here for the time it would take her to drink a whole mug of it.

'Have you cleared out any of your da's things yet?' she tries, but Elise doesn't even answer. She has that faraway look in her eyes again, as though it took all her strength to ask about Aaron and Lee and now she's gone again, retreated back into the person who's been spending every night on the sofa watching endless DVDs since her da passed away and left her rattling about in this house alone.

'Well,' Natalie says. 'The excavation of the motte is going ahead. They'll be arriving today.'

Elise just nods.

'It's important,' Natalie says, 'for the village.'

She pats Elise's hand again.

'Have you been able to get out at all?' she asks.

'Oh stop worrying, Natalie, please.' Elise smiles. 'I'm not so daft as everyone seems to think.'

'I've never thought you were daft, Elise.'

'Well, as far as your two boys go, if the police find anything, if they're in any kind of serious trouble, I'll hear about it, okay?'

Natalie is nodding, though the thought of her boys in serious trouble is making her legs shake. Her two boys. What has happened to her two boys?

'Natalie,' Elise is saying. 'Natalie, come here.'

Elise puts her arms around her and, leaving the muffins untouched, the two women share the hug they've both been needing.

TASTE OF THE MORNING

Fergus could have done with a hug this morning, instead of waking up to an empty bed and an empty house yet again. If it was him who had to leave at 4 a.m., he'd have left a note at least, maybe even risked waking Georgie up with a kiss – and it's her job, he knows that, and she can't talk about it, but still. Hard not to feel pushed away when he feels like she's pushing him away so often these days. He'd thought this morning might have been better. He'd thought he could see a glimmer of hope in the night. Even after waking up alone he'd got up, trying to stay optimistic, noticed the smears on their bedroom window and got some soapy water to clean them down straight away – they like to see out, of a morning, him and Georgie, watch the clouds blowing by, admire the colours of the sky. No sense masking all that beauty with stains of dirt from the winter storms, is there? But now it's 11:41 a.m. and she's not even replied to his texts and Fergus is waiting at Warphill station for Professor McLeod to arrive on the late 11:34 from the city.

Couldn't the train have arrived, just this once, on time? It always leaves the city on time, but something happens out here on the coast that makes everything less efficient than the laws of physics and engineering say it should be. He wants to make a good impression, though, and if at all possible he'd like Warphill and Burrowhead and the coast and the scenery and the secrets buried beneath the motte to help him out a bit.

A real archaeologist, though, out here at last – that's quite something. It took him two months of campaigning. It's a good thing Kaltonn agreed to let him change to the night shift, otherwise he'd not have been able to supervise the dig. *His* dig. Georgie has got her case to work on, that poor creature, but Fergus has got buried lives to uncover. The possibility of finding ancient artefacts under the motte seems somehow so much more vital than his work at the power plant ever did. He doesn't even feel like the same man who used to project manage the nuclear site, all those people and their jobs under him. No, he likes this better, he tells himself. Though he does wish the trains would run on time.

The station is a single platform and the train line is a single line running from the city to Crackenbridge then down through Thormount and Coulderfield to Warphill & Burrowhead Station – they get the one station, combined, Warphill and Burrowhead – where it waits for a while, sitting on the last few sleepers as if interrupted by the steep cliffs of Burrowhead, before making its way back again. Inland they have newer lines, more trains, but out here it's still the original tracks.

It's 11:49 now and he can hear the tremor of the tracks that tells him the train is approaching. Professor McLeod. Nice to hear a Scottish name, south of the border. She studied in Glasgow before moving down – he's googled her – so they'll have places in common. Here comes the train at last, slowing like there's a force field trying to keep it out and it has to battle its way through, five times a day in summer. It's less every winter, mind, but there aren't many folk will be coming out here in the middle of winter.

He watches the windows. There are a few people on, which means there'll be a few disembarking, what with this being the last stop. A family gets off first – mum and dad, two kids, toddlers. That makes him smile. Then there's June, Whelan's wife, from the village; she must have been up in Crackenbridge for some shopping. He waves enthusiastically and she nods at him with a wink that leaves him mildly confused. And finally down steps a tall, solid-looking woman wearing jeans and a short denim dress over the top with buckets of curly grey hair frizzing out in all directions. She holds out her hand and he clears his throat before saying, 'Thank you, thank you so very much.'

'What are you thanking me for?'

'For coming out all this way and for…for taking me seriously.'

'It's my job,' she says with a large-toothed smile – as she rescues her hand from his grip.

'Well, do you want to go straight to the motte, or—'

'Actually,' she says, 'I'd like to see the standing stone you mentioned first. Often we find they're related, and the markings might be important.'

All of a sudden Fergus feels reluctant and he can't explain why. Of course he must take her to the standing stone. He was planning a whole tour, once he'd shown her the aerial survey he's taken with his drone. He just didn't realise they'd have to go there now, today, before he's had a chance to check on it.

'Don't worry, I've hired a car,' she says. 'I'll drive.'

'No, it's just…the markings can be hard to see sometimes.'

The truth is that, while he knows they are there, he can only actually feel them with his hands. His eyes can't make them out, not in a way that's ever clear enough, ever entirely convincing to someone else that what he can feel is more than natural erosion.

'I've seen it all,' she says. 'Believe me.'

So he walks with her to the car rental and soon she's driving, though he's too nervous for chit-chat on the road, soon she's parking beside the field where the standing stone rises from the grass. He can hardly bring himself to step out of the car – he seems to be magnetically attached to the seat. She's not, though. She's up and out soon as the engine is off, and he has to follow. What's he going to say, that he's a bit afraid of the stone because he thinks it gave him a migraine? That his wife thinks he's obsessed with a pointless lump of rock? He could explain about the murders earlier this year, of course, but something holds him back; that feeling again of wanting to make a good impression.

What if she can't see the markings though, what if she gives him a look like Suze did when she found him tracing their curves and lines with his fingers – like he'd lost it, a few years of unemployment and big Fergus has turned into the village crackpot – and she's already marching up to the stone like she's not scared of a single thing, and of course there's no reason to be scared of a standing stone. That's just ridiculous. But then she gasps and he finds himself running the last few paces to explain, to show her where to feel the contours, convince her he was telling the truth – then he, too, gasps and the two of them stand in silence looking at the stone.

It's not possible. He doesn't understand.

The markings are exquisite. They cover the stone from base to tip, an intricate swirling of circles and loops and spirals surrounding illustrations that could be animals, perhaps, symbols he doesn't recognise – he'd give anything to have Georgie marvelling at this beside him. They're clear as the sky, a deep purple against the pale grey of the stone itself. And there's more. The moss, the lichen has gone, and it looks taller – surely it's not possible that it's got taller – and the grass and nettles that had been creeping up its base have been smoothed away; someone has cleaned it up.

Of course, that's what has happened.

Someone has washed the surface until it turned a smooth light grey, freed it from the weeds so it appears to stand taller, and in among all the work the etchings have finally appeared as they were meant to be. Then the fear lodges itself deep in his belly. There are feathers, circling the stone.

'Someone has done this,' he says, like a confession.

'Clearly.'

'But the markings were here before, they're original, I promise you…'

She touches them with her index finger, tracing their curves as he once did.

'I think they're a combination, unfortunately. Some old, some modern. That'll make it harder to date, and harder to decipher. I'd say you have some superstitious residents round here, do you?' she says, with distaste.

'I…I wouldn't say that. I don't know…' He gestures uselessly at the feathers.

'You see the same sort of thing at Stonehenge. They had to set up a security barrier to stop the loons getting in. God knows what they'd do left to their own devices.'

Fergus wishes he could touch the stone again, but his arms feel paralysed.

'You wouldn't believe the nonsense some people *do* believe,' she says, stepping back. 'This animal here, a cow perhaps, a horse?'

He nods.

'There's nothing genuine about that. This is a badly carved modern stick figure imitation, not a Celtic symbol.'

He reaches out then – if she's so dismissive of it then surely there's no harm in him touching it – and sure enough when his fingertips follow the shape of the animal he feels nothing. Nothing except the desire to keep following the shapes. Away from the horse-cow and out to the concentric circles that surround it, then following a line upwards to a shallow dip in the stone, just the right size for a thumb to press into, and he feels the sun pounding on the top of his head, the pressure building behind his eyes.

Suddenly he can see it: the dead mare lying out on the stone slab of the cup and ring yesterday, just how Georgie described, slaughtered for no reason, six dead birds surrounding her in a circle. There are six feathers lying around the base of the standing stone as well. He saw them hanging in Walt's front window, too.

A metallic sensation spreads over his tongue and he thinks, for a second, that he's imagining the taste of blood in his mouth, the blood from that poor creature, the horse's blood. The professor is watching him. He has to step away, forces his hand down to his side. It is only then he realises he's bitten his lip, and the blood he can taste is his own.

WHAT COMES TO THOSE WHO WAIT

'Oh my God.'

Georgie's hand is over her mouth and Trish is beside her and it just hadn't occurred to her but of course, she should have thought of that. Georgie's never had kids, though, her and Fergus they never—

'What is it?'

Trish, impatient as ever.

Georgie wants to cry, though she couldn't even explain why, not really. Her mind is desperately trying to remember if she'd helped with Errol when he was a baby, her baby brother, if she'd changed him when he needed changing – had she? She's trying to imagine it but all she can see is his face at the end, a teenager she'd dragged to a protest he never wanted to attend, his blood soaking her hands.

'Cal, I'm putting you on speaker,' she manages. 'Trish is here.'

'It's a nappy,' he says, his cheerful voice booming its way into the room even as Georgie fumbles to turn the volume down a bit.

It hadn't even crossed her mind that it was a nappy – and she's sure now, she's never changed a nappy, she never even changed her little brother's – but it is; they've found a baby, a tiny baby wrapped in nothing but a nappy, buried in the ground, deep in the soil and the mud without a coffin or a gravestone, without anyone there to so much as hold their hand.

'Seriously?' says Trish. 'It wouldn't have biodegraded or something?'

'Nope, and it's even better than you're thinking, Trish, because it's old.'

'What do you mean?'

'I mean it's an old type of nappy, from before the modern ones came on the market, so I think we should be able to get a date.'

'That is good news,' Georgie says. Her head's started pounding despite all the water she's been drinking and she keeps feeling compelled to look over her shoulder, as if there's something there, someone, begging her to turn around. It's taking all she's got to ignore the impulse.

'That's great,' Trish is saying. 'Really, a date, that's what we need. And that means the kid must have been a small baby then?'

'I'll be more precise with a bit of time, but I'd say they were about two.'

'A toddler,' Georgie says. Oh God, she doesn't want to think about it. A toddler, an innocent little child.

All the remains are at the lab. The bones hadn't been lying in their original positions, and there were some missing. They had most of the skull though, a partial ribcage, the ulna that Shona found. Georgie's guess is that other parts of the skeleton must have been working their way up, through erosion of the soil or the farming itself, to be carried off by animals. They were just a child, barely more than a baby.

'I'll call when I've got more.'

'Wait, Cal—'

'I'm still here, Georgie.'

That pulling from behind her, willing her to turn around. She doesn't want to look, she's too afraid of what she's going to see.

'What about the other crime, Cal. The, er...' Trish is here and she doesn't even know about the rope yet, Georgie had been keeping that to herself, but she decides to go on anyway, her hand pressing against her forehead all the while. 'Any epithelial cells from the rope you found in the woods?'

'What rope?' says Trish.

'Still be a couple of days for that, I'm afraid.'

'What rope?'

For once Georgie is grateful for the way Cal just presses ahead, ignoring questions he can't be bothered to answer.

'Like I said,' he goes on, 'they'll no be prioritising an animal killing—' She hears him almost chuckle before he catches himself. 'But soon as I have anything, Georgie.'

'Is that you, Cal?'

Simon's back. He must have finished his interviews and he's holding something, a glass vial, easing it into an evidence bag.

'I found this in Aaron and Lee's caravan. I'm thinking—'

'Can't see down the phone, Si,' Cal calls out.

'It's a glass vial, unlabelled, a small amount of liquid still inside.'

'Send it over right away, Si.'

'Will do.'

And then he's gone, Cal is gone and Trish is looking at what Si's brought in with him, careful not to touch, and saying, 'You found it in their caravan?'

'In the cupboard.'

'In one of *Ricky*'s caravans.'

'And they're claiming it was there when they arrived—'

'Then it could be his, could be Ricky's.'

There it is, the agenda that always puts Georgie's guard up: Trish's tendency to blame Ricky for everything, especially if it means excusing some of the local kids that she's always so intent on standing up for.

'I'm not sure,' Simon says, more cautious than Trish. 'They didn't exactly seem *innocent* to me.'

'Kids are always like that with the police—'

'In fact they seemed like they could barely be bothered to hide the fact that they were lying—'

The bulb in Georgie's desk lamp suddenly shatters, glass splinters spraying her desk and everyone shocked into silence and Georgie can't help it, she turns away from them both to look over her shoulder at that corner behind her desk and in the shadow she glimpses a baby, a toddler, lying on his back and clawing at the air above him and then he is gone and there's glass everywhere and Trish is saying 'What the fuck just happened' and Georgie thinks she's going to be sick.

HOW GEORGIE BECAME LOST

Leaning her hands against the back wall of the chapel, her head hanging low, spitting into the dirt and wishing she could throw up – but that wouldn't be right, because after you throw up you feel better, don't you, and she doesn't deserve to feel any better, she doesn't want to, not now and not ever. He's dead. Errol is gone. Her little brother is dead and if it wasn't for her he'd be alive and no amount of other people telling her it wasn't her that pulled the trigger is going to change that. She only needs to see the look on her dad's face every time they're in the same room together to know that. Georgie doesn't need to be told that she can't stay here any more, not now.

Conversation after conversation with the fucking cops, round and around, knowing that the truth she was giving them wasn't the version they were wanting to hear and the futility of it, the way her anger would rise and for a second, for a fraction of a second she could see herself fighting, demanding justice, demanding they be locked up, those white men with their fucking cloaks and hoods, before it burst and she'd feel the air kicked out of her lungs; he was gone, her brother was gone and if it wasn't for her he'd still be here.

'There was no need for him to be there,' her dad saying, his head in his hands, that hunch and shake of his shoulders she'll never forget. 'There was no need for *you* to be there.' That accusation in his eyes. 'I made sure of it, I kept the both of you safe, there was no need—'

Her mom, leading her gently away, to the kitchen, to spiced milk and honey but it's her dad's words that remain, her dad's words and Errol's blood; his blood, coating her fingers – she feels it every time she wakes, every single morning – holding him on the ground in her arms and screaming for help that didn't come as crowds trampled around them and car brakes screeched and people fell. She sees it when she's awake, senses it around every corner, chokes on her food as suddenly her fingers are slippery with blood again, her eyes swimming in the haze of fear and desperation in the middle of the school lunchroom but she's seeing it, she's feeling it again, and again, powerless to make it stop.

The smell in the chapel, heavy with flowers, pollen hanging in the heat and the way it makes her head throb and the words, the readings, the hymns, all of it pointless. Her tongue sticking to the roof of her mouth, her lips cracked and peeling. *There was no need to be there.* Her mom, crying beside her, loud lurches of pain, unable to stop.

The way people look at her now, on the street, at school, everywhere she goes, the pity, the knowledge and, behind that, unspoken: the judgement. They're not even surprised.

She was always picking fights, that Georgie.

The day she tells her mom she's going to leave, knowing there won't be any objection, won't be any begging her to stay, not like there would have been with Errol, and seeing the way her mom's eyes take in the information; her mom's eyes still bloodshot and raw, the way Georgie's would be, if she allowed herself to cry.

'I'll go north,' she says. 'Away from the heat. Away from the…'

Away from the slip of blood she still feels, every night, between her fingers and the anger that keeps rising and bursting within her, that she doesn't know how to cope with, not yet, but that's pushing her somewhere as far away as possible from here.

Her mom's nod is slow and sure, like she knew it was coming, knew this was the only way it could end; and then her words:

'It was not your fault.'

Words that Georgie can't believe, that smear like blood on her skin.

Her mom's soft hands on her face, pulling her close, her words: 'None of this, Georgie, none of it is your fault.'

The smell in the chapel, heavy and thick, the sweat and the heat and the flowers, her dad avoiding her gaze, the way he has ever since it happened, every day, unable to look at her, and there is singing around her, voices singing, chanting, and she can't stand it, the noise of all those voices, her mom, beside her, holding her hand.

'One day, believe that I'm proud of you.'

And Georgie is standing, gasping, tripping over as she runs to get out. Then sharp cuts of sunlight, her hands leaning against the rough wall of the chapel, her head hanging low, the heat beating against her back, her neck and she spits onto the ground and will not let herself be sick no matter how badly she needs to be until, eventually, she falls to her knees and starts talking to him, to Errol, as if he was here, because he is here, he's cradled in her arms on the ground and his blood is seeping between her fingers and she's gasping through the heavy thick heat and shaking and whispering *I'm sorry, I'm so sorry, I...* Words, the words she's heard, spoken to her and about her, since she lost him, words about need and blame, about fighting and staying away; words about fault and guilt and she searches for her own words instead, because no one else's are right; *I'm so sorry*, she says, her fingers slipping through soil, *I... I didn't save you and I should have saved you and I'm so sorry, but I couldn't, I couldn't save you.*

THINGS NEEDED, THINGS FOUND

'Are you okay?'

Shona hadn't meant to stumble in on anything she shouldn't, she just wants to know, those bones she found, the one she held in her hand, were they really from a child? The thought of it won't leave her, the way she'd carried that bone with her, snug in her pocket, felt the warmth of it against her skin, and now she can't stop imagining a child, the child it belonged to, a child buried in the field where Ricky Barr grows food, where she herself has harvested potatoes and thrown weeds back into the ground, not caring.

A child.

She'd thought she was looking for a story – everyone suspects her of it, so she might as well start to admit it. She was looking for a story to get her noticed, to get her out of here, true, and she wanted to know why Rachel and Pauly did it, why they killed themselves like that; she *needs* to understand. But this is something else now, this is not something she can use to her advantage, for her own good. She held that bone, in her palm, against her skin.

'DI Strachan? I don't mean to...'

Georgie looks up at her, startled, as though she'd no idea she was there, despite the shadow Shona's casting over the concrete round the side of the police station where Georgie's kneeling on the ground. Then, without a word, Georgie turns away again, back to face the wall.

'DI... Georgie, are you okay?'

Everyone knows Georgie as Georgie, that's how she used to introduce herself when she gave her little talks at the school. Shona remembers her, the way she'd invite them, all the kids at school, to ask her anything they needed to. She'd earnestly tell them about what smoking does to your lungs, what ecstasy makes you forget, as they sat in the assembly hall stifling their smiles and waiting it out, till they could head back to the bike sheds for a fag, head out at the weekend to obliterate their memories. 'Georgie's coming back in next week,' they used to say with a grin, a roll of their eyes, like it was sweet of her to try; like she was clueless.

These days, though, everyone's started calling her DI Strachan. Shona's not sure if she asked them to, or if it's just happened of its own accord. So it feels weird to call her Georgie, but also right somehow – Georgie was always standing up and smiling at them, in those assemblies, approachable, not like now: kneeling on the ground with her forehead against the rough wall of the station.

'What are you doing here, Shona?'

Georgie speaks without moving, knees on concrete, head against the pebble-dash, eyes down. It must hurt.

'I just want to help,' Shona says. 'Can I help?'

'No, I don't think you can.'

'Try me?'

Shona's holding out her hand now, but Georgie doesn't make eye contact, still hasn't moved.

'This is a police investigation,' she says slowly, angrily even.

'That's not what I mean.'

Shona reaches forward and places a hand on her shoulder, another reaching for her wrist.

Georgie turns at last, looks at her in astonishment.

'I thought you were going out with that Kevin Taylor.'

The way she says it makes Shona cringe, but she tries to keep it hidden.

'Kev's complicated.'

'I thought you were after a story.'

'Not exactly.'

'You could damage the investigation, you know. You could ruin our chances of getting to trial. You could—'

'I won't.'

'You grew up here, didn't you, Shona? You're a local, through and through.'

'Yes, I am,' Shona smiles, like how Georgie used to smile at them in the assembly hall; genuine, she hopes, approachable. 'And right now I'd just like to help you stand up.'

A WAY BACK

A summer's day, midsummer and the heat is heavier than any summer they've known before; Deborah-Jane is standing in the stream up to her armpits and her clothes are drenched. Her brother is leaping in and out of the cool water, jumping off the stepping stone in the middle and squealing with joy – she's keeping an eye, of course, 'cause she's the oldest and she's the one in charge out here. Birds flutter overhead and the sun is glinting through the leaves like diamonds and no one knows they're even here, their da is in the town for market and their mam's taken to her room again after telling her to stay on the farm, always stay on the farm – she hates it on the farm. Out here though, there's no one else out here, at least that's the way it's supposed to be, that's why there's something wrong in the bird call that isn't a bird, that must be a kid, in the stifled laugh that follows. Her brother hears it too, freezes where he lands in the stream, waits for her to tell him what to do. He's been slow, learning words of his own, but he understands her; he always understands her.

'It's alright,' she says. 'Let's get out now,' and she takes him by the hand and they climb up the stream's bank, letting their clothes drip onto the moss of the track that leads back into the trees. She knows every noise that should be here; she's alert to every noise that shouldn't. The crunch of someone shifting their weight on some dried leaves up in front, the thud of a stone thrown to scare them, or distract them, send them a different way. She's clasping her brother's hand tight. He's only a kid, a little kid, and she's not going to let anything hurt him. It can't be their da, he wouldn't have followed them out here, would he, to scare them? No, he'd just leave them to it. Wait till they got home to throw his fists.

She's heard stories of a man escaped the prison living rough in the woods, a psychopath who picks off campers one by one, chops them up into little bits and roasts them on his fire. She's heard stories of the dead rising up through the ground, coming for their revenge. She's heard stories of creatures out here that claw at your eyes if you look at them, stories of poisonous bushes that scratch at your skin and leave venom that takes days to kill you – there are lots of stories, in these villages, made up by people who want to scare. But then there's a sudden burst of colour, of screams, there's grit in her eyes and she can't see, she can't see anything through the stinging. She drops her brother's hand without meaning to, she just needs to shield her face, rub that grit out of her eyes, but then he runs. It's just a few steps, that's all, she could almost still grab him and then he's gone, only his stunned scream resonating in the air and then the kids, three of them, all coming out from the trees and her brother's scared voice calling her name and their smirks, their laughter.

'Put the plank over the hole,' orders Alfred – he's always bossing everyone about, at school, in the village, and no one's brave enough to stand up to him.

'Don't you dare,' she snaps.

'What did you say?'

There's one behind her, Whelan, he's a spiteful little wretch, and Camellia is with them too, her long plaits tied with red ribbons, but she refuses to be scared by either of them. She glances all around, arms out like she's slowing everything down, giving herself some time to think.

Her brother has started crying down in that hole they dug.

They dug it on purpose, they must have. It would have been too small to hold someone her age, it's the size of her brother, the size of a three-year-old. Whelan has got the plank and thrown it over and her brother is trapped now, down under the ground. She wants to tell him not to show that he's scared but he's too young to have learned that lesson. He must have found a stick or something down there though because he's scratching at the plank of wood over his head, scratching desperately at the wood blocking out the light.

'Let him out,' she says, calm and strong. 'I'm warning you.'

'You're warning us?' says Camellia with that tinkling laugh of hers, and without a second's pause she's on her, grabbing her stupid long plaits and pulling with all her might, scratching at her skin and Alfred grabs her feet so she kicks him, gets him in the stomach, claws at his face and her brother's calling her name. His voice wobbling. And she's running after Whelan now who's laughing at her and she's grabbing his shirt and throttling him, wrestling him to the ground, kicking and spitting and running and she barrels into someone else, someone who's been watching, standing there watching and she falls flat on the ground and looks up. Everyone goes silent.

'What is going on here?' Nora's voice is so stern and quiet she feels her stomach fall away.

'They've, they've—' She scrambles back to the hole, heaves away the plank of wood and reaches down to her brother's upstretched arms. 'It's okay,' she whispers to him, pulling him to safety, 'it's okay.'

It's only then she looks over and realises that Nora Prowle has the new kid with her too, the toddler. It looks like he's been dragged all the way out here even though he's so puny he can barely walk. Sonny, his name is, apparently, though there's nothing very sunny about him – he's prone to asthma attacks and runny noses and crying fits for no reason. He's not going to last here long. His hair is uneven, tangled on one side and cropped short the other, like he was marched out here halfway through a haircut. It's only fleeting but looking at him there, the way he's shrinking back from her gaze, she wonders about the other kids, where they got the idea for digging a hole in the first place; who they were planning to trap.

They can't have known she'd be here with her brother. No one knew they came here. The hole wasn't for them.

'She kicked me,' Alfred yells, his voice all outrage and injustice, and Nora stands where she is and says, 'Take her shoes then.'

Deborah-Jane is too shocked to move.

Suddenly they're all on her, all three of them, pushing her to the ground and pulling at her shoes, gouging at her skin, all nails and spite, and from somewhere behind her she can hear the new kid's scared little voice, *no no no*, the only word he ever seems to say; she's got to fight back, she's kicking and yelling and lashing out at them but her shoes are gone and they're laughing and standing back as she scrambles to her feet. She refuses to cry. She is *not* going to cry; she marches to where her brother is trying to stop his sobs and she takes his hand and glares back at them, and then, seeing Nora Prowle raise her arm, she starts to run; she runs back to the farm that she hates with the brother she loves, and by the time she gets there her bare feet are punctured with twigs and gravel and the vicious tips of conker shells, and her soles are scratched and bleeding.

LETTING THE LIGHT IN

Pamali dips the soft yellow cloth into her bucket of warm soapy water again, and rubs it against the Perspex window in a slow, circular motion. The first time she had to clear graffiti off here, rather than the glass they smashed a few months back, she scrubbed at it with a scouring brush and was left with permanent scratches that turn the sunlight misty and grey. She's not making that mistake again. A gentle touch, that was always her way before and that's her way again now, and she feels better for it too. That's the thing about anger, it can eat you up if you're not careful, whereas a bit of gentleness, a bit of kindness, that can help you heal.

'What's going on, Pamali?'

Natalie Prowle's voice is so full of sympathy that Pamali leans her head against the hand resting on her shoulder, just for a second, before turning.

'Not more of this, Pamali? I told you to call me.'

'It's a one-person job, Natalie—'

'And with the two of us it'll be half a job, which I'd say is an improvement.'

Natalie has the cloth in her hand already. Pamali's not even sure how or when she took it from her, but she's already rubbing away at the scratches as though they're spray paint that will be removed with enough soap suds, enough persistence.

'It's scratched permanently,' Pamali tries. 'I think I've got everything that's going to come off for now. Honestly.'

But Natalie is still rubbing away, and Pamali wonders if there's something there around her eyes, raw skin, lack of sleep, barely contained tears. It's Pamali's turn to place a sympathetic hand on her shoulder.

'It wasn't your fault, Natalie.'

'But it…'

Natalie straightens her back at last, letting the soapy water trickle down the plastic windowpane and start to drip onto the parched, cracked paving stones below it.

'I'm his mother and he, he attacked you, he vandalised—'

'And you can't do his community service for him, Natalie. Much as we've all seen you trying.'

It's true, Pami has noticed it all: she's seen how Natalie is spending more and more time trying to clean up the village, how she calls in on Mrs Dover and Mrs Smyth and takes them hot meals of an evening, now the meals on wheels has closed. She even took in that little girl for respite care over the past few months, to give the parents a chance to get back on their feet – addiction issues, she'd told Pamali in a hushed voice one day when she'd brought the kid into the Spar for some sweeties. What the courts had Andy and Lee doing, what they call 'community service', Pami doesn't have much time for; what's the point in getting angry young lads like that to stand alone on the edge of the road out to Crackenbridge collecting plastic bottles and food wrappers chucked out of long-distance lorries, how's that going to help them? They should be doing what Natalie is doing – helping the villagers, helping *others*, talking to folk who need company, working together with people.

'Natalie, come on.'

Pamali eases the cloth from her hands, squeezes it out and drapes it over the side of the bucket.

'It's as clean as it's ever going to get, I think.' She smiles. 'Thank you.'

Natalie shakes her head. 'It's never going to be enough, is it?'

'You don't owe me anything, Natalie.'

'My family have always looked after this village, and I'm failing—'

'Come on now,' Pamali says. 'We're all trying our best.'

'My aunt used to help kids get their lives back on track, did you know that?'

Pamali shakes her head.

'And now I can't even…my own son, my boys…'

'Oh, Natalie. Won't you come inside, for a cuppa?'

'I can't.' Natalie looks like she's about to cry for real now, and that's not something Pamali has ever seen before. 'I…' She takes a deep breath and straightens herself up. 'There are too many things I have to do today. My village, my responsibility.'

With that she looks more like herself again, more like the Natalie Prowle everyone in Burrowhead and Warphill knows, and Pamali is relieved to see it. She always seems so tough, Natalie, so together, so in charge.

'Another time then,' Pamali says, deciding against reminding Natalie that Burrowhead is her village too. Instead she says: 'You and I, Natalie, I think it's about time we sat down together and worked out how to put the world to rights.'

EXCAVATIONS

Fergus is amazed at how quickly Professor McLeod gets the dig all set up – the fence around the motte marking the excavation, the trenches neatly measured, her two students setting to work on either side of the mound. They're avoiding the site of the previous trench, the one where they'd found the cauldron; apparently that wasn't the best place to dig at all. Now they know better, because there have been two recent discoveries of similar-shaped mounds dated to centuries before the traditional motte-and-baileys were built. The previous dig had assumed it was one of those: a motte-and-bailey fortification around a central tower. But Professor McLeod thinks they were wrong.

'It could be older,' she tells Fergus as her students finish marking out their trenches, 'a different type of structure entirely.'

The ceremonial cauldron, as she calls it, and his iron figurine both suggest something ritualistic. There could be something important, cavernous, under the yellowing grass.

'Like a cairn?' Fergus says, eventually. He doesn't want her to think he's stupid, uninformed.

She's got her hands on her hips though, eyes flicking back and forth over the scene in front of her, and all she manages is a vague 'mmm'.

Maybe he'll take that as a yes. It's his best place of reverence: the chambered cairns of Scotland. He visited them as a child. The huge, ancient stones, covered in lichen, encircling chambers with bed-like tombs built into the walls where the dead were buried. Artists' renditions showed structures rising metres high and sinking metres deep under the ground, and a passageway leading in, formed by giant stones, a person-width across; just space enough to enter the underworld. As they dig, he checks his phone – still no reply from Georgie – then stands back and watches them delve deeper into the ground. It casts his mind back to that feeling he had as a kid. It was like there was something vital buried in those cairns that he wasn't allowed to see, something just out of reach. His mum was always pulling him away, not wanting him to play in the dirt or ask too many questions. Maybe she just didn't know the answers. She was busy; she was a GP. Georgie reminds him of her a bit – more concerned with lives in the present than the long-gone past. Though Georgie never liked his mother, she thought she was too harsh on him. Maybe she's changed her mind about that now. He needs a sign of some kind, that's what he needs, something to point him in the direction of how to make things better. He could text again, maybe, ask if she has time for a cuppa – they always used to find time for each other. But no, she'll be too busy for that. Besides, there is something real under the ground here, something important. Professor McLeod knows it, or she wouldn't be digging her way down.

'I'd like to help,' he finds himself saying, unaware he'd been walking closer to one of the trenches, but he must have been. He was following her, subconsciously, following her to where they had started digging. 'Is there something I can do to help?'

She gives that brisk nod of hers, a bit of a smile – he'll take that – and soon he's kneeling beside the younger of the two students, with dirt on his trousers, a trowel in hand, following carefully every instruction about how to dig slowly, brush away the soil from every object no matter how small. The first few layers are dried by the sun, flaking and pale, but as they get deeper the soil gets thicker, clumpier. It clings under his nails and in the creases of his hands, and the more the earth feels damp and alive, the more he feels sucked into it, ignoring the pain in his lower back as he works without stopping.

The pain has expanded to his shoulders by the time the shadow settles over his field of view. Must be a cloud over the sun. But then it moves, becomes a shape and he feels his shoulders tighten, straightens his back and finally sees what's happening. It's the shadow of a person behind him.

'Natalie?' he says, standing. His knees are damp.

'We've come to help.'

She gestures to the villagers waiting behind her: June and Whelan Rogers, Mrs Dover and Mrs Smyth, for heaven's sake, they'll not be able to kneel and dig.

'We villagers have as much right to this land as they have.'

Fergus frowns, though Natalie is smiling at him.

'Alright.' She lowers her voice. 'I thought you could do with the support. And I wanted to…'

Fergus thinks that maybe she just wanted to be involved. She's not got the bairn with her, the girl always sleeping in her pram in the museum.

'Where's the wean today?'

'Back with her mam.'

That respite care, that's quite a thing to do, Fergus thinks. There must be kindness in her, that's for sure. But Professor McLeod is striding over to them now and for a second Fergus wants to retreat from the confrontation. That's not what happens though.

'Great,' she says. 'We could do with more volunteers.'

'We need to protect this site.'

'Of course we do.'

'I know what happens at these digs,' Natalie says, her chairper-son-of-the-community-council voice on, at its maximum volume. 'There'll be nothing left, everything taken away to the city, to the university—'

'That is absolutely not going to happen here.'

'I want to make it a site of local historic interest,' Fergus is saying. 'We can put up noticeboards and, with information I mean, and...'

Professor McLeod is already guiding the villagers round to where her other student has been working on her trench and she's handing out tools and instructions and Mrs Dover and Mrs Smyth seem to be setting up the deckchairs that Whelan was carrying for them and Fergus feels a stab of embarrassment. He catches Natalie's eye and feels his face flush.

Kneeling back down, he's glad at least that they're on the other side of the motte and that this patch is reserved for him and the student beside him. His name is Justin, apparently, he's doing a PhD, and he's been telling Fergus all about it. For now, though, Justin is focused on his work so Fergus lets his hands rest back in the dirt and enjoys the cool of the damp soil between his fingers; the pull of the past. He can almost see the sharp pointed arms of his iron figurine pointing him downwards and then, to his surprise, the knowledge that he's not alone, that other villagers are here to help, gives him an unexpected surge of hope as he starts to carefully, systematically, dig again.

NOT ALONE ANY MORE

HQ had told her they were sending DS Frazer, but for some reason Georgie can't quite put her finger on, she hasn't told Trish or Si he's coming. She's glad of it though. A few months back he might have felt like a stranger intruding on her station but now he feels like an ally. The way he'd looked at her when he left in the spring, his words: *You have my number.* She'd never used it, true, but it was good to know someone else saw what she was seeing round here. The layers of it, generation upon generation like closed ranks; you're either from these villages or you're not.

Georgie is not. And neither is DS Frazer.

Although Shona is. Shona who'd helped her up and not asked her any questions; who'd simply said she was there, to help, whenever she was needed. Shona who had held that bone in her hand like it was precious. Shona who'd left with the words *You've got my number,* just as Frazer once had.

He's not coming to help on her case this time though. In fact, the super didn't seem too pleased to hear that Georgie wanted to open an investigation into a historic crime at all – and only a potential crime at that – when there were barely enough funds to keep on top of urgent cases from today. No, Frazer has his own investigation, the report of a murder in the old manor hotel. Another historic case. Could be related, the super had said with a sigh. Georgie had wondered if she wanted Frazer out of the city.

As he pulls up in his shiny car, Georgie smiles at the thought of him having it washed especially for the trip down here. She watches through the window from Trish and Si's office, where neither of them have noticed the arrival outside. As he steps out, re-tucks his shirt, pulls on a suit jacket despite the heat and glances up to meet her gaze. A nod of understanding passes between them. Georgie feels a release of tension, just from the knowledge that within the next minute or two she'll no longer be the only person of colour in the room. It's tiring, being so constantly aware of difference.

Simon is typing up a report on his interviews along with what they know about the dead horse, the ketamine in her blood. His angle: Aaron and Lee Prowle, along with Ricky Barr, could have been involved, because drugs were involved, and this could be the way to finally prove Ricky's hands are dirty. Maybe he's got a point – Georgie's letting him run with it for now at least. He's got some reasonable theories, too, about why they might have wanted a horse dead. It could have been a threat to someone who owed money; it could have been a warning to a competitor. But, below that, there's the feathers plucked and arranged around the stone, the shapes the mare's blood made as it spiralled along the etchings on the cup and ring. There's what he said to her about Rachel and Pauly, the way they died last year, replaying in her mind.

Do you still think it was a suicide?

Georgie blinks, pushes the thought away.

Trish is working hard now too, though she doesn't seem haunted by either of the killings the way Georgie is. Then again, it can be difficult to tell sometimes with Trish – she keeps a lot inside, always has. Georgie thinks that mostly she wants to make sure no one's giving Uncle Walt a hard time about anything. She's getting more protective of him by the day.

'Can I have access to the horse crime scene photos?' Trish asks suddenly. 'The ones that weren't loaded on yesterday. Just in case.

Not the horse itself, I mean the surrounding area, the woods, the approach.'

Simon reaches for the camera, flicks through with a slight frown. 'You've got everything, Trish. What's left are just out-of-focus shots I was using to set up, a picture of my foot I took by mistake, some trees and sky, Suze setting up the perimeter—'

'Yes, they're the ones. Please.'

Georgie walks quietly from the room to let Frazer in before he needs to ring the bell. They keep the front door locked now, all the time – there's not enough of them to have someone constantly on reception and whatever naivety made her trust the villagers enough to leave the door open in the past has evaporated. Not that it was naivety, really. Maybe it was hope.

'Welcome,' she says, opening the door just as he steps up to it.

'Good to see you again, Ma'am.'

'You know full well you can call me Georgie.'

He smiles. 'Only when no one's listening.'

She takes his hand, and he shakes hers warmly.

'Come on in,' she says, inviting him to walk beside her down the corridor with a nod of her head. 'I hear you've got a statement from one Betty Marshall that might relate to our case.'

'That's what we're hoping,' he says.

'Then let's start with you briefing us on everything you know.'

She pushes the door to Trish and Si's office without knocking.

'You know the team, of course,' she says, her voice raised high enough for both Trish and Simon to stop what they're doing.

Si stands up with a smile right away. 'What are you doing here, Frazer?' Between them it's warmth, verging on friendship. Frazer must be seeing quite a change in Simon since he was here last, when Si was so grief-stricken he could barely string three words together, but if he does he's too thoughtful to mention it.

Trish, though, is a different story. She's sitting rooted to her chair, mouth still slightly open where it fell. As Frazer glances over to her with a nod and a simple stating of her name and rank – 'DC Mackie' – Georgie is sure there's a hint of red spreading up over Trish's neck, round behind her ears. She spikes her hair up a bit, as though she can't think of anything else to say or do, and it makes Georgie smile.

'New haircut?' Frazer says.

It's not dislike of an outsider that's making Trish flush like that, Georgie's sure, but something else entirely. In fact it's the first time in a while she's wanted to give Trish a hug. Poor girl; Frazer's got a wife, and a wife he's smitten with judging by the way he's constantly twisting that ring on his finger. But it's good to see a glimpse of Trish's softer side.

'DS Frazer has had reports of a historic murder in Wyndham Manor, the old hotel down the coast, that could date from a similar time to our skeleton. So he's going to fill us in on his investigation, then we can fill him in on ours.'

Trish seems to regain her composure a bit at that, and the office settles down and Georgie is able to sit back and listen. She doesn't interrupt his story, even though she can tell there are pieces that don't fit. He's not been able to find any sign of his alleged victim in any of the missing person reports of the time – he's checked widely – and so it might come down to word of mouth. The housekeeper who was working there, one Mrs Pettigrew, is unfortunately already deceased. He's going to be interviewing the villagers, especially older ones. Unless, he says, their two cases can combine; that would give him something much more solid to go on.

With Cal's characteristic good timing, the phone starts ringing. Georgie answers, doesn't speak, writes down everything he says. Then she turns back to the room.

'I'm afraid it's bad news for you, Frazer,' she says. 'But it's...' She swallows, can't bring herself to say the words *good news for us*.

'The nappy?' says Trish.

'Cal's found an expert, apparently, got her to look at some photos, and she recognised it immediately. Says she got quite excited at the prospect of seeing it in person, rushed up here to take a closer look. Turns out it's one of the earliest types of disposable nappies put on the market.'

'Nappy?' Frazer says.

'Which means we've got a date,' she continues. 'And we've got an age range. We're looking at a burial from between 1978 and 1982 – the years this particular type of nappy was available. And tying in with that, Cal's given me an age estimate of between eighteen and twenty-four months. We're looking at a toddler, buried in an unmarked grave in a field on the Barrs' farm, approximately forty years ago.'

'But it was a young woman who was seen by my witness. A teenage woman.' Frazer leans back heavily against the wall – there's no spare chair for him in here. 'Our cases might not be connected after all.'

'I'm afraid not.' Georgie sits back beside him. 'It's the wrong age and the wrong date.'

'Ricky might not even have been born,' Trish says, with more than a note of disappointment in her voice.

'Or he would have been a young child himself,' Georgie says. 'In fact, he could have been exactly the same age as the child buried in the field.'

'But then who were they?' Frazer asks.

The silence hangs around them thick as the heat, and none of them have an answer.

CROSSED LINES

Georgie leans against the outside wall of the police station. She's finding herself out here a lot today, needing to get out of the office. Only this time she's staring at her phone. He's rung twice already. Her phone was on silent. Thankfully. And then the text message: *I'll call you at exactly 5 p.m.*

It is 4:59 now and there is no logical reason for this to be irritating her so much, but as the time flicks over to 5:00, her phone starts ringing as she'd known it would and she lets it ring, and ring, holding it in her hand and counting to ten before she answers.

'Oh, hello, Georgie, is that you?'

'Of course it's me, Fergus,' she says.

That laugh of his, almost verging on nervous. 'Of course it's you, I mean, I thought it was the answerphone message for a second there, because that's your voice as well, if you see what I mean, but it's not the answerphone, it's you this time.'

She waits for it to stop, for him to tell her what it is he's been trying to phone her about all afternoon. Instead, they both fall into a pause.

'Is there something wrong, Fergus?'

'No, not at all, no nothing's wrong—'

'Then—'

'I was just wondering if you might like to have an early dinner tonight.'

'What?'

'Earlier than normal, I mean, because it would be nice to sit down together, I was thinking, and chat, you know? Like we used to.'

Up the road, Mrs Dover and Mrs Smyth are heading for the village square, arm in arm, and Georgie wonders if they've been down on the beach or something – Whelan is following behind them carrying two ugly, brightly striped deck chairs.

'I miss those long chats of ours over dinner.'

'Mmm...'

'So you'll be home by six then?'

'What?'

'That's why I'm saying early, Georgie, because—'

'There's no way I'll be home by six, Fergus, I'm in the middle of a case here and DS Frazer has just arrived, thank God, and I need to work – you do understand that, right?'

His pause is enough to tell her she's gone a bit too far. She hadn't meant to snap like that, she's being so careful with Trish, with work, and with that scratching at her skin from the heat... 'Sorry, love. Long day, and it's going to get longer. I'll try and be home by eight, alright?'

'I'll be gone by then, Georgie.'

'Gone where?'

'My shift starts at half seven, and I'll need to get the bus up because you've got the car and—'

'Shit, of course—'

'You forgot?'

'I'm sorry,' she sighs. 'I've got a lot on my plate.'

'I know that, love, it's just...'

'What?'

'Well, with you working so late all the time and me on night shifts, when are we going to see each other?'

'I'm not the one put you on night shifts, Fergus.'

'It was the only way I could be there for the dig,' he says. 'The excavation.'

'Yes,' she says, the heel of her hand rubbing against her head. 'I'll...look, we'll find some time, Fergus, I promise. But I've got to get back—'

'Right—'

'Another night—'

'Early evening,' he says quietly.

A noise catches her attention, from further down the road, away from the village – there's someone down there.

'Bye, Fergus.'

That's Andy Barr, gangling his way along the street with what seems, as far as she can tell from this distance, to be a trowel and a large bag of something hanging over his shoulder and what the hell is that kid up to now? Georgie needs to keep a close eye on him, whatever he's doing. She's seen what he's capable of.

EVENING SHADE

'There's no one here,' Kev says. 'No one.' His hand reaching up her shirt and her hand following to pull it away again.

'How do you know?' she says, matching his smile but only just.

It's getting late, true, but the sun's not gone yet and with the farm shut down for the day all the summer workers must be here, somewhere, walking the village, dozing in their caravans, picking their way over the pebbled beach to take a swim in the sea; watching them.

She's seen no sign of Ricky Barr since he had that coughing fit while they were digging out the body then skulked off to get some water at Georgie's suggestion, bent in on himself in a way that almost turned her dislike to pity. It was hard to tell if he was disturbed by the body, if he was even surprised by it – he's got one of those faces that never lets much through. That cough sounded rough as shingle, though, and not a soul asked him if he was alright. Mind you, it was the dirty stare he'd been giving her all morning that put her off talking to him. He seemed to know she was the one who went to the police. Aaron told him, probably. Or Lee. Or... Kev wouldn't have, would he? He's the only one who knew though, for sure, and he's getting too good at his act, too convincing – it's easy to believe he's one of them.

Still, the point is Ricky Barr could be there in his farmhouse, eyes at the window, he could be pacing the borders of the farm. It's not that she's shy, but she doesn't want to be caught in a vulnerable position; wants to be sure she can run, if necessary, the second she needs to. She can feel the high alert, prickling her skin.

'Come on then,' he says, still trying his luck, still grinning playfully. 'Into the woods. No one'll be in there.'

She follows him, not because she's ready to go at it with only a few silver birches for shade, but because she wants to talk to him properly, like they haven't had a chance to all day. She needs to see him the way she used to. The way she's been seeing him lately she doesn't much want him touching her at all. It's like she said to Georgie. Complicated.

The woods are beautiful though, in this light, the dappling effect of all those leaves, starting low enough to caress your neck, rising so high you can't see the top of them, just the twinkling of silver where the sun finds a way to peek through. Wild garlic has colonised the undergrowth, the heavy smell of it sweet and intoxicating, and there are swathes of green shrubs she can't name, that she doesn't even recognise, their leaves almost emerald, polished and dense as laurel.

Kev stops after a minute or so, taking her hand and pulling her to him as he leans against a tree trunk.

'How's this then?' he says.

'It was a baby, in that grave.'

His shoulders hunch up in a shiver before he takes a deep breath.

'That wasn't a grave. A grave would be marked. A grave would be visited and tended and…'

'Loved?'

Kev slides down the trunk to sit in the undergrowth, not caring what else might be down there – the woods are crawling with insects, as they should be; it's their domain after all. Shona sits down beside him.

'I was holding that bone all day,' she says. 'I can't stop thinking about the skeleton, the way it was all curled up like that.'

'I heard the police say the bones had been moved about over the years.'

'Maybe,' she says. 'But it still looked to me like that was the way they were lying when they were buried, curled up like they were trying to defend themselves and...in the foetal position. Like they were afraid.'

He puts his arm around her shoulders.

'Come on, you're the one who wanted a good story to write for the paper.'

'You think that's what I want? Seriously?'

There's a woodlouse crawling along her leg already. She lets it climb onto her finger, moves it over to a clump of twigs.

'Do you really think that's what I've been doing since last year, just looking for a good story?'

'Actually, I only know what you tell me,' he says. 'But seeing as you ask, I assume it's got something to do with Pauly and Rachel, why they did what they did...'

She doesn't speak, but her eyes don't leave his face.

'And seeing as you're working on the farm, I'm guessing you think it might have something to do with Ricky Barr.'

She feels a wave of sadness come over her that she can't explain, places her hand on his thigh. His jeans are warm. He takes her hand and holds it in his own.

'Shona.'

He leans forward and lets his forehead rest against hers and finally she can hear the woods all around: the call of birds out of sight, more different songs than she can count, leaves rustling gently in a breeze she can't feel on her own skin, a bee somewhere distant, its buzzing no more than a gentle fuzz, Kevin's breath matching hers, the warmth of it against her cheek. She pulls back, brushes at her eyes with the back of her hand. His fingers rest against her neck.

'Are you working for Ricky, Kev?'

He moves back at that, as she'd known he would. She tries to stop herself from breaking her gaze; it would be too easy to look away.

'Just tell me.'

'We're both working for him this summer. It was your idea.'

'That's not what I mean and you know it.'

The woodlouse is back. She lets it crawl over the back of her hand, holds it out to him. He picks it up between his fingers and throws it over towards the gorse. Shona stands, turns, then changes her mind. Looks down at him. He's still there, sitting on the dried leaf mulch; he's always been comfortable without needing to be above people. That's one of the things she likes about him. It made him seem less of a bully than most boys, but then again it takes a certain confidence to stay sitting when the only person you're with stands.

'I know Bobby was working for him before he was killed.'

He's not smiling or scowling. He's listening to her, carefully.

'I know Aaron has taken over, selling round the villages and to the school. I know Rachel and Pauly were taking something that fucked them up to the point of making a suicide pact, and I'm pretty damn sure they were getting it from Ricky himself. So I'll ask you again: are you working for Rick—'

There's someone here. She doesn't know how she knows, but she knows. A footstep on the moss, a push past a branch, a quieting of the birds as though they know it too, insects landing in unison and the woods suddenly more silent than they should be.

'What is—'

'Shhh.'

He's getting up now. Quietly. At least he's got the message. She can't hear anything, the sounds are missing, the light still glittering through the treetops and the sun turning golden and she can feel the first chill of sunset on her bare arms. Kev is frowning. She feels her legs tense.

He nods over her shoulder.

'Look.'

She doesn't want her back to him, but she doesn't want her back to whatever is behind her either so she holds her palm to his chest as though that's somehow going to stop him from lunging at her and turns to see what it is he's pointing to.

At first there's nothing there. Bushes, leaves, woodland stretching deeper inland and getting denser the further it goes, twisted trunks and straight-backed pines, bark that's red and gnarled, and then she sees it: lodged up on a branch, higher than her head. It looks like a clump of straw. Kev has taken her hand, interlaced his fingers with hers. Glancing at her, he walks up to the oak, reaches for a branch then lets go of her hand and pulls himself up, a stump for a footrest then a sole against the trunk itself as he makes a grab for it, landing back down on the moss. In his hand is a roughly made straw figure. He pretends to make it dance.

'The fuck?'

'It's a corn dolly. You not see one before?' he laughs, as though the sight of it has banished all the tension in the woods. 'My mam makes them. Loads of folk do.'

'What's it doing up that tree?'

He shrugs and holds it out to her, but she can't bring herself to take it. It's faceless, expressionless, its whole head made of nothing but parallel sprigs of corn tied together at the top, so why does it remind her of a girl, her face covered, her lips sewn shut?

'What?'

'It's fucking creepy, Kev.'

'It's just corn,' he says with a shrug, dropping it to the ground and kicking some dried leaves over it.

'Don't do that.'

'I thought you didn't want it.'

'That's not the point.'

For a moment they both stand there, over the doll lying on the ground, in the leaves, in the dry dirt. Someone must have put it there in the tree.

'Come on,' says Kev. 'If we're not going to find a way to enjoy the woodlands of an evening, we might as well go somewhere else. Let's get a drink.'

Shona doesn't move. She's suddenly aware of a trickle of sweat prickling its way down her back.

BLOOD THICKER THAN WATER

Trish is standing outside Uncle Walt's room in the care home, pleading with him to let her in. Finally, she's found the strength to come and talk to him, but he's barricaded the door against her. It's something he's done before, so the staff have told her, though what with she can't even tell. His chair? The table where they serve his food? He can't have dragged his whole bed over, surely. She pushes her hand through her hair, thinks of DS Frazer then shakes the image of him away. Tries to make her voice cheerful.

'It's me, Uncle Walt. It's your Trisha.'

The smell: disinfectant, old people. She doesn't want him to be here, but what choice does she have? It's just the two of them, and she can't be with him full-time; she wasn't built to be a carer. Besides, she's got to work, to pay for his heating, for biscuits to cheer him up. For whatever care he'll end up needing.

'I don't want to talk to the police. Done that already.'

'I'm not here on… I'm just visiting, Uncle Walt. I just want to see you.'

The staff said they couldn't risk being held liable if something happened to him while he was barricaded in. They've made her sign a waiver. That's what happened when she arrived – not a rush to see him, to hug him, to make sure he was okay; an awkward meeting in the office with a stern woman who reminded Trish of her head teacher and the information that Uncle Walt was misbehaving. If she can just get inside, she'll ask him why. He'll know her, once she's in the room. Simon said he was asking for her by name – that's got to be a good sign.

'I bought you some custard creams, Uncle Walt,' she calls. 'A cup of tea and a custard cream, that's what we need, isn't it? And some old photos to look through? From when I was a kid, remember, we're all in them, the whole family…'

She presses her ear to the door and thinks she can just about make out his breath. And then, at last, a scraping of furniture along the floor – it must have been his chair he was using. The doors don't lock, that'll be why. He won't like the idea of the staff being able to come in whenever they want. She waits a moment then tries the door again and it swings open easily. Inside, Walt is sitting calmly on his chair by the window.

'It is you,' he says. 'I didn't believe it could have been—'

'Of course it's me,' she says, taking his hands and sitting on the edge of his bed.

The staff are hovering by the door, but she gives them a nod and they retreat.

'Close that for me, will you, Trish?' His voice is steady, different to a second ago.

She gets up and closes the door, taking the chance to survey the room before she sits back down. He seems to have stuck some bits of toilet roll over the door frame, hanging down and now trapped in above the closed door. It reminds her of the feathers he'd hung up in his house. No access to feathers in here. There are splashes of water and a sprinkling of salt along the windowsill too. They must let him have salt at mealtimes. Is he trying to stop something getting in, or trying to invite something?

'You're not feeling too lonely in here, are you, Uncle Walt?'

Uncle Walt scoffs at her.

'I mean, there's the common room downstairs, by reception, you could—'

'Shhh,' he says, finger pressed to lips, his voice turning to a whisper. 'I've got all I need from that lot.'

Trish's stomach sinks.

'Please tell me you've not been "borrowing" things from the other residents.'

They could send him home, refuse to take him in full-time – and what would she do then? He's shaking his head though, and he's got that look in his eye.

'You're here now,' he says. 'You're here.'

'Yes, I'm—'

'Now you're here, I need you to listen.'

'But I've come to ask you—'

Suddenly he's the one holding her hands, and his grip is firm.

'I should have told you before, Trish. I don't remember, but… But I can trust you, can't I?'

'Of course, Uncle Walt.'

'My little Trisha,' he says. 'My little girl.'

'Not so little any more,' she says with a smile.

'That's why it's time.'

Prickling at her neck again, Suze's words the other night in the pub.

'There's something I need to ask you about, Uncle Walt, I think, and I'm sure it's not true but I don't—'

'I love this village, you see.'

'I know you do.'

'We all did. That's why we tried to protect it.'

She wants to close her eyes to it, to block his words out, but they're like nails scratching down the back of her neck. She wishes she hadn't cut her hair so short, left herself so vulnerable.

'Art Robertson was the first one of us, when he was still a young man. He was chosen by Nora Prowle. Then he invited me and Big Jack to join him, see, because of how long our families had been in the village.'

'Please just tell me you'd never have—'

'Just listen. The others, they're dead and gone and I'm the only one left to speak, don't you see?'

She wants to make him stop. She wants Suze and Elise to be lying.

'Jack Helmsteading, before, and now Art, gone, all gone.'

She chose to come here; she came here because she needed to know the truth but now she doesn't want to hear it. Whatever it is he's about to say, it's not going to be the denial she was hoping for.

'It's beautiful, Trish. When the night is at its darkest and the creature understands, willingly offers—'

'Stop!' she says but it's too late, she can see it again, the image of that poor horse, her neck severed by repeated slashes of a knife that was too blunt for a clean, kinder cut. There was a sheen to her black coat, or there is now, in her mind, as though she had been regularly brushed, cared for.

'But you need to know how.'

'No, I don't. No one needs to know that, Uncle Walt, and I don't want you telling anyone, understand?'

'But I like having visitors.'

He smiles like he's got a secret and suddenly she's afraid for him, piercingly afraid.

'Has someone been coming to see you, Uncle Walt?'

In the blink of an eye he's a little boy, sitting before her, and she can see he's in over his head, like he's got something precious he's going to take to school and she knows the bigger kids are going to grab it off him in the playground but she can't do a thing to stop it.

'They're coming,' he says.

'Do you mean the Others?'

'It won't make any difference how quiet I stay.'

'Has Natalie Prowle been here?' she says, her voice sterner than she'd intended.

Something Suze said, and Elise, in the pub.

'Natalie is a believer,' he says, with something that looks like victory in his eyes. 'There aren't many of us left nowadays.' Or perhaps it's a judgement of her, of Trish, disappointment in her. 'She comes to see me sometimes. Natalie's my friend.'

'No she's not, Uncle Walt.'

He looks hurt at the tone of her voice.

'I mean… I don't think you should talk to her any more.'

He looks over to the window, eyes misty, and she wonders if she should wipe up the mess. Would he take that as a betrayal?

'Is that why you've locked me up in here?' he says.

'You're not…' She wants to squeeze his hands but he's pulled them away, retreated inside his clothes. 'Please don't say that, Uncle Walt. I'm trying to help you. You know that. Look, I've brought some photos of you and me, from when I was little, remember?'

But Uncle Walt looks at the photos she's brought, keeping his distance from them as though they could burn him.

'I want to go home.'

'What if you go walkabout again? What if you…'

She remembers running to him, out in the woods, after Georgie found him frozen and babbling on the stone slab with the cup and ring; he spoke of nothing but the Others for days afterwards, convinced his ancestors were coming to save him. He used to talk about them as though they would come to help him cure the village. No, not cure. Cleanse, he used to say. But after Mungrid Woods, it was always that they were coming to take him away, to a better place. That all he wanted was to go with them. That was when she'd decided to find him somewhere safe. Somewhere he couldn't hurt himself. She's doing the right thing, isn't she?

'You could have died out there,' she says, and it is true.

'I could die in here.'

Trish doesn't even know if Uncle Walt can see her tears; he seems to be looking past her, over her shoulder to the absence of someone who isn't even there.

NEW FRIENDS OVER OLD

Fergus keeps looking over at her, though he's not even sure why; maybe the way she is so focused, so serious about this work. She insisted on staying when Whelan and the others left. She believes in this dig, in the motte, in whatever they'll find underneath it, just as much as Fergus does. She might be the only person he could say that about. Natalie Prowle.

He's tried telling Georgie so many times how important it is to know what we've come from. Every time, a darkness moving over her face, a shudder, a refusal to look back – and now, today, on the phone, it's as though she doesn't even hear him. His life, his interests, his job, if he didn't know better he'd say they've become…

No, he's not unreasonable, and he's not daft. They *have* become secondary to hers.

God but this is Georgie he's thinking about. His Georgie. And she's not becoming a stranger to him, she's just falling back to that person she was when they first met, when she was still reeling from the grief, the loss of her brother. He needs to turn things around. He needs to find a way to talk to her, to help. He'll leave her some flowers before he goes on night shift, that's what he'll do, some fresh flowers from the garden, in a vase on the kitchen table so she knows he's thinking of her.

Suddenly there's movement, a voice – Natalie – she's standing and calling to the others and this is new, this is different.

She's found something.

Fergus is up, heading over to her, though not as fast as Professor McLeod or her students, running over the site to the far trench; all afternoon they've been at it with nothing but dirt and dry soil and the occasional bit of buried litter for their trouble but now—

'What do you have?' Professor McLeod wants to know.

They're all looking in, peering at the edge of something Natalie has uncovered in the trench.

It's a stone fragment but it's angular, shaped like a corner.

It's shaped as though a person, a human being with tools, has shaped it deliberately. Fergus can imagine it as the cornerstone of a building, and suddenly he can see the walls extending from either side of it and rising above his head. Maybe a family lived here. There could have been a fire where they'd have cooked, a hearth to keep them warm – the smoke in his eyes, he can feel the sting of it – there could have been animals and children and whole lives lived here.

'This could be something,' Professor McLeod says slowly, straightening up. 'Good work.'

And now everyone's excited; there's a buzzing through the group that's infectious. To Fergus it feels like a promise that they're on the right track, that the ground is inviting them in, and even Professor McLeod is smiling her big toothy smile and the students are discussing where to position a new trench to follow the line suggested by the cornerstone fragment and only Natalie isn't smiling. His eyes have been drawn back to her again and she touches him, briefly, on the arm and that's enough to make him follow her aside.

She looks at him with such seriousness that he feels his pulse beating in his neck.

'Can I see the photos again, Fergus?' she asks in her quiet but deliberate voice, her voice that makes her sound in charge, and Fergus simply pulls out his phone because he knows exactly what she means. It's the photos of his iron figurine she wants to see – not the official ones from the university but the ones he took himself, on his phone, the day he found it. She touches the screen when she's looking at them as though she recognises it, that iron figurine, and he almost asks her if she's seen one before. In the museum maybe, or—

'No one's ever dug into the motte this deep before, Fergus,' she says, her fingers zooming in on the screen, though not on the figurine itself – she's zooming in on the unearthed soil all around it. 'As far as we know. Wouldn't you agree?'

'As far as we know,' he says, his words echoing hers.

'You promise me you didn't find anything else out here that day, with your metal detector,' she says, as she passes his phone back to him.

He frowns; he's told her already, and Fergus doesn't lie.

'I promise.'

The sky's dimming now though and he'll have to leave soon – he's got his night shift to get to.

'Thank you, Fergus,' she says. 'I think you were right to organise this dig. I think this is a good thing to do.'

Fergus can feel that pulse in his neck again, but as soon as he starts to worry that his face is about to turn red she's looking away, and the relief leaves him restless and not at all sure what to do with his hands.

NOW MORE THAN EVER

There is such a look of kindness in Pamali's eyes that everything Georgie had wanted to say to her friend melts away and she simply leans in to the hug being offered. It's late, it's dark outside, Georgie is exhausted and she can't stop seeing him, everywhere, that little boy, lying on his back, his hands scratching at the air as if he was being buried alive and every time, every time Georgie feels such a stab of grief and love and guilt that it leaves her reeling.

'Georgie, what's happened?'

Pamali doesn't know; for a whole day now Georgie has known that they murdered a child, a toddler, someone here murdered a baby and buried them decades ago and no one even seemed to notice. They've all been living their lives on top of that crime, walking over the ground and all the while they were under there, an innocent little child.

'No one's told you?'

'No one's told me anything.'

'The shop's been closed?'

'No, I've been open since eight.'

When was it, yesterday? When Georgie had seen Pamali from across the road, had waved but not stopped to speak because she'd been too drawn in by Walt Mackie's carved bleeding wooden face to spend a few minutes talking to her own best friend? Did she mean that no one had been in the shop, or that no one had spoken to her as they grabbed what they wanted from the shelves, thrust some coins at her and trudged out again? Georgie's not sure she even wants to know the answer.

'How are you still smiling, Pami?'

Pamali smiles, as if that in itself is an answer. She's got the kindest smile of anyone around here, that's for sure.

'You're still washing off the graffiti every morning?'

'Sometimes I leave it there for a day or so. Just to see if anyone else cleans it up instead.'

They don't, though. Georgie doesn't even need to ask.

'I live in hope. And Natalie's been—'

Suddenly it hits her: Georgie herself is one of those people who hasn't. She feels another stab of guilt in her throat.

'I'm sorry, Pami, I—'

'You're busy, Georgie. I didn't mean you.'

There it is, her kindness again. It feels to Georgie like holding ice-cold hands under hot running water; soothing and stinging at the same time, leaving her with pins and needles and, also, with warmer hands.

'Don't you feel like giving up on this place?'

'It's not all bad, you know, Georgie. Besides, I've got my plans,' Pamali says, with a mysterious lift of her eyebrows, and she sounds hopeful and young and full of potential and Georgie doesn't know why it hurts her so much – maybe because Georgie herself feels none of those things any more. 'Oh, I can't believe I nearly forgot.'

Pamali is up and heading over to one of the shelves out in the shop, returning with an orange packet, beaming at her and it reminds Georgie for all the world of a Reese's Peanut Butter Cup packet, like she used to eat as a kid, like her and her brother used to share before she lost him and with that thought she feels it again, the shock of it; even after all these years, she can see his body slumped on the ground beside her.

'I ordered them in especially for you,' Pami says, handing her the packet. 'You love them, right?'

'I love them,' she manages, and she does. In fact, she can taste them already: the comforting sticky sweetness of them, the innocence of them, from before she lost all innocence of her own, and right there, in the Spar, at dusk, Georgie leans her elbows on her knees and her head in her hands and she starts to cry.

'Oh, Georgie,' Pamali is saying. 'It's been so hard on you, this year, all this racism and...'

'It wasn't even directed at me,' Georgie sobs. 'It was you they attacked and now...' She shakes her head, tries to straighten up a bit. 'You're comforting me when it should be the other way around.'

'It was directed at both of us,' Pamali says. 'It *is* directed at both of us. Besides, you're the one having to deal with crimes every day. I get to listen to music in here, walk along the coast on my lunch break... It's peaceful, sometimes. And the graffiti – I'm sure it's kids, lashing out.'

'I don't know, Pami—'

'I'm not saying that excuses them, not for a second. But there are folk round here who are as appalled by it as we are, who are trying to find a way to make things better. You don't get to see that side of things; you have to deal with the worst in everyone, all the time.'

Georgie brushes at her eyes, impatient at herself.

'It's my job.'

'Ever considered a different one?'

Despite herself Georgie smiles at the suggestion.

'I thought it would be about helping people.'

'You do help people—'

'I thought if I worked here it would be...well, like you said, peaceful. Idyllic.'

Pamali laughs.

'The quiet English countryside station?'

'A gentle life in a beautiful landscape.'

And she'd thought, by moving here – though she doesn't say this out loud – she'd thought she might finally be able to forgive herself for what happened to Errol. But now, with every suspicious glance from the villagers in her direction, with every body they find, every needless death, it's like she's reliving it again: the violence of her brother's murder, the hatred that sparked it, the anger, the terrible guilt.

'The thing is,' Pamali says. 'That place you were imagining? That perfect English village? The place with no problems? I don't think it exists. I don't think it ever has.'

'Fergus still thinks it's here,' Georgie says, shaking her head. She feels her eyes sting again, but she blinks back the tears. They are not about Fergus.

'Georgie?' Pamali says, taking her hand. 'Georgie, how are things with you and Fergus?'

HOW THINGS LOOK ON
THE NIGHT SHIFT

He'd chosen honeysuckle interspersed with Marguerite daisies. Roses would have been too obvious, and it wasn't supposed to be a romantic gesture. He wanted to remind her of something much more than that; a life together, year after year of noticing the stunning flowers on their climbing honeysuckle, pointing them out to one another with the same awe as the first time they saw it. He's still thinking of the way the room looked as he left for night shift: the lights on but low – he wouldn't want Georgie coming home to a dark house – the small crystal vase positioned perfectly in the centre of the table, his offering of fresh yellow and white petals, green stems, gentle leaves, the table itself cleared and laid with a wine glass ready, so she could enjoy a meal after a hard day, treat herself to a glass of red. He's imagining her doing just that, looking across the table to where he would have been sitting, where he wishes he were sitting.

'This,' says the kid, waving his hand at Fergus, at the till, back up at Fergus, 'is pointless.'

'But—'

'You need to be stacking shelves,' he says.

Fergus looks down the black stretch of his conveyor belt to the empty space beyond and thinks about how it felt to have his hands deep in soil as Professor McLeod watched his work as if he, of all the villagers, he was the one who understood how slowly archaeology needs to progress.

'But I've always been on the till,' he says.

'Not on night shift you're not.'

'What if someone needs me?'

'There's no one here.'

No one but the long shadows cast by row upon row of shelves and this kid, who wasn't even here a minute ago, and Fergus himself – Fergus, on his own, with the tall glass-windowed front of the shop letting in the cold and dark despite the triple glazing.

'But—'

'Restock the juice aisle, eh? Then get yourself over to dried pasta and noodles.'

Fergus looks down the store, the aisles dim now with the reduced lighting, and steps down from his chair. He feels his back twinge as he does so, at the base of his spine, that tension between his shoulder blades.

'Good man,' the kid says and it's not that he's smirking at Fergus, because Fergus is sure someone in a managerial position wouldn't do that, but still, in a way, Fergus is glad when he's gone and it's just him and the tall trolley and carton after cartoon of long-life cranberry and apple and smooth orange from concentrate, even though his back is worse than ever and stacking shelves was just about the very last thing he needed after that day on the dig.

He's starting to feel it now, the tiredness. He knew it would get to him, of course, but it's not even midnight yet and there's hours to go, hours before he can lie his head down and let his back stretch out and please, not another migraine, that would be the last thing he needs but he can feel it in his eyes, the throbbing in the back of his eyes.

He should have left himself enough time to eat something proper for dinner but instead he'd stayed on late with Professor McLeod and Natalie to excavate more of the hand-built wall they had discovered. Then rushing home, picking Georgie's flowers, trying, really trying to make it all look perfect before heading out the door. In the end he'd had to grab a bite from the Food To Go section in here when he arrived, using his staff discount. A cheese savoury sandwich and some salt and vinegar crisps are not cutting it, though; tomorrow, a proper meal, at the very least. He heaves up another pack of six cartons, wrapped together in unnecessary plastic, and lugs it onto the shelf with a groan.

His voice, that moan he just made, seems to echo here with no other people in to dampen down the noise. The aisles feel longer than during the day, must be the dimness doing that, the shadows under the closed meat counter at the far end and the way he can see the rows and rows of almost-identical products repeating without human shapes moving between them to break up the monotony: shelves upon shelves and rows upon rows as though he's trapped in a hall of mirrors and the lights are failing.

It's the same as during the day, he tells himself, it is exactly the same. Nothing has changed. The constant whine of the fridges is still there, the way the floor sticks to his shoes even though they clean it on repeat. But what is it that people bring to a place? More than their bodies, of course, more than the shape and the taking-up of room. It's the sound of them, the heat and the colour and the way that when he catches someone's eye, even if they don't say a word, he can feel some kind of connection that he feels only the lack of in this vast unnatural space tonight.

Maybe that was why he'd stayed at the dig so late: he didn't want to eat his dinner at home, knowing Georgie wouldn't be there.

He heaves up a final pack of cartons and positions them in the final space and looks down the aisle, the neat stacks of juice he has created, then leans heavily on the tall trolley and pushes it towards the storeroom to stock up on pasta and noodles; never let it be said that Fergus doesn't follow instructions. Even before, even when he was the one in charge, managing a whole team at the nuclear site, important work so *especially* then, he was a stickler for the rules. The rules are there for a reason. He used to say that to his team. *Here, we dot every i we come across, and I am keeping you safe by insisting on it.*

Through the window he catches that kid – his manager, he is trying to think of him as his manager – having a fag outside and he looks just past him to the entrance to the twenty-four-hour petrol station and he bites at his lip again, that patch where it was bleeding earlier. The door to the storeroom is locked and he doesn't have a key because no one's given him the key and he thinks about going out to ask the kid but instead he sits down, just about managing to squeeze onto the bottom rack of the trolley, his back pushed uncomfortably forwards but at least he's off his feet.

He's not good without sleep. Fergus needs a full eight hours, he always has.

That's just modern-day luxury though, isn't it? Think of that house they've found in the motte, if it is a house or settlement of some kind; whoever lived there a thousand years ago wouldn't have been sleeping for a solid eight hours in a comfortable bed, would they? Fergus would give anything to know who they were, the people who worked or lived or met there, to be able to spend time among them, to see the lives that have played out right here on the patch of coastline where his own life is playing out today. There could have been a whole extended family living there, right where the motte now stands, living off the land and the sea, hunting maybe, keeping livestock – he'll need to check his dates when he gets home – and that would have been the kind of life that might have suited him. Maybe he wouldn't have needed sleep in the same way if he was connected to the land, the rising and falling of the sun, the life around him but then he hears the automatic door to the shop opening and pushes himself up from his makeshift seat, expecting the kid to be checking on him any second except that no, the kid is still out there, he can see him through the window. Smoking. Is there someone in here?

Of course, anyone could be here. Late-night shopping. Twenty-four hours. That's the whole point.

He can't see anyone now, though. They must have... Maybe they're down one of the aisles, a person could be barely visible some of them are that dark; every one in four lights off and that means the aisles alternate, one dim and one almost completely lost to the shadows of the shelves either side of it. It's not a high ceiling they have here, the shelves nearly reach it and the shadows are so long the ceiling feels like it's almost pressing down on him tonight, though there, that shadow, that's—

It's moving. Fergus can see a shadow moving across the floor and for a second he freezes until he realises, of course, it's the person, whoever the person was that came in. He pushes the empty trolley ahead of him and the building reverberates with the clicking of its uneven wheels. He'll just go see who it is, making that shadow, ask them if they need help with anything, if they'd like him to open up a till for them. It'll feel good actually, to give someone a hand, exchange a few words. Fergus likes to feel useful and he's trying, here, to feel like he's being useful, that he has not turned into such a waste that—

The aisle is empty.

The shadow he saw moving on the floor, it's just the shelves, it must have been just from the shelves and maybe the lights; he stares up at the ceiling, at the fluorescent strips that cannot possibly have been moving as they are clearly, firmly attached and there's no breeze in here anyway. He can feel one, though. He can feel something around his neck, that patch of skin between his hairline and the loose-fitting T-shirt they make him wear, they make them all wear – he wishes he was wearing a shirt with a proper collar and that he was doing something worthwhile and that Georgie still looked at him the way she used to – but there's definitely a breeze in here now. The door? He turns. The door is closed. The windows are closed. He can hear breathing, but there's no one here; he even calls out, a useless hello that echoes back and forth between the never-ending floor and the never-ending ceiling and the row after row after row.

There's someone here. He's sure now, someone doing something they shouldn't be, and Fergus has to check because that's part of his job, surely, to keep an eye out, to keep the shop safe, and he looks around for something to hold, some kind of weapon, even thinks absurdly of calling Georgie, but no, no, there's no one here and he won't give her any more reason to think he's stupid; he's not stupid. He's tired, that's all. He's been working on the dig all day and he's not had a proper dinner and he didn't get a good sleep last night, what with Georgie being awake beside him – not that he's blaming her for his not being able to sleep, he was happy to talk, he wants to talk to her – but it meant he didn't get a full night's sleep himself and he's going to need to learn to handle this tiredness better if he wants to be useful on the dig, if he wants to discover something important and then the door is really opening and the kid is back, the waft of cigarette smoke replacing the absence of smell that Fergus hadn't even noticed was so alienating before it was gone and he holds up a hand in a ridiculous-looking wave and says, 'I need the keys to the storeroom, for the pasta and' – and then the kid has opened the lock and leaves his keys there in the door, just hanging there, and disappears back to the office where he's drinking cans and keeping half an eye on the CCTV. Fergus stands there on his own for a minute. He wonders if Georgie liked the flowers. If they made her smile. He hopes they made her smile. But he's finding it harder than anything to push open the door to the storeroom. It's like he has no idea what he's going to find in there.

A WAY BACK

Their da's waiting for them in the kitchen when they get home. Course he is. Deborah-Jane's feet are stinging and bleeding but she's not going to show it – she can see from his scowl that he's angry enough she's lost her shoes.

'I'll get them back,' she hisses at him, trying to push past, with her brother's warm hand still held tight in her own. She just needs to make it to the stairs and up to their mam's room, but her da's got her by the shoulder.

'You crying again,' he growls.

'Course not.'

'Not *you*.'

Then she sees that it's her brother he's glaring at; her brother whose sobs are silent now but whose face is still smeared with dirt and tears and fear.

'Leave him alone.'

'He's a fucking pansy.'

Her father's arm is raised but she won't let this happen, not again. She pulls her brother behind her, shielding him with her body, stretches herself to be tall, as tall as she can be.

'He's just a little boy.'

'Well you're just a girl.'

He almost laughs then, before dropping his hands to his sides and shaking his head as though she's not worth the effort of standing. He turns, goes back to his chair at the head of the table.

'Who stole them,' he says, his voice quieter, and she feels the chill of fear crawling up her neck.

'No one,' she mutters, backing away, one step then another, her eyes not leaving her father's.

His frown deepens and he clasps the arms of his chair with his fists as though he is trying to crush them. Then they are released as, one by one, he crashes his boots up onto the old oak table, where they leave a scattering of mud among the lines and scratches in the wood.

She is at the door.

She is dismissed.

Lifting her little brother into her arms, she climbs the stairs as lightly and quickly as she can, carries him through to their bedroom and places him down, fully dressed, in the bed beside her own. Then she sits on the floor, pressing the heels of her palms into her closed eyes, forcing away the last sting of grit and trying to know only the pressure of her own hands. It doesn't work.

Since she ran, since she got away from Nora and Alfred and Camellia and Whelan, since they got out of the woods, she's had this image in her mind that she can't shake. She'll not tell her brother about it – she'll never remind him of this, she'll only ever tell him not to be scared, there's no reason for him to be scared – but she can't stop imagining what would have happened if she'd not been able to get him out. If they'd pinned her down and piled mud and earth and stones on top of him until he was trapped down there for good. She mustn't think of it. They wanted to do it, though. She believes that. Those kids, they'd have done it if they could.

'I'm going to get out of here,' she whispers to her brother, voice low even though her da's downstairs and he never comes up these days and her mam's asleep or in her own world next door. 'I'll get out of here one day, you'll see.'

He's pointing to his chest, and for a second she doesn't know why. 'What is it?'

Pointing to his chest, his finger bending at the knuckle.

'Does it hurt?'

'What about me?' he says. He doesn't talk often, her little brother, but sometimes he talks to her.

'I'll be taking you with me, silly,' she replies, as she tucks him up and gives him a kiss on the forehead.

AFTER DARK

Andy liked having the police round today, all except Georgie, who's still mad at him. It was exciting, everyone texting him to see what he could find out. He'd taken the guys some cans and sandwiches at lunchtime before heading out himself – not guys, because there are plenty girls on Cal's team too, and Andy is not any kind of misogynist because that's someone who hates women and Andy likes women, he likes Trish, and he likes Pamali. So aye, he took the drinks and food out to the team of men and women working in the field and he felt like that was worth something, even if he couldn't get close enough to see what they'd found.

They've all gone now though, which is a shame, and he's texted everyone back to say *No Comment* – he learned that was the best thing to say earlier this year, when Georgie was still speaking to him – and he even said not to ask him anything because he needs to keep what he knows as confidential. Which is all good, and he's pleased with that, except now he's back home with nothing to do but sit in the darkened kitchen of the farmhouse and wait for his da to show his face again.

He's been upstairs, his da, since the police left with the bones and Andy started waiting for him to disappear out to Warphill like always or come downstairs and start blaming him for something. His da did neither, though. He's just stayed upstairs and one time there was this strange noise coming from the room like a rasping and then it all went silent and it's been that way for hours now. The not knowing is the worst bit.

It's not that he's afraid of him. He's over all that now. Andy Barr is not the kid he was a few months back – too much has happened for that – and his da doesn't much seem like the man he was once either. It's like he's shrunk. If Andy tries hard, he can seem bigger than him now, give the impression he might just fight back the next time. At the thought of it he clenches his fists, pushes his chair back and lets it scrape against the kitchen tiles, then cringes at the screeching noise it makes. Andy doesn't like that noise. He picks the chair up again, rights it and gives it a quick pat to make sure it's steady. Hardly the chair's fault he hates his da, is it.

He goes to the fridge, grabs a bottle of milk and the cold pizza that's in there from yesterday, and opens it up on the table. There's that familiar smell of the farm all around him, the cold of the floor tiles despite the heat of the air and the way the window frames rattle in the slightest breeze, like someone's shaking them to get in. There's always been shapes in the dark in this house. Since he was a kid he's seen them, learned not to look. But Trish says he's got to stop looking the other way. So. He blinks. His eyes strain to see through the dark, through the heavy, muggy night coming in the windows. The silver of the tap is reflecting light from somewhere. It sticks out from the huge, cracked sink like an old person's neck.

A hand on his shoulder.

He ducks – instinct, that's all – rids himself of the grip and stands, edges round the table.

'Still up then, are you?' his da says. His voice is gravelly, rattling in his throat.

Andy swallows. 'It's no that late.'

'Didn't say it was.'

His da sits down heavily opposite him, and the longer Andy stays standing the less sure he is of what to do with his feet. His da isn't looking at him though; seems barely aware of him. He's pushed the pizza away, is glaring down at the lines and cracks on the table. It's oak, large enough for a family of eight; Andy's always found the size of it threatening, like it was trying to prove a point, with just the two of them living here and this massive, solid old table between them, refusing to budge. It was here before he was born, since his da was a kid, on his own here just like Andy's always been on his own, his grandfather running the farm back then.

Why is he just sitting there?

Andy's got to do something though, can't stay standing here like a lemon, so he pulls out a chair round the other side of the table, sits opposite his father. Then he waits. There'll be something coming. He wouldn't have come down here at all if there wasn't. It's not like his da would ever have sought out his company.

'What have you heard?' his da says, eventually. Eyes still focused on the deep etches in the wood.

'About what?'

His da looks up at him then, just stares at him.

'They found a skeleton in the field. An old one. They've taken it away for forensics.' Andy knows a bit about police work. 'They'll find a way to date it in the lab, from the teeth maybe. I've heard you can tell a lot from the teeth.'

'You can tell how old the person was when they died, from the teeth,' his da says slowly. 'Not how long ago they were buried.'

'Right, well. That's what I meant, isn't it.'

His da pushes the pizza box at him. 'If you're not going to eat that, put it out.'

Andy hates the way the fear creeps up his neck, the way he has to keep working to push it back down.

'It's my tea,' he says. But he needs something more than that. 'There was one thing the police have been asking about...'

He picks up a bit of the cold pizza and folds it into his mouth. His da watches him as though he's disgusted. Andy makes sure to chew loudly.

'See,' he says. 'They're wondering who might have been able to get hold of some ketamine. Any ideas?'

'How the bloody hell should I know.'

'The kids at school, see, they were buying from Bobby Helmsteading, so I figured you might—'

'You don't know a thing about me and Bobby Helmsteading.'

'Maybe, maybe no,' he says. 'But I am wondering as to why you haven't told the police it was our horse they found killed out in the woods yesterday.'

His da lets out a long, barking cough that heaves his chest and leaves his eyes watering. When he's finished, he turns and spits onto the floor. He's the disgusting one, Andy knows that deep in his soul.

'My black mare is none of their business,' he says, wiping his forehead with the back of his hand. He's sweating and it finally occurs to Andy that his da is not alright. That rasping noise he heard earlier, was that crying? That'd be a first. He's never seen his da cry, not once in his life – be good to know what could make that happen.

'So who do you think the body is,' Andy says, just testing something out, a hunch – though the body could be ancient, he overheard that much.

His da doesn't even look up. He's swaying on the seat, his hands clasped around the edge of the old table like he's trying to stop it lurching away. His name is scrawled into it along that edge. RICKY, it says, in wonky capital letters, the Y incomplete, like a child scored it in with a knife and got caught in the act, dragged away. And there's other lines too, letters but no words he's been able to make out, the shape of a dog maybe, and over in the corner there are all these holes, like someone was stabbing at it one time. For some reason, it gives Andy the confidence to push his da again, keep asking the question. He'd never have dared do that, a few months back.

'Well?' Force in his voice. 'Who d'you reckon it is then?'

His father looks up, at last. His eyes are tight, sore. His cheeks lined and weathered, like he's an old man. He *has* been crying. Andy's sure of it now, sure as he is of anything. Why did he come down here? What did he want from Andy, seriously, what the fuck did he expect? Then it dawns on him what that nagging feeling he's had all day really means.

'You know who it is, don't you.'

Then there's the scrape of the chair as his da slowly stands up.

The drum of his boots on the tiles as he walks away.

The scratch of a stone lodged in the sole.

TWO THOUSAND YEARS AGO

The storm is angry. The land has run to rivers of mud. It sweeps away everything that once lived there and grew, and a girl sits indoors by the hearth of her family's home plaiting straw into a corn doll for her child. She watches her fingers as they weave and she tries not to be afraid; feelings can be passed on, between mother and child, and she wants her baby to feel safe in her arms, wants him to know that he is protected. The rain pelts the walls and roof of their home, seeps up from the rough-soiled floor beneath her feet, but she tries not to hear its determined rhythm. The songs she sings are of sunshine and love, and as she sings them her voice cracks until her mother comes to sit beside her, singing the same songs she sung to her children, passing them on again as they were passed to her.

The boy is still a babe, not yet ready to sit nor even smile. When he has finished feeding he sleeps again, and while he sleeps the girl plaits and weaves and tries not to be afraid. She binds the straw to make the doll's head and her mother guards the door – her mother too wants her child to feel safe, to know he is protected – and beyond the cold hearth her father calms the dog that's whining with hunger and her sister cries alone and her brothers fight in the damp muck of their floor and the storm rages on, the day black as night, the night endless. The wet seeps deep into their bones, all except for the baby, who wakes again and feeds and sleeps and lies swaddled and warm, but outside the storm rages on and beyond their home the villagers' fear turns to anger and they blame the girl and her baby boy whose birth brought the endless storm to their village.

They read the signs, like their ancestors did – the people of the village have always been able to read the signs. The flooded land and the bleeding sky tell them what must be done; the land and the sky must be heeded before they are all drowned. The girl plaits straw into her corn doll and binds its neck and places it beside the others in her baby's crib and she reaches for more, the last of the sheaf, and she begins to weave again, trying not to be afraid, as her brothers hit and yell from hunger and doubt and her father's fingers tighten around the dagger he clasps in his sleep. Her mother stays awake, though, and says nothing because she understands too well: the land and the sky can't be ignored, the land and the sky are speaking and her family are refusing to listen. But her girl is asleep, shivering and pale, and her girl's baby is asleep, swaddled and warm, while outside the storm rages and the villagers start to come to the door to force her hand.

You must do what must be done, they say. The land demands it. The storm.

She stands firm. She is a mother.

You know the truth, they say. The rains. The flood.

The land is wrong, she says. The rains and the flood are unjustified.

He is not one of us, they say.

But that is when her daughter arrives at the door, and the villagers see the girl, the fallen girl, her eyes paler than water, her belly still bloated from the life she has brought among them.

He is my baby, she says.

He is not one of us, they repeat.

You must do what needs to be done.

For the good of us all, you must.

And the girl stares at them, eyes swimming, fists clenching, until her mother forces the door shut and the villagers are left outside in the rain. The cold seeps deep inside them, their skin stings with the force of it as they clench their teeth through their anger and the gnawing hunger pains deep in their bellies. What needs to be done must be done. The knowledge claws at their insides and their desperation turns to resolve. They will not plead again. It is because of the father, they say to one another, the lack of the father. We cannot welcome the child among us. We told them; we warned them. Now we have no choice.

We will do what needs to be done.

We are strong, together.

This is how they prepare themselves.

For where did she go, that girl when she ran away, came back swollen and stubborn and refusing to name? The child could be from anywhere, from anyone, he could be carrying disease or plague, the land is telling them, warning them, he is not from here and what more do they need to know? The storm rages on and they starve and watch as their land dissolves by their feet and their crops fail and their animals fall. It is rot, they say, something rotten among us, they say, as the animals are burned and the people begin to gather. It is time.

The girl has finished plaiting the last of the straw she has into dolls for her baby. They are peaceful now, lying in the crib beside him, their eyes of black stone watching. She has made sure they will be watching. The storm rages on and its demand will be heeded, they all know it will be; they all know what is coming. They must pay with blood and air and water. But when they come in the endless night, the fear takes hold.

Kicking against them, running and fighting for life, the rain beating against their home, fists beating against their faces then they are dragged outside: mud slipping and filth in rivers, the rope looped around their bodies, their hands, their feet; her mother and father on the ground, her two brothers spitting and thrashing, teeth shattered with stone to silence them. Her sister is begging and screaming beside her. Taken from his crib, her babe has woken for the last time.

But the villagers have no choice.

They know this sure as they know their own souls. They loop rope around the family's necks and as they fight back they are smashed down again, and again, and again. It is the will of the angry skies and the land and the dirt trying to claim them. They have to make their circle: the circle of villagers, forming beyond the outskirts of the village, on the hill from where they can see the menhir and the woods that hide the ancient stone. They taste salt from the coast and grit in the wind, and they join hands and their voices begin to rise. In the middle of their circle, the vessel is ready and the old woman is holding the dagger. There will be water and blood and air.

The storm rages and the air pulses with their chant, arms rising to the skies and feet bare, pounding, mud seeping through their skin. The ropes tighten. The gasping of the girl, her sister, her brothers, her mother, her father; their last breath. The blade cuts their throats. They bleed. The rain falls. Then they are gone, all except the babe, who is crying: the sacrifice that will placate the skies and honour the land. Three ways of death, three ways, always, air and blood and water, as it has always been.

The babe is held over the vessel. The figures on its sides are pulsing with their chant. The babe is swaddled and screaming as they loop the rope gently around his neck. His screaming turns to a rasp. The dagger cuts his throat. His blood is collected as the storm rages on and the child is offered to the water, with blood, with breath, until silence falls and the skies begin to clear.

They move fast, while the rain holds. They act fast, while the night lasts, for they don't want to see by the light of the day what has been done. They pile the bodies into the grave, edged with stones, throw in the dagger and the pot, the rope and the crib and all the corn dolls the girl had plaited from the last of the straw while the village starved, their eyes black stone and watching. They pile more stones on top, pile earth on the stones, letting the land reclaim them, and they leave with muddied feet and drenched hair, go back to the homes they protect and the village they have saved and they hold each other through the night, close and warm with love.

They will never speak of it again, the villagers. The next day brings light and calm; the ground heals and the birds return. They never speak of it except in songs that are passed down to their children and grandchildren, and on to their grandchildren's grandchildren. The songs they sing are of storms and sacrifice, their meaning hidden yet understood by the villagers alone. For that is the way of the villagers.

Except that when they pass that place, from where they can see the menhir and the woods that hide the ancient carved stone, the ground seems higher every time; it grows into an unnatural mound, steeper than the land should ever be. And when they sleep, they see them – though they never say it out loud, not even to each other – they see them rising up through the earth. Those who did not belong.

Their teeth are shattered with stone.

Their breath is rasping through rope.

Their nails are clawing the air.

Until eventually they wake, shaking and sick, alone even when they are together.

After these nightmares, the villagers look at one another, for a moment, for the first breath after sleep, and they see desperate, raging eyes in the faces of the people they love. Then they shake their heads, look up to the clear skies and remind themselves that their village is safe again, and that what is hidden beneath the ground stays there.

BURIED

A WAY BACK

Ricky is searching in all his secret hiding places: under the bed, though even he knows that would be too easy; down in the basement where the door is supposed to be locked but he can just about reach the bolt if he stands on the crate his sister found for him; out in the shed, in the barn, clambering high up onto the beams where he's not allowed. He searches all the forbidden places on the farm where she might hide, but she's not in any of them. She's not skulking around their feet at breakfast. She's not snapping at the birds or running back and forth until he follows her, out through the fields, over the fence, all the way to the woods where they can play for hours and no one else will know.

That's where he has to look now, though. Because she has to be somewhere and no one else is looking and she's the only one who's ever on his side.

His da has been in a mood all day, stomping mud through the kitchen and kicking at the table legs, cursing 'cause the damn dog's run off again – the dog, he calls her, the damn dog, though Ricky named her Rosie and that's a pretty name. His da's not fond of pretty things. She was his sister's dog first, though she let him choose the name, and if she was here she'd know where to find Rosie, but she's long gone. Ricky is the only one who can find her and he is eight years old and that's grown-up enough to work and make himself useful for Christ's sake, so he is plenty old enough to find Rosie.

The door's open as usual. His mam's upstairs in her bed where she is most days and his da's crashing about in the barn, so he pulls on his wellies and his hat and heads out across the field towards the tumbled down bit of fence, where his sister taught him how to get out of the farm and get back again, unnoticed. A plank of wood to step on, another to hold, then duck under the top. The grown-ups don't know the gap is there because they're too big and stupid, that's what his sister used to say. His hat catches and falls in the mud so he reaches back through to get it and when he does that he scratches his hand but it's okay, it's not too deep. He's off the farm grounds now and on the wild land and that's where they used to go, him and his sister, when he was just a little boy and he couldn't keep up with her and she'd stand with her hands on her hips and hiss-whisper *Ricky* and her voice would catch him like a tickle on the wind. He'd try to catch up as fast as he could, trying to make his steps as giant as hers, trying to be as giant as her; his sister was big and strong and that's how he knows she's doing just fine even if his parents won't talk about her.

For a while there he kept setting the place for her at the table and his da would chuck the cutlery off onto the floor and his mam would pick it up and put it back in the drawer and no one would talk for the whole meal. *Bitch didn't want you around, did she?* his da said once, but that was just him being a bully – his sister used to talk about him being a bully a lot – and Ricky knows she would have taken him with her if she could, wherever it is she's gone. Maybe to Australia because then it would be sunny all the time and she could go swimming in the sea and ride a shark maybe and that's exactly the kind of thing his sister would do.

Now he's at the stream and he's got to wade to get to the other side – this is the bit where his sister used to wait for him, even though she'd pretend she wouldn't and say things like *I'll cross the stream without you if you don't hurry up and then what'll you do?* She always did wait for him though and lift him stepping stone to stepping stone because he was too small to make the jumps. But today he's got his wellies and besides, now his sister's gone, there's no one keeping the stepping stones right and they've grown over with slippery green mush and they're not safe to stand on even. Best walk his way through, feet on the stream bed, wellies keeping him dry, though in the middle the water makes it over his wellies and down through his socks and his feet are squelching and freezing cold but he keeps on going. Through the water and scrambling up the bank the other side, he even sees a couple of the villagers way off in the distance but he knows well enough to steer clear of them. There's the villagers and then there's the Barrs and that's the way it fucking is, his da says, and his mam never says much back, even though she was a one of them and not a one of the Barrs once upon a time. Da says she needs to check her loyalties.

He's at the edge of the woods now and the rain's getting heavier, it clings to the treetops and rustles the leaves. He heads into the darkness of it because the woods in winter are a gloomy place, and that's when they're at their best – so his sister used to say. Good for hiding. Good for disappearing. That's how he knows Rosie must be in here, seeing as how she's disappeared. There's a clearing that vanishes when it wants to, that can only be found by people like him and his sister who need it and properly respect the woods in winter; that's where he'll go. He's not sure of the way exactly, he just used to follow his sister and she seemed to be wandering through the trees and hiding and skipping and sometimes she'd disappear into a trunk only to jump out and make him scream; sometimes they'd build a whole den together, with fallen branches lodged between the trees and leaves for a carpet. He's forgotten to remember the way back out, but he's not worried about that because it means he's going the right way – it's always when you're lost that the clearing appears. He stumbles over a root and his feet are going numb in the wet and he's not going to cry because he's not a baby for Christ's sake and he's sure he can hear something, a barking maybe, could it be a dog barking, Rosie? He starts to run then, through the thinning trees and mist of rain and straight into the clearing that appears from nowhere and there he stops, cold, sick, faced with something he can't believe, something that is like a bad dream but more real than anything he's ever seen.

On the big stone in the middle of the clearing, Rosie is lying on her side.

There's blood everywhere. Her legs are hanging down, motionless. Her neck is wide open and glistening red; he can see her insides. He's too scared to go close. He's too scared. He doesn't want to look. He backs away. He starts to run and run and he doesn't know where he's going until he's back in the stream and back crawling through the fence and not caring that the wood leaves a big scratch along his cheek and as he gets back to the house shaking and crying and words spilling from his mouth that he doesn't even understand his da, for once, listens to him.

His da, who waits till Ricky is sobbing in his mam's arms before standing up from his chair and saying, 'Right. That's it.' Then he goes striding off and it's just Ricky and his mam together, and she pushes his hair back from his face and cuddles him on her knee while the bath is running.

By the time his da comes home Ricky and his mam are building a castle in his room and his da comes right in, which he never does.

'Rosie's safe now, lad,' he says.

For a second Ricky thinks everything's really going to be alright.

Then his da looks at his mam and says, 'No more pets,' and under his breath, 'Your fucking village.'

The door slams closed behind him.

Ricky can't understand why he's being punished when he didn't do anything wrong but he'll never keep a dog again, not for as long as he lives.

When he goes to bed that night he asks his mam, 'Why do they hate us so much?'

She just strokes his hair like she hasn't done since he was a little boy and tells him to have sweet dreams. He doesn't have sweet dreams, though, because soon as he closes his eyes the image of Rosie is replaced by the image of his sister, lying dead, her throat slit, and he has to open his eyes again. Even then he can't stop seeing it. Can't stop seeing her body lying limp like that, her head hanging down like there's nothing left inside. And that's how it stays, as he grows up, turns nine, then ten, and eventually becomes a man, attends the funeral of his father, then his mother, with dry eyes, mourns his wife in public and never mentions her in private, somehow allows his love for his son to turn into resentment and always closes his eyes at night to the image of his sister, not big and strong and free, but small and buried and forgotten, until DI Strachan knocks on his door to tell him that they have found what appear to be human remains in a field on his farm.

FIRST THINGS FIRST

Frazer has been up for hours. He never can sleep out here on the coast, and so he got up before the sun rose and drove out to visit the hotel where Betty Marshall was working when she saw the murder sixty years ago. A teenage girl, her eyes rolled back in her head, a blade at her throat, surrounded, watched, and in the distance: Wyndham Manor. It's still standing. He even got some photos to show Ms Marshall, see if that will jog her memory a bit more. She remembered the name of the girl she thought she saw being murdered, and she knew that of the housekeeper, but all the other staff on his list have first names only and there are no employment records for the temporary staff he's been able to find so how's he going to track them, unless someone here in the villages knew them and is willing to talk?

It was strange, seeing that hotel as it was in the 1960s but for the decades of damp and decay, weeds and insects that have filled it up since the human beings who kept it free of all that natural life stopped passing through. It's not far out of the village, ten miles or so, far enough that it'd be a challenging run – if someone were in the hotel and needing to escape to the village, or in the village needing somewhere out of the way to lay low – but a short drive in his car. It's south along the coast, in the opposite direction to Warphill, and there's not much else down that way. After the Manor the land reaches out into a jagged promontory, the cliffs too steep to get down to the sea, the wind too brutal for anyone to want to picnic there. Even the grass and the trees don't seem to want to be there. It felt to Frazer like a place of bare rock and gulls at the end of the land and once he'd reached the edge all he could do was retrace his route: drive back past the derelict Wyndham Manor with its nettles and gorse, its twisted green ivy clinging around the ornate pillars either side of the grand entranceway, and all the way back to Burrowhead, where he parked outside the police station and started thinking about what it was that he needed to do. He needed to find any relative of Mrs Pettigrew, the housekeeper. He needed to find any relative of Abigail herself. He needed another eyewitness or at the very least a missing person report; he needed to hear his wife's voice. That's why he's still sitting in his car, parked outside Burrowhead police station, phone on speaker, when he allows his eyes to close and finally hears her.

I see you're out on the coast again, Daniel, she says, with a gentle harmonic of laughter in her voice.

Not my choice, he says.

We have more choices than you think.

Her hand is warm where it touches his, and it leads him to an empty concert hall, lush with wood panelling and ornate gold. He takes a seat in the front row, on a cushioned red velvet chair. On stage, his wife is playing one half of Bach's double violin concerto. In her passages, her body sways with the music, her violin singing out its perfection, until the missing counterpoint fills the room with such aching silence that he finds himself struggling for breath.

A single, sharp knock.

He jumps up, the phone clattering into the passenger-seat footwell.

Trish Mackie is standing outside his car, peering in, a smile spreading across her face.

His pulse is racing. Christ, was she watching him sleep? He wasn't sleeping though, was he?

His hand on his cheeks – burning now, and still that perfect note, that longing, and something about the look in Trish Mackie's eyes.

Is she laughing at him?

'You coming in?' she says, that brisk flick of her head. Her words are muted through the glass.

Frazer swallows, reaches down for his phone and waves it at her, ignoring the shake in his hand – *Just a quick call*, he tries to make his movements say, *nothing to worry about, I'll be right there*.

He needs some time.

Trish's expression changes, smile becomes shrug and then she's gone, too, and Frazer is left alone, feeling empty. He looks at the phone he's still holding and hears the beeping tone telling him he needs to hang up. So he does. He is here now, he is too firmly here; in the car park of Burrowhead police station, out on the coast again.

Time to get out of the car.

They're suspicious enough round here already. He doesn't want them asking questions and now here's Simon too, appearing in his rear-view mirror, striding towards the station in that confident way he has. He turns to Frazer with a smile as soon as he catches sight of him sitting in the car, gesturing the sign of drinking from a mug – maybe Frazer could do with a coffee. Okay. Enough.

Simon steps back, waiting for Frazer as he opens the car door.

'I'll get the kettle on,' Simon says, then with a grin at the phone in his hand, 'Anyone important?'

Frazer shakes his head. 'Answerphone.' He looks down at his hands, the way his fingers are subconsciously twisting his ring around on his finger.

'Your wife mind you being sent out here?' Simon asks, though there's a change in his tone and Frazer is surprised; he'd not have expected Simon to be the one to suspect anything. His voice is so gentle, though, Frazer wonders if he's worked it out already. If he's trying to tell him he can talk to him, if he wants to, if he needs it.

'My wife's dead.'

'I… I'm so sorry,' he says, with a soft nod of his head.

Yes, he'd known already, or suspected at least. Was loss that obvious to someone who'd also felt it?

'It was last year. She had… It was breast cancer… It was…'

It was cripplingly fast and agonisingly slow and he wishes he could stop feeling this pain.

'I'm so sorry.'

Simon's hand on his shoulder.

That gentle smile in his wife's eyes, even towards the end.

'Sometimes I feel like Alexis is still here,' Simon says.

All Frazer can do is nod. He doesn't talk so easily as Simon seems to. More of that confidence, perhaps. Does that come from knowing you are in your own place, something more than familiarity, more like owning your home turf? Maybe that's unfair – it can't have been easy, coming out in a place like this.

'It's like he's not finished yet.'

Simon's voice is rough as he says that, gravelled, and Frazer realises that whatever he'd thought was confidence was maybe something else, a determination, a refusal to lie down quietly and accept what has happened. The violence of it. How do you come to terms with that?

'Come on,' Simon says.

Frazer wonders if Simon is going to tell Trish. Not that this has anything to do with Trish. A sudden twist of guilt and an ache to take his wife's hand, tell her she has nothing to worry about, certainly not that prickly Trish Mackie.

'I meant it about that coffee. I need one.'

But Frazer's thoughts are pulling against themselves, because his wife would never have worried about something like that; she'd have liked Trish Mackie.

'I still can't bloody sleep.'

He looks at Simon, sees the bags under his eyes, the raw skin in their corners.

'Me neither.'

Frazer clicks the key and the car doors lock.

'Caffeine, then,' Si says. 'Come on, we have work to do.'

'We?'

Frazer was planning to do some interviews round the village then head home, do his research from the city. Their skeleton has nothing to do with him; this place has nothing to do with him.

'Yes, we. There was something about what your Betty Marshall said, the way she described a group of people, everyone dancing around that night.'

'She's not reliable, I don't think she can even remember—'

'The night she thought she saw a girl being murdered?'

Maybe she did remember. Maybe no one could forget.

Her eyes rolling back in her head, voices surrounding her, chanting, the blade pressing into her skin; Frazer scrunches his eyes shut, just for a second, and the image intensifies: tall figures, cloaked and swaying, the blade cutting into her skin, and a rasping breath from just behind him, scratching at his neck.

HOPE, EARLY

Fergus's back is killing him and he's so tired his eyes ache but he's not going to stop; they've found something amazing and at last everyone will see that what he's been doing is worthwhile and Georgie will be proud of him. Look – a wall made of large rectangular stones, created by the ancestors of the villages thousands of years ago. Creation to offset all the destruction he's seen, proof of a community working together to counteract whatever happened to that poor child they've found in Ricky Barr's field. No wonder Georgie hasn't been herself, that's a terrible thing to have to uncover. The opposite of this, of what he is uncovering. Proof of their ancestors living here and building something.

Imagine them: carrying these stones by hand, through rain or mist or the beating sun, clothes of animal skins and their own skin dark with the soil, streaked with sweat. Or perhaps they used logs to roll the stones on – the menhir could have been moved like that, he's read up on standing stones – the whole village coming together to create a cavern that has survived millennia. Although the standing stone is even older than the motte and his Iron Age figurine. Professor McLeod said it could be Neolithic.

He pauses in his work, allows himself to massage the base of his spine. All this kneeling and digging and stacking and carrying, it's taking its toll, and Fergus's hope evaporates as his mind is pulled back to the storeroom he found himself standing in last night, just a few hours ago, with its broken light and stacks of tins and packets and jars, stacks and stacks and more, surely, than they could ever need and yet there's food banks opening up in Crackenbridge, in Warphill and something must be going very, very wrong. That poor child, in Ricky's field. He can't even think about it. Needs to focus on something else.

There's a buzzing behind him but he doesn't mind that; he's got used to the buzzing of bees since they took Walt's in when he went walkabout. Georgie seemed relieved to get them out of the house, but Fergus liked having them – felt like a family, the wee noises they made, the scrambling and chattering, the sense of them all working away together. Maybe he could get some bees of his own seeing as how there are no other beekeepers left round here, now Jack and Art are both dead. Walt's the only one left, and poor old Walt—

'Ouch—'

He slaps at the back of his neck but the insect is gone and he's just got that stinging in the skin.

'Got to watch out for them,' a voice says from behind him. Natalie. She's been here since first thing, they all have been. She's prioritising, like Fergus himself – she's closed the museum to be here, like Fergus taking on the night shifts at Kaltonn. He's thinking about suggesting Natalie get some work there too, save her signing on. That'd be nice. Mind you, he was so knackered when his alarm went at eight this morning he'd chosen an extra half-hour's sleep over his shower and now he's starting to regret that – he's sweating through his shirt-sleeves already and he was in such a rush he didn't notice the mud stains on his trousers. Still, they'll be getting dirtier today and he doesn't have the energy right now to care. At least he'd had some breakfast, a big bowl of his porridge to keep him going; no Georgie beside him but the flowers still there on the table.

Fergus stands up, a groan escaping his lips as he straightens his back. Natalie looks stressed, and that's not like her.

'Where's Elise today?

'I've not seen her.'

Aye, she's stressed. The worry's showing around her eyes. It's the pressure of the dig, maybe, or something else. The child in the field; it's getting to everyone, he knows it is. And he's heard rumours about her two boys as well, dealing, working for Ricky Barr, targeting the kids, but he'd never repeat things like that. She must have a lot on her mind though.

'Got something!' The shout comes from Justin and Professor McLeod is over in a flash, so Fergus edges round to where she's kneeling and gets down beside her, despite her upheld hand telling him to keep his distance, and moves over to invite Natalie to kneel beside him.

'What do we have?' he says, too eager, his hope returning with a warmth and a comfort, like being reminded of his natural state. His hands reach into the soil; it's cool, this deep in the ground, soothing. But then.

'Is that a bone?'

More than one, there are – my God.

'What is this?'

Professor McLeod looks up at him.

'This could be an important find,' she says, though he knew that, he's not a fool. 'This needs delicate work,' she says, pausing as though she's expecting some kind of response from him. 'Give us some space, please.'

She glances at Justin and for a second Fergus thinks she rolls her eyes. He just nods though, bites back an apology, stands and makes his way over to the grass. What have they just found? It looked like – and Fergus is no expert, of course he's not – but it looked like more than one creature, or more than one person, if it's possible… Could they have found important people, ancient people, a whole collection of ancient skeletons? He knew, he always knew this place was special, spiritual somehow, and this, this is amazing, this is… Has he discovered a ceremonial grave?

HOW GEORGIE MET FERGUS
IN THE FIRST PLACE

She can't place why she recognises him at first when he catches her eye with a sheepish grin, waiting patiently at the bar as she serves the large crowd beside him. You can do bar work anywhere, that's what Georgie has discovered; Seattle and Montreal and Newfoundland, briefly in Tenerife, and in Scotland, the damp west of Scotland just round the corner from her rented tenement flat in the Southside of Glasgow.

'How are you?' he says, as she pours the next pint. He's ginger with floppy hair, a round face and boyish freckles, and he's looking at her like he knows her, and she's wracking her brains as to why.

'I'm good,' she says, conscious of how very American she sounds, more so than anywhere else, compared to his Scottishness.

'You don't remember who I am, do you?'

There's nothing but warmth in the way he says it – he's not annoyed or anything, not taking offence.

'Fergus Strachan,' he says. 'Flat 3/1.'

It's their local. Of course. He lives in her tenement – the upstairs flat. She's only been here a few weeks and she's not one for getting to know the neighbours. What's the point, when every few months she moves on?

'Georgie,' says Georgie.

'Aye.' His smile expands into a laugh though she's not sure what's funny – he just seems to have cheerfulness bursting out of him.

She wipes her hands down her trousers once she's finished the large order and the till has clicked back in place. He's the only one left standing at the bar now.

'What can I get you?'

'Oh no, you're okay – I've got a drink already. I was just…sorry, just thought I'd say hello. I recognised you, see…'

'I guess I stand out.'

'You could say that.'

But he's taken it differently to how she meant it; she can see that from the admiration in his eyes. He's turned her accusation into a compliment.

'Well, you know who I am now, but,' he says.

'But what?'

His laugh again – she smiles this time, can't really help it.

'If you ever need a pint of milk.'

The pub, their local, she's on till 3 a.m. at the weekends – late licence, they call it – and midnight during the weeks and he starts popping in often, Fergus Strachan from flat 3/1. Or maybe he always did. People seem to recognise him when he walks in; there's always someone offering him a pint. He's one of those people who naturally has friends everywhere he goes and so Georgie doesn't know why she thinks he's coming in to see her in particular, but she does. She doesn't do a thing to encourage him – she doesn't even want to make friends – and he never makes a move, never once asks her out or anything like that, but there's the way he beams at her every time he sees her, like seeing her is just about the best thing that's ever happened to him.

Fergus Strachan from flat 3/1. He never questions the fact that she wants to be left alone, most of the time – she appreciates that. If they meet on the stairs as she's on her way out and she isn't up for talking he seems to sense it, offers a nod and a smile and leaves her in peace when she doesn't want to talk. Sometimes he's out there cleaning the stairs for the whole tenement, every week he does it, and the fact that it's always him and no one else starts to bother her. Is he too kind, that man, too willing to do the jobs no one else will do? Is there something innocent about him that's verging on the naive? But here he is in the pub again, surrounded by friends and beaming at her and she starts to smile back, because it's infectious, his way of being in the world.

She hears the clattering of the mop in the bucket and knows he's doing it again, washing the stairs on Sunday with no one out there helping him.

But she can do something about that.

He looks up, startled, as she opens the door.

'I thought you could do with a hand,' she says, almost apologetically.

His smile, his big face, that ginger hair, more auburn in this light.

'I've only got the one mop,' he says.

'Pass it to me then.'

So he does, and she starts on the next step down from where he'd finished.

'You can go, if you like,' she says, conscious of him watching her. 'I'll just get this finished and—'

'I was enjoying the company,' he says. 'I miss a bit of company, on Sundays.'

They're looking at each other now, across the wet step between them, and Georgie thinks that maybe he is someone she might be able to talk to. That maybe she might be able to tell him – not now, but one day – about what happened to her and to her brother but for now she doesn't feel like talking, not to anyone. Though she does understand what he means about company on a Sunday.

'Happy to be of use,' she says.

'Aye, me too,' he says, 'me too.'

And when she gets to the first-floor landing, he takes another turn with the mop.

A DIFFERENT KIND OF HOPE,
A LITTLE LATER ON

Fergus's eyes fall on the coastline, searching out towards the horizon. Behind him, the silence is heavy with anticipation as the archaeologists – the professionals – carefully excavate the remains within the motte.

He'd always wanted to live by the sea. That's one of the reasons he and Georgie moved here – the peace, the quiet, the sea, the sky. When they'd met in Glasgow, it felt like they both wanted exactly the same kind of life. Trying to reach her these days is like trying to cross a stream on a narrow tree branch; he can't balance the right way. Did she even like the flowers? When was the last time they spoke in person – that night, when she stroked his hair? It feels too distant and makes his stomach churn. Looking up, he sees another one of those huge birds overhead. He's been seeing them since the spring. Maybe they're sea eagles, that'd be a thing. They've not had sea eagles round here for a century or more. Imagine if they were nesting on the coast, starting a family.

He'd have texted Georgie about it, if he thought there was any chance of a reply. She never seems to reply to his texts these days though so he's starting to wonder if he should stop sending them. She's busy, she's got a lot on her mind. Awful things. He knows that. So maybe, if he goes quiet, she'll make an effort to get in touch with him when she's ready. It's a new approach, at least, and he has to try something.

He follows the bird's flight as it circles overhead before vanishing in the distance, and where his eyes come to rest, the sky is meeting the sea in a shimmering haze of green that obscures the horizon. It must be more than a cairn, this building. It was important to people, profoundly so. He can sense it. Maybe it was the ancient centre of the village; maybe it was some kind of spiritual resting place. It's going to be okay, he tells himself. We're going to be okay.

I'm going to be okay.

'It's a barrow,' Professor McLeod says. People keep appearing behind him today, without him hearing their approach. 'It probably grassed over naturally in time, though it might have been briefly used as a motte in the Middle Ages.'

'I don't understand.'

'Often the structures built on top of mottes were wooden, the tower fortifications and so on, so nothing remains of them now.'

'But what makes you think it's just a barrow?'

'Well, clearly it's a mass grave. There's no other monument. Preliminary interpretation, I'd say the bodies were dumped here, seven of them at least. Then soil and rocks were just heaped on top.'

'No, they...no, this is a sacred place, I'm sure.'

'I seriously doubt it. There are no ceremonial objects—'

'But the cauldron, the figurine?'

'The figurine was found too high to be part of this site. I suspect someone placed it there.'

'What do you mean?'

'Someone buried it there recently, is my guess. One of your local crackpots.'

'And the cauldron?'

'Could have been useless when they threw it in. It was certainly lying on top of the bodies, rather than buried meaningfully alongside them.'

'But—'

'You're disappointed,' she says, and the way she smiles at him makes him feel like a child. 'Don't worry, amateurs always like to imagine something rather more glamorous than the reality. That's why the professionals have to take over.'

Natalie Prowle is standing right there. She heard it too. Fergus glances over at her, waiting for her to blame him for wasting her time. She doesn't though. In fact, she looks as angry about what Professor McLeod just said as Fergus is. Then she gives him the slightest of nods and he feels inexplicably better. Professor McLeod wouldn't even be here if he hadn't called her; this place should be protected for the villagers, not pulled apart by strangers and removed bone by bone. He wishes he hadn't even found that iron figurine, or wishes he'd kept it, returned it to the ground.

Natalie is sitting beside him now, and he feels a warmth from her even though she's not saying a word.

'I did some research about iron figurines,' he says eventually. 'There have been others found around the country, stylistically similar. They're Celtic. The same age as the bodies they found in the peat at Lindow Moss… The ones that *were* killed ceremonially. That's why I thought…'

'You mean the bog bodies?'

He nods. He's keeping his voice low, though he couldn't explain why.

'There have been similar finds across Europe too. Similar figurines buried with bodies, as though they were some kind of sacrifice. Nobody knows what for though.'

'For the good of the community.'

'Well, yes, maybe. Though I wouldn't have phrased it quite like that myself.' He gives her a smile. 'It's called the threefold death. They can see it on Lindow Man because he was so well preserved. He'd had his throat slit, there was a noose around his neck, and he was drowned.'

'Blood, air and water,' Natalie says.

'You've heard of it?'

She doesn't reply to that.

'There was no sign of a struggle, on Lindow Man's body, and he seemed wealthy and strong. They think he might have been a chief, sacrificing himself when he lost a battle or a harvest or—'

He's not sure why he says it, but somehow he feels like he can trust her, and he wants her to know she can trust him too.

'But actually they think the iron figurine must have been buried recently. It was too high in the ground to have been part of this find, with these bodies. Someone...'

'Someone buried it,' she says quietly.

'As an offering maybe,' he says. 'As a way of asking for help?'

She puts her hand on his arm and his breath catches in his throat.

'Help comes from unexpected places, sometimes,' she says.

He swallows; he's not even sure if his voice is going to work any more. But then Professor MacLeod is striding towards them in the no-nonsense way she has.

'Are you not bored of watching us work yet?' she says. 'We'll be publishing our findings, it's not like we'll be keeping any secrets.'

'But surely it could have been a...a sacrifice?' Fergus says.

She laughs, head full back, and he cringes. 'Call it what you like, but every skull has been smashed in, and the teeth shattered, so I'm calling it a mass killing.'

'So...' The words stick uncomfortably in his throat. 'They were... they were murdered?'

Like the child in the field, like Georgie's case.

'Wouldn't be the first time,' Professor MacLeod says. 'Or the last.' At this she cheerfully wipes her hands down her trousers, pulls on her work gloves and strides back over to the bones her students are still painstakingly excavating.

Fergus looks up to the sky, but there's no sign of the sea eagle any more.

The exhaustion hits him deep between the eyes.

'Are you okay, Fergus?'

Natalie's face is all concern.

'Yes, yes thank you, I'm fine, I… I just didn't get enough sleep.'

'Problems at home?'

'No, no, nothing like…'

God, he misses Georgie. He had tried to reach out to her, before dawn. He'd just got back from night shift and she was there in bed, eyes closed; he'd thought she was sleeping. He was so careful to undress silently, to climb into bed without disturbing her at all, to reach a gentle arm around her. The speed with which she'd pulled away had winded him.

'I'm on night shift, so…'

'I understand,' Natalie says. Her hand, briefly on his shoulder, then away again. 'I'm here, if you want to talk about it.'

'That's kind but honestly, there's nothing… I'm just…'

He shakes his head, eyes out to the horizon. The haze has dispersed. The bird is gone.

'It's okay,' she says. 'It's okay, Fergus. I'll still be here when you're ready.'

TOO MANY QUESTIONS

'Right,' Georgie says, standing in Trish and Simon's office where they've gathered, the three of them plus DS Frazer. He came in with Simon so she's letting him stay – his eyes on their case could be helpful, just so long as she keeps any local eyes away from his. He's interviewing the villagers, of course, so they'll know someone is looking into Wyndham Manor, but she has this feeling that if he does find any information it won't be coming from any of them. 'Our case: there was a toddler, so far unidentified, buried on the Barr farm forty years ago. We have lots of questions and no answers, and I want that to be the other way around.'

The whiteboard is covered with pictures, arrows, and very few names. The only one looking in any way central to what's been going on is Ricky Barr.

'What we know about the skeleton so far: we've dated the burial to between 1978 and 1982, due to the type of nappy. It's a partial skeleton, only about half of the bones have been recovered, but given that it was buried fairly near the surface on a working farm forty years ago, that's not hugely surprising. We've got a partial skull, and some teeth. We're placing the child's age at eighteen to twenty-four months.'

She feels a shudder along her arms, a scratching, tries to shake it away. It was there in the night too, when Fergus reached for her, even as she instinctively recoiled from any touch. He'd woken her up when he got in, clattering around downstairs then clambering into bed beside her when surely, surely, he could sleep down in the spare room if he must take on night shifts even though he knows how busy she is. That would be more use right now than the sickly smell of pollen hanging in the heat of her home, pulling her back—

'Ruling out any connection to Betty Marshall's claim to have witnessed someone being killed unlawfully,' Frazer says, filling in her silence.

'Precisely.' Georgie blinks, swallows. She needs to stop letting her mind fall back there, to the thick smell of pollen in that suffocating humidity, to the dust that caked her knees after she'd fallen outside the chapel. 'So' – she clears her throat – 'as a separate case, we have your witness claiming she saw a girl of seventeen or eighteen being attacked by a group, in the 1960s.'

'Abigail Moss,' Frazer says.

The name tugs at Georgie's mind and she frowns, wipes her hand across her forehead. The weight of this heat, the way it's clawing at her.

'There's no record of her in police files,' she says. 'But you're going to continue with your interviews, see if anyone remembers the name, the family – anything.'

Frazer nods.

'Si?' Georgie says.

'We also have a dead horse,' he begins, standing up to take over. 'Viciously killed, probably also by a group. It would have taken some strength and, since ketamine's been found in her blood, one of the group at least must have had access to restricted drugs. Now, while I was interviewing Aaron and Lee Prowle I found a glass vial in their caravan – and Cal has just confirmed that the liquid inside was indeed veterinary grade ketamine. *They* are claiming it was in the caravan when they moved in. Are they lying? Could it be Ricky's?'

'Or both?' says Trish. 'They all blame each other, so no one can be convicted.'

'Could be.'

'But why kill a horse?' says Frazer.

Simon pauses. 'Well, so far no one has claimed ownership of her. Could be they don't want the police involved in their business? Could have been some kind of threat or warning perhaps, to the horse's owner? But then the dead birds placed around the scene give the impression of some kind of ritual... A lot of folk round here see feathers as a way of warding off evil – you'll have seen them in the windows?'

Si glances at Frazer, but Georgie keeps her eyes on Trish.

'The blood all belonged to the horse, according to Cal, so we've no reason to suspect any human was hurt,' Georgie says. 'But I want to know who did this and why. Until we get forensic from the rope, our focus is finding out who owned that horse.'

Trish clears her throat.

'Now, back to the human remains. I want someone looking into every missing child report in the area in the 1970s and 1980s. I want a list of everyone living on that farm, the full family tree of the Barrs – and find out when they bought it as well, and who from. It was several generations back, and I want a list of exactly who might have had access to that land. How did anyone bury a body there, unseen?'

'Yes,' Trish says, standing now too. 'Exactly.'

Suddenly everyone in the room is standing up.

'Trish, you're on research – the Barr family tree and any reports of missing children. I want to ID that body.'

Trish sits back down and immediately starts typing. At least she's keen. Georgie knew she'd want to be the one on Ricky Barr; she's probably halfway there already.

'Si, for heaven's sake, we need to know who owned that horse. And see what Andy has to say as well, will you? We need to know of any change in his dad's behaviour. Any subjects he's learnt to avoid... Once we know all we can, we bring in Ricky for interview.'

Frazer clears his throat.

'You two get to work,' she says. 'Frazer, with me.'

She stands and he follows her out of the room, into her office.
'Ma'am?'

Georgie hesitates, glances out of the window. All winter there'd been flocks of seagulls pressing their way in from the coast, screeching outside, relentlessly pecking at the tarmac of the car park. The heat has banished them now though. There's not a bird in sight.

'I want complete separation. You're not working with us on our cold case – it's unrelated. But you are in charge of your own investigation.'

'Thank you, Ma'am.'

'Ask whatever questions you need, but you're on your own. No Trish, no Simon. Understood?'

'Yes, Ma'am.'

'You report back to me.'

'Will do, Ma'am.'

'And call me Georgie!'

There's a knock at the door. An impatient one. It'll be Trish. Frazer straightens his back, pulls his suit jacket down. Trish peers in through the small window in the door.

'Come on in,' Georgie calls with a smile.

Trish pushes the door open and stands awkwardly between Frazer and the hall.

'I was just wondering if I could have a word in private now, Ma'am?'

Georgie nods at Frazer, who walks towards Trish and pauses, looking at her – there's not quite enough room for him to pass with her standing there and Georgie sees it, the look between them, the electricity in the air. Trish sidesteps just enough to let him pass her and then he's gone, heading out of the room.

Trish closes the door behind him, though she's rubbing her own hand where he brushed against her – did she see that happen?

'You know he's…' Georgie stops; she shouldn't say anything. It's none of her business. She's not felt this protective of Trish for a while though, that's the truth.

'He's what?' Trish says.

'He's married.'

The slightest pause.

'Aye, the ring gave it away. He's also a pain in the arse.'

Georgie laughs.

'What can I do for you, Trish?'

'Well, actually, I've got something interesting. I'd been putting together the Barr family tree anyway, see, because I thought it would be useful, what with how Ricky was only a kid when our body was buried, and that family—'

'What have you found?'

'There's something weird… I found a birth certificate for someone who doesn't exist.'

Georgie blinks.

'I mean, not doesn't exist, but…it's for a girl, Deborah-Jane Barr. Born 1966, so too old to be our skeleton. Nothing quite fits with our case but…on the birth certificate, it says her mother was Ricky's mother, Isabella. Her father, Ricky's father.'

'I've never heard of her.'

'Neither have I,' Trish says. 'Which is pretty strange for round here. But I did track down an old school photo from 1978, and she's there. Deborah-Jane Barr, twelve years old. And then…'

'And then?'

'No further mention of her anywhere that I've been able to find.'

Georgie feels herself grinding her teeth.

'She never finished school. No exam results – just confirmed.'

'You're saying Ricky Barr had a sister?'

Trish nods. 'She was quite a few years older than him and she's the wrong age to be our dead child. But yeah, it seems Ricky Barr has – or had – a sister who disappeared from the village at some point and hasn't been heard from since. And the family just…'

'Let her go?'

'Forgot about her?'

'What about the rest of the village? The school? Someone must have reported it, surely.'

'There's no corresponding missing person report. In fact, there's nothing in police files *at all* – no mention of Deborah-Jane Barr anywhere.'

'Why would no one report her missing?'

'Covering up that she'd run away?'

'Or something worse?'

'Exactly. So I'm afraid there's another question we need to add to your list. What happened to Deborah-Jane Barr?'

MIDDAY SUN

Shona can see Ricky Barr from where she's working. Maybe that was why he moved her over here to the garden. It was the first thing he did when they all turned up for work, bored of traipsing round the village and curious enough that they'd risk being yelled at for a chance to see what was going on at the farm. Nothing much was going on though – other than the police cordon around the field – and when he saw them he'd just started barking out orders in his usual way, sending them off in their teams to get on with it. Except for her, that is. After barely a glance in her direction he told her to get to the garden: weeding duty. Today, unlike last time, she didn't fight back.

The garden is round the back of the house, mostly, but the nettles have spread round to the front, circling the whole place like nature's version of barbed wire. Her arms are burning with stings already, even through her hoody. That's not what she cares about, though. The spread of them, the way they have encroached, means she's got a valid enough reason to walk all the way around, which gives her a good view of everything. From the front, there's the field where Andy and Lee are working; from the side she can see the police cordon, keep an eye on anyone arriving to have a peek over the fence, nosing around – it's worth knowing who shows their face, even if half the villagers think every damn thing is their business. She's been watching the lads mostly though; she's been watching Kev and feeling increasingly sick about it.

He's just too good, that's the trouble. His act: it convinces. It's convinced the others, that's for sure, they're comfortable around him in a way she hasn't been, not for a while. She can't hear much of what they're saying but she doesn't need to, she can hear the edge to their laughter, the tone of it all, the way they slap each other on the back after a particularly nasty joke. Like a pack. That's what they remind her of: a pack of dogs, young and vying for the top slot. And Kev, in the middle. Winning.

She doesn't want to see it. Doesn't want to watch as the boy he was turns into a man she wants nothing to do with. The decision is better than a cold swig of water – she doesn't have to be here. She can leave. She's going to leave.

Round the back of the house, the windows are edged in knotted cobwebs too dense to see the individual threads, but through the dirty glass she can see Ricky Barr sitting hunched at the table. Head down on his arms, folded against the wood.

She watches him. Watches to see any movement in his shoulders, in his back. Anyone else she might have thought they were sleeping there; might have even wondered if they were crying. Not Ricky. He looks knackered though, worse today than she's seen him, the deep bags under his eyes, the way the lines of his face seem etched further into his skin. Just then, he looks up.

It's like he knew she was there. Like he was waiting for her to have stepped closer to the glass, so he could glare right at her.

They stand there for a minute, neither able to break eye contact, and then he starts to cough and it gives Shona the push she needed to leave the window and walk to the door. Christ, he sounds ill. She steps inside. Maybe she should offer to get him a glass of water. She's not doing that though.

'I don't belong here,' she says.

He gets the cough under control, wipes at his mouth with the back of his hand.

'Right then.' He nods. 'You want back with the lads?'

'No, that's not what I mean.'

He waits for her to explain, that scowl still on his face. A fist pressed into his neck, like he's trying to stop the cough from returning.

'I shouldn't be working here,' she says. 'On the farm, I mean.' She swallows. Hates that she's nervous about saying it, but even with him looking so shattered she's still slightly afraid of what he might do. 'I quit.'

'Right. No bother. I'll pay you for the work you've done so far.'

She wasn't expecting that.

'Okay. Thanks.'

But there are things she wants to say; a reaction she wants to provoke.

'I was the one called the police in.'

He clears his throat, goes to the sink himself and turns the cold tap on.

'I know,' he says, his back to her.

He downs the pint of water he just poured. Seems to give him what he was needing. She's not finished though, not just yet.

'But how do you know?'

'That doesn't really matter, does it?'

He takes a step closer and she finds herself backing towards the door.

'It matters to me.'

She wants to ask if it was Aaron, or if it was Kev. She feels dizzy, like she's not had food for a day, then remembers that she hasn't.

'Well, I'm glad of it,' he says, gravel in his throat.

'Glad of what?'

His mouth is pressed closed now and there's sweat on his upper lip and he flicks his head back, as if to send her away. Glad she called the police? He's started closing the door against her but she's got too many questions to let him.

'It's a little kid,' she says.

His eyes snap to hers.

'What?'

'Buried out in your field,' she says. 'It's a baby. A toddler.'

His face is desperate, pleading, and he's closer to her than he should be and she's suddenly afraid; she's at the door, closing it behind her, leaving him with that relentless cough as she runs, out past Aaron and Lee and Kev, not caring any more if they see her go, past Andy Barr sneaking away to God knows where, past that overgrown field between Ricky's farm and the village where someone's kneeling low in among the weeds and only slowing as she approaches the centre of Burrowhead, the paving stones glimmering in the heat of the midday sun.

OUT OF LUCK

'Pamali? You there?'

Georgie peers in through the Spar's locked door but it's clear enough there's no one in there. Pami never closes for lunch. Mind you, what had she said yesterday about going for walks on her lunch break? Maybe she's out walking. She'll be fine. Pamali is strong, for all her kindness. Georgie is just…she's just worrying. That feeling, that there's something wrong here, something rotten. She can't shake it off.

The Spar is gleaming though, the windows are spotless and she can see inside the floor's been mopped and the shelves are neatly stacked. It's like the opposite of the station; the opposite of her home even: she'd woken up to a pile of dirty dishes in the sink and damp washing from two days ago smelling of mildew in the machine. She'd left the lot where it was and come straight into work, to all the questions she's struggling to answer.

Deborah-Jane Barr. Pami used to come here as a child, she's told her about family holidays, summers spent on the beach, and her uncle lived here and ran the shop before she did so maybe, just maybe, she might remember something about Deborah-Jane. It's a long shot, but she'd trust Pami more than any of the other villagers. Si and Trish, they're both too young to remember, wouldn't even have been born back when Deborah-Jane disappeared, and it was long before Georgie and Fergus arrived.

'DI Strachan?'

Someone's calling her name and for once Georgie is glad to hear it, until the suspicion rises unbidden.

Shona just always seems to be there, somehow, and it can't be coincidence. Not that she has anything against the girl – she was kind to her yesterday, and Georgie's not going to forget that – but she must still be looking for her story and Georgie doesn't want the press to know how little she knows. The wrong thing appearing in print could be just the excuse HQ need to close them down and then what? She's still not found another job for Si, and Trish might not even be able to leave Burrowhead, what with her Uncle Walt in the state he is and Shona is local after all—

'Georgie?'

'Hello again, Shona.'

'Is there any news?'

Georgie shakes her head.

'Not that... I understand of course, you can't talk about the case or... I mean, how are you feeling?'

Georgie feels her head starting to pound in the heat; it's not natural, this weather. There's someone else here now as well, lounging on the edge of the fountain in brightly coloured baggy trousers, smoking an e-cigarette.

'Who's that?' Georgie blurts out without even meaning to.

Shona looks to see, turns back with a grin.

'Name's Orlando. He's one of the summer workers too, in from the city.'

'Should have guessed,' Georgie says. 'Just about everyone I see under the age of thirty is working for Ricky Barr, far as I can tell.'

'Not me,' Shona says. 'I quit.'

Her voice changes as she speaks and Georgie turns to her, surprised, and something else maybe, slightly impressed.

'You quit Ricky's farm job?'

'Yeah. I didn't want to be there any more. The place felt...'

Georgie knows what she means, and she doesn't have the words for it either, not really, but this whole place is breaking, stale and dried out.

'I...'

'What is it, Shona?'

'I might have said something I shouldn't, though. As I was leaving. I was coming to tell you, actually...'

'What, Shona?'

Georgie wishes she could close her eyes to this bloody sun, the way it's sparking off every window on the street.

'I told him it was a little kid, buried out in the field. I didn't mean to, I just wanted to get a reaction from him, something to tell me how he was involved in all this, you know?'

'And did it work?'

Shona shakes her head.

'Right.' Georgie feels heavy, every part of her, like the air is pressing in against her skin. 'Well, you've told me.'

'I'm sorry,' Shona is saying. 'I just want to help, really... I want to help.'

'The best thing you can do is to stay away from all this. Please, Shona.'

Though even as she says it, Georgie knows it's futile – people like Shona don't stay away from things, and a bit of her admires her for it as well, but Georgie has to do this alone and Shona is local and press and still a kid herself and Georgie tells her to stay out of trouble, cringing at how patronising she sounds, as she heads back towards Burrowhead police station, having failed to find Pamali and failed to find any answers.

MISUNDERSTANDINGS
BEFORE LUNCH

'See, Trish, we're going to need an answer, you understand. Have you got my back or haven't you?'

Trish grinds her teeth.

'I wasn't even sure we should come to you first, but Suze was quite adamant, what with your family and everything... We all care about your Uncle Walt, you understand that, don't you...and so you need to let us know sooner rather than later, what with things progressing...'

Trish is damn tempted to hang up the call – bloody Elise, who does she think she is? – but Georgie's just got back to the office and the best Trish can do is pretend it's nothing important and keep her voice, her words, completely neutral.

'Of course,' she says. 'I see what you mean.'

She glances over at Georgie and rolls her eyes; that should imply a local looking for gossip. They're the kind of calls she's usually fielding.

'He's shown up, Trish, right now, that black DS from the city—'

Trish feels conscious of her own pulse, dreads that blush spreading up her neck again and she doesn't know why her own body keeps betraying her when she has absolutely no interest in DS bloody-married two-years-younger-than-her Frazer and fuck, when his hand brushed her hand, she felt a spark of something passing through her.

'—and the last thing we need is him snooping around, do you hear what I'm saying, Trish? If we've made a mistake coming to you then we need to know about it.'

'There's nothing more I can tell you,' Trish says, more abruptly than she means to. Georgie looks up. 'I understand your concern, but it's "No comment".' She hangs up, takes a deep breath. Then another. She shouldn't let her get under her skin.

'Another bloody journalist,' she says, forcing a smile.

'Which one?'

Trish shrugs. 'I... Sorry, I forgot the name.'

Georgie frowns slightly as she picks up a stack of the missing child reports, offering to help with the search for an ID, and Trish feels a stab of guilt. She's been getting nowhere fast. Bloody Elise Robertson. She never asked to be caught up in all this. At least Uncle Walt's safe in the care home. She's got good reasons for wanting him safe in there, for keeping him away from the village just now; it was the right thing to do. She needs to stop second-guessing herself.

'We could arrest them,' she says, and Georgie looks up startled.

'Who?'

'Aaron and Lee Prowle. We've got the ketamine found in their possession—'

'That they say isn't theirs—'

'And Kevin Taylor's witness testimony—'

'That wasn't recorded, and he might deny—'

'We could still bring them in, couldn't we? Maybe they'll give something away, if we put a bit of pressure on...'

Georgie looks at her like she's considering it, or considering something, before shaking her head and saying 'Not yet,' as though she has a plan, a whole other plan that she's not telling Trish about and turning away from her again and her phone keeps ringing, on silent in her pocket.

She checks it when Georgie leaves the room, and later when Georgie is watching her so close she feels like her neck is burning she gets up and leaves the room herself, pretending to need the toilet and hiding in there, door locked, just for a couple of minutes of being away from that look. It doesn't work though, of course, because she looks at her phone and there are the missed calls: Elise and Suze and she wants them to leave her alone. Trish hasn't done anything wrong. It's not fair, this.

Here's what Trish has done: she's cared about Andy Barr, tried to help the kid turn his life around. She's forgiven him when no one else would. That's a good thing, isn't it? Forgiveness? She's cared about Uncle Walt, loved him all her life, and tried to keep him safe. True, she hasn't managed to get anything on Ricky Barr yet; Andy won't say a word on the record about the abuse – he won't even listen if she uses that word, denies it flat out – and the trail back to Ricky from Bobby has fizzled out. There's no proof the drugs were coming from Ricky Barr, just the gossip of everyone in the town and the way all the kids just know it and he always seems to have the money to keep the farm going, buying up more of the land when everyone else is barely staying afloat. She just needs more time. Bloody Elise.

There's something else though, because it's not just a dead horse, there's a dead child too, found on Ricky Barr's land, and the missing sister, Deborah-Jane Barr, who she's not been able to locate; there's some link back to the 1980s when Ricky was a child and Trish wasn't born yet.

Georgie's watching her though and Trish can hardly concentrate on her work and she's supposed to be searching through the missing person reports for a child, an eighteen-month-old child and she looks through the images, scanned photographs of people reported missing in the area forty years ago, never returned. There are more than she would have imagined. Teenagers trying to get away from overbearing parents – was that why Deborah-Jane had run away? – husbands running off with all the money in the bank, or running away from debts their family had no hope of repaying. In every photo, though, the missing people seem to look out at the camera with warmth. With love. That probably says more about the family members left behind than the character of the missing people themselves. It was those left behind who chose the photo, after all, who wanted the police to form one type of opinion and not another.

There are no toddlers though. A couple of closed cases, older kids run off and parents overreacting, calling the authorities only to have the child found by a neighbour a couple of hours later. She'd done that, once. It was Uncle Walt that found her, hiding out in the community shed with a stray cat for company. She'd begged to keep it, then begged for a kitten, then wished for a pet of any kind, then wished her mam would come back.

Christ, her phone again. It's automatic, this time, it's right there in front of her on the desk and she answers it without thinking. On the other end, the voice is gentle, sympathetic, and her stomach sinks.

'What's happened?'

'It's your great-uncle, Walt Mackie.'

'Yes?'

'It's…this is… We're concerned that he might have hurt himself.'

'Oh God, what's he done, please tell me—'

'He's okay now, calm again and we've bandaged up the cut—'

'What cut?'

'We're not quite sure what happened, he hasn't wanted to talk to us about it yet, but he seems to have cut his arms on some smashed crockery, from his mug of tea.'

'His arms?'

A beat of silence and Trish knows, she knows.

'His wrists.'

'I'll be right there—'

'No, no, please don't do that. The doctor is here and Walt is calm again, he's going to get some sleep now, and I think we should let him – I think he needs the rest.'

'I need to be there!'

'Actually…he asked us not to tell you. I'm calling because you're listed as his next of kin and in these cases, it's not always clear residents know what they're saying…'

'He told you not to call me?'

There's a pause on the end of the line.

'Yes, I'm afraid so. He got very agitated and it did take a while to calm him down, so I think the best thing now is to let him sleep.'

Trish feels like she's drunk again, dizzy and out of breath, like the humidity in here is so extreme there's not enough oxygen; Christ, she's not going to faint is she?

'Trish,' Georgie is saying. 'Are you alright? Trish?'

THE SAME TIME EVERY DAY

Simon reaches into his bag and pulls out the package again, the padded brown envelope, the address in Alexis's handwriting. He's opened and resealed it so many times now the top of it is scarred with Sellotape. Rips in the envelope, exposing the bubble wrap underneath, are covered over with brown tape but he can't bring himself to change the envelope, or even move the contents to somewhere more secure. The address: Simon's home, written by Alexis. His handwriting, the elegant sweep of his handwriting; even when he was afraid he took time with things. Alexis didn't scrawl words. He was too much of an artist for that.

Half an hour at home for lunch, that's what Simon has taken for himself every day since he's been back at work. It's what he needs. He carries the package into the station with him each morning, and home again; he's always got it with him. But during his half-hour lunch break on his own, in his own house, that's when he takes it out of his bag and allows himself to hold it. To imagine Alexis doing the same.

Most people, he imagines, would choose a favourite item of clothing, maybe, a jumper to wear, a photo to look at. Simon has those things too, of course he does, but the package is something more. It was an act of trust. Alexis had decided to trust him. He holds the package to his stomach and leans over, grasping it close. And there, with his eyes closed, that's when he can hear the voices again most clearly. He no longer needs to open the package, to play the tapes – he knows them by heart. The three women who had turned to Alexis in their three very different ways.

He thinks of Dawn the most often. She feels like the closest link he has back to the man he loves. Dawn Helmsteading: safe at last, living her life somewhere else, away from Burrowhead and its ghosts. There's a comfort in that, for Simon, a comfort in knowing he helped her, even though it could have cost him his job. Some things are more important than a job, after all.

The sound of Elise's voice inspires a very different feeling though, which is why he tends not to think about her words so often: that stab of guilt, made all the sharper by its uncertainty. This week, it's Elise's voice he's been hearing more than Dawn's, and today it's all he can hear. There is a connection, somewhere, between her words and her memories, her father, old Art Robertson – dead now – and that poor little boy in the field, he's sure of it – he just can't find it. It's buried in there, like the faces Dawn saw hidden beneath those blank billowing masks.

Would Georgie be able to find it?

Is that what he needs? Is that *who* he needs: Georgie?

Then there's the third tape. Natalie Prowle's voice. The anger in the way she spoke, the accusations she made – he can imagine Alexis cringing, the way her words must have cut him – and the knowledge she hinted at, the way it overshadowed the words being spoken and somehow, he thinks, somehow, it is all tangled up together.

UNEXPECTED UNDERSTANDING
IN THE AFTERNOON

'Who were you phoning just then?' Natalie's voice is calm and low compared to Elise's high-pitched fluttering.

Fergus is watching them. Or at least he's watching Natalie, as Elise steps closer to her, brandishing a small trowel and leaving Natalie's question hanging.

'Have you found something?' Elise wants to know.

She must be able to see how the villagers have been pushed back now, how the archaeologists from the university have taken charge. Fergus, Natalie, they've been reduced to the role of onlookers. They are not leaving though.

Natalie blinks, and the mood between them changes – he can sense it even from a distance.

'There are bodies buried here,' she says softly. 'There are people here, buried under the motte.'

She speaks so gently that Fergus finds himself immediately thinking of Elise's grief, of how badly she must miss her dad. He'd been living with her towards the end, so she could care for him; it must have left such a gap in her life. Natalie would understand. That's why she's speaking so kindly, delivering the news as though these are people they know, family buried here, missing relatives finally discovered. He needs to go and offer some support.

Fergus is on his feet, heading to where Natalie and Elise are standing, a little away from the group, and he barely notices DS Frazer walking towards him at the same time until all four of them converge at the edge of the motte. Given her grief and everything, Fergus turns to Elise first, holding out his hand and when she doesn't take it giving her a friendly squeeze on the arm. 'It's good to see you again, Elise. How are you keeping?'

Natalie's eyes flick from him to Elise, who doesn't seem to know what to say. None of them have yet acknowledged DS Frazer, who Fergus is sure must be hovering there behind him.

'It's hard,' he says, 'It's such a hard time for you, I can only imagine…'

He lets his voice trail off. It's difficult, knowing what to say to someone you don't know very well, when they've experienced loss, but it seems to Fergus that surely acknowledging their pain is a place to start.

'It's erm…' He clears his throat.

It's weird, with DS Frazer standing there, because he doesn't know any of them, does he, and he's not even said anything yet and they're trying to have a personal conversation here. He tries again.

'Are you interested in our local archaeology too, Elise?'

He smiles, a little sheepishly, falling back on what he knows.

'Because I thought maybe you might like to join up to my society, my archaeological society, same as Natalie here. We're getting a nice group together, aren't we, and we're going to apply for some funding to make the motte into a community space…maybe get some information signs and…maybe make a sort of hub and…well, what do you think?'

Elise smiles, takes a step back. 'I've got a bit going on just now—'

'Of course you do,' he says. 'Of course, and I'm so sorry. You know I'm here, if you ever need…'

She nods but her eyes aren't even on him, they are behind him, over his shoulder – is DS Frazer still standing there?

'Can I have a word in private?'

Yes, of course he is – that voice isn't from around here. Has he been called in, to help with the body they found in Ricky's field?

'With me?' Elise sounds so young sometimes. 'Well, of course, I'm always…' Though her flutter of words is a little slower than usual.

Frazer steps up to her and Elise steps back and turns, uncertainly, and Frazer seems to be steering her away from Fergus and Natalie and over towards the road. They both watch – Fergus and Natalie – as Frazer keeps walking and Elise keeps walking ahead of him until they are across the road and out of earshot.

'That was kind of you,' Natalie says, surprising him.

He'd expected her to say something about Frazer, about what on earth the police are doing here, at their archaeological dig.

'Tell me, Fergus, why do you care about your archaeological society so much?'

Suddenly he feels foolish, like he does whenever he tries talking to Georgie about it. He can feel himself turning red; sense the apology rising up his throat already. He just wants to get a group together, that's all, wants to find like-minded people he can talk to.

'I think it's your way of trying to make some new friends,' she says, touching his arm in the way he'd just touched Elise's. 'And I've told you already, you don't need a society to do that, Fergus.'

Mrs Dover and Mrs Smyth are sitting side by side on their deckchairs overlooking the dig, weaving something out of straw, now and then glancing in the direction of DS Frazer and Elise Robertson. Natalie seems to notice them at the same time as Fergus. She just gives him the briefest of nods as she heads over to join them, leaving Fergus's arm feeling cold where her touch had been. That's twice she's touched him now, he's sure of it. On his shoulder. On his arm.

'Fergus Strachan?'

The voice is so close it makes him jump – DS Frazer is back already, wanting to talk to him now it seems. And Fergus does have some ideas that might help them, as it happens. Earlier this year he'd done an aerial survey of the whole area with his drone and there are some photos of Ricky's farm – although he's not sure Ricky would like that, and he hadn't exactly got permission to fly over there, but then if it's for the police—

'Fergus Strachan, I have some questions.'

And before Fergus can even take a breath, DS Frazer is launching straight in, right here by the motte. He doesn't even bother to lead him over the road, just starts telling him that he's trying to track down a young woman called Abigail something and has Fergus ever heard of her. It doesn't seem to have anything to do with the bones they found in Ricky's field. He's even asking about the dig, about what they're looking for, whose idea it all was.

Maybe DS Frazer would like to join the archaeological society. He seems very interested in what's going on here, in who's involved, and Fergus likes him. He does. It's just that Fergus had never seen himself and Georgie as different before but now, when he thinks of Frazer and Georgie working together...

Fergus doesn't know if there'd have been any black people here, in the Iron Age. There were boats though, folk travelled, so it's possible. He's read there was lots of trading across continents, via the Mediterranean, the North Sea, Persia. This idea that humans have always stayed in the one place until now, there's no truth in that. Humans are explorers – always have been. Just watch a toddler, that's all you need to know right there. Give a toddler a boundary and they'll want to see what's on the other side.

'So have you?' Frazer is saying.

'Have I what?'

'Come across the name before. Abigail Moss.'

'Oh, I'm sorry, no,' Fergus says. 'But you know, I've only been here twenty years. I'm just a newcomer really.' He can imagine Georgie bristling at that: *How many years will it take, Fergus? These villagers...* 'You could try Walt Mackie, he's been here as long as anyone.'

Frazer frowns slightly.

'You'll know that, of course, I'm sure you're very thorough...'

Over his shoulder Fergus can see Natalie looking his way, and he's pleased to know that she's watching.

'Natalie Prowle next,' DS Frazer says in a way that makes Fergus slightly uncomfortable. 'That one doesn't like talking to the police, does she?'

Fergus frowns, but doesn't reply.

'You lot should be helping her boys, not questioning them,' Elise says, appearing behind him. 'Those poor boys, we've all seen the state of them but yous don't care, do you? None of you are doing a thing to help—'

Fergus is starting to feel like he's letting minutes at a time vanish between each breath. He doesn't feel very well, now he's thinking of it, there's something making his legs feel unsteady and his knees feel weak. Frazer's striding over towards Natalie and as he stares over at them he sees a shadow moving across the ground – it must be a cloud over the sun, that's all – but he sees it moving and it looks as though it's seeping up from the earth, from the soil and rocks, appearing then vanishing as he stares. Dark shapes seem to be stretching towards them, towards Natalie, and nausea grips his stomach, saliva collecting under his tongue and suddenly there are long fingers clawing at Natalie's face, at her skin and that can't be right, Natalie loves this motte, Natalie loves these villagers and he shakes his head, presses his fists into his eyes. When he takes them away to look again Natalie is smiling, holding out a hand then placing it on Frazer's arm in that way she has and Fergus feels a twist of... but no, it can't be jealousy, of course not, that would be absurd.

SECRETS, UNEARTHED

Shona has to get off Main Street, away from the corn dolls watching, half-hidden, behind net curtains and the feathers hanging in windows, away from Walt Mackie's carved face with vines spewing from its eyes and so she takes the lane – the lane that goes down beside the Spar, beside where Alexis Cosse used to live. The lane where Simon was unintentionally hiding just before he caught Kev trying to break into Alexis's old flat the week of the murder. She never did ask him what he was doing down there. What had called him down there, what about it had caught his attention? He was grieving and angry and she'd left it at that; asking questions would have seemed like too much of an intrusion. But now? DI Strachan telling her to stay away only makes her feel more determined to find out what is really going on.

It was cordoned off with police tape for ages afterwards but – for the first time – Shona's noticed that it's gone. Looks like no one's been down here since it was cordoned off, though. Smells like it, too. Rotten, damp and mouldy then dried out in this heat, leaving spores floating in the air; she could almost choke on them. There are two large bins that used to be for the Spar's waste, but after the attacks Pamali petitioned the council to get new, smaller bins, recycling and landfill, so she could fit them by the back door where it wasn't so dark or confined. She wouldn't have said so, but it must have been because she didn't feel safe down that alley.

Shona takes another step, though, further into the shadows. There is something down here. What is it, there in the dark?

There was nothing found down here related to the murder, not that she knows of, but she can see right up to Alexis's flat. It's empty now and no one's going to take it on, no one from round here – even the least superstitious villager wouldn't want to be moving into a dead man's house; not when he had been killed in such a brutal way. It's like how the playground is deserted, even in this weather, even with no other swings for the kids to play on, as though the bloodstain were still visible on the ground. So it's no surprise really that folk avoid the alleyway.

Shona's here, though, and she's staring at the mound of old clothes and sheets that have turned brown and stiff in the waves of torrential rain and blistering heat. She can't bring herself to step any closer, but she reaches out a hand and there's no one here, not a soul, and so there's nothing to stop her as she pulls the fabric at the top.

A beige towel now stained brown and rough with dirt.

A knitted blanket. Hand-knitted, as though it had once been loved, or been gifted to someone who was once loved. Thrown out like it was meaningless.

She keeps going, digging deeper through the waste.

A pair of walking boots, some waterproof trousers, piles and piles of white sheets, mounded so high she almost expects there to be a person huddled underneath them – there's plenty of homeless in Warphill might have made good use of the blankets – but it's just these grey-white sheets, cut into weird shapes and then dumped here uselessly, abandoned, unrecycled, to decay. She pulls them out, lays them on the ground. God but it stinks.

She holds her sleeve over her mouth so she can breathe, backs out of the alley and drags the sheets with her, the biggest ones, and the bits she's got clutched in her hand. Why would anyone cut up their sheets to dispose of them? Why would anyone cut holes in them, like eyeholes? She drops the sheet she'd been pulling and holds the smaller piece between both hands. They're not *like* eyeholes, they *are* eyeholes. It might have been a sheet once, but it's been cut and shaped into some kind of mask. Stitched, by hand. There are holes for the eyes but nothing for the nose, the mouth – it would cover the whole head and face, the breath of whoever wore it left to cling to their skin.

There was something else she'd thrown off to the side. A dressing gown. Was it? Her neck prickles.

She glances over her shoulder – that feeling of someone watching, something moving but there's no one here, no one at all – then runs back to the alleyway and pulls it out. It is a dressing gown, and it's exactly like the one Walt Mackie wears. It could be anyone's, of course, except that when she turns it inside out, his name and address have been written on a piece of fabric and stitched into the lining. She folds up the mask and stuffs it into her pocket, grabs everything else and throws it back into the pile where she found it, then heads along Main Street out of the village, north, following the single-track road that leads to the Burrowhead care home.

CONFESSION AT QUARTER
TO THREE

Georgie stares at him longer than she should. She was planning to bring him in herself; she wasn't anticipating he'd turn up like this, looking like he hasn't slept in three days, saying he needs to report a crime. Last time Ricky Barr was in the station he had a look of disgust on his face and a threat in his voice that made young Andy recoil into himself and put Georgie's teeth on edge. What was that, three months back? Looks like he's aged about ten years. He needs a shower too, he's brought the smell of the farm with him. She regains her composure, swallows down her dislike and invites him to have a seat in the interview room. Offers him the cursory cup of water assuming he'll say no.

'Please, aye.'

His voice is grating, sore. She nods, goes through to the kitchen to get him his water – they're out of the paper cups they're supposed to use and they're expensive, those things, so he gets one of the plastic camping mugs that were donated when the outdoor shop in Crackenbridge closed down. Given the way he downs the water, she doesn't suppose he cares much what kind of cup it's delivered in.

'Are you alright, Ricky?' she says.

He clears his throat and for a second she thinks he's actually going to spit on the floor, but he doesn't. Trish comes through, sits beside her and starts up the tape.

'Want me to fill that up for you again, Ricky?'

'It was my horse.'

It takes her a moment.

'Can you…'

'My black mare was stolen last weekend. I was trying to track her down myself—'

'You lied to PC Hunter?'

'Like I say, I was handling it myself. But my son tells me a horse was found slaughtered in the woods. PC Hunter didn't mention that bit.' He hasn't broken eye contact since he started speaking, but something about him has changed – it's not a threat, in his eyes. 'So I'm here now to tell you it was my horse.'

Georgie swallows.

'Do you have any idea why anyone would want to steal your horse?'

'I could take a guess.'

'Would you, please?'

He looks at Trish, then back at Georgie. A flicker of emotion crosses his face but it's gone faster than Georgie can read it.

'Whenever something goes wrong round here, folk like to blame me. That makes me a target.' He sits back and presses his fist into his throat. 'But don't worry, I'll no be requesting police protection.'

'Trish,' Georgie says. 'Have you got a photo, for confirmation?'

Trish pulls a photo of the dead horse out of her folder, pushes it across the table. Ricky looks at it. 'That's her. She's got a whorl on her stomach, 'bout an inch across.'

Georgie nods. It's as he describes – the mare they found had the same marking. That poor creature, with her eyes staring wide as though she'd had to watch what was happening to her as it happened. The sheen on her coat, where it was unharmed; the dark black matted mess around the chest where the blood had gushed from her throat.

'Do you have any suspects yet?' he says, clearing his voice like he wants to get down to business. He's not here for sympathy, that's for sure.

'We don't know why anyone would do this.'

A single rough bark of a cough.

'It's personal.'

'What makes you say that?'

He waits before replying. Fleetingly, Georgie could almost feel sorry for him. It's as though, whatever he's about to say, it's going to cost him something he'd never want to pay. He's forcing himself to go there.

'They did the same thing to my dog.'

'You don't have a dog,' Trish says, her obvious suspicion making Georgie cringe.

'I did once,' Ricky says, quietly.

'And when was this?'

'I'd have been eight years old. I was the one who found her—'

Trish opens her mouth to interrupt but Georgie stops her with a look.

'Please, take your time, Ricky,' she says in her slow twang, despite Trish's obvious impatience.

Ricky swallows, rubs his mouth with the back of his hand.

'Someone killed my dog in the same way they killed my horse.'

'Can you be more specific?'

'They cut her throat, when I was a kid. And they left her there, in that same clearing in the woods.'

'So,' Trish says, leaning forwards. 'Was this before or after your sister ran away?'

'Been looking my family up, have you?' he fires back.

'We were just wondering where she is now. Any idea?'

He doesn't reply – he doesn't even move – for what feels like minutes.

'I've not seen her since the day she left,' he says.

Georgie stares at him, at the exhaustion deep in his eyes, the red splatters of veins across his cheeks, the haunted way his teeth grind at the back of his jaw and the way his neck never seems to relax, like's he's constantly ready to fight – and at last she realises why he looked so terrified when she started digging in his field.

'You thought it was her,' she says quietly. 'You thought it was your sister, buried on the farm.'

'But it wasn't, was it,' he says, suddenly sitting that bit taller.

'We don't believe so.'

His shoulders fall; he seems able to breathe again. For a second she wonders if she can see some softness in his eyes – she dismisses that thought fast though.

'Look, I don't know who it was killed my dog,' he says. 'I was a kid. It made a fucking impression though and I've no kept a dog since. So doing that to my mare… whoever stole her, slaughtered her out in the woods, they knew exactly what they were doing. Same place. Same cut across the throat.'

He swallows and Georgie can hear the pain of it.

'As for whoever it is buried in my field… They say killers of animals can turn into killers of people, don't they? And I can tell you who was in charge back then, in charge of who got the jobs, of who sold what, of who got to marry who, who got to live in peace, all of it – and it were the same people who had it in for my family all along.'

He stops and looks at Trish; looks at her hard and refuses to break his gaze. Georgie can feel her shoulders clench at the sight of it.

'I've got four names for you,' he says, still refusing to look away. 'Art Robertson. Jack Helmsteading. Nora Prowle. And Walt. Fucking. Mackie.'

EYES, WATCHING

Shona peers into each door she passes – they all have a glass panel in the top so the staff can keep an eye on the residents – and the old people inside ignore her or, worse, look up with hope that she might be here for them, until she gets to the end of the corridor, climbs the stairs, and repeats the process. She doesn't have to go too far. Walt Mackie's is the second door on the left. She pushes it.

His eyes follow her into the room as though he'd known she was coming – or that someone was – as though he's been waiting for her all afternoon and she's turned up late.

'Sit down, lass,' he says.

She perches on the bed, opposite where he's sitting in his chair, a dressing gown just like the one she found wrapped round his body despite the suffocating heat.

'You cold?' he says.

She shakes her head.

'I was wondering if you'd lost a dressing gown.'

He looks down at the one he's wearing, back up again. His face is open and lost, his eyes straying across hers in confusion.

'I found one in the village, Walt. I found a dressing gown.' She pauses. 'It had your name and address sewn in.'

'Ah,' he nods. 'My name is in all my clothes. My Trish likes to do that, in case I go walkabout.' He looks over her shoulder, as though he expects to see her arrive any minute. 'She'll no leave me here alone.'

Shona pulls the mask from her pocket. It looks comical, here, in this heat and this light, with this harmless old man.

'And this?' she says. 'Is this yours too?'

He reaches out and caresses the filthy white fabric.

'This is special,' he says. 'This is the first one I ever made.'

'Why did you throw it away then?'

His fingers find the eyeholes and he seems to massage the frayed edges; he's got that faraway look of someone remembering. They say that the past can seem more real than the present for people with dementia, don't they?

'I couldn't at first,' he says. 'But then they killed Bobby.'

Shona feels her breath catch in her throat.

'Bobby Helmsteading?'

'They killed him because of what he did.'

'Who killed him?'

'He sneaked into the woods and he watched us, and then he copied us, twisting everything up wrong. Something had to be done.'

'What did he see?'

'It was the right thing to do; he was a vicious boy.'

'Can you hear me?'

'But he saw us performing the ritual and that's where he got the idea, to attack poor Dawn.'

He's not looking at her, hasn't looked at her while he spoke, not once. His eyes are raised above her head, flicking back and forth like someone's pacing behind her.

'I would never have condoned that though,' he says, suddenly taking her hand. 'Never, not a wee girl like that.'

Shona wants to pull her hand away but his grip is tight and his eyes are still avoiding hers – she turns: nothing. The crumpled duvet. The bare walls.

'I'm the last one left now,' he says. 'The only one left. But the Others are coming.'

His eyes clear and focus and suddenly he looks at her like he knows her.

'Who comes to visit you, Walt?'

'Natalie, sometimes. She says I can call her Natalie.'

'You mean Natalie Prowle?'

'She likes to talk about the old days.'

He's still clutching onto her hand.

'And I like that too,' he says. 'Things were better in the old days.'

She pulls her hand away at last, and he looks down surprised.

'Old people always say that.'

'You think I'm an old person?' He smiles. 'So I am, I suppose. And I should know then, shouldn't I? Things were better before.'

'When before?' Shona says. 'When we had the strikes?'

'I remember the strikes… We had bad times, true enough, and I'm no saying…but before that, lass.'

'Before that?' She looks at him, straight into his eyes. 'You mean during the world wars? You miss all that killing? The rations, the fear?'

He looks uncomfortable, trying to avoid her gaze, his shoulders hunching in as though her words are hurting him, but she can't stop.

'Or do you mean before that, Walt? Before medicine, before human rights, when there was plague and starvation, when witches were burned at the stake?'

Walt is staring down at his chest now, at the crumbs from his lunch that have collected there, that slowly, painfully rise and fall with each breath he manages. His hands are shaking, she hadn't noticed that, shaking like he can't make them stop and he keeps pulling the sleeves of his dressing gown over his wrists and she's seen that before, that motion, that pulls her back into her own memories where she doesn't want to go.

'Your friend,' he says, suddenly. 'The one who always wore those long skirts, the ones she embroidered herself. She was so pretty, that one. What was her name again?'

'Rachel,' Shona says.

'Rachel,' Walt smiles. 'She's okay now. I thought you'd like to know that.' He pats her hand. 'Some good news, after you came all the way out here to see me.' He leans in closer, his voice dropping to a whisper and his breath clammy on her cheek. 'I summoned the Others to help her, just like we used to.'

She pulls away from him, her hand wiping his breath's moisture from her skin.

'I saved her.'

'No one saved her, Walt. She killed herself. She's dead.'

Suddenly she needs to see some sunlight, something other than his hopeful eyes and his creased old face and his shaking hands and his cut wrists and so she looks up to the window and that's when she sees it.

A row of see-through plastic cups, positioned all along the white painted windowsill, each with a layer of red beneath the clear water that she feels sure must be his blood and right there in the middle of the window – she has no idea how she could have missed it – is another corn doll. He must have made it himself, here in the care home. It's not even made of straw. It's made of neatly ripped pieces of old photographs and three colours of thread have been plaited together and looped around her neck, tied to the curtain rail high above the window, so that the corn doll is hanging, lifeless, against the glass.

SOMEONE WHO MIGHT REMEMBER

Mrs Helmsteading stares at Simon from the other side of the glass. She looks well. Younger than she seemed before, inexplicably hopeful given that she's facing a life sentence having pleaded guilty to murdering her own son.

'Good to see you again, Georgie,' she says, her eyes not leaving Simon's face.

Simon thinks about asking how she is, if she's heard from Dawn, but decides against it.

'I hear you've volunteered to work in the prison library,' Georgie says.

'Oh aye. I've never been around so many books before. I like it, in the library. I like all them books better than I like most people these days.'

'They're treating you alright then?'

'Why are you here, DI Strachan?' At last her eyes are on Georgie, and Simon feels able to breathe again. He can see Dawn in her; hear Dawn's words in her voice.

'Have you heard from Dawn since you've been in here?' Georgie says.

It's like she could be reading his mind, sometimes.

Mrs Helmsteading's lips rise into a smile and the warmth spreads up her face, all the way to her eyes.

'Dawn's gone,' she says. 'And she's never coming back.'

'She's got nothing to fear now. She's not suspected of any crime any more. We're not even looking for her—'

'She's never coming back here. She's a smart girl, my Dawny. And she's safe.'

'Do you think she'd be in danger here?'

'You're not trying to save people again are you, DI Strachan?'

Georgie shakes her head. 'Actually I want to talk to you about something else.'

'Is that so?'

'I was wanting to talk to you about your husband Jack, and Ricky Barr.'

Mrs Helmsteading's eyes flit momentarily about the room, and for a second Simon sees the same haunted woman he followed to the cave, to Dawn's hiding place.

'Interesting,' he says, 'the way Ricky took your Bobby under his wing.'

'Is that what you've heard?'

They both wait a beat.

'That boy told me nothing, and I didn't get a kind word from him since the day he got home and set himself up in my spare room.'

'Does it haunt you?' Georgie says.

'You mean what I did?' she says. 'Or what he did?'

She leans back then, away from the glass.

'I just mean…are you doing okay in here? Do you need—'

'Ask your question, DI Strachan. I've books to be getting back to.'

'Okay,' Georgie says. 'Fair enough.' She takes a breath. 'First up, we were hoping you could tell us about a particular group of villagers we've been hearing about, when they were young.'

'What group's that then?'

'Your husband, Jack. Art Robertson. Walt Mackie. And Nora Prowle.'

Mrs Helmsteading smiles at that, like she's glad to have permission to fall back into her memories for a moment.

'You want to talk about Jack, Art and Walt, when they were young men. Yes, I remember. My Jack was the youngest of the three but he was the first to die. It seems unfair, that.' Her eyes rise to Simon's for a second. 'But aye, he was the youngest. A few years older than him was Art Robertson. And then Walt Mackie, he was older again, by a good ten years. He was in his fifties by the time he took in poor little Trish. But age aside, there was nothing separating them, for a few years there. They kept bees – did you know that?'

Beside him, Georgie nods.

'They're ancient, the bees. They haven't evolved in ten million years.'

'And Nora,' Simon says. 'Did she keep bees as well?'

Mrs Helmsteading laughs. 'She kept children, did Nora Prowle. Her and her husband were foster carers – they'd no time for bees as well, I dare say.'

'But she was part of the group?'

'I don't know about that. Were women ever part of the group, in those days? She was older than them, too. I didn't know her well, and she died when my kids were young, see. I didn't have much time for anything other than them either.'

Next to him, Georgie is pushing the palm of her hand back and forth against her forehead.

'And what about Ricky Barr?'

'What about him?'

'Were they...friends?'

'Didn't have a thing to do with each other far as I know. Back when Nora was still around Ricky Barr was just a kid himself. But then they've never been popular around Burrowhead way, the Barrs. That farm of theirs, taking over more every year, heaven knows how.'

She raises her eyes skyward for a second, and Simon tries to remember if she'd been religious before. He doesn't think so. She wouldn't be the first to find God in a prison like this.

'What about Ricky's father then,' Simon tries. 'What about John Barr.'

'That's a name I haven't heard in a long while,' she says.

'He's been dead fifteen years now, if we have that right?'

'Aye, sounds about like it. Long before my Jack took ill, he was gone. Not many grieved his passing, either, and I don't mind telling you that.'

'So he wasn't a part of their group then?'

Mrs Helmsteading actually laughs at that.

'Well now, there was Art and Walt and my Jack, here.' She touches the glass with her left hand, gently. 'And over here.' She stretches her right hand to the far side of the glass and knocks, once, hard. 'Over here was John Barr, and he wasn't part of any group.'

'Why was that?'

'There was some talk, you know how it is. There was always talk. I remember it all coming to a head back when me and Jack were first married. The others, see—'

'You mean Art Robertson? Walt Mackie?'

'A lot of folk, actually. A lot of the local folk, they didn't like that the Barrs had that farm – didn't like that old Herman Barr had bought the farm in the first place. What right had he, to be over here? It was all too raw back then.'

'What was?'

'When he arrived, it was less than ten years since the war had ended. I wasn't born then, course, but you can imagine. We lost a lot of boys in that war, boys from Burrowhead, from Warphill. And then: a German arrives like that, in our village.'

'He was German?'

'Aye. And he brought his son with him – no sign of a wife – just the son.'

'That'll be John?'

'That's what they told everyone. An English a name as could be. I doubt that's what it said on his birth certificate. But aye, John Barr arrived as a little boy. Ricky's da.'

'And Ricky's mam?'

'Isabella. She was as local as could be. They say Walt Mackie was in love with her, when he was a young man; that he never married because of the loss of her. Don't know if it's true, mind. Could be lots of reasons a man never marries, if you ask me.'

'So when you say it came to a head?'

'There'd been talk about chasing Herman Barr off the land. Buying the farm back, persuading John he wasn't welcome here – why he wanted to stay I don't know.'

'It was his home, wasn't it?'

'Well. But then Isabella chose him and some folk, they didn't like that.'

'You mean Walt Mackie and Art Robertson…'

She doesn't reply.

'And your husband?' Si says. 'He was one of those people too?'

'We almost fell out over it. I stood up for John and Isabella, see. I didn't think it were right, blaming the son for the father's crimes.'

'What crimes?'

Mrs Helmsteading shrugs.

'Moving to a village in northern England isn't a crime,' Georgie says. 'Or are you trying to tell me people thought Herman Barr was a Nazi?'

But Mrs Helmsteading isn't listening to them any more.

'That makes it all the worse, doesn't it?'

'Makes what worse?'

'What I did. The fact that I blamed my Jack for his son's crimes. It makes the way we all abandoned him even worse, doesn't it?'

'I don't know. I don't really think there are better or worse ways for things to play out; just the way that they do.'

'You're lying to me now, though, aren't you.'

Simon doesn't think Georgie is lying.

'Tell me...' Mrs Helmsteading places her hands up against the glass, as though Simon were someone she cared about, someone she loved, and something makes him place his hands against the glass as well, so they are palm to palm but for the transparent barrier between them. 'Do you think my poor Jack will ever forgive me?'

A WAY BACK

Walt can tell Jack hates having to lie to his wife the way he does, whereas Art seems to actively enjoy it; but for Walt there's no one to lie to. A night like this suits his mood, overcast and spitting, everything battered and bruised – on a night like this there's no pretending he's in control, or that anyone can be. The only power here is the churning sky and the salt carried in the wind to sting and scratch; the anger of the land. It's bigger than him, than his trampled heart or his useless hope, bigger than the love Jack has for his loyal wife or the dislike Art feels for his unfaithful one. And Nora, following them from behind like a wolf herding her pack, her dagger held against her heart.

Art has always had his eye on that blade, but there's cunning in Nora Prowle that Art would be no match for. Walt can see it in those tiny, precise fingers of hers, in the way her movements are sharp but controlled. They say she can stitch up the wounded as well as any surgeon. She's stern as a headmistress, that's for sure. But she cares for those foster kids she takes in, and she cares for the villagers too. Walt's not sure he could say that about Art. He cares for himself too much to be a true conduit, that man.

When he thinks about what must be done, something stirs in Walt's blood, makes his fingertips sting. He can feel it running through his veins, down into his calves and back up through his spine. He feels more alive right now than he has in a year or more – he feels nauseous, too, hyper-aware. He's never been to war, never had to fight, but maybe this is what it feels like the night before. Like there's a change coming, that he's about to throw himself into it, to be beaten and hurled and ripped apart and maybe put back together again, and he's trying not to think about how it reminds him of the night he spent with Isabella, how nervous he was, how afraid.

This is different though. He knows what they are going to do. He knows the weight of the hood that will cover his face, his nose and mouth, the heat of his breath collecting on his upper lip because it has nowhere else to go. He knows the way his eyes will feel exposed, vulnerable, as the only part of his face that's not masked in white. Blood, air and water, they are the words that have been passed down and buried deep into the land itself, but Walt would add a fourth word, if he could. He'd add the eyes. None of this would exist without the eyes.

He saw the ritual first when he was just a boy. His father had come back from the war with a stump where his foot had been and a longing to seep into the land and never emerge. He would vanish for days, come home stinking and soaked, gabbling words that made no sense and came from no language, fall onto his bed where Walt's mother would tend to him until he reappeared as a man Walt barely recognised. It was a time of rations and loss, of running through the village in frayed shorts and playing conkers with his brother, as he grew into less of a child, something still achingly far from being on the cusp of a man.

The world around him changed too, into a world that didn't care about the hunger or the loss, didn't care about the ghosts of limbs that had never come home, or men that could never again be the parents they were supposed to be. When his father shook him brutally awake, his large hand was clasped tightly over Walt's mouth to stop him from making a sound. He took him from his bed at midnight, forced a mask over his head and made him follow him out to the river that runs through the woods, to where the white stags appear and disappear between the tall trunks of the silver birch.

It seemed to Walt that his father made him march for hours, over fields and dense wooded tracks, until they found a clearing far beyond the village where the men were gathered. Their robes reached the ground, their hoods hung low, their faces were obscured. Voices like the groan of the wind. Walt would always remember the way the eyes stared at him, the glint of the blade in moonlight, the shine of hair, the black of the blood that soaked it; the circle of men called upon to make a sacrifice when everything they had fought and died for was slipping away.

Nora Prowle's voice rouses him like a slap, even though it's just a whisper.

'It's here.'

'Where do you want this then?' Art sounds out of breath. He'd insisted on carrying the body, slung over his shoulder like that, and a part of Walt hates him for it. Walt would have cradled it in his arms.

Nora points and nods and pulls her hood over her head until all Walt can see is her eyes, her grey-blue eyes peering out from the perfectly cut holes in the fabric, and she is not Nora any more. He wants to transform too. He wants to be something other than Walt Mackie. He pulls his own mask over his face, readjusts the robe around his body, breathes in the heavy air of his own breath masked by fabric, dampened by the drizzling rain and clinging to his skin. His eyes peer out, and at last he can see clearly.

The sky is not black, nor grey; the sky is a pulsing purple, layered and full. The rain that's falling is silver, collecting the light that his senses are too weak to pick up, offering it to the trees. There are three nearer than the rest, their bark shimmering in the glint of rain and their branches, bare-boned but rich brown against the shadows between, and the shadows themselves: lingering, darker than black, stretching out the longer he stares at them. Beside him Jack is cloaked, his eyes a wide brown staring in awe from between neat holes. Art's mask looks more like he slashed it with a knife. It makes his eyes look jagged. Walt can see streaks of skin beyond them.

Nora is holding the dagger. She is presenting it. This is the moment.

Walt stares at the body, unconscious, drugged, but breathing – he can see the movement of every breath. He wants to reach out and touch, but he knows he mustn't. Only the dagger can call the blood; only the rope can gather the air. Nora loops it around, once, her fingers expertly tying the knot before the edges of the rope are passed to Jack on one side, to Art on the other.

Walt's own hands are shaking as Nora passes him the blade.

He has to force himself to breathe, to let the night into his body, to slow down – his pulse is beating too fast with the need in him to do this. It must be slower than this. It must be sacred. The markings on the dagger catch the light of the rain, the glint of the sky and reflect his own eyes back at him. The shadows beyond are getting closer, emerging from between the trees to bring the darkness of the otherworld into their circle. Nora begins the chant and Jack joins her, Art joins them, their voices guttural yet melodic, ancient, echoing around them, reflected and repeated by the shadows and the wisps of touch, of cold, and Walt can feel it now: the faintest scratch down the back of his neck, another on the back of his hand. They are not alone. Their circle of four becomes five, becomes eight, their voices blending together to chant of the threefold death and call the ancestors to return and protect the village once more and his hand reaches forwards, his fingers no longer his own as he presses the blade through skin, and their voices screech around him and their bodies distort as Jack and Art pull the rope and the rain bathes them clean.

REGRETTING TIME

'Oh, Walt,' Georgie says, her words coming slowly, sadly, her Deep South lilt stronger again, the way it gets when she's upset – she doesn't want to see him like this; wouldn't want anyone to end up like this. 'What have you been doing to yourself, Walt?'

He's sitting in his comfy chair and he's got his dressing gown wrapped tight around him; beneath that Georgie can make out the ends of his striped pyjama bottoms, his stockinged feet flat on the floor. She thinks, inappropriately, about bringing him in some slippers. The bandages that have been wrapped around his wrists disappear into his dressing-gown sleeves. He looks old, grey, hopeless.

'Walt,' she says, wishing she were here to comfort him, not question him.

His room is stifling in this heat, though he's got his arms wrapped around himself as though he's freezing and the window is locked shut. She remembers how warm he kept his house, all those cacti and succulents thriving.

'Do you miss your houseplants, Walt?'

'I don't understand.'

'I could bring you some in, maybe. Would you like that?'

He looks at her as though she's talking a different language and then looks over at the window.

'They cleared it all away,' he says. 'How am I supposed to help anyone now?'

'You don't have to help anyone, Walt. We're trying to help you. All the staff and me and your Trish.'

He looks up at her name, his eyes suddenly filling.

'Please don't tell my Trish.'

'I… She misses you, Walt. Wouldn't you like to see her?'

He picks at the edge of the bandage around his left wrist.

'But while I'm here, Walt, would it be okay if I asked you a few questions?'

'You understand, don't you, Georgie?'

'Not yet, Walt. You see, there's been an accusation.'

'But I was trying to help them.'

'Help who?'

'Rachel and the other one, the boy with her…'

'Pauly?'

'Yes, that's right. You remember too. Trish thought I'd gone walkabout, and I let her believe that. I always want to keep her safe, my Trisha.'

'You didn't go walkabout?'

'I went to help them cross over. I'm sensitive, Georgie, like you. I can summon… I wanted Rachel and her boy to be at peace. That's not a bad thing, is it?'

'What did you do, Walt?'

'I wouldn't have hurt anyone; I was offering myself. But they didn't want me.'

'Who?'

'The Others, Georgie. The Others.'

Georgie feels that pull, her gaze drawn over to the corner of her vision where she doesn't want to look – a pull that's getting all too familiar – and she braces herself, looks over to the window but there's no one there, no little child clawing uselessly at the air, no shadows reaching out with clawed fingers.

'Who *are* the Others, Walt?'

His eyes glisten with hope when she asks that, and she realises that she's never simply asked him before. Perhaps she's never wanted to know the answer.

'They're the spirits who protect the village, Georgie.'

He leans towards her and takes her hand and for an absurd moment she thinks he might be about to kiss her.

'They protect us from evil. Everyone who's sensitive can see them.'

The circle of them surrounding her, their bodies elongating unnaturally; every one of them faceless behind their long hoods.

'You're sensitive, aren't you, Georgie? With your heritage? Although…'

They're reaching out, clawing at her skin, at her hair. No. They're not protectors.

'What *are* they, Walt?'

'They're ancient,' he says, his arms now taking in the room and the village and the coast with a wide sweep. 'I believe they were once our ancestors.'

'And you think they'll come when you call?'

'We hope that they will. When we need help, or when the village needs help. Like Rachel and Pauly needed help.'

'So what did you do?'

'I offered myself at the cup and ring, in Mungrid Woods.'

'Just like earlier this year?' Georgie says.

That's what he'd done when Alexis was killed. Was he really just trying to help people by, what, sacrificing himself?

'But they didn't come for me,' he says.

'What makes you think they'd be on your side if they did?'

'I called them but they didn't come…' He's shaking his head, lost and old and hopeless again. 'They left me there alone.'

'It's me you need to call, Walt. For anything, anything at all. If you see something wrong or you're worried about anyone getting hurt, if you need help, you call *me*.'

'Okay, Georgie,' he says, his head nodding back and forth. 'Okay.'

'The thing is, Walt...' She clears her throat. 'There's been an... I'm afraid there's been an accusation. An accusation against you, Walt.'

He's almost wincing as she speaks.

'You've known Ricky Barr a long time, haven't you?'

'A long time,' he says. 'A long time, I'm afraid.'

'Well, Ricky's told us that there might have been a crime committed against his family, when he was just a little boy. Do you know anything about that, Walt?'

'Is Trish...?'

'She's not here, Walt. It's just me. You're going to have to talk to me.'

He's picking at the bandages, working a thread free near the tender pulse point on his wrist.

'Please, Walt,' Georgie says. 'Talk to me. Whatever it is you're keeping to yourself, it's festering. You'll feel better, to let it out. I promise you that.'

Walt looks at her with crystal eyes and cracked lips and says, 'I got blood on my hands, Georgie. It's not supposed to touch human skin, but it touched mine.'

That pulling again, but she won't look; she doesn't want it to be him. Walt is a kind man, and he's always been nice to her and Pamali. He welcomed her into the village when she first arrived. He loves plants and bees and collecting pebbles and she's turning her head against her own will and there, on the floor, a little child, mouth open, gasping for breath, fingers scratching desperately at the air, hair a tangled mess of blonde and blood from the cuts and she shakes the image away, blinks, looks at the carpet, at the window, at Walt Mackie. She doesn't trust her voice to make a sound at all; all she manages is a whisper.

'What did you do, Walt?'

He holds his hand up to his neck. 'We used the threefold death,' he says, eyes closed. Then open, staring at her. His hand still clasped

WHERE THE MISSING GATHER

around his throat. 'The knife is for blood, their breath is for air, the rain is for water.' He takes a deep breath himself. 'Do you have to tell Trish? She'll be so ashamed of me.'

'Who did you hurt, Walt?'

'I tried to keep Trish away from it all. She's a good girl, my Trisha, she'd never hurt anyone – you know that, don't you, Georgie?'

He blinks.

'But you're not from around here, are you.'

Georgie feels her shoulders stiffen.

'You have to tell me who you hurt, Walt.'

His eyes swim, searching the nothingness in front of him and she thinks she's got him. He's about to confess, a frail old man no longer strong enough to hold his secrets.

'Ricky called her Rosie,' he says, his shoulders slumping. 'She was just a pup.'

Georgie can hear a buzzing somewhere, in her hair, under her skin, but she squeezes her nails into her palms and the sound disappears.

'You're saying you killed his dog?'

'It was a sacrifice. Something had to be done...' His voice sounds distant now, like he's given up. 'That family, they were destroying everything. We'd tried...they were carving up the land and coming between the villagers and...we had to do something, didn't we? So we called on the Others for help. We sacrificed an innocent creature. We were trying to protect the village.'

'Who else was there?'

'Jack,' he says, eyes closing again. 'I heard Jack's dead now. Is he dead, Georgie?'

'He died four years back.'

'He was my friend. He loved the bees, like me.'

'Who else was there?'

'Art was there. Nora was there.'

Ricky had been telling the truth. Everything he'd told them, it was the truth. This would have been before Bobby or Dawn were born. Before Trish was born, or Elise. But Art Robertson was there, and Nora Prowle was there.

'They're both dead now, aren't they, Walt?'

He doesn't even seem to hear her, he's that far away.

'Did you know that, Walt? Art Robertson has passed away too.'

'You need a sacrifice that's pure,' he says. 'If you want them to help you.'

'Help you do what?'

'We were trying to protect the village.'

'But what did you want to happen?'

'That family don't belong here, Georgie. They don't – you know it too. Everything is broken now and there's hate everywhere and they…they attacked Pamali.'

'That wasn't Ricky Barr.'

'It was his boy, Andy. Why can't they leave us be?'

'So you thought they'd find their dog had been slaughtered' – Walt cowers at that word, at her tone – 'and just decide to sell up and move on somewhere else?'

'We thought the Others would help us.'

'You thought the Barrs would be haunted into leaving Burrowhead?'

'They have ways no one can understand.' He swallows then speaks more quietly. 'And then I wouldn't have had to see her every day.'

Georgie just stares at him.

'Isabella,' he says. 'My Isabella. But she chose him – she chose John Barr and I was too weak to survive it and I turned into someone else, someone capable of…cruelty.' That last word is whispered so quietly it barely passes his lips. 'So now you know why Trish would be ashamed of me, Georgie, why the blood fell onto my hands. It's never supposed to touch skin but it touched mine. I was thinking about me, not about the good of the village. It should never be personal, not like that.'

He's out of breath, like so much talking is too physical an effort, so much pressure built up over the years that now it's coming out it's leaving a space behind that he could fall into, like what supports him is suddenly flowing away.

'I tried to make up for it, Georgie,' he says, his eyes swimming and his body drooping forwards. 'I tried to help Rachel and Pauly. I tried to get them safe passage to the other side. I tried to stop the foot-and-mouth from spreading. When was that?'

'That was twenty years back, Walt.'

'We tried to stop it spreading through the village. How were we to know Bobby was watching? I was trying to help... I was trying to help people... Are you going to arrest me, Georgie?'

'No, Walt. I'm not going to arrest you for killing the dog. I'm going to ask Trish to come and visit you.'

Suddenly he straightens up again, shaking his head and clasping his wrists and it seems to Georgie like his strength is still there after all; the thing that supports him just needed to find a new footing.

'Now is there anything else you need to tell me, Walt? Anything at all? Anything about Jack or Art or Nora Prowle...*anything*?'

She holds his gaze and he stops breathing as though she were holding his throat with her bare hands.

'You have to keep her safe, Georgie.' He lunges forwards, clasps onto both her arms. 'I'm begging you. You have to look after my Trish.'

Georgie can't move; she's trapped here and she can't imagine ever getting away.

'Will you promise me, Georgie? Because I'm the only one left. I've failed all the others and now I'm the very last one and when I'm gone it's going to be up to you.'

HOW LOVE CAN BE LONELY

Georgie is standing outside Walt's care home and her phone is ringing and the screen tells her it's Fergus, her Fergus, and for a moment she can't even bring herself to answer. But she shakes it off, holds the phone to her ear, listens to his voice as he asks her to meet him for an early bite to eat. 'It's important, love,' he says. 'I need to see you,' he says. 'It's for us, for you and me. Please?' And so Georgie agrees, and half an hour later they are sitting together in the pub in Warphill. The Queen's Head.

It's got the smell of a pub that used to be thick with smoke, yellowing walls, ceiling tiles lumpy with faux plaster, carpet with a texture like damp moss. The air is heavy with lager, the lights dim, the windows misted – keep the sun out, keep the outsiders out, make sure there's no peeking in here; folk need their privacy. Is that what people come in here for, some privacy? The lad Ben who works the bar is slumped forwards over a paper – the *Mail*, some headline shouting about immigration – and he barely looks up when they walk in.

'I'll order,' Fergus says, in the forced cheerful voice he only uses when he's upset. 'What do you want, love?'

She tries to think what would be safest in here.

'Cheese and tomato pizza,' she decides.

'That's a good idea.' He keeps trying to smile. He looks a mess, here in the pub's lights; his skin seems heavier than usual, more lined, and there's mud under his fingernails and in the creases at his wrists. 'I think I'll have the same.'

Ben's not the owner, of course, just some kid in his twenties who needs the money. The pub is owned by Mrs Smyth, who inherited it from her late husband who inherited it from his father – or something like that. If someone other than a family member had got their hands on it they surely would have gutted the place and started again. Mind you, there'd be a cost involved in that. Fergus is asking Ben how he's doing, how his folks are keeping – Georgie has no idea who his folks are. How does Fergus know so much about him all of a sudden?

'He's a good lad,' Fergus says, sitting back down.

Georgie frowns at him.

'He works double shifts here and in Kaltonn to pay the rent. You know what the landlord's like. Is there something you could do to help the youngsters get on their feet?'

She feels exasperation sweep over her. Does he have no idea what her job is, what her remit is – must be – as a detective inspector?

'I just meant…'

'What, Fergus?'

'His landlord is Ricky Barr.'

Georgie rubs her fingers hard against her forehead. 'And what, you want me to arrest him unless he drops his rent for local kids under thirty, is that it?'

Fergus laughs, uncomfortably, like he can't think of how else to avoid a fight. Then her phone is vibrating in her pocket, and it's Cal, somehow she knows it's Cal before she's even opened the message: *Epithelial cells have been found on the rope.* The rope used to lead the horse. Her first case – her *current* case. They're checking the database for any DNA match. That's good. That's something solid. She thinks about Aaron and Lee, the way they look at her with that angry mix of threat and hate and suspicion, and she wonders if they come drinking in here.

'Is that about the case?' Fergus says, seeming to regret the question as soon as it's out of his mouth. 'I mean, obviously you can't… actually what I mean is that I was thinking maybe…'

'Get to the point, love.'

She smiles, to soften it.

'Right,' he says. 'You're right. What am I like, eh?'

It hits her in the chest, that sudden protectiveness, though what she could need to protect Fergus against she doesn't know.

'The thing is,' he says, 'earlier this year I was using my drone to take an aerial survey of the whole village and surroundings, do you remember?'

'Of course.'

She could almost reach out for his hand, but she doesn't.

'Well, I got some photographs of Ricky Barr's farm, and the field where…'

'Where we found the remains?'

Fergus nods, and she realises he couldn't even bring himself to say the body. She'll be patient though – she knows him well enough to know he's going somewhere with this, and her instinct is finally telling her to listen.

'Well, I brought one along, one of the photographs I mean. This one's the clearest of the field, and it looks like… I don't know what you'll think. You'll know if it's useful, not me, I know that.'

He holds it out to her, over the table, and she takes it from him, their fingertips meeting for a moment.

'There's something…see there?'

'The colour changes, and that dark band there—'

'Exactly! I mean, sorry to interrupt, but that's what I was thinking—'

'Fergus, this is actually helpful.'

She didn't mean to sound quite so surprised. He lets it go though, just gives her one of his big smiles, and she realises with a pang how much she's missed them.

'Can I take this?'

'Course, it's for you.'

'I'll get Trish on to it right away. We need to check the land boundaries, find out what this was in the field, a wall maybe, could be, some stones left under the ground or… Fergus, this is… Thank you. Really.'

'My pleasure, Georgie.'

She pulls out her phone and sends the text while he waits, while he seems to be just sitting there watching her.

'Any more tricks up your sleeve to help me with my job?'

'Well, there is…'

He pushes his hand through his hair, leaving a few specks of mud behind. She would never comment on it, of course, but he does smell like he could do with a shower.

'The other thing is the er, the archaeologists, they've…'

Georgie slips her phone back into her pocket and keeps her hands firmly on her side of the table.

'They've found the remains of an extended family under the motte. All ages, some very young.'

Suddenly Georgie is sitting up straight, leaning closer to him. His excavation couldn't turn out to be related to her case, could it? It couldn't actually be important?

'When were they buried there?'

'Oh, a long time ago, Georgie, a long time. They don't know for sure yet, but possibly early first century AD.'

Nothing to do with her then. She leans back. God but these seats are uncomfortable.

'It's fascinating, isn't it?' Fergus is saying. 'They weren't buried ceremonially, according to the professor anyway.' He swallows. 'She thinks it looks more like a mass grave. Like they were all just sort of…'

'Dumped there?' Georgie's not certain, but it looks like he cringes when she says that. 'Why would that have happened?'

Fergus straightens himself up, like she's given him the go-ahead.

'My theory is that they were trying to attack the village, maybe trying to steal some land or something, and the villagers fought back and won and then buried all their enemies.' He grins. 'That would have been good, wouldn't it?'

Georgie raises her eyebrows.

'But Professor McLeod says it could just as easily have been the other way around. That people attacked the village and won, then killed the existing residents, or some of them anyway, and dumped their bodies as a warning to the rest of the village. Then they could have taken over and—'

'Become the new villagers? The ancestors of today's villagers?'

'Well, it's possible. Maybe the bones will tell us more. There weren't any artefacts found, no weapons or anything.'

'Then what makes you think it was an attack? Could have been one group of villagers slaughtering another, couldn't it?'

'It seems unlikely—'

'Why's that then?'

A cough from closer than it should be. Georgie looks up. Ben, standing there with two plates, each with a greasy looking pizza on.

'Cutlery's over there.' He swings his head sideways to show a wicker tray on the side of the bar with knives and forks wrapped in blood-red paper napkins.

'Thanks,' Fergus is saying. 'Thanks very much. This smells good.'

Georgie looks down at her plate of food and can't even imagine eating it.

Her husband is tucking right in though. There's nothing self-conscious about him, it's almost endearing. She used to find it endearing. She wonders if he's been eating at all – the kitchen sink has been full of dirty dishes all week, but now she thinks about it they've all been hers. He pauses mid-chew, sits back to look at her as though he could read her mind. Suddenly he looks serious, almost sad.

'How's work going, really?' he asks her.

She's not sure where it comes from but she could almost cry.

'It's awful, thinking about what might have…' he begins.

She can see it on his face again, how hard he finds it to even say out loud.

'...what might have happened to that poor wee bairn in Ricky's field.'

'It is,' Georgie says. 'It is.'

His expression is the same one he gets when she talks about Errol, when he gives her the space she needs to remember him, the softness she needs to be able to speak. There's no one else she's ever been able to talk to about what happened – no one but Fergus. And he never even asked her. She just knew he would listen without judging.

'Do you know who they were yet?' He reaches towards her across the table but stops short of touching her arm. 'Forty years has to be easier to navigate than two thousand, right?'

'You'd think.'

He has such kind eyes, her Fergus. She's ashamed of herself now, for being so frustrated with him all the time, for being less kind than he is.

'I...' She glances over to the bar, where Ben's head is down low staring at his tabloid. 'I think they might have been a...well, an innocent kid who had nothing to do with the Barr family at all. Just a little kid who had no one looking out for them, no one to report that they were missing, no one to miss them once they were gone.'

'You mean they weren't from around here?'

Neither of them talk for a minute. Georgie can feel something in the shadows, sense it beyond the edge of her vision. She wills it to go away, but as the time creeps on it only gets stronger.

'Professor McLeod says that in some cultures they sacrificed the innocent,' Fergus says. 'If they needed to ask the gods for something, they'd sacrifice an innocent creature, or even...'

Like Walt, like that poor dog, like the horse.

'...Or even a child,' he says.

It's happening again. They're gathering. Her skin is starting to sting with scratches, she can hear that rasping noise over her shoulder.

You're sensitive, aren't you, Georgie?
With your heritage?
Nails scraping against her neck, making her whole body tense.
'Do you not want your—'
Georgie pushes her plate away.
'You eat it, if you want to.'
Fergus looks down at the food but doesn't move to take it. Her tone has sliced the air between them and left behind a separation sharp as glass.
'The thing is…' Fergus is speaking, his voice distant somehow. 'The other reason I wanted to, to talk is that…'
Clawing at her neck, whispers like stifled screams.
'I… I think you're angry with me, Georgie.'
What did they do to that poor child?
'I think you've been angry with me for months now and I don't understand why.'
'I know, Fergus,' she says, pressing her hands against her eyes, rubbing her temples. 'I…' She shakes her head but something's clinging to her hair, refusing to let her go. 'I visited Walt earlier. He was talking about sacrifice too, in between reminding me that *I'm* not from around here.'
Fergus actually smiles at that, and suddenly the shadows are gone.
'I didn't find it funny, Fergus.'
'I…'
She glares over her shoulder – there's nothing there, no creatures, no Others, no local kids staring at her as though waiting for an opportunity to slash her throat.
'Do you not understand what I'm saying, Fergus?'
'I'm not… Look, I know people here sometimes say things they shouldn't, the older generation especially and…and people like June and Whelan and even Walt. People who are supposed to be our friends. I get it. They make stupid remarks and it sounds racist, I

know they can sound racist sometimes, but they'd never hurt anyone, not really. You know Walt. It's like Trish says—'

Trish again. Georgie's neck tightens.

'—these villages just need a bit of help, not judgement,' he says.

At least Trish hadn't known about Uncle Walt killing Ricky's dog. Not before this week at any rate, Georgie is fairly sure of that. She hadn't known about the sacrifices, Walt had kept her away from it all. So what is it she suspects Trish of? Of being racist herself? Of forgiving the villagers their racism? Of being somehow on the wrong side? It's a hazy suspicion; it slips through her fingers, flickers through compassion. Just like her thoughts about Fergus, too, her Fergus. Is she wrong?

Then she hears Walt's phrase again: *we take care of our own.*

'Words matter, Fergus.'

'I know that. I'm just saying that there are levels, aren't there? There are different stages of things. These villagers, most of them anyway, they're not real racists.'

'Yes they are.'

'Not Walt and Natalie, not—'

'Yes they are. And their words have consequences. You think Andy and Lee would be attacking people because of the colour of their skin if they hadn't seen it normalised every day?'

'But they don't mean any—'

'Trish is forever letting them off the hook. It's white privilege, that's what it is.' Georgie wishes she could close her eyes to it all, will herself somewhere else, but instead she says what he needs to understand. 'And you're as bad.'

'What?'

'You don't call them out, do you? You let them say what they like, the us-and-them implied in the way everyone talks – you let it go. You excuse them.'

'I don't have a racist bone in my body, Georgie.'

'But you enable them. You forgive them. That makes you complicit.'

He looks like he can't even imagine how to reply. She can see the shock, the pain, on his face. His big open face.

In some cultures they sacrificed the innocent.

What did Walt do?

What did Walt Mackie really do?

'I have to get back to the office,' she says, standing up, his photograph in her hand. 'Look, thanks for this. But I need to go.'

And she leaves him there. To her shame, she just leaves him sitting there looking as though she has just kicked the life out of him, and she gets in her car alone and starts the drive back to Burrowhead.

SURFACING CONNECTIONS,
PART ONE

Trish has pulled together all her research and now she's going to make her case: to Simon first, and then to Georgie. To start, she's got the Barr family tree dating back to the arrival of Herman Barr in the 1950s all the way down to Andy, his brute of a father and his dead mother Genevieve. Andy might have turned into a different kid if he hadn't lost his mam when he was twelve – not far off the age Trish was, either, so she knows what she's talking about. Amanda, her mam's name was, though it's rarely spoken in Burrowhead these days; Trish isn't one to talk about her and Uncle Walt isn't either, and none of the other villagers ever knew what to say in the first place. She had Uncle Walt though. Thank God for Uncle Walt. Young Andy's got no one to turn to, not really.

She's been spending a lot of time with him this year, trying to show him how he doesn't have to end up like his da; how we make choices in life above and beyond whatever DNA we might have inherited. His mam died of leukaemia in her mid-thirties. She'd never had much to do with the villagers, of course. Everyone always thought she felt herself too good to be mixing with the rest of them, though why she married Ricky in the first place no one could tell. She'd come up from London, sounded like she'd been to finishing school for fuck's sake, and before she got sick you'd see her walking the cliffs in those beautiful dresses like something out of a catalogue photo shoot, always on her own, while Ricky worked the farm, covered in muck with manure-caked boots.

Andy used to cling to her skirts. She dressed him in cute little outfits, denim shorts and a striped T-shirt with braces, maybe, or dungarees with some kind of hand-stitched animal faces on them; sent him off to school in the smartest version of their uniform Warphill Primary had ever seen. While the other kids were fighting and getting filthy, Andy Barr was ironed and polite. Until she got ill and died, that is, and Andy grew into Andy Barr, his da dragging him out to work in the fields, all weathers, even though his mam had only just passed and he was still a kid by any decent standard. It was like the only way Ricky knew how to keep in control, of himself and of his son, was with the biting cold of manual labour and a brutal punch, or the threat of one at least.

So that's the base of the trunk of the family tree: Andy Barr on his own there. Above him Ricky Barr, and Genevieve, deceased. No suspicious circumstances.

'This is impressive, Trish,' Si says, beside her.

'Tell me about it. I've been going through all the old files as well, anything relating to the Barrs – gave myself a bloody paper cut.'

She holds her finger out and Si smiles. 'You'll live.'

'Aye, well. Here, Ricky's parents,' she says. 'John Barr and wife Isabella Barr, née Dover. On her side, she'd been a cousin of Mrs Dover's late husband.'

'Christ, this place. I wouldn't want you looking into my family tree, who knows what names would turn up.'

'The curse of the villages.'

'One of many.'

She snorts. 'I know, right? Go back far enough and I bet every one of us is related. Except for Georgie and Fergus, of course. And Pamali.'

'You're forgetting the Barr family,' he says.

'As if I could. Here, beside Ricky, is Deborah-Jane Barr. Her whereabouts, of course, are unknown.'

'The missing sister,' he says.

They both lapse into silence and stare at the family tree.

Above John Barr sits old Herman Barr. Date of birth: unknown. Location of birth: Germany. Question mark. Wife – and presumably there was one once, since there was a son – name unknown. It's a funny-looking family tree. Starting with just the one man at the top, bulging in the middle and then shrinking in again to the single boy at the bottom. One more chop of the axe and the whole thing would fall.

'So you've found no sign of any other children missing?' Si asks.

'None from the Barr family. Which is why…' She turns to her desk and lifts up a large photocopied map of the area. 'Land boundaries in 1980. Georgie's idea.'

'But the Barrs have owned that farm since Herman arrived in, what, the 1950s?'

'In '52, to be precise. Not all of it, though. Look.'

'Is that the field where our skeleton was found?'

'Yes it is, and you'll notice that the boundary runs right through it.'

'The body wasn't buried on Ricky's land at all?'

'Oh no, it was – but only just. It was buried, so far as I can tell, right on the edge of the Barrs' farm. Like…'

Trish shakes her head, sucking her finger with the paper cut – there's still a bit of blood flowing from it.

'Like it was buried by someone who didn't belong there?'

'And I've been thinking, if it *was* one of the Barr family who buried it, they'd not have done so in their own field, one that's actually used for farming, would they? The chances of it being dug up must have been pretty high.'

'It's quite something it stayed buried this long.'

'Exactly. Whereas, if you wanted to frame someone…' Trish raises her eyebrows. 'Look. Bordering the Barr farm in the 1950s, see here?

That strip of land was owned by one Art Robertson. From the edge of the field where we found the child's remains, all the way up to the edge of the village.'

'In fact,' Simon says, 'all the way here. Right here. To the police station.'

NEW ROOTS

Andy Barr has a bag with all his tools slung over his back and he's sneaked out of the farm so his da doesn't see him, nor any of the others. He's keeping his distance from Lee and Aaron these days – his da's not taught him much but he knows he doesn't want the jitters the way those two have. Making your own choices, that's the thing, that's what Andy is all about these days, just like Trish has been telling him. Andy likes Trish. Andy likes having a bag of tools on his back, and a place to take them and all.

Cutting through the edge of the village, glancing at the police station but sticking to the back lanes, then out to the overgrown field that no one uses and no one even looks at. It's their secret, this field. For now. Andy Barr and Pamali Patel. He heads in through the boundary of tall willowherb and takes a spot beside her.

'Evening, Andy.'

'I've got all the tools,' he says with a grin. 'I've got trowels and forks and secateurs and a scythe.'

Pamali laughs that joyful laugh of hers and obviously Andy would never say this because it would just sound weird but he's started to think that maybe Pami is a little bit like his mam, from what he remembers of her, because she loved gardening too and she had a good laugh, especially when it was just the two of them, sitting out on the grass somewhere in the summer. She forgave him too, when he fucked up.

'I'm no sure we'll need the scythe, Andy,' Pami says.

'Better safe than sorry though, eh?'

'For now,' she says, 'I was thinking we could sow cauliflower in here and then salad leaves over there, lettuce and rocket and Swiss chard, what do you think?'

Andy nods and he thinks that's a very good idea actually, that way when they're ready to open, folk can come and collect a few salad leaves, for their sandwiches or whatever, he can see that. He's never heard of Swiss chard though.

'And I have some good news,' Pamali says. 'We've got another volunteer coming to join us.'

Suddenly Andy is leaning back on his heels and he's not sure about this.

'You know Natalie Prowle?'

'No, no, Pami…'

'She's keen to come and help.'

'She's Lee's mam.'

'I know that, Andy—'

'Lee's not a good guy—'

'Are the two of you not friends any more?'

'That's not what I mean…'

'Well, I think maybe we can give Natalie a chance,' Pamali says, and he knows what she's referring to. 'Everyone deserves that, wouldn't you say?'

He looks down at the vegetable patch they've made, the two of them, working here together this week: cardboard down over the grass, compost on top, a layer of manure, then the rows of seeds they've sown together and when he looks up Natalie Prowle is walking towards them already.

'You don't mind me joining you,' she says to Andy, and it's not a question so he doesn't bother replying. 'Thought you could do with one of the local villagers helping out too, give the community food garden a bit of credibility, eh.'

'I *am* one of the local villagers,' says Pamali, and Andy can't help but smile because he's never heard Pami sound strict before but she's sure standing up to Natalie Prowle and Andy likes that very much.

'Of course you are,' Natalie is saying, 'Of course, Pami, I didn't mean—'

'And so is Andy.'

Andy looks at her, willing her to deny it.

'I just meant I'm one of the original...one of the...'

Andy is scowling at her now and he's not sorry for it and Natalie is looking back at him and he didn't want her here, true enough, but not as much as it looks like she doesn't want him here. He pulls out his tools and tells her that he and Pamali are planting the cauliflower here and that the patch over there is going to be for the salad leaves and the Swiss card.

'Chard,' Natalie says.

'That's what I said.'

Natalie puts her hand on his arm and he shakes it off.

'How is your da, Andy?'

Andy just shrugs.

'You know, if you ever need to talk...'

Natalie Prowle has been after his da for as long as Andy's known his family weren't welcome round here, and that's about as long as he's known anything. Natalie is standing up now though and that's fine with him. She's over talking to Pamali and telling her that she's got cabbages and kale and, if it's alright with Pamali – another one of those questions that's not really a question – she's going to plant them in beside the salad.

Andy doesn't like that idea. He does not like that at all.

But it's okay, because now Pami is telling her to start a fresh bed of her own over there because she's not wanting the bigger plants to take over the salad leaves.

'They could smother them,' Pamali is saying, 'if we're no careful,' and all Natalie can do to that is nod.

So she'll head over to the side and clear herself a fresh patch then, so she's saying, though before she goes she whispers to Pamali that she needs to watch her back, and Andy knows full well she's talking about him. It's no bad advice though because now he thinks about it, Andy reckons they could all do with watching their backs when Natalie Prowle is around.

SURFACING CONNECTIONS, PART TWO

'Now here's a thing,' Simon says. 'Nora Prowle.'

Finally they're getting somewhere. Names and family trees and case files and land surveys are all laid out in their office – and Simon's got what he knows, too, held close. There are boxes everywhere, labelled in faded handwriting and filled with all the petty crimes of the villagers from the past fifty years. He closes the file he's holding over with a slight frown, rubs the outside of the flimsy beige cardboard folder with his thumb.

Trish is watching him intently. 'She died in the 1990s, right?'

The old police files smell dusty and damp and they're making Simon's throat itch.

'Aye, '96. Her husband was the village police officer from '63 till his death in '92. They lived right here, in the station.'

Simon remembers the smell in that cell at the back, the one Georgie always thought was rotten. The one that reminded him of the stale sea air.

'After he died the place was empty for a while—'

'I remember that from when I was a kid,' Trish says.

'I wasn't even born yet.'

'You youngster.' Trish shakes her head, smiling.

'Aye, but from what I've read, they made a right mess of converting it—'

'Folk were not best pleased. Especially when they reinstated it as a police station.'

'According to these records,' says Si, 'there were three different officers stationed here, each of them leaving within a year of arriving, before Georgie made a go of it.'

'She's got some staying power,' Trish says, the admiration only slightly grudging. 'But where are you going with this?'

'Well, while Nora's husband – Jacob Prowle – was the village police officer, and even after his death, Nora Prowle was taking care of foster children. Remember that?'

'Vaguely…I was a kid myself at the time. There were never that many children staying with her, but there was always at least one passing through, appearing at the school then disappearing again, staying with her for a few months until they went back to their parents or were adopted or whatever – sent back to the care home they came from.'

'And Natalie is her niece, right?'

'She's proud of it, too. Told me once her aunt Nora could have got any kid back on track.'

'Probably wishes she were still around to help her with Aaron and Lee.'

'Maybe so. We kids were all scared of Nora Prowle, that's for sure.'

'You, scared of someone?'

'When I was four, maybe. Not since, mind.'

Simon laughs. 'Well, the Prowles never had kids of their own,' he says. 'And their closest relative was Jacob Prowle's brother—'

'Aye, his half-brother, I remember him a bit too. He married Sally, who was way younger than him by the way, and they became Natalie's parents.'

'Know what happened to them?'

'He died years ago, and apparently her mam is living in a camper van in Spain.'

'Alright for some.'

But at the mention of Spain Simon's mind clasps on to his version of the Mediterranean, turquoise sea and warmth and the life he could have had with Alexis—

'You've had an idea, haven't you?'

He swallows, forces his mind back to today.

'Thanks to you,' he says, pointing to the boundary as it was in 1980. 'This is the bit of land owned by Arthur Robertson when the little boy was buried, and it includes the field and the lane, here, that ran between the police station – the Prowles' family home as was – and the Barrs' farm. And then we have this.'

He opens the old file again, held together by a paper clip in the corner.

'We couldn't find any missing child reports, but I've got a closed case here. A little boy drowned on the beach in 1979 when he was nineteen months old. His name was Sonny Riley. His guardian is down as Nora Prowle. No named parents.'

'One of her foster children died in her care?'

The front door of the station slams and it makes him jump.

'Was presumed dead,' he says. 'They never found the body. Nora's testimony said he'd disappeared while playing on the beach. Her husband was the investigating officer who closed the case.'

'They can't have got away with crap like that, not even in the Seventies.'

'Out here, in the 1970s? A boy with no family, no one to ask any questions?'

'But someone would have noticed, surely, known who he was or…'

As Georgie arrives in their office, Trish's voice trails off. In fact, they all three stand looking at each other in silence for a moment. Georgie's face is closed and something in her stance makes Simon feel almost afraid.

'You first,' she says. 'Simon, what do you have?'

'It was Trish's idea…' he begins, wanting to give her credit, especially as Georgie hasn't so much as looked at her since she got back, and he fills her in.

'It says he was drowned,' Trish says, quietly.

Georgie's eyes snap from Simon to Trish.

'In Nora Prowle's care, and with her husband the only police officer, who knows what strings might have been pulled,' she says. 'You trust everything written in ink?'

Trish purses her lips.

'But it'll be hard to prove anything,' Simon says. That is, without the evidence Alexis sent him, each tape not enough on its own but all together, building up a picture. *Don't trust the police.*

'But what is he doing buried on the edge of the Barrs' field?' Georgie says. 'Who buried him there?'

'And who was he really?' Simon says, quietly.

'It could be innocent,' Trish starts.

'Or it could not,' Georgie snaps. 'Now here's what *I* know. Art Robertson, Nora Prowle, Jack Helmsteading and Walt Mackie—'

Trish winces, but Georgie doesn't pause.

'—killed Ricky's dog when he was just a little boy. They were performing sacrifices to "protect the village", which, as far as I can tell, is a combination of controlling the villagers and keeping outsiders away by means of fear and violence.'

'No, Uncle Walt—'

'Stop it, Trish. He was the one who told me.'

Trish looks like she could cry.

'This is good work from you two,' Georgie says, her voice softening. 'But…I think they murdered that little boy, just like they murdered Ricky's dog. And Walt Mackie is in the middle of it all—'

'He would never—'

'Trish, I'm sorry, but I'm putting you on leave while we tie up this case.'

'*What?* Why?'

'Ricky's testimony,' Georgie says. 'Art Robertson. Nora Prowle. Jack Helmsteading. Walt's name belongs with theirs, and you know it as well as I do.'

'Uncle Walt would never…he was trying to help. Look, I know he's confused—'

'I'm not sure he's confused at all,' Georgie says. 'And he's right in the middle of this, whether you like it or not.'

Simon shifts uncomfortably. Trish has been so good to him, the past few months. She's kind, Trish, when she's not being so prickly. In a way, it would be easier to tell her the truth than Georgie, even though he knows he can't.

'Simon, I want you on research,' Georgie says, still staring at Trish. 'We've got a name now, thanks to you both. Sonny Riley. Find everything. Parents if possible, social care records, medical records.'

'I'm on it,' he says. 'And I'll check in with Cal, we're still waiting on the DNA analysis from the cells on that rope…'

'You heard me, Trish,' Georgie says. 'You're on leave.'

Trish is standing in the middle of the room, feet planted, mouth open. Simon wonders if she's actually going to refuse.

'Just go, Trish,' Georgie says, quieter but firmly. 'Now.'

Trish stumbles to the hall and Georgie pushes the door behind her and sits down as though she has nothing left and suddenly Simon sees her as hurt and scared and alone.

'Do you want me to…I don't know, arrest Walt Mackie?'

She shakes her head. 'We'll need more, Si. We need to know who Sonny was, why they would sacrifice him in particular; we need physical evidence. There must be something. Knife marks on the skeleton, something small that might have been missed. Get onto Cal. Walt is the last one alive and if we're going to convict—'

'You don't really believe—'

'You know as well as anyone what the villagers are capable of.'

Simon knows more than she thinks, too. A sacrifice would fit. A human sacrifice.

He's been keeping it secret so long he doesn't know how to start talking. But sooner or later, he's going to have to trust her.

HOW LOVE CAN BE MISSED

Trish's mam is telling her she can have a sleepover. With Uncle Walt.

She's hardly ever allowed to have sleepovers, hardly ever allowed to spend all the time she wants with Uncle Walt, but Trish doesn't need to be told twice.

She's grabbing her bag and pyjamas and her big waterproof and telling her mam she'll walk over despite the storm – a bit of rain never stopped Trish and she's tired of the heaviness of the flat, the way the walls press in and her mam's gaze stares out through the window and the heating pulses and nothing changes – and soon as she's downstairs and outside she's running, racing towards Burrowhead and Uncle Walt's house.

It isn't even dark yet. They'll be able to spend some time with the bees and then they'll make homemade pizza with that bread Uncle Walt always has ready and Trish will be allowed to sprinkle on whatever she wants, cheese and sausages and frozen peas and chocolate digestives and a whole tin of sweetcorn and one time roast potatoes, left over from the night before. But first: they'll go and see the bees.

Trish has grown into the next size up of beekeeper suit, a white one like the adult suits, only a little bit smaller, and she knows exactly what she's doing, though she still lets Uncle Walt take the lead, because they're his bees after all and she can see how much he enjoys teaching her. They buzz around her head and settle on her arms and hands and they know her, just like they know Uncle Walt. He'd been right all along – they never did hurt her, they never have, not once, Trish has never had a bee sting in her life.

The bees and the pizza, the sleepover, the storm; all she's thinking about is the excitement of it and the crackle of thunder and lightning that night, sleeping in Uncle Walt's spare room that's her bedroom, all painted with bees on the walls, her camping sleeping bag on the bed instead of sheets and duvet because when the weather is too cold for camping outside, they camp inside instead. Her and Uncle Walt. Her mam's always trying to stop her going camping too, says it's dangerous, like the bees, like she doesn't trust Uncle Walt or something, but Trish is too strong for her – Trish is old enough to do what she wants and Uncle Walt never tries to stop her.

Then the morning: rain against the window, the phone ringing, Uncle Walt's voice, the way he looks in on her and tells her to stay cosy, he has to go out – he'll be back soon. He gives her a hot chocolate in bed.

He always likes to treat her, Uncle Walt, and she loves hot chocolate.

She sips it at first, savouring it, trying to make it last until he gets home again.

Rain pelting at the windows and she doesn't know where he could have gone in this weather but still, he loves the rain, just like she does.

Hot chocolate finished, cup drained clean, and Trish thinks maybe she'll go and find him. She's up and dressed and ready for a day of exploring the woods in the rain, when the door opens and Uncle Walt comes home.

'Sit down,' he says. 'Sit down, my Trisha.'

There's something in his voice. So many things, like stone and sand and the soft brush of feathers against her face and she starts to know something is wrong.

When she doesn't sit down he pulls her into a hug instead.

From somewhere he says the words: *There's been an accident.*

From somewhere she hears *An accident at sea, your mam, your dear mam, we don't know why*—

It's hazy, like the world through the mist of horizontal rain that's so sharp in her eyes she has to squint till there's almost nothing left until she starts to understand that her mam is gone, that her mam sent her away to Uncle Walt's house for a reason, that when she'd called out goodbye and tried to hug her as she ran for the door, bag in hand, coat half on, Trish should have, she should have at least turned, she should have—

There are people outside of the window, out on the street, the village is here, the villagers are all here, looking in and looking so sorry for her and she looks at Uncle Walt and from somewhere he's saying that there was a search, that the boat is missing, that they found some smashed wood, the beach, the storm, and through it all Trish is thinking that she never felt she needed a da before but that if her mam has left and run away to sea then she's not going to have anyone to look after her. She might be nearly in the adult-size beekeeper suits now but she's not sure she knows how to live all on her own just yet and she never knows what setting she's supposed to put the washing machine on, she always has to ask her mam even though her mam replies without getting up from the sofa and she always said she was looking out at the sea, even though Trish could only see the sky when she lay on the sofa the way her mam liked to. Maybe that's why she's gone to sea now, because she must have loved it very much to spend all her time looking out at it like that and from somewhere, from a long way away, Uncle Walt is talking to her, he's hugging her and stepping back and looking at her face and hugging her again and saying *My Trisha*, he's saying *Oh Trish* and he looks into her eyes and holds her arms and says: 'I am here for you, Trish. I promise you that. I will spend the rest of my life being here for you.'

SURFACING CONNECTIONS, PART THREE

Trish is stumbling out of the station and she's wondering if she's just been fired and actually it doesn't even seem to matter, she's not wanted in the station any more than she's wanted in that care home. Uncle Walt, what have you done, what have you got yourself involved with? Elise Robertson making accusations, Suze whispering in the pub, close and low, so close there's no need to make any threats; they know Trish could never do anything to hurt Uncle Walt, they know he's all she's got left and so they know she'll have to keep their secrets, what they're saying, what they know…and he's trying to protect her from whatever is going on.

Sun stinging her eyes, the last and sharpest rays, and her head is throbbing so badly it feels like it's being sliced into. This fucking heat – she'd thought it would be cooler out here than in the station but it's even worse and she's running but she doesn't know why or where until she's at his house: Uncle Walt's house. It's all locked up. She left her key at her place because why would she need to get in today, when he was safe in the care home, and her house is twenty minutes in the other direction and so she hammers on the door, bashing it with her fists, kicking at it with a sudden anger that she can hardly explain.

'My God, Trish, what—?'

Please no. There are tears in her eyes and please God, no.

It's him though, of course it bloody is: DS Frazer in his designer bloody suit with his posh accent and his big brown eyes—

'Nothing happened, I'm fine.'

'My God, Trish, are you… You're kicking a door.'

His hands are on her arms and he's trying to pull her away.

'I'm *fine*.'

'You reckon?'

His face is close to hers, all concern and kindness and—

'Would you please stop helping.'

'Were you trying to break in?'

'Of course not. No one breaks into homes round here.'

'Right, they just kill each other and scrawl racist graffiti every-where.'

'Now you're getting it.'

For a minute they stand awkwardly side by side, not quite sure what to say next. Trish forces herself to stay still even though she suddenly wants to get away from Uncle Walt's house. Whatever it is in there that she thought she might find, she doesn't want to know what it is now. Frazer's watching her. Christ he looks like he wants to give her a hug. Actually no, that would involve touching her and he's far too standoffish for something like that; instead he just gives her a formal nod. There's a slight sheen of sweat against his black skin and fuck, is it racist of her to be attracted to his skin? It is beautiful though. She wonders if that wife of his is a black woman, or if she's white, white as Trish, pale and freckled and prone to embarrassing flushes around the jaw and seemingly immediate sunburn. He turns away and she suddenly finds him so irritating she could scream. Here it comes. I need to get going. You should go home yourself, Trish, stop acting crazy.

'Do you…do you need a drink?'

'Yes, I fucking do.'

And that's how they find themselves in the downstairs lounge of Frazer's B & B on the edge of the village, floral wallpaper and antlers above the door, each with a glass of the complimentary port for guests only.

'Not much choice round here for a drink then,' he says.

Trish snorts into her glass.

'Pub in Warphill is the closest, but I'd no recommend it.'

'What did you do, growing up here?'

'Pub in Warphill.'

He laughs. 'Of course.'

'Mostly we'd get carry-out though. Cans, vodka, whatever we could get our hands on. Used to drink out by the community shed. Up on the cliffs. In the graveyard.'

'Classy.'

She smiles, but she doesn't like that word. So what if she's no got class – that just means she's not got money, right, never had any growing up, and that's true enough and not something she's ashamed of either.

'We made do,' she says, not meaning to sound so defensive as she does. 'I know it's a different kind of life—'

'No one's is perfect,' he says. 'It was no...well, no fun growing up in the city either.'

She doesn't want to go there – comparing childhood memories is not what Trish does – so she takes a large gulp of her port instead and fills up her glass again. Their conversation seems doomed to be full of fast bursts and uncomfortable silences. She doesn't know why she's so crap with people, but he is too, right, he's totally crap with people. She looks down at the full glass she's cradling in both hands.

'I'll buy them a bottle to replace that one tomorrow,' she says, thinking she can see a hint of judgement in the way he's looking at her.

He grins. 'I was just admiring your style is all.'

'It's medicinal.'

'Yes it is,' he says, finishing his own and refilling his glass.

It does seem to Trish like there's a lot going on under the surface, with DS Frazer. He's matching her drink for drink, at least, and he's not got quite such a stick up his arse, away from the station, away from Georgie. Maybe it's some kind of defence mechanism, the formality he falls back on all the time. Like he's scared no one is going to take him seriously. She takes him seriously, though.

'What's happened, Trish?'

'What do you mean?'

'I mean…why were you kicking your Uncle Walt's door?'

Well, maybe he's the one doesn't take her seriously. He's not laughing at her, though, he's got that genuine look on his face again, like he actually wants to talk to her. Like he's here because he wants to be. Fuck it.

'Georgie's taken me off the case.'

'What?'

'Potential personal involvement.'

He looks down at his hands, back up into her eyes.

'Because of your Uncle Walt?'

He speaks softly when he says that, and it makes something in Trish ache.

'Ricky Barr has been accusing him of God knows what…'

Silence. Silence while she waits for him to say that's ridiculous, that's unfair, it'll blow over, no one could ever suspect your Uncle Walt.

'I might need to talk to him too,' is what he says, eventually. 'I mean, I have to talk to everyone, so…'

Fine. Trish downs her drink. Skirting the subject it is. She grinds her teeth for a second while he watches her with those big damn eyes—

'I'm sorry, Trish. I'm sure it'll be nothing. I mean it might be nothing. Maybe you'll be back on the case soon or… I mean, I don't know, obviously, I'm just trying to be honest with you…'

She holds up her hand. 'Enough. Stop digging. Jesus.'

He laughs, the relief warming his face, inviting her to smile back.

'Remind me never to ask you for a reference.'

'I'd give you a good one.'

Trish's leg is touching his leg and she didn't mean to do that, it wasn't on purpose or anything but it's happened and he's not pulling away or anything and she's not moving away either, neither of them are moving away.

'How are, um...' She sips her drink. 'How are your interviews going?'

He looks surprised at the question for a second, like he'd forgotten why he was in Burrowhead at all, until he clears his throat. Does his formal summary thing again.

'Well, the housekeeper from the manor hotel – Mrs Pettigrew – is dead.'

'Right.'

He takes another sip, slower this time. Her leg, still touching his leg.

'There seem to be no records – literally *no records* – of the summer staff who worked at that hotel through the 1960s.'

His eyes, looking right into hers.

'And as for my interviewing the villagers? Well, no one knows anything about anything,' he says. A pause. 'Except that I suspect every one of them is lying.'

Is he about to trust her with something?

'Folk round here don't open up to the police.'

'Do they open up to you?'

'Especially not to me. I'm the traitor, see.'

'How so?'

'Born and bred, generations before me all local, Uncle Walt... Uncle Walt used to run the community council. Used to run the village, some people say.'

'Sounds ominous.'

'So for me to have joined the police, the establishment, taking orders from the city...'

'Why did you?'

'Same reason as everyone, I guess. I wanted to make a difference.'

'That's not why everyone joins the force.'

How is he doing that, making this sound intimate when all they're doing is talking about the job? Maybe it's the lighting in here, the way the overhead lights are off and there's only the lamps, the small puddles of light on the side tables, the warmth of it, the quiet glowing of the room.

'Then why did you?'

He smiles. 'I wanted to make a difference.'

'See.'

'And I needed the money.'

'Aye well.'

'And I was fed up of feeling powerless. That's part of it, isn't it? If we're being honest. Wanting to be in control rather than be under control.'

'I feel under control every bloody day.'

'You're angry about something.'

Getting personal again. She doesn't mind so much though, this time.

'About what though?' she says.

'I don't know.'

She's laughing despite herself. 'Neither the fuck do I.'

Her thigh leaning against his thigh on the floral sofa with too many cushions in the lounge room of his B & B and men don't do that unless they know they're doing it, right? She is so fucking crap at this stuff and he—

'Trish?'

'What?'

'Have you heard of Abigail Moss?'

'Well you've been talking about her a fair bit. Have you heard of Deborah-Jane Barr?'

'I'm serious. Before this week, that name ring any bells?'

His arm, against her arm now. She swallows, suddenly feels her pulse beating faster than it should, his arm... It's a small sofa though, the kind of sofa you'd see in a granny's house, barely a two-seater really so maybe he just...

'Abigail Moss?'

'I don't...' She is trying to remember, though. 'It's weird, it's like the name is familiar but not a face or a family or anything I can put my finger on. Do you know what I mean?'

They seem to be sitting closer together, leaning closer – is she imaging this?

'Thank you,' he says.

'I've not helped.'

'But it's more than anyone else has told me.'

'Could be that I've been thinking about the name, though. Hearing you say it—'

'In fact, this is more than anyone has spoken to me since I got here.'

She's getting a bit light-headed now. Why the bloody hell does that keep happening?

'It's not easy is it, this place?'

God but his eyes are so big, big and gentle and sad – though what DS Frazer has got to be sad about she has no idea.

'I should get going.'

'Stay for another?'

'Why, are you lonely?'

There's a fraction of a pause before he says it.

'Yes.'

It takes the air out of her lungs, that does. She can't get her voice to work. She can hear her own breathing, and his too, beside her.

'Look, I...' He reaches for her hand, stops, leans away from her, laughs awkwardly. 'There's no need to look so horrified.'

'What about your wife?'

There's that sadness again.

'She's... I'm not... Sorry, I thought Simon must have told you, she...'

'She left you?'

No reply.

'Or what, she's dead?'

Shit.

Oh shit, how had she not worked that out? My God she is such a fucking idiot and the poor man all this time and what a way to put her bloody foot in—

'Subtle,' he says. 'I like that about you.'

Fuck, he's going to hate her. He's going to… He's…wait, is he smiling?

It's okay. Is it okay?

Should she say sorry? She should probably have said sorry but it feels like it's too late now and she's just kind of staring at him and he's staring back and…

Maybe it's okay. Maybe it's all going to be okay and his leg, his leg is still there against hers and maybe…maybe she's not such a complete idiot. Things have gone a bit hazy in a good way and she's leaning into him and letting him know it's alright and he's about to kiss her now, he's holding her face gently and they're kissing and she lets her hand run through his hair, pulling him closer, Christ she's been wanting this for a long time DS bloody Frazer what is she like but my God kissing him feels—

He's pulling away—

Please don't let him be pulling away—

Fuck.

'What?'

'Trish—'

'Let me guess—'

'I'm just not ready for—'

'Right.'

Great, knocked back by DS bloody Frazer and how could she have been so stupid to think, what, they were actually going to—

'I'm serious, Trish, I really—'

She's reaching for the bottle again and pouring herself a glass and downing it.

'Trish, please, it's the timing and the case—'

'What about the case?'

'I told you, I...I need to interview your uncle.'

'You leave Uncle Walt out of this.'

'It's my job.'

'Piss off.'

His hands out, like he's trying to calm her; she fucking hates it when men do that.

'I have had the shittest day—'

'I know, Trish—'

'But here's the thing. You leave my Uncle Walt alone. Do you hear me?'

He doesn't reply, his jaw set in that stubborn way of his, the formal DS again and fuck him fuck him fuck him, Trish is not going to let him or anyone hurt Uncle Walt.

'Do. You. Hear. Me?'

And she's storming out of another room and letting another door slam shut behind her and Christ that kiss, that was, that was...

Fuck.

Fuck.

LOST IN THE NIGHT

For the first hour on the tills he tries to ignore the creeping dread of the half-light and the shadowed aisles and he tries, he tries, to smile at the late-night customers with their bottles of bargain wine and shrink-wrapped salmon and the economy mince packets, the way the blood collects there on the flimsy little slip of white paper designed to collect it by someone who never anticipated how much, just how much red could seep out of that chopped-up meat. But the time keeps moving on and the lights flicker out, a few first, over the meat counter, over the cheese, letting the edges sink into darkness as though no one would notice it was happening – but he notices. Fergus, he can't stop seeing the shadows, no matter how hard he presses his fingers into his closed eyes, trying to make them work better; there can't be this many shadows, really, and the customers, the way their teeth look rotten and fractured, that's his mind playing tricks on him, not everyone round here has teeth like that, those empty eyes.

He is so tired. That's what's happening; he is so tired. How long since he had a proper sleep? Even trying to calculate it causes his head to throb but there were a few hours last night, weren't there, between around 4 a.m. and 8 a.m., and then the night before, what had happened the night before? He can't remember. Georgie's face, all he can remember is Georgie's face when she accused him of being a racist, the stabbing pain of it. Everything he thought they had, everything he was, has always been – she doesn't even know him, not at all, how can she know him if she said things like that, but no, he won't think that, there must be a way back, he will find a way back from this because what else does he have, how can he – what is there here, for him, without Georgie?

She thinks it's him. She thinks it's his fault. She's so angry and how, how—

'I said can I pay by card?'

The man's eyes, hollow like they've been plucked out by, but no, that was Alexis, that was months ago, this man is fine, he's—

'This machine's no working!'

'Sorry, sorry,' Fergus is fumbling to press the keys he's supposed to press and every time he looks up he sees, just for a fraction of a breath, a tall figure, eyes hollow, skin stretching and teeth that are broken and rotten and—

'Well finally.'

The man picks up his bags with a glare and storms off, leaving Fergus holding his receipt and the time keeps moving on and it's later now, it's black as tar outside and it's seeping in through the windows and there are hardly any lights left. Sitting in the pub, staying on after Georgie walked out, just sitting there because he had no idea what else to do; picking up her cold pizza and eating it because at least that way if anyone saw him they would just assume he was having his tea, not that he'd just had the life kicked out of him. He's tried everything. He's tried to reconnect, to give her space; he's tried to remind her of what they'd had; he's helped on her case – he's even done that. None of it has worked. Instead he was left sitting there, on his own, chewing cold pizza and feeling his world dissolve around him until he ended up here: aisles stretching from the tills for miles, rows and rows of matching products in the shadows and the darkness at the end, disappearing into the depths of the meat counter and the cheese counter and the baked goods and something else, a mound of earth and rock that shouldn't be here, that's just in his mind, he needs to stay alert, this is—

'Shut the alcohol aisles,' says his manager, less like a kid now and more like a shape of something older than his years, his pupils dilating until his eyes are wells of black and his lips peel back. 'Now, mate.'

'Yes,' mutters Fergus. 'Yes.'

'Then refill the tinned veg, eh?'

The storeroom again, the single bulb hanging from its cord in the middle of the vast storeroom and in the shadows there is a noise, a scratching. Stacking, stacking his wire trolley and wheeling it out and Georgie's voice, over and over again, *you enable them*, her eyes, not blank like the others he keeps seeing but bright and furious and he loves her but *You don't call them out, do you?*

Does he?

Has he, ever?

Oh God, his head, it's worse than a pounding, it's sharper than that, needles in the back of his eyes and he needs to sleep, he knows it, but he can't, not yet, he needs to know what they'll find tomorrow, he needs to go back there, those people, those poor people buried in the motte, thrown there, he has to find out who they were, he has to help them. When he bites into his nail he tastes the earth, the dry soil baked from the heat, the relentless heat and it tastes of salt and blood and his T-shirt, his red T-shirt that is his uniform now is stained with sweat marks and mud and it stinks, even he can tell that, no wonder the kid looks at him with disgust whenever he comes down to the shop floor. He's not here now though, no one is in here now and there's a bright puddle of light right in front of the doors to fool people into thinking the shop is welcoming and then, beyond it, the aisles sinking into shadows and the angry hiss of the fridges and the scratching, the clawing and scratching – what is that?

Nothing. There's nothing there, nothing here and he feels sick, the tiredness, the ache of it in his body and Georgie, the way she looked at him, fired her words at him like he was a suspect and all she could see was the bad in him but he's not, he hasn't, he only ever wants to help people, that's all it is, he doesn't want to fight with anyone and he's sitting down on the floor now, he can't stack any more shelves, these tins of soggy carrots and peas and *It's white privilege*, she'd said and how can they come back from *That makes you complicit*, how can he come back from that, from being complicit, from the weight of her blame and the look in her eyes—

'Are you ill?' the kid's saying – but how does he even know, is he watching, is that what he does up there in the office, watch to make sure Fergus is doing his job?

'Do you need to go home? We can't be paying you to sit here on the floor, you understand, so tell me—'

'I'm fine,' says Fergus. 'I'm sorry.' He's always sorry, he's sorry for everything, and the kid is gone and out of the shadows come tall, elongating shapes that reach out to scratch their nails down his cheeks and then there are tears, running down his cheeks, and he's alone here holding tins of vegetables and placing them neatly on the shelves and the kid had asked if he wanted to go home and he wants to go home so much, there is nothing in this world he wants more, but he can't go home, not after what she said, not after the way she's looked at him, like she…it's not hate, if she hated him that would be okay, maybe, it's that she has no respect left for him. He's useless. She thinks he's useless, he's not done the things he should have done or said the things he should have said and he can't go home, the shadows moving closer, that pain, slicing away behind his eyes, and the more he stands here holding these tins of carrots the more he knows, he's on his own, with these shadows moving closer and no one to help him defeat them because he's all on his own.

ONE FINAL THING

It is the deepest part of the night when Walt feels them arrive. He senses the shadows crawling across the windowsill, darker than the sky. The heat has been pressing in for days and Walt knew – he always knew – that one day he must do what he is about to do. He will offer himself to them and they will welcome him among them. There is a balance in knowing that he can right a wrong, at last, and if he does it now his Trish will be safe from it all.

He reaches the window and presses his hands into the shadows and waits, eyes closed, for something; for the glass to smash or their fingers to reach their way under his skin through the cuts he made for them. He waits, he waits, but there is nothing. He waits; he starts to fear that he was wrong. They are not here. He opens his eyes and then he understands: down there, the lass from reception. Outside, having her cigarette. They are not coming in. They are calling him out.

His door is not even locked. That's what the care home thinks of him: an old man too frail to leave his own room. But he has drunk the water and made his own rope out of the twisted threads of cotton from his pyjamas and he can make his way down the stairs, clinging on to the banister, because they are calling, at last, they are calling him. They are granting him safe passage.

There's no one down in the common room, just the snoring of the old people who have accepted their fate. The emergency lights in the hall are on as always. The reception desk is empty, as he knew it would be – the lass outside, smoking. The doors have number pads and he knows the codes. It's not hard, down here, to listen in when you need to, especially when everyone around you thinks you've lost your mind. Sitting in the common room, pretending to play draughts, to watch daytime TV; listening to the receptionists, waiting for someone to say what they shouldn't. Memorising. He holds his breath though, as he enters the code, as the first door clicks open and he is one step closer to freedom. The door, the internal door, closes behind him and he knows his whole life is behind it and in front: he turns the latch and pushes the handle and he is out, where the air is cooler and fresher and, yes, carries the promise of a storm. He peels off the bandages they wrapped around his arms and lets them flutter away in the breeze, looking up to the clouds, looking up and calling them to gather.

He doesn't see Shona, who's sitting over the road, smoking, with her back against the conker tree. She didn't know what else to do, she's not on the inside, Georgie has been nice enough but she's not in the police, she's not part of the investigation. She has his mask, though. That strange mask that would cover his head and face, the hand-cut slits for eyes, the way it makes her skin crawl. Walt hadn't even asked for it back. He was too busy collecting the biscuit crumbs fallen down his chest by the time she'd left. But he wasn't always an old man. Once he was younger, strong and capable. He might not always have been sweet; he could once have been strict and cruel and violent. So she's been sitting and smoking and doubting Kevin and wondering where she should go, if she should leave this place for good, move to the city, write for a real paper, all the while something stopping her from catching the last bus home to Warphill, and when she sees Walt Mackie in frayed pyjamas and dressing gown, nothing at all on his feet, wandering out of the care home then shuffling down the road towards Burrowhead, she knows this is what she's been waiting for, and she silently stands up and follows him.

Kevin Taylor, meanwhile, has been sitting slouched against a different tree, on the edge of Ricky Barr's farm, near enough to the caravan park that he could claim he was just having a fag but near enough to the farmhouse that he can keep an eye on the door. That bloody Orlando and his *vaping*. He doesn't like the smell of real fags apparently, looks at Kev as though he's some kind of poor relic every time he starts to roll one up. The caravan smells of sickly fake fruit every evening – bloody pomegranate is the latest – and Kev's rollies are unwelcome. So it works well enough as an excuse, to be sitting out here.

He doesn't know where Shona is. Hasn't seen her since they were in the woods, since she'd backed away from him as though he might've been the one made that fucking corn doll and disappeared off into the village and he'd not followed her, because he knows well enough that when a girl doesn't want to be followed the best you can do is stay away. A lot of blokes don't get that, but he does. Basic common sense, basic respect. He might not respect many folk around here, but he respects Shona. She'll come back though; he's got to believe that or he'd have nothing to stay here for. He'll have to leave soon anyway else he'll be too far in to ever get out.

The sounds are fucking strange out here, though. It's not just his mind playing tricks on him, it's like he keeps hearing the scrape of footsteps but when he turns there's nothing, when he shines the light of his phone around there's not so much as a mouse scurrying along the ground. It wouldn't have been a mouse anyway, that's not the noise he keeps hearing. It's slower than that, more like a dragging on gravel – Christ, at times he could almost convince himself there's something scraping at his skin. He slaps at the feeling, must be some kind of insect trying to get a bite of him but there's nothing there, just this scratch at the back of his neck every time he thinks the place has gone silent. It's not letting him rest.

Walt could find the way with his eyes closed; he can hear them calling to him, just like he has before, when the village needed him.

It's on his skin, the insistent pulling, the urgent scratching if he slows. It's on the wind: the hiss and the voices just for him. His dressing-gown belt has come loose from its knot and it falls to the ground, trailing along the tarmac and so he steps onto the grass verge, where his gown can be in contact with the soil instead, with the earth. He can feel his voice starting already, that low hum coming from the back of his throat, wordless and animal.

He keeps moving but suddenly he's in the air, on the ground, with a deep throbbing in his ankle and his knees and his hands; he is lying sprawled on the road and it wasn't the kerb he fell over, there are other powers at work, something is trying to stop him but it mustn't win. They need to know he is strong enough this time. That he is ready. He pulls himself up, ignoring the shooting pain that fires up his leg, and he hobbles on; holds out his wrists and lets them scratch at his self-inflicted wounds.

Shona almost rushes forward when he falls. He looked frail enough before, his bare feet dragging along the road, his head rocking back as though his neck hadn't the strength to support it, but he pulls himself up so fast she hangs back – she'd help if she were needed, but she also needs to see where this is going. He's holding out his arms and turning off the main road and she feels a bit sick as she realises she's being led back to exactly the place she was trying to avoid. Maybe it was inevitable. Maybe she had to end up back where she started, maybe she was looking in the right place all along. Ricky Barr's farm. Walt doesn't even hesitate – he's approaching the old trees by the edge of the potato field, the trenches the police dug, the spot where she found the bone and there's the strangest groaning noise coming from him, halfway between a note and a moan and suddenly he's kneeling down, getting lower and lower and disappearing from view and Shona finds herself running because he is climbing down, into the ground, into the grave.

Kevin hears the sound of a door being pushed open; nothing like the strange whispering noises of the dark, the rasping sound of breath the wind makes through the elder trees on the edge of the woods. It's so loud it reminds him that the sounds he was hearing before must have been in his mind, surely. The person standing in the doorway doesn't put the lights on inside, so it's hard to make out who it is but for the rattling cough that tells him it's Ricky Barr, sneaking out of his own farmhouse. Kev takes a last drag, silently treads the remains of his roll-up into the ground. Ricky is moving, heading out to the field where they found the body, and he's carrying something long and sharp. That's what makes Kev crouch, tells him this is what he's been waiting for. It's not curiosity making him watch, it's something like fear, a twisting knowledge that if there's violence here tonight he needs to witness it.

The sky is shimmering purple again and Walt welcomes it, his head rolling back, his eyes open to the sky, arms out and palms held upwards. Forty years to get here, forty years of seeing that tiny baby every time he closes his eyes. He was trying to save the village and he has failed – *I am here* – he was trying to save his family and he has failed – *I have come* – and he scratches at his wrists and lets the blood swell free. A hiss of leaves, a buzzing around his head, the sharp sting against his neck and he knows. They have come for him. They are stretching their way from the shadows, shapes emerging between the trees, rising from the ground and he is no longer one, he is many and they are closing in; he lets his head swing back and his knees sink into the ground and the earth starts to drag him under and suddenly he is back there. A storm more violent than any he had seen before. Trees ripped from their roots, the pier smashed, the land flooding. A newborn baby cradled in his mother's arms. A father she is refusing to name. The villagers form a circle around him as the storm rages on in the blackest of nights, one by one nodding their agreement: it must be done, for the sake of the village. *No.* It must be done. *Please, no.* And then there is loss and grief and regret and Walt getting deeper in, always deeper, missing that little boy, seeing him in his dreams while

Shona's rooted to the spot. It's sick, what she's watching, but she can't move, her limbs won't let her and the branches are closing in. This can't be happening. She's fainting or something, she's unconscious, a night terror, it feels like a night terror; her eyes are wide, her mind is desperate but her body won't move and that noise, it's setting her teeth on edge, making her whole body rigid with tension. Every rasp of his voice is a nail scratching down her spine and

Kev, crouching low against the ground, feet sinking into the soil as though it were quicksand and Ricky approaching the black lines of the cordon where they found the bones and what the hell is that noise? Like a trapped animal, a fox shrieking, but he sees Ricky pulling the rifle from his shoulder and aiming it down into the grave and there's someone down there, Christ not Shona, please God not Shona looking for more evidence and that noise, that fucking wailing, what the hell is

Stop, but Walt can't control it, the chant is being dragged from his body like air from his lungs and the terrifying noise of it, a desperate, guttural, inhuman screaming as the creatures close in around him, more appearing all the time, surrounding him, scratching at his skin, clawing at the back of his knees and he was wrong, he was trying to help but he was wrong about everything: they're not kind or good, they're vicious and sharp and full of revenge and they're reflecting the very worst actions of his life back at him. He falls into the dirt. Their faces are ancient and scarred, their eyes caverns of hatred. They clasp their thin fingers around his neck. He wanted them to take him somewhere better but this, this, not this, their teeth are shattered and their claws gouge at his face. They're not here to help him, they are here to claim him, to turn him into one of them, and then it is him, he is here: Ricky Barr. The son of the woman Walt loved. He is coughing and retching, the most violent cough Walt has ever heard, and when Ricky leans over blood spews from his mouth and finally Walt understands.

Forgive me.

Sudden, shooting pains down his arms, in his chest and he's clutching his stomach and he can't breathe. His voice cracks and falters, his chest is imploding, the pain, the pain. He's reaching out to Ricky but it's too late and he collapses into the earth and his eyes are swimming with water. The creatures are gone. They have left him in peace but the skies have opened and the rain is gushing and at last he lets it happen, he lets his eyes roll back and

There's a voice.

Shona can barely hear it, but there's a voice shouting something at her and at last she can make out the words.

'Fucking phone?' the voice is saying. 'Have you got a fucking mobile?'

Ricky Barr, pointing a gun at her. No, chucking it onto the ground. She's shaking her head; the words won't come.

'We need an ambulance.'

From behind her.

'I don't know. Heart attack or… I don't know.'

It's Kev, he's here.

Shona is running, at last she can move and now her legs are faster than she can control, she's running and falling and Kev is covered in dirt as though he's done the same but it's not Kev that she runs to: she runs to the graveside, kneels by the grave and Ricky is down there, beside Walt Mackie, leaning on his chest, pushing and coughing and Shona can see his eyes, Walt's eyes, and she knows he's gone already and there is a rifle lying on the ground and Kev is standing over it. Ricky keeps pushing on Walt's chest, uselessly, desperately, like the rhythm alone is keeping him going until another violent coughing fit erupts and Shona sees him wipe the blood he's coughed up on the back of his hand and he stumbles to standing, pulls himself out of the grave. He looks at Kev, looks at the gun, picks it up, nods, just once, and walks away and then there is the wail of a siren – it's all happening too fast, or her brain has got too slow, but the ambulance has arrived and they're trying to resuscitate him. They've got better tools, there's an oxygen mask and electric pads and shouts of clear and the longer it goes on the clearer it becomes: Walt Mackie is dead, and Shona and Kev are retreating into the woods in the commotion, the woods on the edge of Ricky Barr's land that lead all the way to the motte, that hide the cup and ring, and they walk in silence until they get to the clearing.

'He's dead,' Shona says.

'You saw everything?'

'As did you.'

Kev nods, tries to pull her into a hug, but she resists him.

'Whose side are you on, Kev?'

'Yours, Shona.' He purses his lips. 'Always have been, always will be.'

Her legs are ready to drop and she wants to be sick but her body won't let her, all she can do is shake, and Kev is shaking too, he looks pale and afraid and young and at last she gives in to the hug. They hold each other like it's the only way they can stop from collapsing, and in the deepest part of the midsummer night, they breathe.

BEGUN

THE END OF SOMETHING

The air is filled with chlorine. It's too strong, it's suffocating. Just like in that pool Uncle Walt took her to when she was a kid, as a special treat – her mam would never have thought of it, didn't even want her to go, her mam who exists more as an absence than a presence in Trish's mind. It was the first time she'd been in a pool like that, with the slides and water fountains and wave machine. A special treat with her favourite Uncle Walt who was so much fun, who used to throw her up in the air and catch her again, spin her round in circles by her arms so her feet rose up off the ground and she felt like she was flying.

She'd been excited for days and it was the school holidays and she had her new swimming costume that Uncle Walt had bought her, but then they got there, got changed in their separate cubicles and all the while she felt like she could hardly breathe; the smell was too much, the heat, the humidity. She couldn't let it show, not Trish, not in front of the other kids – not in front of Uncle Walt. It was his special treat for her, so she pretended she liked it, got in the water for a splash about, careful not to go further than Uncle Walt could reach. She laughed along with the other kids and eventually let go of Uncle Walt's hand and then the wave machine came on, dragging her further to the deep end and all the while that chlorine in her eyes, in the back of her throat, in her lungs – she could have screamed, but everyone was watching. A kid, another girl from school, grabbing her hand and saying they should go on the big slide, a bright red tube of a thing, swirling and circling above the water, closed in like a tunnel, and she could hear other kids screaming with delight so she tried to look all cool and said, 'Alright then, aye, let's go on the big slide.'

She asked Uncle Walt if it was okay.

Willing him to say no; willing him to stop her.

'Of course it's okay love,' he'd said. 'This is your day. Enjoy yourself.'

No choice then, not with everyone watching and Uncle Walt smiling like he was so proud of her.

Climbing the steps, chlorine filling her mouth, her nose, her eyes burning with it, climbing the steps right to the top, and her eyes spilling over as she watched the queue of kids disappearing into the slide. Kids grinning and squealing and going too fast, too close together, and she knew it was all wrong – she could imagine them, piling in after her, leaping onto her at the bottom of the slide where the water cascades down into the pool. The weight of bodies pressing her under the relentless waves. They're pushing her now, already, because she's hesitating, because it's her go and they won't wait and she scrunches her eyes and steps into the torrent of water hurtling down the slide and then she's in: water everywhere, choking, scrambling for breath, trying to slow down but there's a kid behind, yelling, and she has to keep going; she opens her eyes and everything is red-black in the tunnel of the slide and she peels back the cloth over his face, the room flooded, the chlorine in the back of her throat, eyes streaming, and she forces herself to speak.

'It's him,' she says. 'It's Walt Mackie.' It's her Uncle Walt, lying dead in the morgue in Crackenbridge.

How was she to know, in that slide, in that panic, as her lungs filled up with sloshing water, how was she to know that Uncle Walt would be there at the end, waiting to catch her, waiting to check she was okay. He was, though. He was right there. He saw immediately that she was scared, hoisted her out of the slide before she tumbled into the deep end of the pool. He held her tight and laughed kindly and said, 'You came down there mighty fast, Trish, you've got some courage in you,' and he looked proud of her, in front of all the others, and said, 'How's about I buy you a slushie now, hey? You can choose the flavour.' Then all the other kids, they weren't laughing at her at all, even though her eyes were leaking and she was spluttering up swallowed water, they were jealous of her Slush Puppie, jealous of her Uncle Walt. She chose the purple flavour, and he had one too. Her and Uncle Walt.

She's outside the morgue now, outside that chlorine-filled freezing sweltering silent clamouring room and she's sitting on a chair that someone must have got her and Cal is beside her, not saying anything, but waiting for her to pull herself together. That's what she's got to do, of course – that's what Trish does.

'You've got a friend wants to see you,' he says at long last, once she's finished wiping at her eyes and the tissues he gave her are all used up and scrunched tight in her fists. She's not expecting it, the way DS Frazer's face pops into her mind, but it does. Who else would be here to see her, who else would Cal describe as a friend? Georgie's her boss, and Si – he would just have said Simon, wouldn't he? – and she tries not to think about how she must have very few friends if it's Frazer who's come to see if she's okay, after last night.

'Will I let her in then, aye?'

Trish frowns, nods.

Elise Robertson wouldn't have come to mind as a friend if she'd sat here for another hour trying to cry her way to a name.

When she sees her eyes though, how red they still are, sore and raw around the edges despite being perfectly dry, it makes sense. Her da is gone too, not that long ago, the pair of them are orphans with no one left, so maybe there is something they have in common. That's how friendships start, isn't it?

'Trish,' Elise says, taking the empty chair next to her and glancing at Cal.

'Call me if you need me, girls. You sit here for as long as you need,' he says, before gently closing the door behind him and leaving Trish and Elise alone in the white, empty corridor beside the morgue in Crackenbridge.

Trish waits. She didn't ask Elise to come here, after all. It's up to Elise to do this. Trish's mind is still swimming in chlorine, in the heat of the care home where he'd begged to come home and she'd left him there, thinking he was safe.

'We need to talk,' Elise says.

So she's not here to offer sympathy. She's not got any advice.

'What, you want me to sit here drying your tears?'

'Do not be a bitch to me today.'

Elise shakes her head. 'I've got something that helps much more than that. It wasn't your fault.'

Trish looks at her but doesn't respond.

'It was someone else's fault. I know who did this.'

Trish's eyes are stinging but she can't blink.

'In fact, I think you do too. You're not ready to see it yet though, so I'm here to help.'

'What am I not ready to see?'

'My da. Your Uncle Walt. Jack Helmsteading. Nora Prowle.'

Chlorine, scratching at the back of her throat, at her eyes.

'They killed Ricky Barr's dog,' Trish says.

'They did.'

'Looks to me like I'm seeing just about as much as you are, then.'

'And Natalie is at the excavation site right now…'

Elise looks at her as though she's supposed to understand what that means.

'What?'

'The excavation. Natalie's been wanting the motte excavated for years.'

312

'I thought she was pissed off about it?'

'She thinks that's where the knife is buried. Her Aunt Nora's old knife.'

Trish scrunches her eyes tight, opens them again – yes, this is real.

'The carved blade, the one that has to be used for the threefold sacrifice – we can't find the right one. My da, Nora, Jack Helmsteading, your Uncle Walt; they had it back then. They used it for the dog. But now it's missing.'

'You don't seriously believe all that crap?'

'Natalie does.'

'And what, she's in charge of you?'

Elise takes a deep breath, like she's forcing herself not to rise to Trish's taunting, followed by another.

'We *were* just looking for evidence of Ricky Barr's dealing. That's all. Trying to provoke a bit of a reaction.'

Her voice has got more serious now, and it makes Trish feel nauseous.

'We had no idea how things would escalate. We wouldn't have pushed him the way we did, if we'd known what he was capable of.'

Serious and cold, hard-edged – Trish finally realises that Elise is furious, that's how she's been keeping her tears away. Trish admires that.

'But now, we're going to get him for manslaughter…'

Walt was on Ricky's land.

'Or murder.'

Walt had escaped from his care home where he was supposed to be safe, where they'd made her sign a waiver – a waiver saying that *she* was the one responsible since he wouldn't cooperate, *she* was the one responsible if he was injured as a result of his own actions – to walk all the way to Ricky Barr's farm. Where no one was there to see he needed help. Where he had a heart attack, that's what they're saying.

But Ricky was there.

Ricky was there when Walt was dying; he was there when the ambulance arrived. He's not even denying it.

'You do understand, Trish. This is all between us.'

Ricky fucking Barr.

'We need to work together. And I've got something: Kevin Taylor was there. Ricky told the police he was doing CPR but Kev saw Ricky pointing a gun at Walt, so I'm going to have a word with him right now, see if he saw something more…threatening. You get back to the station, Trish.'

'What?'

'Dry your eyes – again – and focus.'

For a second Trish wants to hit her, wants to punch her right in the face.

'Look, I know this is hard,' Elise adds. 'But we need to know what the police know, and with Suze stuck up here with Cal nosing around and DI Strachan so secretive about everything since what happened to Alexis and…'

'I'll deal with Georgie,' Trish says, with a final glance at the closed door to the morgue, towards Uncle Walt.

But he's gone now. Uncle Walt is gone, and Trish is going to deal with all of it.

REASONS TO RUN AWAY

DS Frazer's eyes are on the road and he's not taking them from the road and he is focused on driving, he is absolutely not going to let himself think about anything other than driving and my God he kissed Trish Mackie and all night he couldn't stop thinking about kissing Trish Mackie and the way she shouted at him and stormed off and he misses his wife so deeply he could curl into a ball and cry but now he's left Burrowhead because he woke up to a name, a name that Trish gave him: Deborah-Jane Barr and that kiss was everything he'd been needing and not needing and he is focused on the road, he is driving to the city, to the care home where all this began.

The villagers are lying to him but Trish isn't, not Trish. There is something honest about her, unfiltered, like the truth just comes blurting out of her mouth whether she wants it to or not and those eyes of hers, so bright and sharp and aware – Trish Mackie and thank fuck, a proper road. No more of those winding single tracks to navigate, a full lane to himself until he reaches the main road then it's a straight drive to the city and there's plenty of questions he needs to ask once he gets to the care home. He catches sight of his speed; taps the brakes. DS Frazer obeys the limit. It's who he is, even when the evening before keeps coming back to him in flashes. He can see the city though. The tall flats to the east, the floodlights and seat banks of the rugby stadium. By the time he's passing the larger houses, the ones with a generous garden out front and gates to keep their two cars safe, he's convinced himself he's not thinking about Trish Mackie at all.

The receptionist at the care home buzzes him in quicker this time, and she doesn't seem surprised to see him – he even wonders if she's called the police again herself, if someone else is on their way round. But she's looking at him with such recognition now; it's him she's been waiting for, despite the touch of suspicion behind her eyes.

'Betty Marshall again, sir, or...?'

He shakes his head.

'Actually I'm looking for Deborah-Jane Barr,' he says. 'From Burrowhead.' He holds her gaze and doesn't let it go.

'Got a bit more time on your hands today, DS Frazer?'

He deserved that, and he takes it with a smile.

'I'm sorry I didn't listen before. That was...stupid of me. My mistake.'

'We all make them.'

'We do. And there's not so many folks in the city like to admit they're from Burrowhead. You were trying to tell me though, weren't you?'

She nods, like she's still considering her words.

'Would you like to sit down?' he asks – there are comfy chairs in the corner of the reception, three of them, arranged around a low table with a vase of flowers and some magazines. Like a private doctor's surgery.

Her gaze rests on the chairs, but she doesn't move towards them.

'It can be hard,' he says, 'to start talking, when you've spent a lifetime not saying something.'

'I don't know what you mean.'

'The thing is,' he says, 'they've found a body.'

'Where Betty told you to look?'

'No. No, it's on a farm.' He waits for a moment. 'It's on a farm owned by Ricky Barr.'

Her hand is over her mouth now and he wishes he'd insisted they take that seat.

'Deborah-Jane?'

She takes a deep breath, gives a single reluctant nod.

'I prefer Debs these days. Haven't gone by the name Barr in forty years. And I haven't wanted to talk about why in just as long.'

Frazer waits. He's not here to push her into anything. He's here to ask her about what happened on the farm that once was her home.

'But if you think it's Betty Marshall's murdered girl... If I knew what had happened to her I'd have told you before. All I know is that I believe Betty's story.'

'I believe her story too,' he says. 'And I've looked into it. Wyndham Manor, where she claims the murder took place, has been closed for decades. I've not been able to track down any list of employees yet, or even speak to the current owner. As for Abigail Moss—'

'Let me guess, no one in Burrowhead has heard of her.'

Down the corridor, through the locked doors, it must be breakfast time for the residents – he can hear the rhythmical clicking of the food trolley on the pristine tiled floor again.

'No one even seems to have heard of you.'

Debs frowns slightly, then speaks with a quiet sadness in her voice.

'But what about my brother, DS Frazer? He owns the farm? So he's still there then, he's still alive?'

'He could be in trouble now, though. The body they found on his farm, it was a small child. A toddler. And I was wondering if you might—'

But Debs is swaying on her feet and Frazer is holding out an arm, guiding her gently over to the chairs where, this time, he'll give her all the time she needs.

REASONS TO STAY

Simon knocks, once, hard, on their caravan door with his left hand; in his right he is holding the paperwork.

'Aaron,' he says, leaning to the side to look over his shoulder, 'and Lee. I'm here to search your caravan.'

'Of course you are,' says Aaron Prowle, his voice sounding for all the world like his mother's with that I'm-in-charge tone of hers. 'Would you like us in,' he smirks, 'or out?'

'You're welcome to stay,' Simon says, stepping up to the door and backing Aaron into the caravan. 'We can chat while I search, if yous like.' He pulls on his gloves and starts in the kitchen. 'What would you like to talk about?'

'Me?' Aaron says.

'Or your brother.'

'Fuck off,' mumbles Lee

'You know,' Si says, glancing over, 'I saw your mam on my way over here. Helping Pamali clean the Spar windows again. Did you know she does that every morning?'

'She what?'

'Funny, isn't it? I think it's funny.'

'What's funny?'

'You two, scrawling graffiti everywhere, and your mam, cleaning it all up.'

He's got his back to them and he's doing it on purpose now, letting them glare at each other while they think he doesn't know, work out who can say what, who should deny it. The kitchen cupboards are clean, as he knew they would be – whether it was Aaron and Lee or Ricky himself keeping drugs in here, they'd have made damn sure there were none left by now.

'We're no doing that,' Lee says eventually.

'Is that so?'

'You got proof?'

'No need to get defensive now,' Simon turns and smiles at the pair of them. 'All I was saying was, that's quite a mother you've got there. I guess you could say you owe her.'

They've gone quiet, sullen and scowling and Lee's doing that thing with his leg again, the relentless tapping of his heel on the floor.

'I've got to check in here now,' he says, head flicking at the door. 'Maybe you want to take that breath of fresh air after all.'

They scuff their way to the door and disappear outside and Si sits on the bench that doubles as a bed. He's not sure what he's doing here. Forensics are coming to do the full search, just in case, he doesn't even need to be here, Cal's team are on their way and Si would bet money that even they won't find anything but there was something – his mind keeps falling back to Alexis, to what Alexis sent him, to the links he's trying to make – there was something that made him need to get here first, to look them in the eye. He heads to the door, has to crouch to get out and there's that other kid, the student, Orlando. Striding over towards him. That's all he needs.

'How's it going, mate?'

Simon shrugs – everyone wants to know what they know, what they've found, who they suspect.

'I was hoping I'd see you again.'

He's wearing jeans today, instead of those festival trousers, and he looks slightly less ridiculous, slightly more—

'Look, I've got an internship. An investment bank, back in the city. Starting next week so…'

'So?'

'Am I free to go? You wanted us to hang around, right—'

'Oh, aye,' Simon laughs, shakes his head. 'Go, go.' He's sure someone must have told them they weren't needing to stay put, once all his interviews were done.

'And what about you?'

Simon doesn't get it at first.

'What about me what?'

'Are you going to leave? I mean, you don't have to stay here, do you?'

It's none of his damn business whether he stays or goes, that's what Simon's thinking, as Orlando is pulling a card from his pocket – typical, kid like that with a business card.

'Look, if you're ever in the city…'

The card is being held out to him and Simon's taking it without even meaning to, it's just when someone holds something out for you it's automatic.

'We got a good scene. I could show you round… Fuck, man, you don't have to live here, right?'

He doesn't hang around for an answer either, he's striding off back to the farm like maybe he's going to finish his day's work because that's the right thing to do and you never know when you might need a reference, even from some hated farmer from the back of nowhere and it gradually dawns on Simon that he is holding Orlando's business card with his mobile number on it.

Walking away from the caravan park and back to the station, back to the case, back to his life, he holds the card over the bin that's always overflowing by the fountain and he thinks about dropping it in, while his fingers hold it tight.

CLUTCHING AT STRAWS

'Trish, you don't have to be here,' Georgie says, her southern states twang even slower than usual. 'You... I'm so sorry, but you shouldn't be here.'

Trish looks devastated. Georgie can't get the sight of Walt out of her mind, the last time she saw him, his wrists all bandaged up and the look in his eye, like he was seeing something no one else was. It was as though – she shakes her head, not wanting the thought to settle – he knew it was coming. Folk used to say that back home, that you can tell when your time is up. But that's nonsense. Georgie's seen the shock of death, the way it punches the breath out of your lungs.

'This is where I need to be,' Trish is saying. 'Please.'

They're all here, together, this morning. Georgie, Si, Trish.

Georgie was on the phone to Cal first thing, confirming and reconfirming Walt's cause of death: heart attack, no suspicious circumstances – Cal repeating himself for her benefit. *He was an old man, Georgie. He was unwell and his mind was wandering – you'll have seen it.* And she had, of course. What's worse, at the end of the day, a fast death or a slow disintegration into dementia?

'Georgie?' That's Trish's voice. 'Did you hear me?'

'I'm sorry, Trish. My head—'

'I know who did it.'

She wasn't sure what to expect, from Trish, whether she'd show the pain or turn it into another fight. A fight seems to be her choice.

Georgie feels the dark pressing in, the storm that arrived last night still refusing to leave, like the heat itself. The clouds are low and the rain is soggy and dense, the moisture clinging to everyone's skin like sweat.

'Ricky Barr has motive.'

Georgie shakes her head, just slightly. Get the shadows out.

'Do you mean his dog, from forty years back?'

Trish glares at her.

'It was a heart attack, Trish, that's all—'

'He had a gun! Kevin Taylor saw it.'

Georgie rubs the sweat off her forehead and goes to turn on the overhead light. This weather is insane, so dark out there it could be dusk, and in here it's sweltering.

'What Kevin Taylor saw was Ricky giving Walt CPR,' Georgie says quietly, still standing by the door. 'He phoned the ambulance, he gave a statement, everything backed up by Shona as well. He tried to save Walt's life.'

'He terrified him into having a heart attack.'

This is going to be difficult. Trish looks ready to scream and Georgie's never seen her break down, not really. She saw the panic in Trish's face when Uncle Walt went walkabout earlier this year, and she saw the relief in the way she held him when he was found. But the loss she's experiencing now, the lack of any hope.

'Look, Trish—'

'Listen to me!'

'Ricky's done nothing wrong—'

'Except get Natalie's sons into drugs so bad she loses her mind, and get Rachel and Pauly hooked so bad they kill themselves, and then scaring my' – she swallows – 'scaring Uncle Walt into a…a heart attack and watching while he…while he…'

'Ricky tried to save him, Trish. We've got two witnesses. Poor Walt died of a heart attack. There's no proof of Ricky doing anything other than trying to resuscitate him—'

'You just…'

'I just what, Trish?' Georgie's voice has gone flat as slate.

'You just don't like us, do you.'

Us. That makes Georgie a version of *them*, right?

'That's why you're siding with Ricky Barr. After what happened to Alexis, to Pamali, you've decided you don't like this village any more and so you're siding with the one person who's hurt it more than anyone.'

'Ricky Barr,' Georgie says firmly, 'was a victim. *That* is all we know for sure.'

'What, because someone nicked his horse?'

'I think it's time you took a break, Trish.'

'I'm fine right here.'

'No you're not, you need a sit-down and a deep breath,' Georgie says.

Trish is shaking, Georgie can see it even though she's doing her best to hide it by swivelling back and forth on that chair of hers. She wishes she could give her a hug. Instead she sits down, to make what she's about to say seem like less of an accusation.

'I'm sorry, Trish, but what I said yesterday still stands. We have to consider Walt a suspect for the possible murder of that little boy forty years ago, along with Art Robertson, Jack Helmsteading and Nora Prowle.'

'There is no way – absolutely no way – that Uncle Walt could ever have hurt a baby. A fucking two-year-old. No. Way.'

'Trish—'

'No!'

There's a dripping, a quiet, irregular dripping behind her and Georgie turns to see the water collecting in the corner of the window frame and dripping down onto the floor. She stands, slowly, picks up the wastepaper bin and places it under the leak.

Fergus didn't come home after his shift. Or at least she was up and out before he got back, out to deal with more death while he carries on with his pointless minimum wage job and his amateur archaeology and Georgie doesn't even know whether she's more annoyed or worried but either way she doesn't want to think about it.

'It's a motive though,' Trish says quietly.

She's not breaking down, then, or backing down.

'Isn't it?' She glares at Georgie again, in that piercing way she has. Simon seems to be avoiding her stare. 'If Ricky *believed* it was Walt, Art and the others buried that kid – if he thought it might even have been his own sister – well, that is a motive for murder. And then the horse, bringing it all back again...' Her voice trails away.

'Walt died of a heart attack, Trish. I'm so sorry, but he shouldn't have even been on Ricky's land.'

'Ricky had probably called him there, to threaten him or—'

'Trish, you're just making this up now.'

Trish's hands are clenched into fists.

'We need to investigate Ricky Barr for murder. Put that bastard away for life.'

There's something scratching at Georgie's neck, but every time she turns there's nothing there, nothing but this feeling. It's been there all week, been there for months.

'I think we all need a cuppa,' she manages. Keeping her voice slow and kind. This is Trish, after all, and she's just lost someone she loves. 'I'll put the kettle on for us.' She gestures vaguely at the kitchen and leaves the room, pulling the door over behind her but letting it hang open a crack rather than sealing it tight with a twist of the handle. Then she waits, silently, in the hall, resting her pounding head against the wall.

Georgie doesn't want to be this person. She doesn't want to suspect people she once cared about, doesn't want to push her husband away every time he reaches out, doesn't want to be annoyed by his inadequate job or his hobbies or the bloody washing or the weeds smothering everything else, the mess of their house that seems to be worse every single time she wakes; she doesn't even mean to think in those terms, she doesn't want to feel like an outsider in the village where she's lived for decades just because of the colour of her skin. But she does. To all of these things: she does. A life spent trying to think the best of people, undone and unravelled in one year of gulls screeching and relentless violence.

'But I *know* Ricky is to blame.' Trish's voice, raised. Simon must have been trying to talk some reason into her. 'This is *all* about Ricky Barr.'

'We don't know that. That's the whole point.'

Georgie can tell from how Simon speaks that he's trying to be kind; he has reason enough to hate Ricky himself, all those barbed comments about 'people like him', the barely masked homophobia. She heads to the kitchen before they realise she's been standing out there listening, splashes her face with the cold water from the sink. Beside her, a shadow sways. The door. The bare light bulb. Her eyes playing tricks on her. She splashes her face again, flicks on the kettle and prepares to do her job.

THE WAY POWER CAN FADE
OF A MORNING

Fergus has to force his legs to carry him to the motte – every push on the pedals feels like a strain against some invisible chain holding him back. He even stops a mile from the house, checks the wheels, checks the brakes. It's not something wrong with his bike, but he wishes it were; that would be a lot easier to fix.

He's so tired and he's been trying for so long he doesn't know how much longer he can keep it up. How long, really, can you stay where you're not wanted? Georgie has started seeing him as the enemy, that's what's happened. Even though he's done nothing wrong. She thinks all the villagers are racist, because of the attack on Pamali, the threatening notes, because of Andy and Lee and the comments people make and she's blaming him, blaming Fergus, for not standing up to them, for being who he is and wanting everyone to get on – and why can't everyone just get on?

That makes you complicit.

He'll never be able to stop hearing those words.

He's standing at the motte, the trenches running through it like deep scars, the brown earth drenched from last night's downpour, soil turned to mud. A whole extended family buried in a single grave, blocked up with large rectangular stones all the way around – no path in, no tunnel for relatives to visit, no relatives left to do so – then hidden under mounds of earth and debris, like the way folk dump their rubbish in the old quarry today. But why? He could cry for the land, for the people discarded and forgotten.

Professor McLeod, she must understand how important this place is.

Maybe – and the thought creeps up on him, he almost doesn't want to imagine it – but maybe he could do a course at the university, now he knows her personally, build up to a PhD researching this very site and the people buried here. Would that be so ridiculous? He could move to the city. Even get a job at the university, eventually. But Georgie. Is he going to…is he thinking of…

He feels a fresh stab of guilt, shakes the thoughts away. He just wants to talk to someone about the mass grave, about who they were, why they were abandoned. Instead of standing here staring at a damaged hulk of earth. The rain is getting heavier again. The ground soggy beneath his feet. Mud seeping into his drenched shoes, his wet socks. His hair is clinging to his forehead – probably good it's getting a soak, it's been a few days since he managed a shower. Then he realises that the fence Professor McLeod set up is different, it's higher; there's a gate now. Why is there a gate? He pushes it, rattles it. There's a *locked* gate.

'They've gone.'

Natalie is standing behind him, a large bright-red umbrella keeping her dry. She raises it high enough to offer Fergus a bit of protection.

'I don't understand.'

'They've taken everything back to the lab for analysis. The bones, I mean. Protect them from the rain, supposedly. If you ask me they decided it was time to run their tests and experiments and whatever they do behind our back so they've taken it all away from us. Pushed us out.'

'But…but we don't even know who they were, those people.' He looks at her, searchingly, as though she might have the answer. 'Villagers who were attacked?'

'Or people who attacked the village. More fool them.'

It's like his legs can't support his weight; he slumps down on the ground, in the mud. Natalie, to his surprise, kneels down beside him.

'I know this must be a shock to you, Fergus,' she says. Her voice is gentle, intimate. She doesn't normally have that tone, that ability to make you feel necessary. 'But I need to ask you something.'

'Anything,' he says.

'You found that figurine. You were surveying the area long before the university team showed up. You've spent time with the standing stone, with the cup and ring.'

'Aye.'

'Well, there's something that used to belong to the village that's gone missing.'

'You mean the henge?'

She works hard to hide her surprise, but she's not quite fast enough. Surprise is maybe the wrong word, though; actually she looks impressed.

'That's not what I mean, but you're right. There was a henge here once.'

'I thought it might have been under the motte.'

She shakes her head. 'The motte was never big enough for that.'

'You're right.'

'What I'm looking for is something that used to be in my family, and it's gone missing. It went missing years ago. It was stolen from us, I think. And I've been wondering if it might have been buried somewhere, like your iron figurine.'

She's never referred to it as his before. It makes him smile.

'I've not found anything else, Natalie,' he says. 'I wish I had.'

Although, if Fergus had found anything else, he'd have handed it over to the professional team. When he thinks of that, he's quite glad he hasn't found anything else. Then he has an idea.

'There was a dagger,' he says.

For a second her eyes light up.

'In the museum. It's in the case beside the old cauldron.'

'Oh, that.' She pats his arm, kindly. 'A nice thought, but I made that display myself. That blade is nothing special, anyone could have had one of them.'

It's a strange way to describe an Iron Age knife, but he doesn't want to contradict her.

'You should think about joining the community council,' she says.

He's not sure why he never asked to join other than a vague sense he hadn't been living here long enough, coupled with the idea that they'd ask him, if they wanted him – it's never said that the council is invite only, but it does feel that way. A chosen group.

'And…' She pauses, like she's choosing her words carefully. 'How are things…?'

He closes his eyes. 'What do you mean?'

'I mean how are things between you and Georgie, Fergus.'

He shakes his head.

'I'm still here, you know, if you want to talk.'

He doesn't know how she knows. Did someone see him in the pub? He doesn't know who could have said what. He no longer has the strength to deny it, though.

Maybe he could just stay here, by the motte. He doesn't know where else he's going to go; he's too tired to think. But he can't… he can't stay where he's not wanted. He can't do it any more. It's worse than being alone.

'When you're ready,' Natalie says, touching his thigh just for a second then standing herself up with the faintest of groans. Maybe she's got a bad back too. Maybe she's just like him. 'You're not alone, Fergus.' And then she is holding out a hand to help him up.

TWISTING INTO THE AFTERNOON

'Cal? Tell me you've got something.'

'There's nothing on the bones we have, Georgie. I'm sorry, but I've been very thorough. No sign of trauma at all – from the evidence we have, it's entirely possible Sonny Riley, if it even is Sonny Riley, died of natural causes.'

Georgie is alone in the room. Simon's next door. Trish is out in reception, where Georgie sent her.

'But I do have something for you, Georgie. Something you're going to like.'

'Tell me.'

'Our DNA results are back from the skin cells on the rope, and there's a partial match to the DNA we have on file from one Lee Prowle.'

Georgie pauses. The spite in that kid, the look on his face as he glowered at her from the cell she had him in earlier this year.

'Lee.'

Footsteps, out in the hall.

Georgie shouts. 'Trish, sit out in reception, *now.*'

'Poor Trish shouldn't be at work today,' Cal says, his voice all sympathy. 'That girl's got enough to be dealing with—'

'Cal. The DNA. Did you say partial?'

'Well, we've got a familial match.'

Georgie waits. She can hear his breathing down the line, wonders why he's hesitating the way he is. Maybe it's just her, being impatient.

'That is to say,' he continues at last, 'a parent or child of Lee Prowle held that rope.'

'Lee doesn't have any kids. He's practically still a kid himself.'

'Aye, don't we all know it, the young fool.'

Cal chuckles down the phone like this whole case is a bit of a joke, but Georgie cuts off his laughter.

'Are you saying it was Natalie Prowle?'

'Looks that way.'

'Natalie Prowle. Head of the community council. Runs the beach clear-up. Natalie Prowle was involved in killing a horse. Are you serious?'

'Serious as can be, Georgie. Who else could it be, seeing as Lee's da is long gone.' He clears his throat. 'You friends with her, aye?'

'I wouldn't say that, no. But…Natalie?'

Simon touches her shoulder. He's come in to see what's happening. Trish is gone, finally out in reception like she was told.

'Cal, I'm putting you on speaker with me and Si. Is there anything else?'

But there's nothing else, no evidence the child was murdered, just evidence that Natalie Prowle of all people had held the rope that was used to lead a horse out into the woods where it was killed. And for what? Was Natalie there, looking into that poor mare's wide-open eyes; was it Natalie who had hacked into her throat with a blunt knife? There's the family connection though, the Prowles, Nora… Maybe her aunt Nora had taught her how. Ricky's dog was the only other animal they knew of that had been killed in the same way. And what was it Trish had said about Natalie losing her mind?

'No other DNA, no sign of other people?'

'None. Sorry, Georgie.'

'Okay. Thanks, Cal.'

Then he's gone and Simon is biting at his thumbnail.

'What is it, Si?'

'Natalie Prowle.' He shakes his head.

'I know, it seems too bizarre to be true.'

'But it doesn't,' he says slowly. 'I mean… I think I might have…' He clears his throat, the way Cal had earlier. 'She'd have needed to get hold of some kind of tranquilliser.'

'Through her boys.'

'Exactly. Aaron and Lee had the ketamine, found in their caravan – that's pretty solid. And then there's… That is…'

It's not often Georgie sees Simon looking afraid to speak, but he does now. She knew he'd been holding something back, she'd just assumed it was something to do with Rachel and Pauly, with their suicides that Simon no longer believes are suicides. Not something about Natalie Prowle.

'I need to tell you something, Georgie. It's…'

Suddenly, that prickling at her back. The squawk of a gull in the distance, a sound she hasn't heard in weeks, sending a chill down her neck.

'Tell me, Si.' She lets her hand rest for a moment on his, an offer of reassurance that reminds her, stingingly, of the only comfort she had to offer him as they sat out by the playground, Alexis's body still lying cold on the ground below the swings. 'It's time to tell me now.'

TRUSTING TIME AT LAST

Simon is conscious of his breath, of the way the air fills his lungs then leaves them deflated again. He looks over his shoulder towards reception, to where Trish is sitting down the corridor and through the double doors.

'Do you think she's okay?'

'Not really, no,' Georgie says.

'I should be there with her, taking care of her. If I could be in two places at once—'

'You're a good friend to Trish,' she says. 'And she knows that.'

He shakes his head. 'But I've not known who to trust—'

'What is it, Si?'

'Let me explain. I… I might be about to lose my job, after I tell you how long I've been sitting on this—'

'No one is losing their jobs here today, okay? Now what is it you need to tell me?'

He swallows, stands slowly and goes over to his bag, pulls out the brown paper package he's been carrying with him everywhere.

'Before Alexis died,' he says. 'Before he was murdered, he sent me this.'

He holds it out and her fingers tremble slightly. His eyes don't leave the package.

'Before I open this,' she says, 'thank you, Si.'

He nods, manages a smile.

Inside are three old-fashioned cassette tapes. Each one is labelled in Alexis's neat handwriting. Dawn Helmsteading. Elise Robertson. Natalie Prowle.

Georgie doesn't ask him if there was a note, and he's grateful for that. It was personal, written for him alone. In silence, she walks over to the old cassette player they have in their office and puts Dawn's tape in first. It's similar to the recording they found on his mobile phone, but not identical – must be from an earlier session. Dawn, describing the way she was stolen from her bed as a little girl, carried to the playground, the screeching of the wind, the covered faces; the noose, the knife.

'I think the recording on the phone must have been taken while they were out of the office,' he says. 'Maybe he'd gone round to her house or something.'

'Could be,' Georgie says. She's already holding the tape labelled *Natalie Prowle*, but Simon holds out the other one to her.

'Start with this,' he says. 'Elise Robertson.'

She'd come in for interview voluntarily before, told them she'd had two hypnotherapy sessions with Alexis, though neither recording had been found when they searched his office. She'd resisted the whole idea of hypnosis in her second session with him, but in the first…her voice fills the room, birdsong on the edge of shrill. Alexis is there too, his breath, his guidance:

'Tell me about your father.'

'He's no keeping well,' Elise starts, 'he needs care and we can't afford it and I don't want him going into that home outside the village, it's no right…'

Simon closes his eyes and tries to picture what Alexis was doing, like he always does. Elise's voice gradually slows – was he moving his fingers side to side, tapping gently on her hand, encouraging her with repetitive, soothing motion? He'll never know; all they have is what's on the recording, what Elise is saying during this one session that she kept hidden when she was sitting in the interview room three months ago.

'… and it's true he's got a temper, like all men his age, don't they, it's a generational thing, but he never hurt me, he'd never and when I was little…'

Alexis lets the pause rest for a few seconds before prompting her.

'Go with that, Elise. Tell me about when you were little.'

'He was my da and he never knew I was listening, otherwise he wouldn't have…'

Simon opens his eyes to see Georgie watching him. He gives her a nod.

'… and he wasn't himself that night, when he came in – I was up in my bed and I heard his voice and it was him but not him, he wasn't making any sense and it was… scary. Him and my mam, they had rows but no like…'

'Go on, Elise…' Alexis's gentle voice.

'He's…he's laughing like he's…laughing but not, like he's crazy and everyone knows they've all been burned, with the bodies on those big pyres outside of the village and the smell…'

'What bodies, Elise?'

'The cows. All the cows,' she says. 'All the cows.'

'Why were people burning cows?'

She doesn't answer but Simon knows why – twice there have been bad culls of livestock hereabouts, from mad cow disease in the 1990s and foot-and-mouth in 2001.

'It's cold out of the bed but I get out anyway because of the voices. I'm too scared to be on my own so I go down the stairs one at a time and I can see into the living room through a little crack and no one knows I'm there. Da's in the middle, soaking wet and dripping onto the floor and he's got his arms wide and he's staring up at the ceiling and there's a creepy mask over his head and he's laughing that manic laugh that doesn't sound like him at all but I can't leave. Then I see the eyes. The eyes staring out and I know they see me and it's no my da, the eyes staring at me through the crack in the door—'

She's out of breath, talking fast, urgently.

'—just those eyes, those eyes and suddenly the mask is pushed back and the eyes are in a face then there's a voice, *Bobby*. It's him, Bobby Helmsteading from school, but different somehow, he reaches a finger through the crack in the door like he's going to scratch me and then another voice, *Shut that door*, and the door is slammed and I can hear my da laughing like he's crazy and I want him to stop but he's laughing and…'

'Stay with me, Elise.'

Nothing but breathing, Elise's desperate breathing.

'It's okay, Elise. You're okay, stay with me.'

'What the fuck was I talking about? Why am I… What… I feel sick.'

'You came to me, Elise. Your dad's ill, I'm trying to help—'

'I don't like this feeling.'

'That's okay,' he says. 'That's okay. Everything is okay.'

'Turn that off!'

Georgie doesn't move.

The tape keeps playing, the way tapes do, the hiss of the machine. But Alexis had turned the recording off. Eventually Simon reaches forward and hits Stop.

'The dates?' Georgie says.

'Fit with Dawn's story. Must have been 2001, from the cull of the cattle to stop the spread of foot-and-mouth. Art Robertson lost his farm, what was left of it. A lot of folk round here were badly hit. Dawn would have been four.'

'You think Elise is describing *that* night? That Art Robertson was one of the men who attacked Dawn, along with Bobby; that they went back to Art's house after Walt scared them off and Elise saw them when she was just a kid?'

Simon is sure of it.

'Is the tape enough to prove it, though?'

She shakes her head. 'We don't know what we can believe from these hypnosis sessions, not really.'

'I know,' he says, and he's remembering Alexis, how much he believed in his work, how it got him killed.

'Even if it's true, who were the others? Dawn described a group.'

It's Simon's turn to shake his head.

'And Elise is describing a group.'

'I don't know how it all connects. And then there's this.'

He's holding the third tape now.

Natalie Prowle.

Her name written in Alexis's gentle, sloping hand.

But the phone is ringing.

THE SHAPES YOU CAN SEE WHEN YOU LOOK THE RIGHT WAY

The thing about Natalie Prowle, Fergus thinks, is that it takes some doing to break down her walls. He doesn't mean it in a violent way, of course. He doesn't much like that expression actually – breaking down walls makes it sound like something needs to be smashed. Getting someone to trust you, to show their real selves, that's something that takes a gentleness, a kindness, the ability to not get angry if you're pushed aside again and again but to make yourself available for that one time – however long it might take – when you are welcomed in instead.

The standing stone outside Warphill looks ancient now, vital, the way it rises magnificently out of the ground. Untouched by storm winds or the brutal excavations of a team from the city who care more about their publication record than the village. It seems to Fergus this must always have been his home, in a way; it just took him a while to find it. True, someone has been adding to the carvings, but now he and Natalie are side by side, now he's no longer looking at them through the lens of Professor McLeod, he can see they've followed the shapes of the original engravings faithfully. They've cleared the lichen and enhanced the curves that give the stone its meaning, eased back the weeds that had been clinging to its base.

'It was you,' he says and it's not a question, he doesn't need her to reply – that she invited him here, suggested they come together, is enough. She does answer, though.

'Someone had to,' she says. 'There were…oh Fergus, there were cans and fag ends all around, as though kids come here to drink and smoke, leaving trails of litter on this ancient site. Sometimes, when I visited, I could barely even feel the markings.'

'I'd noticed that myself.'

She nods as though she'd known, but he's not sure how she could have.

'When I was a girl we came here on Sundays to sit with the stone, and the markings seemed immovable, like nothing could touch them. How does something last untouched for thousands of years, only to disintegrate in the space of a generation?'

'I don't know,' he says, and it's the truth. Although he does know there are other things at work here, industry and unemployment and capitalism and frustration and disposable versions of everything that used to be saved and cleaned and reused.

'So yes,' she says. 'It was me. I've been coming here every week to clean up, collect the rubbish, scrape the weeds and moss off the stone. I haven't been etching with tools or anything like that, no matter what that professor said; I've only ever used my fingers to trace the lines. Have you ever done that, Fergus?'

'I have,' he says. He doesn't add it was on the day he had to call the police, when he felt a pull so strong the village was laughing about him hugging the stone for weeks afterwards. He doesn't care any more though, not now he knows Natalie feels it too. She's reaching out her hand, following the shapes carved into the standing stone, and he does the same, beside her, the two of them tracing the ancient lines that must be a message from their ancestors, reaching out to them down the years.

'It's older than the motte. The barrow,' he says, correcting himself then regretting it – it's always been known as the motte to the villagers, so why should he change that?

'By a long way,' Natalie says. 'It must be Neolithic.'

'That's what I think too, and the professor didn't tell me I was wrong about that.'

Natalie smiles with a kindness that Fergus appreciates. She's not laughing at him; if anything she's sharing the joke about how the professor treated the whole village as a bunch of kids in her lecture theatre. Or worse, a community outreach programme she'd been tricked into attending. The community being them, Natalie and Fergus, Walt and Mrs Dover and Mrs Smyth, June and Whelan, everyone who loves this place the way he does. It's such a good feeling, to be part of a community like that. Fergus feels a glow just from thinking about it.

'I used to think the standing stone and the motte were in a line, like…'

'Leading somewhere,' she says, finishing his sentence for him.

'I thought they might lead to the henge. Wherever it was. But it doesn't work. If you follow a line from the standing stone to the motte, then it just leads on to the coast. There's nothing there, I've walked it so many times, flown over with the drone, but…'

'What about through the cup and ring?' she says. 'More likely the standing stone and the buried stone of the cup and ring are related, I'd say.'

'But that doesn't work either. It leads further inland, away from the villages, deeper into the woods and then through the hills, the lakes, eventually just…'

'On to the city.'

From where they are standing, though, the land has given them a natural vantage point – they are higher here than the coast, higher than the dip of the woodlands. They can see all the way to the motte, and to the clearing of the cup and ring. Together they stand and look out, the horizon over the sea vanishing into haze and wisps of low-lying cloud clinging to the trees, to the roofs of Burrowhead in the distance.

'It's not a line,' she says.

'What do you mean?'

'It's not a straight line they were leaving to guide us, it's a cross. Here, starting from the standing stone, travelling through the midpoint between the motte and the cup and ring; keep following the central line of the cross. Where does that lead you?'

'It leads you to Burrowhead.'

'It leads you to Burrowhead,' she repeats.

RUNNING OUT OF LAST CHANCES

'You've got a cold case from forty years ago and a dead horse, Georgie. It's a waste of police time and resources.'

It's the chief super, on the phone.

'We just need another day, Ma'am,' Georgie says, voice calm, her twang pronounced, the way it always gets when she's upset and determined not to show it.

'I take it you still don't have a name for the child from said cold case.'

Something is pulling at Georgie's skin.

'Actually, we've got a lead, Ma'am—'

'Look, I've got to tell you the truth here, Georgie.'

Georgie feels a twist in her stomach before she realises where the conversation is going. This isn't about Sonny Riley or Ricky's dead horse, not really. No one from headquarters cares about either of them. Too far away and too long gone for them to bother with. It must be easy, to look at a place like Burrowhead and imagine you can simply blame it for its own problems as you brush it under the carpet.

'I'm sorry, Georgie, but we're stretched too thin and I can't keep this up. I need to save somewhere now we've been hit with these new cuts.'

'I see, Ma'am.'

It's been coming, of course it has, but Georgie thought she could last out the year at least, find a placement elsewhere for Trish, for Si.

'I'm sorry. I really am…'

Georgie is barely listening by the end. The buzzing that won't leave her in peace has turned to a high-pitched ringing in her ears.

'We can't afford to keep Burrowhead station going. So that's that, I'm afraid. You're being closed down. I kept you going for as long as I could.'

She's trying to work out whether to fight or not, to point out the inconsistencies – after all, if they close her down then that's even more work for HQ, isn't it? Or is it that with her gone they can just turn a blind eye to it all. Not take over the policing of the area so much as leave it to destroy itself like a snake swallowing its own tail.

What will happen to the village without her? Maybe they'll all be glad to see the back of her.

She realises the chief super has gone and slowly hangs up the receiver. For the briefest of moments, she imagines pulling the phone from its socket and hurling it across the room. She's been fighting for this station for so long she can hardly remember why. But Si's watching. This is his career too, his income.

'Bad news?' he says.

They're not daft, her team, they're sharp. Still, she'd expected him to look a bit more worried. He's good though, he'll get something else. If he's willing to leave the village, that is.

'They're closing us down then?' he says. 'I've been expecting it.'

'You have?' Georgie presses her hand against her forehead. 'I've been fighting it.'

'I know.'

'And now I could scream.'

But instead the smile on Simon's face makes her smile too – maybe the sight of Georgie actually screaming and hurling phones in the office would be enough to make them both laugh.

'It's okay, Georgie. You don't need to worry about me. I've been thinking maybe I need a change of scene anyway.'

His face looks lighter, when he says that. So he has been looking ahead, rebuilding his life, or at least making plans to. It makes her feel better to know it. He's a good man, Simon.

'But what about Trish?' she says.

'Maybe...' He lowers his voice, though there's no way she could hear. 'Maybe that's a conversation for another day.'

'We might not have long,' she says, leaving it vague until she has a plan, until she has something concrete to offer him, to cling to herself.

'Then we need to listen to this,' he says, and he presses Play on the last and final tape and Natalie Prowle's voice fills the room.

LOST

It's not like the other recordings. Georgie can tell that immediately.
Natalie wasn't seeing Alexis for therapy – she was after something
very different. She needed to find something she'd lost, and she
thought Alexis could help her remember.

'It was a family heirloom,' she's saying, before the hypnosis even
starts. 'This big.' Georgie can imagine her holding out her palms,
the length of a small knife between them. She says she saw it when
she was a kid, Aunt Nora used to show it to her, let her trace the
carvings on the handle – made her feel grown up, important. And
she *promised*.

'What did she promise?' Alexis's voice appears for the first time, and
he sounds cautious, reluctant. Georgie wonders if he'd only agreed to
see her because he needed the money. Or was there something else?

'She promised that it was *mine*.'

There's an uncomfortable pause on the tape – her voice was
insistent and sharp, and Georgie can imagine Alexis trying to find
the best way to diffuse her resentment.

'I'm not sure what you want me—'

'Elise told me you've been doing hypnosis. I want you to help me
remember. There must be something, some clue she told me when
I was a kid so I'd be able to find the blade when I was old enough.
I remember exactly what it looked like – dark metal, polished, and
the handle was thicker, large enough to grasp, engraved with these
beautiful markings...'

'Markings of what?'

'Are you going to help me or not?'

'That's not really how this works.'

'She used to keep it in her bedroom, in that bloody police station where she lived, she kept it on her wooden dresser by the three-piece mirror—'

'Maybe you should start there.'

'The dresser is *gone*, obviously, we had to sell all the furniture at auction.'

Georgie's not sure, but she thinks there might be a waver in her voice.

'Could the knife have been sold at the auction as well?'

'Of course not,' she snaps, then takes a deep breath. 'I told you, I searched everywhere. I was the one sorted through everything after she died. The blade was gone.'

'Then I doubt a hypnosis session would help.'

'You won't even try?'

'I'm not doing that any more. It's not...'

'What?'

'It's not reliable. Not in the way you want it to be.'

'Elise was right, you're just a hack, aren't you.'

There's a shuffling on the tape, a scrape of something – Natalie is standing, storming out of the room.

'That's it?'

'All there is,' Simon says.

'This tape.' She points at the silent machine. 'This is the only one where no one was under hypnosis. He didn't have a legal right to make it – not without her permission – as I'm sure he knew, but at least we can trust what they're saying. And it was recent.'

'After he'd seen Elise, making this the most recent of the three tapes.'

'Do you think he'd stopped the hypnosis because...'

Simon looks at her. This is what he's been piecing together.

'I think he'd just found out about Dawn's false memories. That her da was innocent after all, and her brother guilty – her mistake coming from the very hypnosis sessions he'd performed to try and help her remember the truth. He would have blamed himself. Of course he would.' Simon swallows. 'But he also suspected there was something bigger going on in these villages. He'd started recording his sessions on purpose. Avoiding electronic records, keeping it off his computer – it's like he was worried someone was monitoring him. He was trying to piece it all together, trying to find the links between the villagers. And I think he was...I think he was afraid. He posted the tapes to me the day before he died.'

Georgie feels that scratching at her neck again, the heat, sweat running beneath her collar – or something else. That feeling of being watched. Is that because it feels like Alexis is still with them, waiting to see if they can join the dots?

'When Dawn was kidnapped, when she was a little girl. She said...'

Georgie looks at Simon, lets him finish the sentence.

'She said they held a knife to her throat.'

'The same one Natalie describes here?'

'No way to tell. As you know.'

Georgie smiles.

'But what we do know,' he continues, 'is that Natalie was intent on finding this blade. She couldn't find it among her aunt Nora's belongings after she died – long before Dawn was kidnapped – so maybe someone else had it and hid it. Natalie's been out at the excavation all week.'

'You think someone buried it?'

'I don't know. But I think it was the same knife used by Nora, Walt, Jack and Art to kill Ricky's dog forty years back. And we know that happened at around the same time – within the same few years anyway – as someone buried poor Sonny Riley, whoever he was.'

Georgie nods at him to continue.

'We know, twenty years later, Dawn was threatened with a knife, and we suspect that Art Robertson might have been involved, along with Bobby Helmsteading. It's all in the same four families, travelling down through the generations. As for today, we know that Aaron and Lee had a vial containing traces of ketamine in their caravan, and now Natalie Prowle's DNA has been found on the rope used to lead Ricky's mare to her death.'

'Okay, Simon. Now we bring in Natalie Prowle.'

CONFRONTATION, 4 P.M.

It's not that Fergus feels them coming, but when he hears the car down on the road he gets this itching on his back, enough to make him step away from Natalie, which in turn is enough to make her take a step back from the standing stone. Someone's coming, that much they both know, and there's a silent understanding between them that they don't want to be seen kneeling together, tracing the curves and markings of the standing stone, trying to decipher the message that their ancestors left for them to find.

The henge, he thinks. Stonehenge of the North, the site where they would once have met at the most sacred times of the year, where they would have been bound together and reached for the gods, sacrificed, celebrated. Imagine if he could find it. Natalie understands. Georgie never would. Sometimes he thinks she wants to abandon Burrowhead, let it slip unseen into irretrievable poverty – an ancient village that's been here for millennia, that was once so important people placed monuments that have outlived homes and wars and churches, isn't there something profound in uncovering that, in preserving who they were and how they lived?

He wishes he felt something different, watching her walk from the passing place in the road, over the soggy yellow grass towards the circular path around the stone that Natalie has watered and tended, decorated with shells and feathers. It's Georgie, just like he knew it would be. His Georgie. Georgie in her trousers and shirt, open at the collar because of the heat, raindrops speckling her face, her hair pulled back into a knot so that her dark curls are visible only from the back, though he can imagine them as easily as he can imagine his own expression: apprehension covered by a smile that he's trying to make welcoming. He wishes he could meet her halfway, hold out his arms in the offer of a hug; he wishes the sight of her brought with it the happiness, the safety, the warmth it used to.

That makes you complicit.

He wishes she would look at him, see him for who he really is. But her eyes are avoiding his gaze.

Simon's with her, too. He's in his uniform – must be damp and sweltering. How would Fergus have greeted him, before? *Si, good to see you. We've been meaning to invite you round for a Sunday roast, how are you doing, how are you holding up?* But none of that happens. In fact Fergus, standing there, feels a stab of invisibility as Simon walks straight past him with barely a nod and stands in front of Natalie.

Look at me, Georgie.

'Natalie Prowle,' says Simon. 'We need you to accompany us to the station for questioning.'

'What?' Fergus says, pushing his way to stand beside Natalie, facing Simon, facing Georgie. 'What's going on?'

They can't arrest his friend and pretend that he's not even standing there.

'Georgie?'

'Fergus,' Simon says. 'I need you to step back, please.'

'We're doing research here,' he says. 'You'll have to go harass someone else.'

'Please, Natalie,' Simon says. 'Come with us and we'll talk down the station.'

'Am I under arrest?' she says, calmly.

'Of course you're not under arrest,' Fergus says, glaring at Georgie, daring her to look at him, to shout at him, to take *him* to the bloody station for questioning if she wants, but at least to acknowledge him.

'We're not arresting you at this time,' Simon says. 'But if you don't accompany us—'

'Look at me!'

Georgie's eyes, at last, on his.

Oh God, the sadness in them. He can't take it.

He can't do this any more.

'Okay,' Natalie says quietly.

'No—'

'It's alright, Fergus. I've been expecting them.'

'I don't understand.'

'Yes you do,' she says. 'That's the whole point.'

Georgie. It was Georgie who just spoke.

Fergus thinks he's going to be sick. His migraine is forcing its way up over his eyes and the sky is pressing in around his head, the colours of it a swirling dark purple and Georgie says he understands – but what does he understand?

They've gone now, though. Georgie and Natalie and Simon, they've all gone. He didn't even hear the car leaving.

Is it over?

His legs are heavy as marble. Eyes burning, he forces his knees to bend, makes it down to the grass and collapses against the stone.

Is his marriage over?

Is he the one in the wrong?

But those people buried under the motte, human beings, women, men, children, he wants to help them. To be buried with no one to remember you, dumped under the ground without so much as a funeral rite – the thought of that being the end, dumped and forgotten, that can't be right. He opens his eyes to the haze, the wet smear of the air all around and he's back at the motte before it was the motte, when it was a hole scraped out of the ground. When it was a grave.

Lying within the earth are bodies. Each one of them is limp and broken. Their faces have been smashed with rocks; Fergus can see it in their broken teeth, their broken bones. He's watching a pile of bodies being encased with blocks of stone, each one carried by four men while the women circle the tomb, throwing in soil as they sing.

They wear cloaks of animal skins on their backs, and as they work the light fades to dusk, to a desperate, drowning night. The grave grows and Fergus watches until the bodies are hidden deep out of sight and only then do the men stop bringing their stones, the women stop shovelling the soil. Before them: a mound of earth and rock they have created to smother the lives they stole.

Then, one by one, the people who carried the stones and the people who watched; all the people of the village walk away, heads down, avoiding each other's gaze through the night. Fergus knows where they are going. He knows the route, he has walked it himself many times; they return to Burrowhead and leave him alone in the darkness at the freshly made mound of the motte. Except he is not alone.

There is a scratching. A clawing at mud and rock.

Shadows deeper than night seep up from the ground, elongating around him.

They rise together. Their clothes too are made of animal furs and hand-woven rope; their faces are bloodied where they were beaten, their teeth shattered. Every one of them has a sharp, single cut at their throat. He sees them rising through the earth, from the under-world to the air thick with storm clouds and haze. They reach out to him, clawing their way from shadow to appear with a hiss of breath, a rasping as they get closer; their fingers are long and pointed, their nails scratching at his skin but he is not afraid – not like the others who have seen them. *Let me help you*, he says, his voice less than a whisper, *how can I help you?* Cold stone at his back, white light, the shadow of a cloud moving over sun, the sharpening of the air around him. *What is it you need?* But it is daylight again and the rain is cold and fresh and clean, it soaks his shirt and leaves it transparent, clinging to his skin, and he stands, his legs his own again, tilts his head back and welcomes the rain into his mouth. The sea is deep green turning to violet, the swirling froth of pure white in the waves, the horizon a haze of purple separating the land and the sea from whatever lies beyond with an indistinct murmur of life and death and he feels like he could reach out and touch it, and it seems possible, to Fergus, to exist there in the border between.

BEGUN

In Burrowhead station, Natalie Prowle is sitting upright and proud on one side of the interview room, looking across at Georgie and Simon.

'Why am I here?' she says in a way that makes Georgie think she knows exactly why she's here and she's not going to make this easy, which suits Georgie just fine.

'I'd like to talk to you about a dog, Natalie,' Georgie says.

The conversation is being recorded, the rain is pelting down outside, and finally the temperature has lowered enough in the station for Georgie to feel like she can breathe.

'A dog?'

Georgie sits back a little, thinks about that old expression: rope and hanging. Thinks about what the villagers did to that slave girl two hundred and fifty years ago, what they did to Pamali earlier this year, what they did to the little boy buried in Ricky Barr's field.

'Did you know that the Barrs don't have a dog?' she says. 'No? They haven't had one since Ricky's dog was slaughtered by a group of villagers when he was just a child.'

'I don't know anything about that.'

'Which part?'

'What?'

'The slaughtering, or that there is no dog today?'

Natalie's eyes flick to Simon, then back. Georgie can hear Simon utter a single, cynical laugh beside her – Natalie is looking in the wrong place for an ally.

'Have you visited the Barr farm recently?'

'That's not a crime.'

'So you have been there?'

'He's got my sons there.'

'He's hardly keeping them against their will.'

'They're just kids!'

'They're eighteen and twenty, quite capable of making their own decisions.'

'You're not—'

'Not what?'

'You're not going after them, are you?'

'That depends, have they done something wrong?'

'If you lot would do your jobs you wouldn't have to ask that question.'

'I can't think what you mean.'

'Ricky's the one brings the drugs in and everyone knows it! You should be helping my boys.'

'I see, I see,' Georgie smiles. 'Thank you for that, but first, can you tell me anything about a ceremonial knife—'

'*You've* found it?'

There it is: the shock she was hoping for.

'The poor child's makeshift grave was my crime scene.'

'It was there, with the body?'

'Why would it be?'

Natalie opens her mouth, closes it, opens it again.

'That blade belongs to me.'

'Well if you want it back then you'd better start talking.'

She glances at the door, sits up taller. She doesn't believe she's done anything wrong, Georgie realises. Natalie is convinced of her own innocence. Or justification.

'Okay,' Natalie says. 'But I want you to understand, that knife has been in my family for generations. Kept safe, and kept as a secret. It's got…sentimental value.'

'Why do you think it would have been buried with a dead child?'

'I don't know. It doesn't make sense… It was… It's a ceremonial dagger that was used for ancient rituals, generations ago – you can see them carved into the handle. Just animals I mean, it was used for animal sacrifices. That was what… I'm talking about the Middle Ages here, or before that even.'

'What's carved into the handle?'

Natalie closes her eyes a fraction longer than a blink, looks over uncertainly at the door then seems to make a decision.

'It depicts the threefold death,' she says. 'Blood, air and water.'

'Meaning?'

'The sacrifice, the ritual would be…the blade would be used to cut an animal's throat. A rope would be tied around their neck. The body would be drowned in water. It's an ancient ritual, they've found signs of it across Europe.'

'That is interesting,' says Georgie, nodding her head in the way Fergus seems to when he's learning about ancient history. 'Particularly because that's how Ricky Barr's horse was killed.'

Natalie's shoulders tense, her jaw tightening.

'I had nothing to do with that.'

'You sure?'

'What evidence do you have?'

'We'll come to that. But to set the record straight, we didn't find any knife buried with the little boy. His name, by the way, was Sonny Riley. It's a nice name, isn't it? Sounds like he would have been a fun-loving kid, given the chance.'

For a second Natalie looks regretful. That's what Georgie has been waiting for.

'Did you know that when you hold a rope you can leave some of your skin cells behind?'

'What?'

'We found the rope, Natalie. In the woods near the cup and ring.'

She's looking around, like there's someone else here, like there should be someone on her side. Georgie wonders if she's about to demand a lawyer.

'On the rope we found some skin cells, and from the skin cells we got a strong partial DNA match to your son Lee.'

'What? No, no, Lee would have had no reason—'

'Well someone from your family held the rope used to lead that horse into the woods. Lee, Aaron… We have reason to suspect them both, as it happens.'

She's not daft though, Natalie. She's taking a minute now to think it through.

'What's a partial match?'

'It suggests a relative of Lee's was there.'

'Relative?'

'A parent, actually.'

Georgie recognises the look on her face now, the realisation that they have her, and that maybe it'll feel good to confess, like a relief, a chance to explain at long last.

'We found a vial in your sons' caravan containing traces of ketamine—'

'That wasn't theirs—'

'I think it's about time we brought them both in for questioning, wouldn't you say, PC Hunter?'

'Aye, and forensics are doing a thorough search of their caravan as we speak. And that car of Aaron's—'

'Leave them out of it,' Natalie shouts. Then, calm again, quieter: 'They had nothing to do with it. It was me. It was all me.'

She straightens herself up, smooths her hair back as though she needs to be looking smart for what she is about to say, professional and upright.

'I've been trying to clean up this village for so many years. Do you know every week I clear litter off the beach? Soggy food wrappers covered in flies and fag ends and goddamn condoms, *I* clean that up…'

She wants to be congratulated. Georgie gets that same sense from the community council, the bristling when they approach someone who's not one of them, to tell them how to live differently, the letters they send to the station demanding more speed cameras, a tourist tax to raise money, a neighbourhood watch scheme – as though the neighbourhood needs watched by the neighbours any more than it already is.

'The knife, it means something to me. It was left to me, it should have been mine and…can I get it back? I mean, after, if I…how can I get it back?'

'Where did you get the knife you used to slaughter that poor horse?'

Natalie blinks.

'That was just a carving knife. I had it in my kitchen at home. I'm sorry I had to leave it in the horse like that, but I couldn't… I'd never normally leave anything dangerous lying around, you know that. But the *real* blade, it's important.'

Natalie still doesn't look guilty – she still doesn't really think she's done anything wrong. She's the one been cleaning up the village, after all. Ricky Barr lured her sons away so she stole his mare, killed her like he was killing her family. Sacrificed her like her aunt had sacrificed his dog all those years ago – except without her precious dagger. Georgie knows righteousness when she sees it. She knows how to use it, too. Trish was right about one thing: this is about so much more than a dead horse.

'If you want to know more about that knife,' Georgie says slowly, 'then I have some questions about your aunt Nora that you're going to have to answer first.'

FOR ALL THE WRONG
RIGHT REASONS

Trish is walking and thinking, walking fast and thinking about this village, thinking about Uncle Walt and how he was trying to tell her something and she'd not wanted to listen; she's thinking about Elise crying that time she'd seen her at the bus stop, the day after her da's funeral, how she'd seemed so vulnerable. Then there's what Suze had told her, how they'd trusted her that night in the pub, how that has to mean something, especially if they've arrested Natalie – and they were about to. Trish sent a text to warn her, though she's not even sure why.

She's thinking about Aaron and Lee, the way their faces are blank and drawn, their eyes twitching; she's remembering one summer when they were maybe eight and ten and they were playing at burying their mam in the sand and giving her a tail like a mermaid. She can still remember the smile on Natalie's face as she called out to Trish to get a photo, her happiness in that moment; and she's thinking about Andy and how afraid he is, how afraid he's always been. Rachel and Pauly, they weren't angst-ridden teenagers who killed themselves last year, they were on something, they were taking something hallucinogenic and dangerous and everyone knew it, and then his car is there, right there in front of her and he's stopped at the stop line outside of the village – of course he has – and he's checking left and right and she's standing there beside the road.

DS Frazer.

The blood rushing to her face.

The way he was that night, just yesterday, yesterday evening when, for a moment, they seemed to be on the same side and how he looked when he told her about his wife, and that kiss, the warmth of that kiss and then he started accusing Uncle Walt of something, of what she doesn't even know, and she was so angry and out the door and then everything dissolved and Uncle Walt was...seeing him in the morgue like that, his face, she's been fighting all morning to stop herself thinking about his face until now, now she's thinking about DS Frazer and how his case is a big fat dead end, so why is he even still here?

But there's, oh great, there's a woman in his car. Some older woman is sitting beside him and he's meeting Trish's eye, just for a second and what is that look supposed to be, that look like he's, what, that he's sorry, that he wants...no, it's that he's driving on past and not even stopping and great, that's just great that is, he's speeding up, driving fast now towards the village in the direction of the police station. Maybe he's decided he's got no interest in someone who's off the case, is that it? All about work now, well, fine.

Maybe she shouldn't have yelled at him yesterday.

But she'd kissed him and he'd pulled away and what the fuck was she supposed to do and shit, she'd actually waved when she first saw his car, what an idiot and now his car is gone and Trish is standing on her own like a muppet on the pavement and she wants to cry and she misses Uncle Walt like a part of her has been dug out and she'll never be able to put it right again.

BURIED

'My aunt, Nora Prowle, was a good woman.'

Simon scribbles in his notepad with every word. Georgie likes that; he's being more official than anyone round here would be expecting. It's putting Natalie on edge.

'She devoted her life to raising foster kids, whichever ones needed her the most. They never stayed with her that long – just long enough to get them back on track, give them a chance in the world. It was a brave thing to do, and selfless.'

It's not a question and no one in the room feels the need to answer.

'She was a strong woman, my Aunt Nora. She did what had to be done.'

Natalie sits back, the chair legs creaking under the pressure.

'What did she do?' Georgie says eventually, quietly, slowly.

Natalie looks almost smug as she replies.

'There was a problem in the village,' she says. 'This was before I was born, and before you came here, when old Herman Barr was still alive. He'd arrived from Germany with his money and his kid and started buying up the land. At it for years he was, no matter how folk tried to stop him, to reason with him. The local farmers, the Mackies, the Robertsons, they were struggling, had been for generations. Those years were tough on everyone but the Barrs. Then the storms arrived and the land kept flooding, destroying the crops, and there were strikes all over – by the 1970s the Barrs were paying way under for any land they wanted, because people were that desperate. Folk had to watch it happening. And his kid had married a local girl, the pair of them always in the village, walking round like they owned the place.'

'According to you, they did own it.'

'Not the village itself,' she says. 'Folk knew they couldn't ever let go a their houses, no matter how much he was offering. But the surrounding land. The fields, the farms… They were buying up our heritage.'

'Of course they were,' Georgie says softly. 'Please continue.'

Natalie looks slightly uncomfortable, but she shakes it off.

'The villagers back then, well…there was a bit of superstition around. So a few of them – including your Trish's Uncle Walt – they got together and made a plan. They didn't want to hurt anyone, mind. They just wanted the Barrs to leave.'

Georgie takes a deep breath. 'So they resorted to murder.'

'Of course not!' Natalie's look is outrage – a little too much outrage, Georgie thinks. 'My God, I'm talking about the dog.'

She's looking between them as if searching for a nod of understanding. Neither of them provides one.

'She was trying to get the Barrs off that land, that's all. They don't belong here. Ever since they arrived they've brought violence, drugs, they've ruined this village…'

'But what was the point of killing the dog?'

'The sacrifice calls the ancestors to help rid the village of evil,' she says. 'It's the threefold death. And don't you dare laugh at me.'

'No one here is laughing,' Simon says.

'But we do want to know what happened to a young boy named Sonny Riley.'

Natalie frowns.

'You recognise the name?'

'No, I… Maybe…'

'This is serious, Natalie. We need the truth.' Georgie's voice is stern, unforgiving.

'It could help you, down the line,' Simon offers, softer.

'I think he was the one she used to talk about,' Natalie says quietly.

She seems subdued now, almost confused by their questions, as if she doesn't want to realise where they're leading.

'My aunt, like I told you, she used to foster, take care of young kids who had nowhere else to go and...it was so sad, she was heart-broken. I remember she cried when she told me.'

Georgie tries hard to keep her face passive.

'I think it was Sonny Riley, I think that was his name. The little boy who died,' Natalie continues. 'It was...it was terrible. It was so tragic. Aunt Nora told me that one minute he was playing happily on the beach, they were all there – it was a happy day, it was supposed to be a happy summer's day but the next minute...' She shakes her head. 'He was just gone.'

'He drowned.' Simon says. 'According to the case file, he drowned.'

Georgie looks away and feels it before she sees it, a punch to her lungs: a child, a little boy, lying on his back on the floor, matted tufts of hair and a bleeding scalp, his fingers clawing uselessly at the air; her throat clenches around the force of it.

'He loved being in the village though, before the accident...' Natalie is saying. 'Nora used to talk about how much the kids loved it here.'

'And who knew about this?'

'Everyone, I guess,' Natalie says, lips pressed tight. 'It was a village tragedy.'

'Then you'll be able to tell me where his grave is?'

'I...' Natalie shakes her head. 'The body was lost, wasn't it? I mean, they never found...that's what I'd assumed. There must have been...'

Suddenly she's sitting straighter again, eyes clear.

'Are you charging me with something? Do I need a lawyer?'

Georgie sits back and swallows. The horse. The only thing they can charge her or anyone with is the horse. Cal found nothing on

Sonny's bones, no sign of any violence at all. Nora Prowle and Art Robertson, Jack Helmsteading and even Walt Mackie, they're all dead. If there ever was a truth to discover about the death of Sonny Riley it died with them. Walt was the last one who might have known and now he's gone too – just like he said would happen.

The shout from down the hall almost feels like it's coming from within her until it resolves into her name and Frazer's accent and something in his tone that tells her this isn't over yet.

Si, left sitting with Natalie in the interview room; Georgie, with Frazer, in the main office of Burrowhead police station and standing in front of her is a woman saying her name is Deborah-Jane Barr. Saying she knows who is buried in the field. Saying she was there, she saw it. Saying she heard him screaming.

A WAY BACK

It is a moonless night, unforgiving, the way the darkest nights can be, when Deborah-Jane sneaks downstairs to find her father sitting bolt upright in his chair with his rifle laid across his lap. She freezes in the shadow of the heavy wood door, not daring to breathe till her eyes have confirmed what she needs to know: the old man is fast asleep there, the grunting noises are his snores, the rifle has fallen lopsided against the arm of the chair. A sliver of drool is running down from the corner of his mouth and collecting in the creases of his skin. The fool. He imagines he is protecting the family when all he's doing is giving the villagers all the more reason to hate.

Not that Deborah-Jane cares about the villagers of Burrowhead; far as she is concerned he can shoot the lot of them. He'd never actually do anything about them though, her mam makes sure a that. She'd put her own body between his rifle tip and the village if she had to, though that makes her sound a damn sight more heroic than she is. There's a photo of them from their wedding day, faded and yellow with age, but it's the only one they have and for Deborah-Jane's whole life it's sat on the tall, locked cabinet in the kitchen and she's stared at it and wondered who the hell those people were. Her da looks like a kid, grinning like he can't believe his luck and her mam is defiant, proud, walking towards some future that never happened. No sign of the baby in her belly, though the villagers have made sure Deborah-Jane knows it was there. It's creepy, looking at a photo of someone else and knowing your heart was already beating inside them.

Then she hears something. Her da, waking? Her mam, upstairs? Time to go. The front door pushes open silently and she's out. It's a dark night, true, but she knows her way sure as she knows her brother's face: across the field, the mud sucking at her feet like quicksand, under the low branches of the dead cherry tree and along the lane that leads towards the village. But not all the way. She's headed to the house that sits on the edge of the village, larger than the others, blocky and stubborn, a cell at the back, bars at the windows.

She can see it already.

It's not that far – they live close, the Barrs and the villagers, closer than they should. The shadow of it calls out to her and it feels like the house is on her side somehow, the way it lets her disappear into the dark edges sheltered from the moonlight by those thick walls. She wonders if the building doesn't want its inhabitants; they said in school that it was the oldest building left in the village, still standing, saved from ruin because of how it was taken over. Maybe it never wanted to be taken over though, not by them, by the police and the Prowles, maybe it wanted to rot.

Light is seeping out from between the windows' bars: someone is home. The front door is locked, as always – the only one in the village you could say that for – but the side door that leads into their home, she thinks, she hopes, maybe that will have been left open and give her a way in. She pushes: nothing moves. Tries again: it doesn't budge. But there, overhead, a window has been left ajar, a window into their parlour that has no bars on. If she could just find something to stand on—

Voices.

No, not voices.

She hears one voice.

A child; a little boy.

No no no no

She knows who it is at once. Sonny, the new kid who doesn't want to be here. She can imagine him shaking his head side to side in that pleading way he has, his little voice getting louder as he gets more desperate, the wobble of a cry, but this isn't like all the times she's heard him cry before. There's something wrong. There's something very wrong but she's not tall enough to see in, needs something to stand on, *no no no no* followed by the sharp unmistakable sound of a slap. They're in the room, the parlour, and Sonny is the only child staying with them and he's not saying no any more, everything has gone silent except for the desperate inhale of a smothered sob and the scrape of something against the floor, a chair leg, a table, she doesn't know and then scrambling, kicking.

'Nora!'

The shout comes from another room, a man's voice, then Sonny again, *no no no*, his word, the only word he ever says, turning into a scream and then a slam, his scream still there but quieter, distant, footsteps, a scratching, a scratching of nails against wood, or is she imagining that?

Deborah-Jane steps back, starts searching for something to stand on. Why didn't she bring a torch? She could kick herself, so sure, wasn't she, that she knew the way, but she doesn't know her way around their square patch of garden, the roses all thorns, the trees dark and twisted. Over there, by the concrete. Nora calls it her patio – boasting in the village. Folded to the side, leaning against the wall: two chairs. She grabs one, carries it to the back window, struggles to get it opened up, stands on the rickety frame and peers in.

A table, pushed back from the centre of the room.

A hatch in the floorboards.

The scratching of nails against wood.

Scratching, wheezing.

She pushes the window – it won't open further, it's on a latch.

Scratching.

Wheezing.

All she'd wanted was to get her shoes back.

Scratching.

Silence.

'Let him out, Nora.' The man's voice again, Officer Prowle, out of sight.

Deborah-Jane squats down, keeps her face hidden.

'Have you learned your lesson?'

Nora's voice, close.

'You know I'm trying to help you.'

She knocks on the floorboards.

'I'm trying to teach you.'

The silence.

'I told you to let him out.'

They're both in the room now, Nora and Jacob Prowle, Deborah-Jane can't see but she can hear.

'The fuck have you done?'

She knows what she can hear and what she can't; she can picture them opening up the hatch, pulling his body out, the panic in their eyes. The air is clawing at her neck, telling her to run, the trees getting taller, their twisted branches reaching out like broken limbs and she stumbles backwards, falls on mud, drags the chair to where she found it, shaking, telling herself he's okay, he's bound to be okay, he was just pretending to go silent, playing dead so they'd let him out, that must be it. She needs to get out of here but she can't, her feet won't let her move, her legs aren't her own any more. She keeps seeing her little brother's face, hearing his cries from down in that trap the kids built in the woods.

Time distorts around her; she's on the ground, hugging her knees to her chest; she's standing, trying to force herself to leave the shadows and run down the lane; there's a door opening. They're carrying something. Wrapped in a sheet. It's him. It's Sonny. But he's holding her hand as well, leading her along the shadows, following them to the lane. His clothes are too big for him, hand-me-downs frayed at the edges with holes stitched over roughly with thick red thread, his hair is cropped short and uneven, there's a trickle of blood down his forehead that she thinks is coming from his scalp, and he's leading her: back to the farm, to the dead cherry tree with the low branches that she knows as well as she knows her own brother's face. They're digging in the mud. They've got trowels, they've got hoods pulled up over their heads and the night is deep and black, cruel and unforgiving. A rasp of breath. Low and throaty. Sonny has let go of her hand. Her feet won't move. The soil is sinking, pulling her down as Nora looks up, straight into her eyes and then: a shadow shifts, a thin arm reaches out and there are more of them, figures in the dark, billowy and swaying. She shouldn't be here. She should never have seen this and she feels a scratch at her cheek and she gasps: they've seen her. She has to go. Backing away, slowly. Nora's eyes, arms reaching out. She has to go. She has to move. Her hair clasped, pulled from her scalp as she turns and runs and runs, thrashing out with her arms, breath clawing at her throat as she twists and kicks and hurls herself over the fence and scrambles and runs until she is deep in the woods. She swipes into the air, keeps moving, thrashes at branches and tree trunks and she can't see where she's going. There's only the spongy slip of leaves beneath her feet, the gravel in the back of her throat, the tangy smell of blood on the air and the tall shapes that surround her, that run with her, that grow as she grows and get faster as she gets faster. They are running together now, they are growing taller than the trees and rising into the sky and the next morning she is safe in Crackenbridge, in a shelter, under a false name, and there is a tightness in her chest telling her that she has lost something she should never have let go, that she has seen something she should never have seen, and that there can be no going back.

REUNION TIME

Georgie drives carefully up the bumpy, muddied track that leads to the front door of Ricky Barr's farmhouse. In her passenger seat, Debs is looking nervous. It had taken a bit of persuading to get her to come with Georgie and see Ricky Barr. It's the right thing to do, though, Georgie's sure. The look in Ricky's eyes when he'd talked about his sister – he'd thought she was dead.

But she wasn't dead; she had escaped. She'd witnessed that violence and run away, because she was a child, because she was terrified, because no one listens to kids if they're contradicted by adults and carers and the police; because the balance of power is wrong. Yes, her memories are blurred, but her testimony, the matching dates, the partial skeleton – it might be enough to identify the body as Sonny Riley, parents unknown, who had been living under the foster care of Nora Prowle. Could it be enough to prove what had happened to him? Could they prove murder? Manslaughter? They're both dead, anyway. Nora and Jacob Prowle, they're dead. She has cleared Walt's name at least, Trish will be glad to hear that, but the truth is there's no one left alive to convict.

Simon is with her, sitting in the back. He's got such a kindness to him. Trish would have brought too much hostility with her. Simon though, he was the one who suggested the Prowles would have buried the body on the Barrs' land so they could blame them, should it ever be found; that Jacob Prowle could have destroyed any reports of Deborah-Jane being missing and ensured that *she* was never found.

Simon was the one who had put his arms around Debs when she broke down after telling them her story. She'd been too afraid to ever come back. She was a coward, she said. She was brave, Simon told her. And it's never too late to return.

Out of the car, the ground sinks beneath her feet; at last the soil is wet again, damp like fresh manure, not parched like it has been for weeks. She glances at Debs, presses the doorbell, which makes no sound, then reaches out a closed fist to knock several times on the wooden door. Simon's behind her. The three of them; she hopes they don't look too threatening. That's not something she'd normally worry about when it came to Ricky Barr. It's Andy who answers the door, though.

He looks at Georgie as though he's afraid of her. She's been avoiding him since the court case, since he got away with his racism and that violence against Pamali. She didn't know what she'd say to him – that he deserved a harsher punishment, that there was no excuse, no matter what sympathy Trish might have been showing him? That she was never going to forgive him? He looks sheepish now though, his shoulders deflating, his eyes flicking nervously to Debs.

'We need to come in, Andy,' she says.

'Yes, Ma'am,' he says.

Beside her, Debs is smiling. They've never met, of course. Aunt and nephew. They couldn't look more different. It's like Deborah recognises him though, like she knows him from a long time ago. Georgie wonders if Andy looks like Ricky did, when he was still a kid.

He leads them, in his usual awkward, lanky sort of way, to the kitchen. The last time Georgie set foot in here it was to escort Andy Barr back to the station for attacking Pamali. Georgie suddenly misses her friend like an ache. The kitchen is brighter than she remembers, though; maybe it's the lights. They seem to reflect off that huge oak table and the place feels almost welcoming today, Andy almost considerate.

'We need to talk to your dad, Andy,' she says.

'Yes, Ma'am. I… Would you like to have a seat?'

'Thanks, Andy,' Debs says, and he looks at her with a slight frown that turns into an uncertain smile.

Then his footsteps taking the stairs two at a time, that heavy pounding that teenage boys seem convinced they need to use when they're moving about the place. Ricky's own footsteps down are different though, slower, more cautious. He treads lightly. The sight of him: dishevelled, old, lined, stubbled and a hint of saliva caught in the corner of his mouth. He's ten years younger than Deborah-Jane but looks ten years older.

'Ricky,' she says.

His mouth falls open and he leans on the back of one of the kitchen chairs. His face, always etched with bitterness, blurs into someone else, someone Georgie barely recognises.

'Ricky,' Deborah is saying. 'Oh Ricky, I'm so sorry.' She's moving closer to him, reaching out, but he seems unable to move. 'I'm so sorry I didn't come home sooner.'

'I thought…'

'I'm sorry.'

'I thought you were dead.'

'Oh, Ricky—'

'All these years, I thought—'

'I'm sorry,' she says. 'I'm sorry.'

Deborah is standing right beside him now but there's no touch between them. Perhaps, after forty years, a hug would be weird; they hardly know each other. The air is charged though, and for once in this farmhouse it's not with anger. Ricky just shakes his head. Simon starts to quietly explain that she witnessed a murder, that she ran for her life, though as he talks Deborah starts to cry. Georgie thinks she can hear someone outside, Andy maybe, too scared to come in, too curious to leave.

'You got out then,' Ricky says eventually. 'At least you got out.'

Deborah rubs her hand over her face, takes a deep breath.

'But you stayed here, Ricky. Why?'

It's gone quiet out in the hall now. Maybe Andy has gone upstairs after all, not wanting to be anywhere near the police – or not wanting to be anywhere near his dad. Or her. Maybe it's her he's afraid of. She'd have thought he'd want to know who that woman was, standing on his doorstep looking at him like she knew him, like she was fond of him. There's no sign of him though, and it feels like Deborah and Ricky have forgotten Georgie and Si are watching them. Georgie would rather leave, let them have their moment in private, but she can't bring herself to move, to make a single sound – the best they can do is stay still and silent and let it play out.

'Not to prove a point, Ricky? Please tell me you didn't stay here all these years to prove a point.'

'I'm as local as any of them. Why shouldn't I have stayed?'

Georgie can imagine him, as a boy, thinking himself more local than the locals, desperate to prove it too. Beating up outsiders, picking on anyone more unwanted than he was, more different than he was, weaker than he was; that's what bullies are made of, and that's what Ricky Barr is.

'What have you done, Ricky, to get these villagers to accept you?'

But the cough he's been holding back takes over, and he can't seem to stop it, the rough growl in his throat, his lungs, his eyes watering with the force of it. Si stands, gets a glass of water. Deborah is watching, looking scared. Georgie suddenly understands.

When he's stopped coughing at last, spat into his handkerchief and taken a drink and refused to sit down, he tells his sister.

'It's lung cancer,' he says, with not a hint of self-pity in his voice. Just the facts. 'I've been seeing the doctor in Warphill, after hours. Didn't want any gossiping about me...' He swallows, his expression softening again. 'It's terminal.'

Debs has got her hand over her mouth.

Georgie is conscious of her own breath in the room, too conscious of her own presence. He'd told no one, not the villagers, not the police. Had he told his own son? Andy hadn't looked like a kid who'd made peace with his father. He'd looked like a kid who was ready to abandon him.

'I've not got long left,' he says. 'Months, they reckon. If that.'

A movement, the slightest movement of the door and Georgie knows – Andy is there, Andy has heard.

'Ricky,' Deborah says, her voice like a gasp. She puts her arms around him and to Georgie's surprise he lets his head fall to her shoulder.

'I thought it was you they'd buried, out in that field. I thought the old man had killed you.'

'No,' she says. 'He'd never have had the guts to kill either of us.'

Georgie wonders what he did do to them, what his father did to him in turn, what the village did to all of them, but now is not the time to ask.

'And he had nothing to do with the child in the field, either. I saw Nora and Jacob Prowle burying their foster child, that new kid Sonny, remember? The little one who was always crying?'

Georgie can feel something circling around her, just like at the cup and ring months ago: billowing figures, their sharp nails reaching out to scratch at her skin, just like they do every time she closes her eyes.

'They saw me, Nora and Jacob – that's why I could never come back here, not even to get you. I'd have been next. I thought if I ever came back they'd have killed me too, I was a witness so they'd have had to and they hated us so much and I was—'

'It's okay—'

'It's not okay. I'm so sorry, Ricky. I left you when you were just a little kid, but I was terrified of them and I just ran—'

'You're alive, Deborah. You're here and you're alive.'

The door to the kitchen finally swings open and Andy Barr is standing there, looking older than Georgie has ever seen him, and more vulnerable at the same time.

Ricky touches Deborah's face, just softly, and for the first time ever Georgie can see how Ricky Barr might once have been kind.

'Andy,' Deborah says, her hand reaching out to her nephew, though Andy stays where he is and Ricky doesn't turn around.

'You're here and you're alive,' Ricky says, the words repeating almost like a chant, or a prayer. 'You're here and you're alive.'

FOUND

Trish avoids Main Street and the fountain, she avoids the twitching net curtains of Mrs Smyth and Mrs Dover's front rooms and she avoids Uncle Walt's house – not because she's afraid of being seen there, but because she is too sad to set foot inside. The feathers are still hanging at the window, the plants drooping in the heat because she hadn't been watering them as often as he would, hadn't been stroking them, caring for them in the gentle, loving way of his; and besides, since he died, they seem to have given up, drooped in their pots on the windowsills, on the front porch, throughout his home.

But not everything that belonged to Uncle Walt has given up.

She's been checking on the bees, and they at least have been thriving in this weather, the heat and the moisture, the pollen and seeds floating through the air. They've been finding new wild flowers and heather, dipping in and out of gardens, dozing in the bright centres of roses and diving through the swathes of hardy geraniums that edge the track that leads to the overgrown field of the old community shed. It might have become a haven but for the rough rain and frost of winter, the storms of the spring, the relentless sea winds that have rotted the wood so badly the roof is sagging. The walls are ready to peel off at the first touch of an unkind hand.

Trish is not unkind, though. She might be a bit prickly, she might be a bit too ready to get angry at folk, say what she thinks, but she's not unkind. She's like Uncle Walt, in that way. She loves the village, like he did; she can see it needs some kindness.

So it is with a cautious, gentle touch that she reaches out to the rotting front wall of the community shed, having carefully made her way through the brambles and gorse, the nettles, dock leaves and the blanket of buttercups that no one else has touched. Maybe no one else has even seen them. Who comes here any more? She does, and Uncle Walt did, because this is where he keeps his beehives, during the season. Far enough away from the village that no one will be scared of them, no one will get jumpy and anxious about stings; no one will swat them and kill a creature that does more good than any other on the earth. Here, the bees are safe, in among the nettles and the thorns and the wildness of what nature can do when finally left alone. This is where he brought her when she was a little girl. This is where he taught her to ride her bike, to tell the difference between a mushroom you could forage and one that might kill you; this is where they came to build a secret snowman that none of the other kids would try to topple with their stones encased in ice. If Uncle Walt had something else precious, besides her and the bees, then this is where he would have put it.

The beehives are all around, close to the fence so as to have a bit of shelter, more from any prying eyes than from the elements – there's houses that look over the field, like Simon's place, but they can't see the beehives nestled along the fence. All they see is the mounds of weeds, the derelict shed: an eyesore. They don't see what matters. But today, Trish is not here for the bees, though they have recognised her, come to say hello, buzzing lazily around her hair in the heat, and she likes having them for company, makes her feel a bit closer to Uncle Walt again. Today, she is here for the shed.

She pushes the door and, to her surprise, the padlock falls off and the door swings open. Inside, willowherb rises to the roof and the floor is moss and grass, a padded tapestry of mulch that her feet sink into. The smell is dry, rotten, sticks in the back of her throat and she starts to cough, wonders if there are seeds permeating the air, things that shouldn't be inhaled. At first glance it doesn't look like anyone's been in here for years, but then she sees it: a slightly flattened patch of grass by the far wall, where there's a window. It's a large step but she makes it, treads in Uncle Walt's footprint.

The window has a wooden sill, cracked and rotten, with a metal nail sticking out from underneath it. It must have once helped to secure the frame in place, when the shed was built, but the wood around it has rotted away and the nail has remained, bent upwards as though hammered wrong, creating a makeshift hook. Hanging on it, beneath the scratched and cobwebbed window, letting the sun in like light through latticed lace, is a knife.

Its blade is old, but clean. It has been cared for.

Metal can last, if it's kept free of rust, it can last a long time, and this has. It's polished, sharp – it must have been sharpened recently. The handle, also metal, would be wide enough for a comfortable grip. It is covered in carvings, stick figures with long, pointed arms and heads that rise to strange peaks. They circle the knife, by the base of the handle, leading to another figure, its head falling from its neck. There is a rope dangling around what remains of the throat, twisting up into the intricate knots that form the decorative cusp of the handle. There are strange semicircular markings that she can't understand at first, and only as she moves her head does she realise they must be depicting waves.

She imagines clasping her fingers tight around it and closes her eyes.

The rest of the villagers, though, don't have their eyes closed at all; they are making their way through the heavy storm heat towards the community hall in Warphill. There are more than usual. More people, more bodies. The fountain seems to be glistening with sweat as they pass – as if stones could glisten, as if they could feel the heat – and the road that connects the villages is busy, at least would look busy from above, with people crawling along the sticky road like ants; clever ants, mind, as there's one speeding past the others on a bicycle. Even Georgie has her eyes wide open as she leaves the station, leaves Frazer and Simon to write up everything that has happened, Natalie Prowle under arrest and Ricky Barr united with his sister and Frazer all set to drive home to the city tomorrow and Burrowhead police station all set to be closed. Her job is finished here.

She thinks that perhaps *she* is finished here.

Which is why she doesn't follow them, all the villagers making their way to a community council meeting, even though she doesn't trust them and she knows they've been watching her and keeping things hidden; after all, if she's leaving this place, then they're welcome to their sordid secrets. A wee boy, she thinks. That poor wee boy. They killed a little boy and dumped him in a shallow grave on someone else's land and left him there, unremembered and unacknowledged. And who asked about what had happened to him? Who questioned them? Who spoke up? Who searched for his parents or told his story or mourned him after he was gone? This village deserves whatever it gets. That is why, as the villagers continue to make their way through the streets towards the community council meeting, Georgie sets off, deliberately, in the other direction.

OUT OF OPTIONS

Georgie and Fergus live a little way outside of Burrowhead – far enough along the coast that their house stands alone, neither touching nor seeing any other houses, but close enough that you can walk it, if you have the time and inclination; and today Georgie needs the walk. The path leads away from Burrowhead and follows the coast, not down by the beaches but up, along the cliffs, their edges steep and jagged, brutal, nurturing, filled with seabirds' nests and hidden caves, glittering with quartz, streaked with colour and intricate as coral. Georgie, despite everything that has happened this year, loves these cliffs more than any place she has ever set eyes on. She too had wanted to protect this village, in her way. She'd wanted to save it. How was she to know it had no interest in being saved, and certainly not by someone like her, *not from around here*. She could dwell on the colour of her skin, on her gender, her accent, her job, but really what it all came down to was that one simple phrase: not from around here.

Just like poor Sonny Riley. That poor, innocent little boy.

But as she follows the cliffs, as the moisture hanging in the air becomes denser and falls in large, satisfying drops, she realises that she does have options. Her and Fergus have options. They could talk it all through, now her job is gone and there's nothing holding them here. Fergus, after all, has been going on about archaeology for months – maybe he could do a course. He could be the one with a job for a while, with English Heritage or the National Trust or something. He'd enjoy that. A fresh start for them, away from here, away from the otherness that has driven a wedge between them.

As the track turns away from the coast, leaving the sea behind – it has turned an extraordinary colour of green with clear white peaks on the waves – she notices the coppertips, the montbretia as they call them round here, not in flower yet but their lush green leaves spilling forth along the edges of her path, calling out to be touched. They are such gentle-looking plants, especially at this stage, almost furry with the way the long leaves flop over, like a shaggy haircut, before the fiery tips of the flowers emerge in late summer. Her own front garden is full of herbs: mint, rosemary, oregano, thyme; herbs that flourish in the local climate, that release gentle scents as she lets her fingers brush through their leaves. At the door, she pushes the handle absent-mindedly, leaving work behind. It's time to talk to Fergus. He'll understand, now; she'll be able to explain now that *she* understands – they can leave, together, they can start again. But the handle won't budge. There's an unpleasant lurching in her stomach, the door is locked and that means—

Her keys in her bag: pulling them out fast, unlocking the door. Calling his name even though it's futile – he'd not have locked the door if he were inside. But then where is he? Their conversation in the pub coming back, the way he seemed to sympathise with the villagers more than with the way she'd been feeling; he was always trying to understand them. Trying to see their point of view. Fergus was always trying to see everyone else's point of view – but what about hers? Should she have explained to him – but then, really, should she have to? She had reason to be short tempered, living here, didn't she? That note she'd been sent back in the spring, *Foreign Bitch*, she's still got it. She keeps it, to remind her of what she's dealing with. In the silence of her house, though, her steps falter and she finds she can't propel herself forwards any more.

Upstairs: empty cupboards.

The bathroom: razor gone.

The look on his face when she left him sitting in the pub and he knew – he must have known – that she was angry; the look in his eyes at the standing stone, that look of hurt, of betrayal. And yes, anger too, from her Fergus. She didn't want to see it. She doesn't want to remember it now.

What has she done?

Down to the kitchen: everything still in place. He's not taken his mugs or cereal that she doesn't eat. Maybe…maybe…

Outside, to the garage: his drone is gone.

Fergus is gone.

Georgie has crumpled to the garage floor and then, suddenly, she is back to a crisp autumn day, an October, and she is allowing herself to feel something that she hasn't felt for years, not since her brother died. They stand side by side outside the cottage on the coast, the For Sale sign swaying in the breeze, Fergus's hair blowing wild as Georgie's own and the small front garden is dotted with dandelion clocks, their seeds escaping, dancing through the grass and over the low wall that edges the path to the door.

'It's perfect,' Fergus breathes. 'It's so perfect.'

'Let's wait till we see the inside, hey?'

He turns to her with a boyish grin and she knows the inside could be a disaster of crumbling plaster and damp and he'd still love it, and she'd still love it.

Light seems to float into the hallway and that feeling, she can't shake that feeling.

The kitchen needs modernisation but as she looks she can imagine it all taking shape around her: widening the windows out to the back garden, an Aga, perhaps, a deep stone sink, maybe they could get a dog – Georgie would like a dog, they'd always had one back home, ever since Errol turned ten and started begging every single morning for a puppy, a huge basset hound puppy he'd wanted, and none of them, not her mom or her dad and certainly not Georgie, had ever really been able to say no to Errol. And there it is: the first moment in years she's been able to think of him without a stab to the stomach making her retch. Her brother Errol, as a happy kid. Their happy family. Before…

Fergus taking her hand – he always seems to know how to do that just as she's about to fall back into the dark – and leading her upstairs, to the low-ceilinged bedrooms with their views over the garden, over the landscape and up to that vast sky, changing in the breeze, the colours of the clouds glinting and melting as she watches, the beauty of it and Fergus, looking around, sizing up the room.

'We could put the bed here,' he says.

'Keep the curtains open.'

'Wake every morning to the sunrise.'

And that feeling, that feeling, familiar but distant and longing and warm; Fergus is excited, she can see it, though he's trying to remain professional, he's checking the old fireplaces, looking for any signs of damp, asking about electrics and that feeling, she can't shake it and she doesn't want to, she lets it take her over as she stands by the bedroom window watching that extraordinary sky and she feels hopeful, deeply, innocently hopeful.

The garage floor is a cold, uneven concrete and Georgie needs to stand up, but she can't. Her legs won't stop shaking.

Months of wondering if she should leave him, if their marriage was over, if there was something to save, to reclaim, and she's the one left here, alone.

No, this can't be it.

He'll be somewhere, he can't have gone far – where can he have gone?

She feels sick.

She has to find him.

She doesn't know where to start.

Can't even think of who his friends are, who might give him a bed for the night, a sofa to crash on.

Oh God, Fergus, what have you done?

There's Walt, but Walt's dead and Trish is dealing with her own grief and Si would have told her, wouldn't he, and Pamali would have called if she knew anything. Then she realises that it's her own friends she's thinking about. Who are his?

Georgie doesn't even bother to lock up behind her. The sea is festering – it was stupid to think of it as vibrant, with that storm churning it up. The air is soupy and damp, her shirt clinging to her skin and she's heading back out to the cliffs, she's walking faster and faster, she's running, racing out into the rain and letting her feet take her wherever they need to go.

THE INSIDERS

The villagers arrive separately at the community hall, not speaking to each other as they walk, not even acknowledging where they're going. If someone were to stop them, to ask, they'd each have a different story to go with: heading up to see my cousin lives in the new flats; to the pub for a bevvy, end a the week; got to get the dogs a walk, eh. They're good, the villagers of Burrowhead and Warphill, at knowing what they can say to strangers and what they can't.

Nevertheless, they are all making their way one by one, apart from Mrs Dover and Mrs Smyth who are walking side by side, talking about the new potholes that have caved into the road, how they'll fill with water and the inconsiderate young folks will drive through, splashing them as they pass; they've seen it before. Mrs Dover and Mrs Smyth have seen everything before. They glance at the young ones from the school and shake their heads. They'll be up to no good, no doubt. The young ones glance back at Mrs Smyth and Mrs Dover, share smirks about the state of them, plastic rain-coats, floral skirts over thick ankles, granny sandals, purple tint to their grey hair; smirk as though they'd no be seen dead in a room with them 'cause no one needs to know – no one not from around here – that they're all headed to the same hall.

There are a few folk missing, mind. Lee and Aaron Prowle, no sign of them. No one's seen them round for a while, must be hanging out at Ricky Barr's caravan park, and that says it all to anyone who knows enough to be walking this way. Poor Natalie, what will she make of her sons being missing again – they don't know, not most of them, that Natalie's in a cell in Burrowhead Police Station – and then a course Andy Barr will be back at the farm like he always is, him an his da, same and same, that's the way it's always gone in that family. Still, most folk are here, most folk you'd expect. Elise Robertson of course, that girl's got a love for the village that no one could argue with. Suze will show up too, she never did fit right with the police lot – though it's handy to have someone at the police they can trust. Not that they'd ever say that out loud.

So one by one they keep their thoughts to themselves and their heads down until they arrive at Warphill community hall, where the front doors are locked and only folk who know, folk from around here, circle down the side alley to the back door that leads through the kitchen – kettle's on, ta much. In the hall plenty of chairs are laid out so one by one they collect their mugs of tea and take a seat, waiting for Natalie Prowle to arrive and start the meeting. But she doesn't arrive to start the meeting.

They wait till five past, ten past – not like Natalie – and at twelve past Suze arrives. They knew she was on her way. She'll know what's going on. Sure enough Suze makes her way into the centre of the circle, standing, clearing her throat. Except then there's a bang of the door shutting hard and footsteps they weren't expecting, and their faces turn, collectively, as Trish Mackie walks into the community hall.

She's never been at one of these meetings before; they all know that.

Course, she must've known about them. Her Uncle would have told her. Though Walt Mackie had such a thing about protecting Trish he'd never actually brought her along. There's a rustle of whispers like breath passed round the circle, until Trish walks straight up to where Suze is standing and Suze reluctantly, trying to hide her frown, takes a seat in the front row where she's always sat before, and the room flickers with silence.

'I see you're all here,' Trish says.

As soon as she speaks they look, every one of them, straight at her. She is carrying something, wrapped in a blanket, and she doesn't put it down. Instead, her eyes make contact with every person in the circle: Suze and Elise, Mrs Smyth and Mrs Dover, June, Whelan, Ben from the pub, Bessie Wilkie, Colin Spence from Warphill, Terry and the lads from the garage, Camellia Taylor and young Esme, even Shona from the paper is here and Kev too; they've lost people, same as Trish has. They've all lost people and now it's time to fight back.

'Here's what I know,' she says. There's no waver to her voice – she is hardened and angry and certain. 'Natalie Prowle has been arrested for stealing and killing Ricky Barr's horse. She's in a cell at Burrowhead station. The police believe she acted alone.'

Trish pauses. Imagine Natalie killing that fucking horse *alone*, Christ's sake. They'd told her the truth in the pub: Elise was good with horses, knew how to lead them where she wanted them to go; Natalie could get hold of the tranquilliser; Suze was supposedly covering their tracks. Together they'd killed that horse and Walt had told them how – so she'd had to keep quiet, unless she wanted Uncle Walt dragged into it. She had to feed back any information Georgie had.

She'd wanted him to stay her kind, innocent Uncle Walt, so she'd gone along with it for a while. But now he's gone.

'She was copying what happened to Ricky's dog,' Trish says.

'What happened to his dog before any of us were born,' adds Elise. Trish gives her a look and she shuts up.

'But more importantly, she'd been investigating Ricky Barr, who's been bringing drugs in and getting local boys – like Aaron and Lee – to sell them on to the schoolkids. It's no just weed either, no just ecstasy and a bit of speed. Rachel and Pauly got themselves caught up in it, though what he was selling them I don't know – something unrefined and dangerous, and they ended up dead.'

She looks at Shona, at Kevin Taylor, and they look back, not questioning, not contradicting her words. They know it's true.

'Elise, Suze?'

The pair of them are watching her now, a hint of fear there to match the change in Trish's tone.

'The truth is, you two, along with Natalie, stole Ricky's horse and slaughtered it. You cut its throat out at the cup and ring just like what Nora Prowle, Art Robertson, Jack Helmsteading and my Uncle Walt did to his dog forty years back. And Mrs Smyth, Mrs Dover? If you weren't there at the first crime, I'd say you knew full well about it.'

'It was a sacrifice,' says Mrs Dover. 'Not a crime.'

'Well, now we're all in this together, aren't we.' She looks around the room, challenging anyone to contradict her. 'In fact, I'd say yous all knew about the horse, eh? Natalie get you to vote on it at the last community council meeting?'

No one laughs, and Trish is glad – they are afraid of her.

'You were trying to scare Ricky out the village, but Ricky Barr's no going to be scared by a dead horse. All you did was freak out young Andy, and I'm not having that boy caught up in all this. He's not to blame, you hear me?'

No one says a word.

'Some of you planted that iron figurine that Fergus found. You didn't want it traced back to the community council but Fergus, he's easy to manipulate, so you got him to arrange the excavation as a way of searching under the motte.'

'Is that so?'

The voice comes from behind her, from the door that was locked. Fergus is standing there, tall, broad, the way he is, but he's not shrinking in on himself and he's not apologising either – he looks like he's here on purpose. He waves the key at them.

'I was invited,' he says.

He looks like someone who might actually know what they're doing and it takes Trish by surprise for a second; he's only ever been

Georgie's useless husband to her. She wouldn't have thought that about a woman. They need to be sure, though. Sure he's not going to be reporting back, spying for the police.

'Georgie know you're here?' Trish asks him.

'No. And like I say, I was invited.'

Suze nods. 'It's true. Natalie invited him along before she got herself arrested.'

Trish stares at him.

'Well, now you're here,' Trish says. 'Are you in?'

'I'm in. And I'm not an idiot.'

He walks, deliberate and proud, to the circle, and sits on the last remaining seat. He's seen her, anyway, he's seen them all – and if he's here under false pretences then she'll deal with it later. She's not going to stop now she's started.

'You see, Natalie has been searching for something for a long time. That's what the excavation was all about. But she didn't find it in the motte, or buried on Ricky Barr's farm, and she didn't find it in Art Robertson's house after he died.'

Elise is watching her, pain flitting across her face, anger too, though Trish decides to save that for another time.

'What she was looking for was a blade.' Her fingers tighten around what she's holding. 'An engraved iron dagger that depicts the three-fold death. It has been passed down the generations in this village, kept hidden from anyone outside. It's the blade that must draw the blood if the threefold death is to be sacred. And it's come to me.'

She lets the blanket fall to the ground and holds up the knife for them all to see. The room is silent, and she knows she has them.

'The thing you all have to understand is that *I* am angry. I am really fucking angry.' That conversation with DS Frazer, before the kiss – she's not letting herself think about the kiss – how much more she might have told him, and how glad she is that she didn't. 'I've been angry for a long time, but it's only now I understand where the anger is coming from.'

She can see the image of her mam, when she was still young, still present, in her way, with that sadness she always carried in her eyes, but that's not why Trish is here, that's not what she's here to talk about.

'You see, Natalie, Uncle Walt, Art, Jack, they all had it wrong. Not that they didn't have their own reasons to be angry, and God knows they did. Natalie, raising those two boys alone, relying on government handouts to keep going year after year, and how she kept going, my God! Running this council, cleaning up the neighbourhood, volunteering at the museum, the PTA – we used to laugh at her, at the school, but I'm not laughing now. No wonder she was angry. But she looked the wrong way for revenge.

'I'm not talking about Ricky Barr or anyone else here – I'm talking about the fact that she was looking backwards, to the old ways of life, the old rituals. That's not how we're going to fix this village. I don't remember the days when Uncle Walt lost his farm, but over these few years I've watched him trying to keep himself alive on out-of-date bread and reused teabags and economy custard creams from his useless state pension – and let's not kid ourselves, the likes of us won't even see a state pension. There's nobody, not the government, not the city, coming to help us. But here's what I know.

'Ricky Barr's grandfather arrived here, an outsider with more money than any of us had, and we were too busy fighting among ourselves to pool our resources and stop him. He bought up land and passed it down to his son, to his grandson, and Ricky has been systematically buying up the shops and property of these villages and setting the rent too high for locals to afford. He fair paved the way for the big Kaltonn to move in – and they're not halfway to replacing the jobs that have been lost from local businesses.

'He might not have had anything to do with that poor toddler buried on his farm, but he's the dealer who's getting our kids hooked on drugs, the bully who gets teenagers to work for him for less than minimum wage because they're so desperate for a place to live.

Seasonal work. No contracts. No rights – Shona and Kev could tell you about that. He's got the police on his side, make no mistake about that. He beats his son, always has, while the authorities do nothing. One man now owns the majority of property and land from the peninsular to Crackenbridge, and that man is Ricky Barr.

'Now I don't believe in feathers for luck. I don't believe in corn dolls or sacrifice but here's what I believe: this village used to be protected. It was protected by people like my Uncle Walt. Those people have gone now. Too many of our people have gone, and someone has to take their place. The police aren't up to the job, so it's up to us. This is our village and we need to start protecting it.'

THE OUTSIDERS

It is strange, inexplicable, the way they all find themselves walking towards the playground that looks out over the rough shingle beach to the sea. Four people, coming from four different places, converging one evening as storm clouds thicken to stone and the ground drinks every drop the skies have to offer.

From the centre of Burrowhead, Pamali Patel finds herself too restless to go home, having locked the Spar, having looked, as she does every evening, at the fresh graffiti on the windows, on the walls. The latest scrawl, down the side of the shop, sprayed in red paint: ALA IS A CUNT and a misdrawn swastika. She used to think staying here, carrying on regardless, was an act of resistance, but it's going to take more than that, she knows: an act of resistance has to involve some action.

Last year, when the spring was filled with golden light, she'd drawn a sketch of the village as seen from the coast, a huddle of pretty houses dotted with climbing roses in defiance of the jagged cliffs and brutal rocks below. Now, if anything, the landscape seems the other way round – it is the village that's jagged and sharp but if she stands on the edge and looks out, something changes: the cliffs are speckled with wild flowers, growing up through the stone, the beach clasping the last of the sun with a shimmer of pink gold and the sea, the sea, deep emerald green to turquoise to jade, up to an icing white where the waves crash against the shore. Nature needs to come back into the village; they need to regain their connection to the land, to plants, to growth. These are her thoughts as she arrives at the playground, avoiding the swings, as all the villagers do these days, and taking a seat on the wooden bench that has its back to the village and faces out to the horizon. Which is why she doesn't see Simon approaching from Burrowhead police station.

Having avoided the centre of the village and skirted Ricky Barr's land, he's been following the barely visible sheep track to the playground, where he comes often, drawn to the last place where Alexis lay under the sky. Simon sees Pamali though, realises with a pang of guilt that he hasn't spoken to her in a while, but stronger than that is the warmth of seeing a friend he's missed – ridiculous, with them living in the same village, but this year's been slipping through grief and sleepless nights and self-imposed isolation that maybe it's time to lift. His pace quickens, he calls her name, she turns, a flicker of alarm on her face replaced with such a genuine smile he runs the last few steps.

'Pami,' he says, sitting beside her, welcoming the hug she offers and for a moment they hold each other – they've both been needing a moment like this. There's no need for either of them to apologise for not being in touch; they both feel it. The rain has cooled the heat and Simon wants to tip his head back and drink it. Underneath their silence they can hear the waves lapping against the pebbles below and there – Simon sits up and points to the figure making his way up the zigzagged path that leads up the cliffs.

That's the way DS Frazer is drawn to Burrowhead playground: scrambling up the cliffs from the beach he'd sworn never to set foot on again. Except that there was something different about it on this visit and he couldn't persuade himself to leave until he'd walked the rocks, veined with quartz and iron oxide, searched for the tall caves that appear in the shadows and disappear soon as he's close enough to touch. They're inviting him in then changing their mind, calling him closer then shutting their doors, like Trish Mackie and her sparking anger. But down here is where Dawn must have hidden, a cave in these cliffs that the villagers deny knowing but one day he is determined to find.

Today is not the day, though; today the beach wanted him to walk slowly over the smoother pebbles, rounded and curved by centuries of the tide; it wanted him to take his shoes and socks off and stand on the thin strip of sand where the waves meet the land, to allow it to cool his toes. Today he feels the tug of a promise that it could be beautiful, that it could be different. It wasn't until the chill of the water had spread up his legs that he made his way over to the path, the zigzagged, weathered, half-accidental drift in the rock that leads up to the village playground. Moss-covered, with the occasional twist of a nettle, he finds wild flowers he can't name, delicate blues and pinks – extraordinary, the things that can grow on a cliff face like this. Then he sees her, a tall figure walking from the south: DI Georgie Strachan, as distinctive round here as he is. He raises a hand but she doesn't see him yet; her thoughts are too stubborn, too unresolved for noticing wild flowers or figures climbing the cliffs.

She sees the playground though, sees that from a distance, through the rain. She's searched everywhere, run all through the village, even hammered on doors, but she's found no sign of Fergus. He's gone. Fergus is gone. So she's back here, at Burrowhead playground, where it all started. Alexis's murder and, twenty years before that, Dawn's kidnapping. A group of locals led by Dawn's own brother, drugging her, carrying her out here to slit her throat, tie a rope around her neck and drown her in the salt-heavy sea. A threefold death for no good reason; violence inflicted by the villagers on a child, simply because they could. Just like twenty years before that, when a group of villagers, grown men and women, stole a young boy's dog and slaughtered it to terrify him, to show him he'd never be welcome. And a little boy, a toddler, was killed and buried with no one to fight for him, no one to remember him. She thinks that maybe she might arrange something, a memorial, to acknowledge that he was here, to force the villagers to see.

The sight of Simon and Pamali on the bench jolts her back to the moment. Si doesn't seem to have the anger that she does, at least it's not coursing through his blood the way hers is and Pamali – she doesn't know how Pami remains who she is, how she's kept hold of that kindness of hers.

'Georgie,' Pamali says, moving up on the bench so Georgie can sit beside them.

'It's good to see you,' Georgie says, her voice cracking against her will.

'God Georgie, what's wrong?'

'I… I think—'

'Here he comes,' Simon says.

Georgie looks up to see DS Frazer reach the top of the path, attempt to brush the wet sand off his trousers.

'What's going on?' he says, facing them all on the bench, looking behind him as though hoping there might be a chair to sit on, so he can stop towering over them.

'They're closing the station,' Georgie says.

Frazer nods – he'd known it was coming, just didn't know it would be right now.

'I'm sorry.'

'I'm not.'

The waves are crashing in now, the rain getting in their eyes, soaking their useless summer clothes.

'What'll you do?' Frazer asks, seemingly ignoring the weather. He's not wearing so much as a hat.

Georgie just shakes her head, stares out to the wild sea below them.

'Well, I've got some news,' Pamali says eventually, her voice breaking the heavy silence with something lighter, fresher. 'I'm building a community food garden,' she says.

'A what?' Simon says.

Pami laughs, and her joy seems to lift the air for a moment, though for Georgie something else rushes in to replace it, something crackling with static that makes her shoulders tighten.

'I'm turning one of the disused fields into a series of vegetable patches,' Pami says. 'Anyone who wants can work there, anyone who needs the food can help themselves.'

Georgie shakes her head. 'It's not going to work, Pami. You'd be better off...'

'What, leaving? Giving up? Young Andy is helping me build the raised beds – it's been really good for him I reckon.'

'Andy Barr?'

'Andy Barr.'

'Andy Barr is helping you build a community food garden?'

Pamali's whole face lights up.

'That's amazing, Pami.' Simon says. 'That's... What a thing to do.'

'Thanks,' she laughs. 'Though now Natalie...we could do with a few more pairs of hands. I might try to inspire some other local kids to get involved, you never know.'

There's a crack of thunder in the distance and Georgie counts the seconds, like she always does, to see how far away it is, to know how quickly it's closing in. Natalie might be under arrest, but her boys are two of those local kids Pami is talking about, Lee and Aaron Prowle, and they're mixed up in something nasty.

'What *will* you do, Georgie?' Frazer asks, quietly.

It's as though he knows Georgie is backing away, like she's been pushed so far and now she's in the shadows, the violence clawing at her.

'Your Fergus loves it here,' Si says.

'You'll be staying here with him, then?' asks Frazer. 'Maybe get a transfer to Crackenbridge?'

Georgie doesn't answer. She doesn't have an answer. She looks around them; the four outsiders.

'Here, have a seat, Frazer,' she says, shifting over.

His face creases in a frown. They all go silent for a second as the waves intensify, crashing against stone as the tide turns.

'We'll not bite…' says Simon.

'No, it's not…look here, move over a bit more. What does that say?'

As Georgie moves over, the plaque of the bench is revealed, and they all read it, Georgie, Simon, Pamali, Frazer.

'That's her,' he says. 'My God, that's—'

'Who?'

'That's the woman I've been asking this whole bloody village about! My witness saw a murder – she says she saw the murder of Abigail Moss.'

Pamali reads the plaque. She's seen it many times, but she's not sure she's ever really read it properly before. She reads it out loud now.

'To the memory of Abigail Moss.'

'*Someone* knows what happened to her,' Frazer says, his voice loud, his whole body suddenly full of furious determination. 'Someone put this here,' he's saying. 'It's not even that old. Look! Someone from *this village* put this here.'

He looks between them and Georgie shivers at the accusation in his eyes and that's when she turns, sees her sitting cross-legged beside the bench: a little girl, stringy pale hair, tattered clothes. Georgie blinks and she is gone. Frazer is pacing in front of them and behind him, beyond, the sea is getting rougher and Georgie sees them, the gulls, a whole flock of them, circling high above the tideline.

'I am not leaving until I find her,' Frazer is saying. 'I swear to every fucking God there is, I am going to find out what they did to Abigail Moss.'

Georgie looks from Frazer to Pamali, to her soft, serious expression, then over to Simon's blue-eyed face lined with loss, making him seem a decade older than he'd looked last year. Frazer's deep black skin is shining in the rain and there are shapes moving on the beach, birds or shadows or something seeping out from the rocks and there's a tugging, a tugging at her wrist, at her shirt cuff and she doesn't want to turn, to see. The sun is gone, it's gone behind the gathering, blistering clouds and she knows they're here, the creatures, they're here and they are gathering around her and there's a light down on the beach that shouldn't be there and the dread of it is colder than the sea in the depths of winter. It's in the way the shadows move across the stones, backlit and stretching closer and she knows: the unnatural light is coming from the cave she's heard about, the cave she's seen when she was trying not to look. The little girl is beside her, gently tugging at her fingers. Her dress is in tatters. Her face is bruised and stained with dirt, marks around her neck that shouldn't be there. She's pleading. She's silently pleading, with her eyes and her hand that is pulling on Georgie's own; she's pulling at Georgie's hand and her fingers are cold as the sea and Georgie can taste salt on her lips, stinging her eyes and the little girl breathes, she breathes, her eyes stare and plead and she tugs on Georgie's hand and she is whispering, she is whispering, *Please help my mammy.*

THE MISSING

The storm hits in January, the worst they've seen in a generation or more. It starts and won't stop: the gales howling through the houses like screams and the pier smashed to splinters; boats wrecked, homes flooded and left brittle with sea salt and despair. What should we do? the villagers ask one another, what can we do? And they start, for the first time in a long time, to acknowledge the answer. Not with words but with looks, with nods, as a silent understanding passes between them.

All the while, young Amanda Mackie stays at home with her new baby boy, and she holds him close in her arms and lets him sleep beside her, snuggled into her chest. She is keeping him for herself, she's decided, and that's how it's going to be, no matter what her mother says or her father, no matter what the school says or the villagers say. She pushes away anyone trying to tell her otherwise with a glare of daggers.

As the baby sleeps she knits clothes for him to wear and toys for him to play with, using the chunky lambswool that Deborah-Jane Barr gave her: the only gift she received when the baby was born. She loops the yarn into hats and jumpers, stitches it into figures of boys and girls, spacemen and animals: a whole community of friends for her son to play with, so that he'll never need to play with those waiting for him outside. But outside the storm gets worse and the nights seem endless, sheep drown in the river that burst its banks and the villagers whisper to one another: but he can't have been from round here. If he was one of us then she would have said. No, the father can't have been from around here.

What about those workers, from overseas?

They were here and then they were gone.

Oh, that stupid girl, to let her head be turned by the likes of them.

Then, quieter, hushed and under their breath: it has happened before.

But Amanda Mackie stays inside and doesn't care about what they say, she doesn't care about school or exams or what she'll do or who will pay for it. She cares only about her baby, sleeping soundly again in her arms. She shuts her eyes against her mother and shakes her head to her father and slams the door when they say they are calling her uncle to come round too.

Manipulation, that's what it is, for everyone knows Amanda Mackie loves her Uncle Walt more than anyone, but the storm winds have blown down a tree that smashed into the fountain and now the water won't flow any more. The angels' faces are barely recognisable and the stone basin is swirling with rotten leaves and stagnant salt water that no one can drink. Down south, they hear, there's been another bomb. The Irish again. At the horizon the storm clouds condense to anger and they know, the villagers of Burrowhead and Warphill, they don't have long left if they are going to act. And act they must.

The sea knows when a wrong has been done, they say to each other, their voices louder now, rough and sure.

The sky knows, they say, the rain and the clouds; who are we to ignore the signs we have always heeded before?

They gather together and listen to the radio, they listen to the words and they nod to one another – we must be on our guard, they say, for it is true, and for days afterwards they repeat those words as their own, talk about how their home is being swamped by people from different cultures. Then they look towards the Mackie family house where Amanda is refusing to give up her child, refusing to name the father, knitting coloured children and animals instead of accepting the corn doll the village gave her. Pretending all the while that the storm outside is not destroying their village. Her own village. Pretending she doesn't know it is her and her baby who are causing the storm to rage on.

Walt Mackie finds himself surrounded, as they press in around him and the rain pelts the roof over their heads. It must be done, they say, you know what must be done. His brother's eyes are pleading. His sister-in-law's are red and raw. The worry, they say. Her future, they say. Her age.

He closes his eyes.

The village, they say, the storm and the boats, our home, we must protect our home. For the good of the village.

Walt Mackie does not want to open his eyes, but he knows that eventually he must.

So it is that Amanda, raw herself and sore and fighting back exhausted tears, looks into her Uncle Walt's kind face and says the words just once: please no.

It's for his own good, he says.

It's for you, too, your life, your future, he says.

It's for your parents, have you seen the state of your parents?

It's for the good of the village.

She turns away and holds her son closer.

He'll go to a good family, he says. To people who will love him.

He will be happy, he says. Then quieter, whispered because he knows these are the words that will win: He will be happier than he would be here.

And for a moment, the briefest of moments, she feels her body relax and her shoulders fall and her face drops to her baby's head so she can smell his hair and kiss his perfect skin one last time. She'll never see her baby again, but she will grow up and she'll even finish school, she'll fall in love and, twelve years after her first child was born, she'll have a baby girl and call her Patricia, though she'll always be known as Trish. Her only child, her little girl: Trisha.

It'll be to Trish that she writes her goodbye note, when she can't stand it any more, before stealing her father's boat from the shed during a storm as bad as the storm that raged when they took her baby. The night will seem endless on that day too, but the sea, the sea will welcome her as she rows out away from the village as far as her strength can take her. She'll never come back after that, she'll never go looking for her lost son and she'll never find out what became of him; she'll never know her Uncle Walt gave him up under a false name, gave him to a care home in Crackenbridge where he developed asthma and grew a full head of blonde hair. She'll never know that he was fostered by Nora Prowle when he was just a toddler. She'll never know that her little boy hated Burrowhead every bit as much as she came to hate it herself. She'll never know that he was there for all those years, alone, buried under the ground beneath her feet and no one, no one, will ever know that he was hers.

ACKNOWLEDGEMENTS

This book would never have made it into the world without the help of a lot of people, and I am deeply grateful. I want to say a special thank you to my agent, Cathryn Summerhayes, who will always be an inspiration – Cathryn, I don't know what I would do without you. Thank you to my editor, Jenny Parrott, for her wisdom and insight. And thank you to my thoughtful copy-editor, Sarah Terry, and to the whole team at Oneworld and Point Blank for their hard work and skill: Julian Ball, Thanhmai Bui-Van, Lucy Cooper, Francesca Dawes, Jennifer Jahn, Juliet Mabey, Laura McFarlane, Anna Murphy, Paul Nash, Aimee Oliver-Powell, Mark Rusher, Tom Sanderson, Molly Scull, Ben Summers, Harriet Wade, Matilda Warner, Hayley Warnham and Margot Weale. Thank you to Alice Lutyens, Sophia MacAskill, Jess Molloy, Luke Speed, Anna Weguelin and everyone at Curtis Brown, and thank you to Scottish Book Trust and Creative Scotland.

For their invaluable feedback and advice, my heartfelt thanks go to Viccy Adams, Jane Alexander, Margaret Callaghan, Ally Sedgwick, Chris Sedgwick and Liz Treacher. To Aoife, Ari, Brigit, Kate, Mairi, Nick, Seamus and Steve – your kindness and support mean the world to me, thank you. And finally, to Hazel and Michael, thank you, with my love, as always.

© Michael Gallacher

HELEN SEDGWICK is the author of *The Comet Seekers* and *The Growing Season,* which was shortlisted for the Saltire Society Fiction Book of the Year in 2018. The opener to her Burrowhead Mysteries crime trilogy, *When the Dead Come Calling,* was published in 2020, followed by *Where the Missing Gather* in 2021. She has an MLitt in Creative Writing from Glasgow University and has won a Scottish Book Trust New Writers Award. Before she became an author, she was a research physicist with a PhD in Physics from Edinburgh University. She lives in the Scottish Highlands.